W9-BMU-468

LETHAL GAME

LETHAL GAME

CHRISTINE FEEHAN

THORNDIKE PRESS

A part of Gale, a Cengage Company

A Cengage Company

Copyright © 2020 by Christian Feehan.
GhostWalker.
Thorndike Press, a part of Gale, a Cengage Company.

ALL RIGHTS RESERVED
This is a work of fiction. Names, characters, places, and incidents either are the product of the author's imagination or are used fictitiously, and any resemblance to actual persons, living or dead, business establishments, events, or locales is entirely coincidental.
Thorndike Press® Large Print Romance.
The text of this Large Print edition is unabridged.
Other aspects of the book may vary from the original edition.
Set in 16 pt. Plantin.

**LIBRARY OF CONGRESS CIP DATA ON FILE.
CATALOGUING IN PUBLICATION FOR THIS BOOK
IS AVAILABLE FROM THE LIBRARY OF CONGRESS**

ISBN-13: 978-1-4328-7399-8 (hardcover alk. paper)

Published in 2020 by arrangement with Berkley, an imprint of Penguin Publishing Group, a division of Penguin Random House, LLC

Printed in Mexico
Print Number: 01   Print Year: 2020

*For Brian and Domini,
because this book wouldn't have
happened without either
of you pushing me to get it done
when it seemed impossible.*

FOR MY READERS

Be sure to go to christinefeehan.com/ members/ to sign up for my private book announcement list and download the free ebook of *Dark Desserts.* Join my community and get firsthand news, enter the book discussions, ask your questions and chat with me. Please feel free to email me at Christine@christinefeehan.com. I would love to hear from you.

ACKNOWLEDGMENTS

This book was complicated and needed a tremendous amount of detail work. Domini was my go-to person, and she put in so much extra time. Brian really pushed me on this one when I was tempted to just put it under the bed and forget about it. It was important to me for so many reasons, but difficult to write. Domini, thank you again for always editing, no matter how many times I ask you to go over the same book before we send it for additional editing.

THE GHOSTWALKER
SYMBOL DETAILS

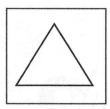

SIGNIFIES
shadow

SIGNIFIES
protection against evil forces

SIGNIFIES
the Greek letter psi, which is used by parapsychology researchers to signify ESP or other psychic abilities

SIGNIFIES
qualities of a knight—loyalty, generosity, courage and honor

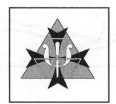

SIGNIFIES
shadow knights who protect against evil forces using psychic powers, courage and honor

nox noctis est nostri

THE GHOSTWALKER CREED

We are the Ghost Walkers,
we live in the shadows
The sea, the earth, and the air
are our domain
No fallen comrade will be left behind
We are loyalty and honor bound
We are invisible to our enemies
and we destroy them where
we find them
We believe in justice and
we protect our country
and those unable to protect themselves
What goes unseen, unheard, and
unknown are GhostWalkers
There is honor in the shadows
and it is us
We move in complete silence
whether in jungle or desert
We walk among our enemy
unseen and unheard
Striking without sound and

scatter to the winds
before they have knowledge
of our existence
We gather information and
wait with endless patience
for that perfect moment
to deliver swift justice
We are both merciful and merciless
We are relentless and implacable
in our resolve
We are the GhostWalkers
and the night is ours

1

We're taking heavy enemy fire.

Like they all weren't aware of the helicopter lurching from side to side as they came in low trying to put down where the wounded soldiers waited for transport. Malichai Fortunes kept one hand on his medical kit and the other on his rifle. He could shoot the wings off a fly with that rifle.

You're up, soldier, Joe Spagnola, his team leader, said. *Want you back in one piece.*

Roger that. Malichai jumped without hesitation, landing in the snow and moving out of the way just in case Rubin Campo, another GhostWalker teammate, landed on top of him.

They both were dressed in white with splotches of gray to better blend into the environment around them. The moment they were on the ground, the helicopter was up and away, skidding sideways through the sky, dodging the deadly fire from three or

15

four bunkers, with heavy artillery shooting continuously.

The moment Malichai saw that the helicopter was out of target range, he was up and running in a crouch, toward the coordinates of the small group of soldiers who had been shot down and were now pinned on top of that very cold mountain, surrounded by the enemy, with no supplies or medical aid and low on ammunition.

A hail of deadly machine-gun fire ripped across the mountaintop and zigzagged in a pattern up and down, seeking to find them and the wounded soldiers.

"Coming in," Malichai called out, hoping his own soldiers weren't going to shoot him.

He and Rubin leapt over the ring of rocks and landed just inside the circle the soldiers had made for themselves. Other than the rocks, there was little cover, and the men were freezing. Malichai had seen some pathetic setups, but this was one of the worst. Added to the fact that the soldiers were all wounded, the rocks didn't make the best fortress. The enemy had enough firepower to blow those large boulders forming their stronghold to kingdom come.

Five men with various wounds lay in misery, but with their weapons ready. One attempted to sit, but Malichai waved him back down. They were all shivering continuously. The snow was stained red in places.

"I'm Malichai, that's Rubin." Deliberately, he left off any mention of rank. "We're here to pull your butts out of the frying pan. Give me your assessment of each patient," Malichai added to the one obviously assuming leadership.

"Jerry Lannis took the worst hit. His leg and arm. They were launching mortar fire and grenades. He shielded the rest of us when one of the grenades landed close. We did the best we could to help him . . ." The soldier trailed off as he indicated a man lying in the most protected spot the small space had.

Rubin immediately went to Jerry and uncovered the man's body. He glanced up at Malichai with a slight shake of his head. *If he makes it, he'll lose both the arm and the leg.*

Get started on him.

Rubin glanced around at the other soldiers, all looking at him with hope. He ducked his head over Jerry's arm, looking for a vein.

Rubin was a GhostWalker, enhanced psychically as well as physically. He was one of the ultra-rare — a psychic surgeon. If his assessment was that Jerry was going to lose his arm and leg, then no one could save those limbs. Rubin would do his best, and that meant Jerry would most likely live, but there was little chance he would live with all four limbs intact.

"We've got supplies. Not a lot, so you'll need to ration." As he spoke, Malichai tore open the thin packets with the blankets in them that would provide enough warmth to survive in the time they had to wait for extraction. He examined each man, making quick assessments.

The appointed leader went on with his report. "Jack Torren has two bullets in him. One caught him on the hip and the other along his ribs. Ribs are broken. Hip's intact. We're not sure how."

Jack sent Malichai a faint grin. "I guess I'm too mean to die. I tell them I have superhero bones."

"Barry Clarke has a broken arm and hand. Arm on one side, hand on the other."

"Nice," Malichai said. That was at least two mobile, if Jack's hip was really fit enough to allow him to run.

"Tim Barrens went down with a shot to the head. He's been in and out for some time. Mostly out, but when he comes to, he knows he's a soldier and he's with us and has to stay quiet, so he's comprehending things around him."

Malichai was already working on Jack, cleaning him up and setting up a bag of fluids to hydrate him as quickly as possible. He would need some of these men on their feet, fighting and willing to keep going, although they'd dug in and defended themselves so far in the face of an enemy outnumbering and outgunning them.

"You were a very welcome sight," the leader continued.

"Tell me about your wounds," Malichai instructed.

"Name's O'Connell. Braden O'Connell. I took a hit, a through and through, on my thigh. I was lucky, it didn't hit anything that's killed me yet, although I'm very weak."

That alarmed Malichai. He cursed under his breath. Would the kid have lasted so long if the artery was nicked? Regardless, he was probably bleeding internally.

"I wasn't certain but didn't want to move around too much just in case. I see to everyone as best I can, but I'm no medic."

"When are they coming for us?" Jack asked.

Immediately there was silence. Even the guns of the enemy had fallen silent. Malichai felt the eyes of the soldiers looking at him. Trusting in him. He sent them a small grin and continued to finish cleaning up Jack before moving on to Barry.

"Well, Jack, the deal was, I jump out of the helicopter and fix you up so you could get your superhero ass in gear and carry us all back home."

The others grinned but no one pointed out he hadn't answered the question. No one asked again. As far as Malichai could tell, Barry's left arm had suffered a clean break. Someone, most likely Braden, had splinted it. He'd done a good enough job that Malichai wasn't going to mess with it. He examined the wrist. There was a lot of bruising and swelling. Again, Braden had splinted it, but it was obvious Barry had continued to use it in an effort to help defend their position.

Malichai stabilized it and then wrapped it. "You're going to need fluids as well, but we'll set up after I've examined the others." Barry wasn't too bad off as far as life-threatening injuries went. He'd lucked out.

Tim lay quietly. Too quietly. Malichai swore under his breath and put his hand over the man's open eyes, slowly lowering the eyelids. Tim was dead. The headshot had quietly killed him, probably in the late evening hours and no one had been aware, leaving him to "sleep." He turned to look at Braden. Braden knew. He saw the gesture and the way Malichai had dropped his head down and briefly closed his own eyes.

"I'm sorry," he said quietly, mostly to Braden. The soldier had tried to keep them together and alive since their team leader was gone. The helicopter carrying these men had been shot down during their extraction. The other one carrying the rest of their team had thankfully gotten away.

"He was a good soldier. A good man," Braden said, emotion crossing his face. He struggled to contain it. "And a very good friend."

The others looked over at Tim and then at each other. "How's Jerry, Rubin?" Malichai asked deliberately, wanting to keep their attention on the living. "Full name, by the way, is Malichai Fortunes, and that's Rubin Campo. Just dropped in to see how you boys were doing and get you ready to come home."

Heads swiveled toward Rubin. Rubin had always been a man of very few words, and he lifted his gaze to Malichai, giving what amounted to a death stare. Malichai gave him a faint grin in return.

"He'll be ready to travel in a couple of hours. He needs a transfusion and he's

21

badly dehydrated. I've already got lines into him and am giving him the blood we brought for him."

"What about his leg and arm?" Jack asked.

Rubin shook his head. "A better question is, what about his life? We've got the enemy coming straight at us in the morning. The helicopters will have to set down right above us on the ridge. We have to be able to get him up there without losing him. We'll need all of you."

"No way can a helicopter land up there," Braden said. "You see those bunkers on your way in? They have heavy artillery. I mean heavy. They'll take out the helicopters every time."

"That's where we come in." Malichai took pity on Rubin. "We're going to make certain they can't shoot down our birds as they come in to get you."

There was a small silence. Braden let out his breath. "That's suicide. I'm serious. They've got every kind of weapon known in those bunkers and experienced fighters handling them."

"We have the intel," Malichai assured. "It's the only way any of us are getting out of here. We knew that when we volunteered to haul your butts out." Deliberately, he sounded cocky, but even though both men were enhanced, the bunkers weren't going to be easy to take down — and they had to be down, or they'd just keep losing helicopters.

"Your job is to get stronger. Get warm. Hydrate. Start getting those muscles to work," Rubin added to fill the silence as the others looked at them as if they were insane.

"It isn't the first time, you know," Malichai added. "That's what gave us the idea. A SEAL did something very similar on a different mountain a few years back."

"Weapons change all the time," Braden pointed out. "I'm telling you, that's suicide. I tried getting close to them, and they unleashed hell on us."

"We think they're going to sneak up on us and take us out," Jack added. "We're taking shifts, trying to stay awake, but they could kill us just about any time."

"You're too valuable to them right where you are. They know we're going to keep sending more troops in to try to bring you home," Malichai explained. "You're the bait."

The team exchanged looks. They didn't like that.

"I can help out," Braden offered.

"I could probably get up and running," Jack offered as well. "Barry can watch Jerry for us. I'm a damn good shot. You brought us some ammunition, right?"

They had, but they weren't taking the wounded with them on what amounted to a suicide mission — not to mention, being enhanced was classified. They weren't to expose others to those enhancements if at all possible.

"Your job is to make certain you're ready for a run up the mountain to the clearing just above us. The helicopter will set down there. If we clear the bunkers, we'll have help getting up to the extraction point. If not, it's all on us."

"We aren't leaving Tim behind," Braden said decisively.

The others murmured their agreement, all nodding and looking at Malichai as if he was challenging their firm statement. Malichai had no intentions of leaving Tim behind if it could be helped. The man was a soldier for the United States. He belonged home, not here, where his life had been taken far too young.

"No, we're not leaving him behind," he stated quietly, hoping everything went as planned and there would be no need to go back on his promise. No matter what, the living came first.

He looked across the small space to

Rubin, who was still working on Jerry. It didn't look good, not with the way Rubin was so gently and meticulously working on the man. That was another body they might have to transport out when the time came. He hoped not.

Jerry had saved the others at a great cost to himself, but he could live without a leg and an arm. He could have a decent life. Malichai didn't want to think too much on what that life would be like. He had to keep telling himself that at least Jerry was alive. Tim was never going to get that chance.

"Braden. I'd prefer that you stop moving around until you absolutely have to. I think you're losing blood internally. It's best if you just stay as still as you can and hydrate. I'm going to set up a transfusion for you as well."

Rubin, when you have a minute, will you check him out? I've got a bad feeling.

Rubin didn't look up, but he nodded.

There was a small gasp that seemed to go around the little encampment. Braden wasn't their commander, but he'd taken command when he had to. He'd been the one to dole out the supplies and ensure that the wounded were cared for. He'd done it by crawling from man to man. He'd defended them when they'd taken heavy fire.

25

He'd risked everything crawling around the bunkers at night to get intel on the enemy.

"The transfusion will help get you home. You're fine, but we just want to be more careful." Malichai said it more for the other men than for Braden.

Braden shrugged. "Save the blood for the others. Especially Jerry."

Malichai flashed him a smile. "You don't all have the same blood type, Braden. We brought a supply for each of you because we weren't certain what condition you were in. They're jamming communications."

Braden glanced at his watch. "Won't be long and they'll launch their nightly show of force, warning us, I guess, to stay put. They know we're sitting ducks here, but they just keep throwing ammo at us and then leaving us alone."

"What do you do?"

"We just have to hunker down and take it. I tell everyone to treat it as a Fourth of July fireworks show. We can't waste any more ammunition returning useless fire. We're not going to hit anything. They could blow us up right here if they really wanted to."

Malichai didn't like that, but it was the truth. They were alive because they were being kept alive in the hopes that more helicopters would come to rescue them.

The whine of a lone bullet was their first warning. Then all hell broke loose. Machine-gun fire erupted from three different locations, the sound and sight insanely beautiful in the cold, crisp night. The incoming looked exactly like fireworks, long white streaks spewing into the air, small white starlike dots filling the dark sky and then the occasional explosion of red and orange roaring flames.

If one could get over the horrific noise and the fact that those bullets could end a life, the murderous assault was exactly as Braden had said it would be — a Fourth of July fireworks display. Braden even began to point out the difference in one bunker's shooting from another's. They ducked and stayed under cover as best they could. Many of the bullets hit too close to home, but the men had endured the assault every evening, so they had already positioned themselves in the best places to stay safe.

Malichai noted that the two most seriously wounded, Tim and Jerry, were both tucked in tight behind the largest boulders. Rubin had covered Jerry's body with his own during the barrage of machine-gun fire. Malichai had been close to Braden, setting up his transfusion and the saline bag to hydrate him. Braden was the most exposed of all the soldiers and Malichai had instinctively covered him as well.

Braden nudged him. "Bunker three is worst. They always chip away at the rocks, making certain the slivers they break off and the sparks hit us. They're in the best position to take us out, but bunker two has the best and most accurate shooters. They're the ones that have taken out the helicopters. They're all capable, I guess, but bunker two seems much more experienced."

As far as Malichai could see, Braden O'Connell deserved a commendation, and if they got out of this mess in one piece, he intended to put the man up for one. Someone had to know how he conducted himself in the field under fire, even wounded as he was. He'd gathered intel, hoping to pass it on to anyone coming to rescue them.

"Do you have any idea how many men are manning each bunker?"

"I couldn't get close enough. They have traps set out to warn them if anyone is sneaking up on them. I tripped them twice. Once at bunker three and once at bunker two. By the time I got to the first one, I knew what their traps were like." He fished in his pocket and brought out a torn scrap of paper. His hand shook as he gave it to Malichai. "I drew them out the best that I could. It isn't one hundred percent reliable."

Malichai thought Braden was the epitome of a soldier. Even wounded, the man had crawled to the bunkers during the night, trying to get intelligence on positions, number of the enemy, and what weapons they had. He took the paper and looked it over carefully. There was far more firepower available to the enemy than they'd known. He didn't want any of the helicopters coming near their position until he and Rubin had a chance to take the guns out.

The two GhostWalkers worked as quickly and as efficiently as possible once the terrible barrage of bullets stopped. The noise had been deafening. More, the bullets had hit all around them. The constant mortar fire hitting close to their shelter was terrifying. There was nowhere else to go. They were in the last of the boulders before they were at the top of the peak. They lived with the certain knowledge that sooner or later, the enemy would get tired of taunting them. They wouldn't be that difficult to kill once the boulders were blown to bits.

It was bitterly cold at night, the temperature dropping drastically. Even with treating their wounds, giving blood, fluids and painkillers, the men weren't going to last unless they got them out of there.

"We're going to do this as quietly as we can," Malichai told them as they handed out ammunition. "We don't want you to try to help us. You just rest. Drink water. Try to sleep if you can. Don't make noise or call out to us, you'll just get us killed."

"They have excellent night vision goggles," Braden warned. "I learned that the hard way. I'm not certain any of us could come to your rescue." He moved as if he might try.

Malichai put a hand on his arm to stop him. "Just take it easy. You especially, Braden. I'm going to need you when we make our move. Don't worry so much, I've got a few tricks up my sleeve."

Braden looked him over. Malichai knew there wasn't much to see, other than he was combat-hardened. His experience showed in the lines in his face, in the calm he displayed under all conditions and in the flat, cold look in his eyes. The soldier nodded, a little reassured.

"You ready?" Malichai asked Rubin.

Rubin bent over Jerry. "I'm heading out now, but I'll be back in time to haul your ass out of here. I want you alive, soldier. You got that? You have a family waiting for you at home. Jack's right here if you need anything."

"I'm with you, buddy," Jack assured and reached out to grip Jerry's wrist.

Jerry attempted a faint grin. "I'll be here. Just lying around. Give me a gun. I'm right-handed."

Rubin looked up to meet Malichai's questioning gaze. No one wanted Jerry to take his own life. A decision had to be made. His team knew him better than they did. Both men looked to Braden.

"He'd never do that with us needing him. He knows every gun counts," Braden whispered to Malichai.

Malichai gave the thumbs-up to Rubin, who put a gun on the man's chest. "It's loaded. Just point and shoot. Just make certain it isn't pointed my way."

"Depends on whether or not these meds wear off before you get back," Jerry said.

Rubin gave him a grin, another pat and then turned his attention to Jack. "He's a tough one, but you keep him down until I get back."

Jack nodded while Jerry made derisive sounds. "That's my momma, telling me I have to behave myself."

"You keep that in mind." Rubin crawled back toward Malichai, staying low. Together, they pulled out their gear and shed their snow clothing.

Their garb was specifically constructed for nighttime raids. They reflected their surroundings and, with their enhancements, it was easy enough to fade into the night. They both were capable of lowering their body temperatures to confuse the night vision goggles and still function without impairment. It was one of Malichai's least favorite things to do.

"Helicopter will be here at dawn," Rubin reported. "We'll be back by then."

They had to be or that meant they were dead.

Malichai regarded Braden as he shoved weapons into each of the carefully hidden compartments in his clothing. "You stay put. Jack, if he gets some wild hair that he's coming after us, either sit on him or shoot him in the leg."

"Not sure that will stop him," Jack said. "But I'll be glad to follow those orders, sir."

Braden let out a groan. "You're giving way too much authority to a bloodthirsty individual, sir."

Malichai heard the strain in their voices, although they were trying to hide it with jokes. He gave them a small salute. "At dawn. Be prepared to move out fast."

"I'll get right on that, sir," Jerry said.

Rubin turned and looked at Malichai. Crouching low, they moved to the very edge of the boulder line. The big rocks progressively got smaller, forcing them to go down onto their bellies. Movement always drew the eye. Someone from each of the three bunkers had to have been given the job to watch for anyone trying to sneak out of the encampment, especially after Braden had tripped a few of their traps.

The mountains of Afghanistan were home, in spite of the continual conflicts, to many wild animals, including snow leopards, lions, jackals, fox and the roaming ibex. Any number of animals might have triggered those traps, if Braden hadn't left tracks for their enemies to find. It didn't matter, they had to take out those bunkers in order to give the helicopter a chance to land safely and take the wounded home.

He signaled to Rubin to make his way to bunker two first. That was the one with serious firepower and the most experienced of the enemy fighters. If they couldn't get to all of them, they had to at least kill those in bunker two. It would take an hour to make it across the snow-covered ground if they didn't want to be seen. During that hour, the hope was the fighters would be taking a much-needed break, eating and, if they were lucky, going to sleep. Malichai would approach from one direction, with Rubin coming in from the opposite side.

Malichai proceeded to move inch by slow inch. He didn't drag himself because he couldn't afford to have drag marks be seen in the snow. He had to use his hands and feet to propel his body forward. Always, he had to keep his body inches from the ground. Without his enhanced strength, he could never have accomplished such a thing.

Months earlier, he'd been shot in the leg, but thanks to Rubin's psychic surgery and the efforts of Joe, another teammate who was very skilled in psychic healing, his leg was stronger than ever. He felt very confident crossing that long expanse of snow to get to his intended target.

His enhancements were not as specialized as some of the other GhostWalkers' because he was considered an "all-around" soldier. He could find water in a desert twenty-five feet down below the surface. He could go up the side of a sheer mountain, or swim for long periods of time underwater without taking a breath. He was extremely fast underwater. His sense of smell, eyesight and hearing were all very acute.

He often felt like the man who wasn't master of anything yet could manage to make his way through numerous pitfalls. If he did have one claim he could make, it was taking apart or putting together explosives in record time. He had a feel for them. He almost didn't have to look at them. It was instinctive. But that was it as far as his enhancements went.

They maintained silence until they both reached their destinations. *In position,* Rubin reported.

They were always careful with telepathic communication. The truth was, many people had undeveloped psychic talents. They could trigger a warning, just by making the wrong person vigilant for no reason that individual could put his finger on — it was just a feeling.

In position. Rubin, we can't chance them making any noise. We have to do this one right. Even if they were able to kill their enemy, they had to do it swiftly, so the others didn't find out. *Most likely number is five. There will be a lookout behind the bunker.* Malichai had to get to him first. He would be in the best position to get away and raise the alarm. *Making my way around to guard's location now.*

He spoke in very small bursts of energy, keeping the output as low as possible. Once again, he began to move, inch by inch. He "felt" for the traps Braden had warned him about. He had encountered the first row of them approximately twenty feet out from the wall. The traps had wrapped around the reinforced boulders with more traps every few feet. A virtual minefield of alarms and real bombs that would be triggered by weight had been constructed to protect those inside the bunker.

The traps gave off energy that he felt through the hairs on his body. He had trained over and over to be sensitive enough to know when there was a trap, a bomb, anything at all that would harm him or those relying on him.

Malichai made his way around the bunker. Due to the rock formation, it was quite a distance to the back. There were no breaks in the rock and he finally went up, once again using his strength and the tiny gecko-like hairs engineered into his hands that allowed him to hold not only his own weight but that of another man as heavy as him. The hair was microscopic, but each was divided into a thousand fine projections, sticking out like tiny brushes. Unseen, they were only felt. Malichai'd had to train for months in the proper way to "stick" to a surface, and then learn to get unstuck. Once that had been accomplished, he'd trained to climb fast and in silence. He could hang upside down or stay on a ceiling if needed.

He clung to the side of the rock, surveying the enemy camp and counting the six men in the bunker. The guard would make seven. Sleeping quarters were toward the back of the bunker. Two men were lying down. Two were drinking what looked like tea while another stood with a pair of night vision goggles looking toward the encampment where Braden and the others were, while the sixth man swept back and forth with his night vision binoculars over the snow-covered ground.

Malichai slowly crawled down the rock wall and made his way toward the back of the bunker where the guard would be. It was darkest there. None of the light from the fire reached the outer perimeter. Once in the darkness, he stalked the guard. The man was facing out away from him, thinking all danger would come from outside the bunker, not inside. Malichai didn't waste time. Coming up behind him, he slammed his knife into the base of the man's skull, his hand over the guard's mouth to muffle any sound, and then carefully lowered him to the ground.

It's done.

Rubin was on the wall on the opposite

side. They took the two men sleeping first. They were a distance from the others and no one so much as turned to look at them, leaving them alone so they could get sleep. They crept up on the two men drinking tea and killed them quickly, catching the small glass vessels they drank out of. The sentries watching the enemy were the last ones, and they managed to kill them as well.

They left the fire burning brightly, and this time used the back entrances to the other two bunkers. Bunker one held only five men, and they used the same configuration as bunker two. One man guarded the rear of the bunker against the off chance that they would be attacked from that side. Two watched the enemy camp and the ground around the front of the bunkers while the other two rested. It was the same in bunker three.

When all the enemy were dead, Malichai and Rubin snuck back to camp. Above the bunkers were caves where they were concerned that more of the enemy lived, so they didn't dare blow up the weapons. They disabled the larger ones and made their way back, arriving just before the helicopter was due.

Malichai indicated to Braden and the others that he wanted them silent as they made their way up the slope to the rendezvous point with the helicopter. They didn't want to make any noise at all and tip off any of the enemy who might be staying in the caves that they were escaping.

Rubin took Jerry on his shoulders. He'd been given painkillers, but it still had to hurt like hell. Rubin didn't say anything or ask questions, he just started up the slope. The moment he had traveled a few feet, a barrage of deadly fire hit just below them. Rubin caught Jerry in his arms and dove for cover.

Malichai swore. That answered the question whether or not there were more in the caves. Or at least, someone had showed up and discovered the dead.

"Shit," Malichai hissed. "We missed a few."

"That's impossible," Rubin denied, but he had his rifle out and ready after securing Jerry.

"I'll get them out of there." There was no choice. If they were going to get the wounded into the helicopter, they would have to make it safe for the helicopter to put down. Malichai had no choice, he had to go.

Braden shook his head. "You're crazy, man. You can't face that kind of firepower."

"Do you have any better ideas?" Malichai asked. His gaze was on bunker two. The bunker was positioned to cover the mountain from almost any angle. Naturally, the enemy would have set up there. They didn't need the other bunkers in order to control the entire area. He had to clear that bunker and get rid of the weapons. There was no point in hesitating. He had to do it now, before the helicopter decided it was too risky and left them and before any more of the enemy decided to show themselves — if there were any more. Wouldn't they already be out in force if there were? He couldn't think about that.

Without further preamble, he left the safety of the boulders, sprinting from his position down the slope toward the bunkers. Malichai charged into the gunfire, running low, using a zigzag pattern with his enhanced speed. He had to leap over larger rocks and go around others. Bullets flew at him, never stopping, hundreds fired from the machine gun, tearing up the ground as he ran. Rocks exploded, sending pieces flying into the air. The bullets whipped around him, ripping at his clothing, tearing holes in the material and slicing pieces of skin. Still, he was up. He was running, his entire mind focused on the task in front of him.

No matter what, he had to silence those weapons. Bunker two contained at least three enemy. Three different weapons were being wielded. They meant business too. The sound was continuous, a booming thunder rolling over top of him, so loud his ears hurt. He had enhanced hearing and no matter how he tried to turn down the volume, with the heavy barrage of murderous machine-gun fire, there was no way to do so.

Mortars hit the ground on two sides of him, nearly simultaneously, letting him know that bunker one had at least one fighter still alive. No way could Rubin and he have missed that many of the enemy, even at night. Reinforcements must have arrived to take over, at least three or four, more likely five. Had they been random? Men arriving? Had they been in the caves? Were there more? He could drive himself crazy wondering.

He dove for cover, rolled and came back up, hurling grenades over the barrier of bunker two. He tossed grenade after grenade into the bunker. The enemy continued to fire at him until the grenades inside the bunker began to explode, one after the other. Bunker one's fire was continuous, the bullets hitting all around him. One nearly parted his hair. He actually felt it burning along his scalp.

He heard Rubin's rifle and then the fall of a body in bunker two. It was quieter after that and Malichai took another chance. Ignoring the firepower the enemy threw at him from bunker one, he ran the last few feet and leapt over the barricade, landing in the snow, his weapon ready and tracking, looking for anyone left alive in bunker two.

The smell of blood and death was heavy in the crowded bunker. Shrapnel had torn into bodies, ripping through them, leaving behind bloody shells he knew he wasn't going to get out of his head for a long time. He had no choice but to wade through the blood and gore to reach the still-intact mortar gun.

The barrage of bullets coming from the machine gun in bunker one was a steady stream, zipping across the thick stone barricade and into the bunker, keeping Malichai pinned down. The mortar gun was lightweight, sitting on a tripod, the weapon resting on the metal plate. He swung the entire apparatus around so that it faced bunker one rather than the boulders his wounded were camped behind.

He turned the explosive power of the mortar gun on the enemy. While he fired round after round into bunker one, Rubin's rifle also engaged, and he never missed. If he pulled the trigger, someone inevitably went down. After what seemed like forever, bunker one fell silent. Malichai waited. There was no way to know for certain, but they couldn't keep the helicopter waiting forever. It was all about fuel.

Everything was still and quiet. Malichai knew he had to check bunkers one and three, although there had been no gunfire from three. They had to be able to load the wounded into the helicopter. It was waiting for the clear signal to land. He stepped out from behind the shelter of bunker two, heart pounding, mouth dry. Nothing stirred. He began to make his way over to bunker one when machine-gun fire erupted from behind the walls of bunker one. It was fast. Furious. And bloodthirsty.

Malichai didn't know how many times he was hit, but it felt like a dozen. Maybe more. Pain blossomed, spread like wildfire, all up and down his leg, from his calf to his thigh. There was no coming back when his leg was that torn up, flesh shredded, pulverized even. He knew he was a dead man as he crumpled to the ground. The bones in his leg were shattered. He felt that, the bursting pain that traveled through his system so

43

bright and hot he nearly passed out. He fought that feeling, ignoring the bullets still spitting at him. He began tearing off wrappings with his teeth and slapping field dressings over wound after wound. It was almost automatic, although he knew it was futile. There was so much blood, but he pressed the dressings over the worst of them. Five of the worst, where the blood was a fountain, spouting up like a whale.

Dr. Peter Whitney had developed a drug called Zenith. That drug would stop bleeding and force adrenaline into the body, allowing a wounded man to get to his feet. It was supposed to promote healing, but after a few hours, it began to do just the opposite, breaking down cells until the wounded died unless he was given a second drug to counteract the first. Whitney had been the man who conceived the GhostWalker program and psychically enhanced the soldiers who tested high in psychic ability. He'd also genetically altered them without their permission.

Second-generation Zenith had been developed by Whitney's daughter, Lily. She was a brilliant doctor and researcher. She was also one of the orphan girls Whitney had experimented on. For some reason, Whitney had chosen her as his successor and he had officially adopted her. She was married to a GhostWalker from Team One. Second-generation Zenith was supposed to work without the ugly side effects. He hoped so. Zenith was all he had to keep him alive.

He waited, breathing deeply until the drug hit his system. When it did, the heavy load of adrenaline from five patches was almost too much to handle. The dressings were already stopping the bleeding and sealing the wounds from the outside. He knew that didn't mean he wasn't bleeding internally, or that it could miraculously heal the broken bones, but the adrenaline gave him the necessary strength to move.

Malichai began to drag himself across the snow-covered ground. Jagged rocks were just below the surface, making it a struggle to keep going. Each time the shooter behind bunker one rose up to aim at Malichai, another rifle barked and then a third. Braden and Jack were clearly helping to keep the enemy pinned down while Malichai painstakingly made his way to the bunker.

It seemed he had used up quite a lot of his strength dragging his wounded leg behind him. He left a long trail of blood in the white snow. That trail of blood was an arrow, pointing out his position to the

enemy. It didn't matter that he wore specialized clothing to help hide him or that his
enhancements would have kept him from
being seen — the blood trail was a dead
giveaway.

Although Rubin and the others kept the
enemy pinned down, the machine gun was
firing continuously so that bullets hit the
ground mercilessly. He didn't care. He
knew, from the way he was bleeding, in spite
of the Zenith, he was a dead man anyway. It
wasn't like he had a whole hell of a lot to
lose. He had to give the helicopter a chance
to land and take the wounded home.

Using the enormous strength in his arms,
he dragged himself across the rugged, freezing ground until he was nearly on top of
the enemy, right under their wall. He
smelled them. Blood. Fear. Stink of the
unwashed. He knew he smelled the same
way. He lay there breathing, hoping no one
poked a gun over the wall and finished him
off before he got his task done.

He took the last of his grenades and tossed
them over the wall, trying to hit the enemy
squarely, just judging the distance by the
sound of their moving around. The explosions rocked the wall so that debris fell on
him, but there was no movement. He
couldn't get off his ass to go check to make

certain he had actually gotten the last of their enemies.

Malichai listened for movement. For groans. For anything at all that would tell him even one person was still alive. When time passed and he heard nothing at all, he began the slow, arduous journey back across the ground toward the slope. He still had to make it back to where the helicopter was landing, and it seemed a million miles away. In the distance he could hear it coming in, and he was thankful, but he knew, in the back of his mind, that he wasn't going to make it.

He should have told Ezekiel he loved him. Funny, he'd never said it to him. Not to him, not to Mordichai either. Then there was Rubin and Diego. They weren't brothers by blood or birth, but they were brothers just the same. He hadn't told them either.

"Shut up, Malichai," Rubin said distinctly. "Conserve your strength. You're not going to die. You do that and Ezekiel's most likely gonna shoot my ass."

That was true. Zeke could be like that. Malichai peered up at Rubin. He was there, rifle slung over his shoulder, his image wavering in and out as if he were more of a mirage. Malichai poked at him with a finger.

"You real?"

"Real enough."

"You getting me out of here?"

"Something like that. You weigh a ton, Malichai. I'm going to tell Nonny not to feed you so much."

Rubin hoisted him on his back and rushed toward the helicopter already set down in the snow and rocks, stowing the wounded inside as fast as possible.

2

"What the hell do people do on vacation?" Malichai asked aloud. He shook his head and turned away from the mirror. Staring at himself didn't improve his looks any.

He was a big man, with obvious, defined muscles running through his body. What wasn't so obvious was the fact that even as muscular as he was, those muscles were loose and he could move fast and use the speed and strength of them, and that his reflexes were astonishing. He had strangely colored eyes, always had them, even as a child, but the enhancements done on him in the service had further changed them so that they looked gold. Old gold. Florentine gold.

His lifestyle was beginning to take a toll on him. There was no getting around it. He went out on missions as often as possible. Mostly, they rescued soldiers shot up and needing immediate transport out of a hot zone. He was fast, he was strong and he was very adept at fieldwork. There were few better at triaging a wounded soldier or finding a vein and getting a needle in fast before the vein collapsed. He was dedicated to bringing his soldiers home alive if possible. So, he volunteered every single time they had to go in with guns blazing.

So, yeah, he'd been shot a few times. He'd seen more than his share of hand-to-hand combat. He'd taken on the drug cartels a few times. What else was he supposed to do? He wasn't the kind of man women looked at and wanted for themselves. He didn't know if a woman could live with him — he could barely live with himself. So, a home and family were out for him. He understood that, but he didn't have to like it.

He'd grown up on the streets of Chicago with his two brothers, Ezekiel and Mordichai. Later, Ezekiel had discovered Rubin and Diego Campo fending for themselves as well, and they'd banded together. Schooling had been intermittent, just what Ezekiel could provide for them. Mostly they looked for food and kept the predators off one another. Malichai had grown up fierce, using his fists, learning every form of underhanded street-fighting known to man, and

50

he'd learned it was life or death. He'd chosen life.

He sighed and walked to the door of his rented room. It was small and he covered the distance quickly, too quickly. Once he opened the door, he was expected to actually do something. Go somewhere. Enjoy himself. He'd forgotten how to do that.

He lived in the Louisiana swamps and he'd learned he loved it. He liked his "family" there, particularly his teammate Wyatt Fontenot's grandmother. She insisted on the entire team of GhostWalkers calling her Nonny, which they did. Eventually, he had begun to feel as if he had a grandmother for the first time. She cooked amazing meals for them. There was always food on the table. He was always hungry. He was now.

Satisfaction, now that he had an actual purpose for leaving his room, settled in his gut and he stood by the door, automatically listening for anyone on the other side. There were at least three people in the hallway, but that was okay, he had already identified them. Like him, they were staying at the little bed-and-breakfast.

He went into the hallway and, without more than glancing at the others who were huddled together arguing about which direction they would go, he continued toward the staircase. The two men and one woman always seemed to be arguing, so much so, that he had deliberately tuned them out. They spoke in what they considered hushed tones, but a man with his enhanced hearing had no problem listening to their ridiculous arguments if he wanted to — which he didn't.

Malichai made his way to the dining room. A prickle of awareness crept down his spine and his gaze swept the nearly empty room. One other person sat by herself at a table in the corner. She was reading a book — a romance — and he smirked when he saw it. She was a gorgeous woman and he tried not to stare at her. She was a blonde, but her hair was so thick, he doubted if the color could be natural. Most blondes had finer or thinner hair than that. He must have been looking too closely because she glanced up. He could tell that first glance was simple idle curiosity but then she stiffened, and her gaze wholly focused on him.

Her eyes were gorgeous, a startling blue, like jewels. So deep blue they were almost certainly contacts. She glanced back down at her book, but he could tell she wasn't reading it anymore. He'd probably scared her. He wasn't like some of his fellow

GhostWalkers, who seemed to walk into a room and have half the female population enthralled — and that had nothing to do with their enhancements and everything to do with their good looks, charisma or both, none of which he had.

The breakfast was set up buffet style with a long row of warmers laid out on a table. He would have his back to the room when he served himself food, but he seemed to be the last man to breakfast. The moment he'd walked in he'd become uneasy, but no one was there but the two of them — the blonde and him. Was the threat coming from her? Was it even a threat? He was on vacation. Didn't that mean there was no threat? Hell if he knew.

He dished himself food, standing sideways to keep her in sight. Her gaze jumped to him and she lowered the book partway, both feet coming to the floor, when she'd been relaxed, one leg curled up under her. He sent her a cocky grin.

"See you're readin' my favorite book."

She narrowed her eyes at him. "You have no idea what I'm reading."

He was an enhanced GhostWalker with the very sharp eyes of an eagle. "It's a romance titled *Toxic Game*." He hoped he didn't have to describe what the book was about because he didn't have a clue.

She glanced down at the book as if she couldn't believe he knew the title. When she looked back up at him, his heart went a little crazy. The sun hit her just right, turning her blond hair into a waterfall of ice and gold sparkles. The strands actually dazzled his eyes for a moment, so that he lost sight of her. Her image blurred. He could only see that amazing, overpowering shine.

He blinked to bring her into focus. When he managed to get her back in his sight, he found himself staring into her vivid jeweled eyes, eyes blazing blue flames at him.

"You do not read romance books." Her chin went up. "There's absolutely nothing wrong with wanting to read about men who believe in monogamy. I doubt you'd know anything about that."

He took a chair facing her and drank his coffee slowly, studying her furious little face. She was beautiful all riled up. His heart was going a little crazy and all at once he felt very much alive. Maybe this vacation thing wasn't going to be so bad.

"What makes you think that? If I read romances, clearly I like happy endings and prefer books where men and women are faithful to one another." It was all about thinking fast on one's feet. Any Ghost-

Walker should be excellent at that.

"I think you're so full of —" She broke off as a woman came into the doorway, clearly agitated, so much so that she seemed to completely miss that Malichai was even in the room.

"Amaryllis?" It was Mrs. Stubbins, the owner of the bed-and-breakfast. "I know your break isn't over for another fifteen, and you were up half the night already for me, but would you mind helping out in the kitchen right now? There's something wrong with the dishwasher and I can't get Jacy to settle down . . ." She trailed off when she noticed Malichai sitting at his table. "Oh, I'm so sorry. I thought everyone was finished."

"I was late coming down this morning," he said. "Is there something I can do to help? I'm not bad with fixing things like dishwashers. Fixed Nonny's a time or two." Mostly she never used her modern dishwasher and critters ate the wires, but he wasn't going to say that.

"No, no, you're a guest," Mrs. Stubbins said.

Malichai had been ordered to take leave and to continue with his therapy by swimming in the ocean. The women and little girls were happy to gather around the Fontenot table in the kitchen with brochures spread out and decide his fate. They'd chosen the little bed-and-breakfast in San Diego, California. A beachfront property, it was reputed to have amazing cuisine, which was the only thing he cared about. The owner had been investigated because one didn't have a multimillion-dollar piece of high security equipment running around without knowing everything about where he was going or who he might be coming in contact with.

Mrs. Stubbins was a widow — the widow of a soldier who had lost his life fighting for his country three years earlier. She was struggling financially, mostly because her daughter'd had two operations on her heart and those didn't come cheap. Malichai liked her and everything he'd read about her in the file they had on her.

She bit her lip. "Besides, I think that dishwasher is just old and has given up the ghost."

"Mrs. Stubbins, if I didn't help you out, my grandmother would have my hide. Lead me to the broken-down piece of equipment and let me see what I can do."

He rolled up his sleeves, revealing the tattoos up and down his arms, and went to her, keeping Amaryllis in his sight the entire time. She left the book and came around the table hastily, as if she feared he intended Mrs. Stubbins harm.

"Please call me Marie. You're sure you don't mind?"

"Not at all, Marie. Give me something to do. I'm not very good at vacations."

Amaryllis trailed after them. He didn't like her behind him, so he deliberately, and gallantly, stepped aside to wave her past him. She hesitated for just one moment, but then hurried to catch up with Mrs. Stubbins. She actually slipped on by her and was in the kitchen first, so she had her back to the wall and her eyes on him as he strode in. She didn't seem afraid so much as leery of him.

Marie Stubbins swept her hand toward the large commercial dishwasher she'd already pulled out. "I tried to check it out myself, but I have no idea what I'm doing."

"I can look it up on YouTube, and maybe find a checklist we can go over ourselves," Amaryllis suggested sweetly. "That way Mr. . . ." She trailed off, expecting Malichai to supply his name. Marie had been the one to check him into his room on his arrival.

He didn't. Instead, he sat on the floor and looked at the impressive amount of tools Marie had laid out. "Thanks, Amaryllis. I'd appreciate the help. While you do that, I'll look this over and see if I can find anything that jumps out at me." Ignoring her, he looked up at the owner of the bed-and-breakfast. "You say it just stopped working?"

"It was working fine last night, but then this morning when I went to turn it on, it wouldn't budge."

Malichai was very aware of Amaryllis staring at him indecisively, and then she flounced out of the kitchen. He couldn't help smirking. They were off to an excellent start.

"Don't worry, if I can't get this thing going, I'll help Amaryllis with the dishes, and we'll figure something out."

Marie looked as if she might protest, but clearly she was too defeated. She just flashed him a wan smile. "I don't know how to thank you. We can take a day off —"

He held up his hand. "I'm always looking for food, woman. I think I'm always starving, and my grandmother says with what I eat I should weigh a thousand pounds."

Marie laughed. "I can cook. I'll make certain you have plenty of food."

Amaryllis must have set a record for running, or her small tablet was close. She rushed back into the room and pulled up short when she heard Marie laughing. Malichai glanced at her and his breath caught in his lungs. It was the first time he'd allowed himself to really see her body. She wore a pair of yoga pants that fit her like a glove. The little racer-back tank clung to every curve — and she had them. She might be on the shorter side, but she was breathtaking.

He peered into the machine as if it were his life's work. He wasn't going to get caught staring at her and reveal that she had the upper hand. That woman had an impressive body packed into those yoga pants and that tank.

"I'll leave you two to it," Marie said. "No worries, though, Amaryllis, I haven't forgotten I owe you hours of time, including last night and this morning. I'll bus tables and clean up the dining room while you do this. I have that appointment with Jacy's doctor this afternoon, but I can do dinner . . ."

"I'm fine with cooking dinner," Amaryllis said. "I haven't poisoned anyone yet."

Malichai thought that might be a pointed jab at him, but Marie didn't seem to take it that way. She laughed as if she found Amaryllis very funny.

Malichai waited until Marie was out of the room before he turned and looked at Amaryllis again. She gave off the kind of energy he felt when he faced an enemy in combat. There was something else as well. If it was at all possible, he would have thought she felt very much like a fellow GhostWalker. They normally recognized one another, although there were a few who were shielded from the others, and they could shield an entire team when needed. He was far from home and the only women he knew who were GhostWalkers had been previous experiments Whitney had deemed failures.

He ignored the little lift to her chin. "You got anything for me, a starting point, because just looking at this, it all looks good. She said it worked fine last night, but this morning . . . nothing."

"You're really going to fix her dishwasher for her?" Sarcasm dripped from her voice.

Malichai looked her up and down. "I don't know what your problem with me is, and frankly, I don't care, but Marie seems like a very nice lady with too much work and too many problems. If I can fix her dishwasher, it's a very small amount of my time to help someone who seems deserving. If you don't want to help me, that's okay. I'm capable of looking up the same things you are."

She stared at him for a long moment, the

clock ticking in the background. She blinked, a sweep of her long lashes. "You really are planning on fixing it for her, aren't you?"

"I told you so."

"Men like —" She stopped what she'd been going to say. "People aren't usually that nice."

She'd been going to say men like him. He didn't ask questions. "I told you, my grandmother wouldn't like it if I didn't help."

She studied his face. "You don't have a grandmother."

"Technically, she's not my blood, but I claim her and, thankfully, she claims me. We all call her Nonny and she's the center of the family. A good woman. She's lived her life in the swamps of Louisiana, is as smart as a whip and about the kindest woman I know."

Amaryllis glanced down at her tablet. "Start with the switch on the door. The latch, I mean. No, wait. It's an assembly of latch switches." She held out the tablet. "Like that. It says if it's defective then the door can't lock, and the dishwasher won't work."

Malichai watched the little video providing information on the door latch switches before carefully inspecting the assembly. "Is

Marie really okay? She looks very upset, too upset to be frazzled over a dishwasher breaking down. It also sounds like you've been pulling extra duty to help her out quite a bit." He kept his voice low as he examined the switch housing.

"Jacy's been pretty sick again. She has a heart condition. Marie lost her husband and Jacy's all she's got. She's very worried."

"Is it her heart again?"

"I have no idea. I don't think Marie does either. But she's scared."

"That's too bad." He didn't know what else to say, but it worried him. It wasn't right that the widow of a man dying in the service of his country was facing financial ruin and the possible loss of her daughter because Jacy had a heart problem. "Give me something else to check. This looks good."

"The thermal fuse. You'll have to access the control panel and you'll need the meter. Do you know how to use that thing?"

"I'm surprised she has such good tools."

"Her husband had them. He was really the one to come up with the idea of a bed-and-breakfast. He would be the mainte-nance man and she would be the cook. They'd both do the household chores to-gether. They bought this place as a fixer-upper and just when they had everything in place, he was killed. His teammates still drop by occasionally, but she never asks them for help."

He checked the thermal fuse twice before ruling it out. "I don't think this is the problem either." He glanced over his shoulder as Marie came in carrying far too many dishes. "Whoa, woman, you're not a pack animal. You're going to hurt your back. I can get those for you."

Marie laughed. "Malichai, that's silly. I do this every day, or Amaryllis does."

Marie had registered him, but still, just hearing his name said in such a friendly tone surprised him. Some of his teammates were married. His brother Ezekiel was married. The women in their "family" were also GhostWalkers, every bit as lethal as their male counterparts. They sometimes joked and teased with him, but outsiders, as a rule, didn't. He put it down to his looks. He knew he was intimidating.

"That doesn't mean you should, ma'am," he countered.

"Marie," she corrected again. "Just please, call me Marie. If you call me anything else, I'll feel far older than I already do."

He doubted if Marie was even thirty yet. He glanced at Amaryllis. "We're narrowing this down fast. Hopefully, if we don't need a part, we'll be using the dishwasher for all these dishes. Otherwise" — he lowered his voice as if entering a conspiracy — "I haven't told her yet that I volunteered the two of us to do the dishes for you."

Amaryllis covered her smile with her hand. "As I often clean the kitchen and do the dishes that don't fit into the dishwasher, it isn't unexpected."

"You hear that, Marie? She's beginning to reach the conclusion that a man can be helpful at times."

"I didn't say that," Amaryllis hastened to deny.

When she smiled, those blue eyes of hers lit up her entire face. She had smooth, beautiful skin and it looked radiant when she smiled. Her voice was extremely pleasing. Soft and melodic. He noticed it in particular because it seemed to get inside him somehow and replayed almost every word she said to him.

Marie put the tub of dirty dishes down and went back for the warmers, shaking her head and laughing softly at their antics.

"She's pretty terrific," Malichai observed. "She's going to be another Nonny. Growing up, I wasn't around too many women. My brother Ezekiel raised us. He was a kid himself, but I didn't view him that way. He was tough as nails and when someone tried to take our food or our territory where we slept, he beat the holy shit out of them. When Mordichai or I didn't follow every dictate, which was almost never, he beat the holy shit out of us."

"Why does it not surprise me that you didn't obey every dictate?"

He grinned at her. "I can't imagine. It's not the thermal fuse. What's next on the list?"

"This says to check the timer or the electronic control."

He scowled up at her. "Woman, seriously. Don't try my patience. Cough up a little more information than that."

She flashed a genuine smile and his heart went into overtime. The more he looked at her, the more beautiful she was. That smile of hers was enough to trigger a serious reaction in his body, one that wasn't welcome when he was sitting on a kitchen floor trying to repair a dishwasher.

"I'm so sorry, I thought maybe you were born with dishwasher files in your head or something. Let me read this."

"Dishwasher files in my head?" he echoed. "The only thing I know about dishwashers is Nonny doesn't always like to use them. It doesn't even make sense. One minute it's okay and the next, not so much and she needs volunteers for dish duty."

"She sounds fun."

"She is fun. She's more than that. Nonny sits in her rocking chair looking out over the swamp, a pipe between her teeth, with a shotgun inches from her hand, and she is the swamp. The people. She knows every plant and what their properties can be used for. She puts out food and clothes for those less fortunate, and she always has a pot of gumbo or fish stew on the stove for any of us who come in hungry."

"She sounds amazing."

Malichai nodded. "She is amazing. What is most amazing about her is she claimed us right away. I remember going home with her grandson Wyatt that first time. I was shot up all to hell. We all were. We arrived very late, came up the river and tied up at this pier. I can't explain to you, but I never had a home. I lived mostly in the streets of Chicago and there I was, in the swamp, this sultry, beautiful weird world all its own. We walked up the stairs to the porch where she was just sitting in that rocking chair, her pipe smelling like spices. She looked at me and I swear to you, it was like coming home."

He hadn't ever told anyone that story, not even Wyatt. He didn't understand why he'd told Amaryllis. He looked up at her. She was staring down at him as if she thought he'd grown two heads. Malichai sighed. That was just like him. Impressing her with a child's tale hadn't been his best idea, although to him, that had been a defining moment. No matter what, he clearly would never be considered the cool ladies' man.

"You continually surprise me, Malichai, in a good way." There was genuine surprise in her voice.

"I think that's easy enough to do, honey. You don't have high expectations of me."

Color climbed up her neck to her face, turning that pale complexion a soft rose. "I'm sorry. Am I coming across as a hag?"

"You're coming across as someone protecting her friend from a stranger. I know I don't look like a nice guy. I expect a little bit of resistance when I'm helping out a woman who works far too hard."

Amaryllis studied his face for a long time. He could feel that look, drifting over his face like the brush of fingers, barely there, but taking his entire focus.

"I don't know why you think you don't look like a nice guy. You look tough, like you can handle yourself, but you don't look mean."

He sat back and looked up her. "Then why are you afraid of me?"

At once the wary look crept back into her eyes. "I'm not afraid of you."

That was very decisive, and he wanted to smile, but held back. Yeah. She was afraid of him, but not in the way he'd been talking about. He was dangerous to her in more ways than was good for either of them.

"Good. Then we can get this done before we have to do the mountain of dishes Marie is piling up for us." He turned back to the machine, making certain that he could keep her in his sight at all times without appearing to do so. He was still uneasy. There was something a little bit off about Amaryllis. "What do you have for me?"

"I'm looking. Apparently, dishwashers drain any standing water out as a first step."

"Wait. There can't be leftover water if we didn't start it."

"There's standing water in the bottom that didn't drain. If you didn't hear the pump, then it's possible the timer is the cause. Is the timer on that one electronic or manual?"

"First, the damn thing won't start so I'm not hearing a thing, but" — he held up his

hand to stop her before he could finish —
"I'm looking."

She laughed, the sound settling somewhere in his gut, creating a strange rolling
sensation that should have been small, but
wasn't. God, she got to him. The longer he
was in her company, the stronger the attraction to her became. And she smelled so
damn good, he was afraid he might throw
down the tools any minute and spread her
out like a feast on the counter so he could
devour her.

He forced his attention back to the dishwasher. "It looks like it's a manual timer."

"According to this, the timer supplies
power to all sorts of things. The pump motor, inlet valve . . ." Her head went up and
she frowned at him. "Do you even know
what an inlet valve is? Maybe we should call
someone."

"I know what an inlet valve is."

She narrowed her eyes at him. "You are
lying to me. You don't have a clue."

"Baby, have some faith."

She rolled her eyes. "Beside the pump motor and inlet valve, the timer thingy provides
power to the heat circuit and to the drain
pump motor in the right progression. The
timer uses a series of electrical contacts that
are driven by a small motor. All of that is

encased in the timer housing. I'm reading this and hope it makes sense to you."

"Yeah. I've got it now." He glanced a second time to make certain the machine wasn't plugged in. When he did so, he watched Amaryllis out of the corner of his eye. He was very leery of things that didn't add up, and she was one of them.

"I have to check each of these for continuity with the multimeter. There's a schematic drawing that shows which is the inlet and which is the pump. Hopefully, we can figure out what's wrong right here." He busied himself checking the first one. "How long have you known Marie?"

There was a small silence. He glanced at her over his shoulder. She was fidgeting. Her eyes met his and she shrugged. "About a year. I met her in the grocery store. She needed help and I needed a job. She was, for me, like your Nonny, or more like a sister and mother all rolled into one. I didn't come from the best circumstances either. Marie showed me that didn't matter. I could still make something of myself."

"That's good. Did you know her husband?" He didn't know why he asked when he knew the answer, maybe to catch her in a lie. She had no way of knowing his team had investigated Marie before his arrival.

"No. He had already passed away, but she talks about him so much that I feel as if I know him."

"I think this is it, Amaryllis." He loved her name. "We're going to have to order the part and rush it here. So, it looks like dish duty for us for the next few days."

"She isn't going to like a guest doing the dishes. I can, but really, thank you for this."

"Put the part number in and see who has the best price and the fastest delivery. I'm doing the dishes because I told Marie I would and I'm a man of my word. Besides" — he carefully put the tools away — "you'd like to get rid of me so I'm sticking around just to bug you."

"That's mean."

"No, I'm expanding your horizons. Pushing your comfort zone. Showing you that even rough-looking men can be nice." He finished closing up the machine so he could stand up. Sitting on the floor so long had stiffened his leg. He stumbled a little but caught himself.

"What's wrong?"

"Nothing." He sounded gruff. Maybe even harsh, his voice clipped and abrupt. He was looking better and better to a woman he really wanted to impress.

She didn't ask again. "Stop fishing for

compliments. You do look tough, but you know you're good-looking."

He coughed to cover his snort of derision. By no means could he be called good-looking. There were some seriously good-looking men in his unit — and he wasn't one of them. He didn't mind her thinking that though.

"You want to wash or dry?"

"I'll dry. I know where everything goes."

"You just want to see my tattoos."

"There is that," she agreed. Once again, she gave him a small smile and that look that he wasn't sure how to interpret. "The ones I can see are beautiful. Someone does good work."

He nodded. "Started going to him when I was in my late teens. Still go back to Chicago so he can do the work on me. You have any?"

She shook her head. "No, but I always wanted one."

"What would it be?"

She shrugged. "Something very personal to me. Maybe the flower."

His gut tightened. He turned to survey the stainless-steel sink, not wanting her to see his face just in case his expression changed. "I don't know much about flowers. My name's all about the Bible. Malichai was either just a book or a prophet or both, although my mother couldn't even get the spelling right. That was so like her." He wasn't above pushing a little bitterness into his voice, although he'd gotten over that somewhere on the streets of Chicago. "Much rather have a pretty name like yours. Is the flower pretty?"

"I think so. It always looks radiant to me. Very striking depending on the color. The ones I like the most are scarlet."

He glanced back at her as hot water filled the sink. "I can see you as scarlet. You're a beautiful woman so having a name like Amaryllis really suits you."

She flashed him a small smile. "Are you a prophet or a book?"

No one had ever asked him that before. He read to people from the book of death and called it the bible occasionally. Okay. More than occasionally. But he felt more often he was the prophet, letting his enemy know he was doomed.

"If I had to choose, I'd choose to be identified as the prophet."

She pulled a fresh towel from a drawer and stood next to him. The moment she was close, he found he took her in with every breath he drew. The more he breathed, the more he was aware of her. Every cell in his body seemed focused on her. He knew when she took a breath. When she let it out. He breathed with her. In. Out. Together. As if they were already exchanging breath.

Malichai had never felt so intimate with a woman, and he wasn't touching her. He didn't need to. He felt her on his skin. Her breath moved over him. Her scent surrounded him. When he handed her a plate, their fingers brushed and lightning struck him deep, forked through his body, spreading an electrical charge through his veins so that she struck at his heart and cock simultaneously.

He could barely think, his head pounding, but it was imperative for him to sort things out. Amaryllis was the name of a flower. Many women were named after flowers. Just because she had that name didn't mean she was one of Dr. Whitney's experiments. He'd taken infants from orphanages, female children he'd considered throwaways, and he'd experimented on them. He'd worked to enhance psychic abilities they may have had. He'd introduced animal DNA into their bodies. He'd given them cancer. He'd conducted all kinds of hideous experiments in order to be able to create the perfect soldier — him. Malichai.

Whitney had done all those things to the

little girls just to perfect what he would do to those men he deemed worthy of his program. He kept the girls and trained them as soldiers, and then, wanting more babies to work with, introduced them into a breeding program. Several of the women had escaped. Some still went out on missions for him. It was impossible to tell one from the other. If Amaryllis was involved in any way with Whitney, she was a danger to him and to national security. If an enemy of their country ever found her and took her, they would take her apart to find out just how Whitney had created his GhostWalkers.

If Amaryllis really was part of Whitney's program, how was it possible it would be a coincidence that she just happened to be at the bed-and-breakfast he'd chosen to visit? She'd said she'd been there a year. If he could confirm that with Marie, he'd feel much better.

"What do people do on vacations?"

She was keeping up with him, drying nearly as fast as he was washing. She paused though and looked at him like he was insane.

"They don't volunteer to fix broken dishwashers, and they don't do the dishes. You're paying to relax and have fun. Read a book. You know, your *favorite*. Go to a movie. Sit in the sun and tan. There's one of the most beautiful beaches you'll find around here right out the door, and you can sit and stare at the waves."

"Is that what you do?" He was curious about her daily life.

"I work."

"You must get time off."

"This is seasonal work for the most part. We're at our heaviest time of year. I work when Marie needs me."

"Honey, that seems like it's pretty much all the time."

She shrugged. "I don't mind. And when it slows down, I take time for myself. I like it here. I have my own room and bathroom. The beach is right there if I ever get time to visit it, and I love to read."

"What kinds of jobs do you do around here?"

"I'm usually the cook now. Marie always did it before, but more and more I'm doing it, at least for breakfast. We work together in the evening. Naturally, we tidy up rooms and clean them thoroughly after each guest leaves, although during the heavy season, we hire a crew to help with the rooms. It's a good life."

"And you meet all kinds of men." Malichai didn't like the fact that he felt jealous.

He was happy he didn't sound it, but he felt it, a dark, swirling, chaotic monster that reared its ugly head, shocking him at the intensity of that inappropriate emotion.

"I'm too busy to meet men, unless you count surfer boy."

She gave that soft little laugh that pierced right through his skin and sent another lightning bolt zigzagging from his heart to his groin.

"And none of the others I met, including surfer boy, ever offered to do dishes with me, so I missed out."

"I'm interested in knowing more about surfer boy. He makes you laugh."

"He's so stereotypical. The blond hair falling in his face. Never wearing anything but board shorts. A tan that is going to give him skin cancer in a few more years. The way he talks. Sometimes if he calls me 'dude' one more time, I consider tripping him as he runs up the beach with his surf board tucked under his arm, looking like one of the television shows."

"Does he actually surf?" Malichai took a deep breath and turned his head in order to look at her. Up close she was even more dazzling. More beautiful. And more potent.

She leaned one hip against the counter. "He does. And he's good. I figure his parents must be very wealthy and they can't take him calling them 'dude,' so they shipped him off to sunny California with the idea he'd drive us all crazy. Once we were all locked up, property prices would go down and they could come to California, buy all the real estate and send him to the next state with a beach and do the same thing."

He laughed because she was so funny. "Your conspiracy theories need work." *This* was fun. He was having fun. He was going to kiss Nonny for teaching him how to wash dishes.

"When you meet surfer boy, you'll understand completely."

"Does he have an actual name?"

"He's taken a surfer name. He is called Dozer. And yes, if you're silly enough to ask, as I was, even though Marie warned me not to, he will explain just why he has that name."

"You're setting me up to ask him, but I prefer that you just tell me. I'm not about to ask some pretty boy surfer who will call me 'dude' until I want to twist his head around so he'd face backward when he walks."

She pressed the towel to her mouth, muffling her laughter. "I've wanted to do that very thing a million times. Okay, he dozes the waves. You know, like bulldoze. He's the bulldozer and he's destroying the waves."

Malichai turned slowly toward her, although he knew it might be a mistake. He couldn't seem to help himself, but he had to see all of her when she was in full-blown laughter. There was no mistaking the beauty of her delicate bone structure. Her form was all feminine, but he could see the muscle hidden beneath her soft skin. She moved with grace, her foot placement exact for balance and speed. He didn't want to see those things.

He only wanted to see her. The woman. He wanted to be that man on vacation, who met the summer fling. The one woman who would seduce him into a long stay and he'd dream about the one who got away forevermore. That sort of hokey hogwash he'd heard about. Instead, he was very much afraid he was meeting Amaryllis, one of Whitney's experiments.

Whitney had decided at some point that he would pair a female soldier with a male soldier. He felt between the two, they would be able to move in and out of situations that called for stealth. Men tended to be intimidating and noticeable. A couple was viewed as less threatening. He decided to give the couple complementary animal DNA or anything else that he decreed might help his soldiers succeed. He paired them so they could give each other blood if needed. He specifically targeted psychic improvements that went with his physical enhancements. Then, lastly, he heightened the pheromones between the couple so they would be intensely physically attracted to each other.

Malichai knew that Amaryllis was definitely beautiful enough and sexy enough to entice any man to her, but she was flirting — with him. They were working in a kitchen. His leg hurt like a son of a bitch. Maybe he would feel attraction toward her, but like this? Like this unrelenting ache that wouldn't just go away? Like a need to feel her touch on his skin? Or her breath on his body? He swore to himself. He didn't believe in that kind of physical attraction, not that fast.

"I look forward to meeting Mr. Dozer." He forced himself to continue their conversation.

She pressed the cloth tighter over her mouth, holding it with both hands, her blue eyes alive with sheer merriment. "Don't. Oh my God, you cannot call him that. Not in front of anyone. You have to keep a straight face when he introduces himself and calls you 'dude.' If you don't, anyone within hearing distance will laugh and he'll be so hurt. He's really a nice boy."

"You keep calling him a boy. How old is he?" Malichai was hoping he was fifteen or sixteen. He couldn't keep wanting to deck a kid.

"I'm guessing he's pushing thirty, but he seems like a kid. He's happy all the time. Smiling all the time. The world seems like a wonderful place to him and when you're with him, you feel that. In spite of the theatrical aspects of surfer boy, you can't help but like him."

He didn't know about that, but he'd give it his best shot. Right now, he was going to get something to eat before he starved, and then he had to rest his leg. The girls had chosen the beach for him. A sunny, beautiful place. He'd watched them, Bellisia, his brother's wife, with Zara, Shylah, Pepper and Cayenne huddled together over a table with Nonny and the three little viper triplets. All of them had given input, looking up places in books, and on the Internet. He'd promised the women he would go where they pointed. It hadn't mattered to him. The choice had been random and it had led him straight to Amaryllis and trouble.

3

Malichai glanced at his watch as they finished cleaning the kitchen and setting it up for making dinner that night. Amaryllis had already started the huge casseroles of lasagna and slathered butter and garlic salt on loaves of sourdough bread she was serving for dinner. He didn't understand how she was still on her feet.

"What are you still doing in here?" Marie asked as she walked in. She had a little girl by the hand.

Malichai smiled at the child, knowing from long experience his looks tended to intimidate children. He crouched down so he was closer to her size. "You're every bit as beautiful as your mother is. I'm Malichai. What's your name?"

The child blinked at him and then slowly smiled. "Jacy."

"That's a really nice name."

"Do you know my daddy?"

Malichai glanced up at Marie. She was standing very still, almost as if she were frozen or would shatter if she moved. There was no help there.

"No, honey, I'm sorry I didn't have the chance to know him, but he was a very good man."

The child nodded solemnly, her blond curls bobbing up and down. "You're like him. I can tell." She reached out and touched one of the smaller scars he had on his jaw. It curved down his neck. That was one that had nearly killed him.

"Jacy." Marie's voice was filled with warning.

"I don't mind," Malichai said. "My friend Wyatt has triplets. Three little girls, and another set of twins were just born. All girls."

Marie's eyes widened and she exchanged a look of shock with Amaryllis. "Five? They have five little girls?"

Malichai nodded. "We all live close and help raise them. It's easy to fall in love with them, although the triplets are little tornadoes. We have to watch them all the time. What one doesn't think of, another will." He didn't bother to try to keep the affection from his voice.

Marie laughed, the sound genuine, rolling

through the kitchen, making Amaryllis and Jacy smile. "I can't imagine having three the same age and then twins. How old are the triplets?"

He flashed a grin as he straightened up. His leg was giving him fits and it took effort not to wince. He felt Amaryllis's gaze on him, but he didn't look to see if she'd observed any weakness. "They're around two. I'm not so good with ages. How old are you, Jacy?"

"Five. I go to school," she added proudly.

"Very smart," Malichai said. "I've been doing dishes."

"Are you Amaryllis's boyfriend?"

"Not yet, but I thought I'd take her out to get something to eat. We've been working all day together, and so far she hasn't hit me over the head with a frying pan." He winked at the little girl. "That probably means she likes me. *And*" — he lowered his voice conspiratorially — "we both have the same favorite book, although she's not as fast at reading as I am."

He stole a quick glance at Amaryllis. She had her hand over her mouth, muffling her laughter, but her eyes were dancing as she looked at Marie, shaking her head at what she considered Malichai's nonsense. He wasn't so sure he was acting for the child.

He liked Amaryllis. The more time he spent in her company, the happier he was. He liked the way she worked so hard to help Marie. She had compassion in her, a good work ethic, and she knew how to cook. He admired all three traits. She also had a great sense of humor, something he considered an absolute must in anyone who was friends with him.

Jacy nodded solemnly again and then looked up at her mother. "Can Amaryllis go eat with Malichai?" She stumbled over his name but managed to pronounce it adequately.

"I believe she can. We have time before we have to serve dinner tonight."

Malichai sent Amaryllis a grin. "I guess that means you'll have to show me where the best place to eat lunch is. We're a little late for it, but that's all right."

"This is the best place to eat," Amaryllis said. "But there's a nice little café just down the block. We can get our food and eat on their patio overlooking the beach."

"Sounds perfect. We won't be long," he assured Marie. "Is there anything you need while we're out?"

"Malichai." Marie tried to sound stern. "You're a guest here."

"Maybe, but Nonny wouldn't want me to

be a self-centered guest. Doing a few dishes or lending a hand where it's needed is a good thing and I don't mind. We'll be right back." He switched his attention to Jacy. "I was going to put on your mom's apron, but it didn't fit. Do you think I can find one in my size?"

The child studied him and then shook her head. "I don't think so, Malichai, but Mommy sews on a machine. She could make you one."

He nodded. "That sounds perfect. I've needed one for a while. Maybe she could make me one and I can do dishes until the dishwasher is fixed. That's a fair exchange, don't you think?"

Jacy thought it over and then agreed. "Yes."

Malichai gave Marie a triumphant smile. "Looks like I'm your official dishwasher in exchange for an apron I can take home with me. The girls will get a kick out of it. If you can, would you mind putting pockets in it so I can put some things in it for the girls to find when they're helping me?"

"Do you really want me to make you an apron?" Marie asked.

"Yes, please, if it's not too much trouble. I can do dishes, since I don't have the first clue how to do this vacation thing. I'm having fun just getting to know the three of you." For him, it was far better than sitting alone on a beach.

Amaryllis put her hand on his arm. The moment she did, a tingle of awareness crept down his spine and entered his bloodstream, like tiny little champagne bubbles. He felt them moving through his veins, spreading through his body, a slow assault that just kept growing.

"If we're really going to do this and we want time to enjoy it, we'll have to leave now," she said.

Even her voice seemed to stroke along his nerve endings. He wasn't so certain being alone with her, even in the light of day with people around them, was all that good of an idea. He turned his hand and caught hers, threading their fingers together.

"You're right, let's go." He waved at Jacy and let Amaryllis lead him into the open air.

The moment they stepped outside, the view was amazing. "The bed-and-breakfast has the perfect location. No wonder Marie has a waiting list to get in half the time." He nearly groaned aloud. That was a big mistake. The investigation had turned that piece of information up. He'd gotten a reservation because there had been a cancellation.

"It is lovely, isn't it?" Amaryllis said. "Marie loves it. If Jacy wasn't so ill, she'd be doing great financially. She works hard all the time. She doesn't have relatives that can help her, so since her husband was killed, she's done everything alone."

"Will Jacy live?"

"She has a good chance. Marie is very careful with her. She keeps her away from most people at the inn to cut down the chances of her getting something that her immune system couldn't handle right now. Jacy's very inquisitive and it's hard on her not to interact with so many people. Marie didn't look so defeated this afternoon, the way she did this morning, so I'm assuming the visit to the doctor went well. She texted me twice and said things were looking up, so hopefully Jacy was just struggling a little like she does in the mornings and isn't really sick."

"I don't get sick," Malichai assured her, feeling guilty that he'd gotten so close to Jacy. "Even when I was a kid, I didn't get sick like most kids do. I must have a very strong immune system. Either that or my brother beat me up so often it scared any illness out of me." He laughed when he said it and was happy when she laughed with him.

They walked along the sidewalk, sand stretching all the way to the ocean waves on one side, brightly painted buildings on the other. The sun was hot, but it wasn't the perfumed, humid heat of the swamp, it was different. He would have said dry, but the slight breeze carried salty mist from the sea with it.

Amaryllis didn't seem to notice that they were still holding hands, so he didn't make the mistake of calling attention to it. He'd never walked anywhere holding hands with a woman and he found, with her, he liked the feeling.

"Now that I think about it, I don't get sick either," she said. "That's kind of weird, isn't it? That neither of us was prone to child-hood illnesses."

He shrugged, not wanting to think too much on that coincidence. "My brothers tell me that just means when I get sick as an adult, I'm going to get whatever it is far worse than anyone else. They usually laugh like hyenas when they inform me of what I have to look forward to."

"Your family sounds . . . nice."

He heard the wistful note in her voice. "They are." He followed her up the stairs to the little café sandwiched between two larger stores. One store sold all kinds of gifts for tourists, and the other catered to locals with a beach-themed clothing line. He noted the buildings, exits, entrances, stairs, rooftops and escape ladders as well as the cars in the lots and the various people walking along the sidewalk. Filing each small bit of information away, his gaze drifting quickly over faces and clothes, Malichai was able to make a mental map of the area and those working, playing or residing in it — and he did that in seconds.

The café was efficiently run. The space was small, so rather than have tables and chairs everywhere, the café utilized the area by giving their employees the ability to move around and be fast. The majority of the seating was outside under a very large covered patio. Customers ordered, took a number and went outside to sit at one of the tables. The moment he was seated, Malichai stretched out his leg, trying not to groan at the relief he felt being off of it.

"What happened?" Amaryllis asked.

Malichai figured there was no need for pretense. Clearly, he hadn't been nearly as good at covering up the injury as he thought he'd been. It didn't make sense that it hurt so much when by now, it should be almost completely healed. He reached down to rub along his thigh where the cramping was the worst. Most of what he did was classified. Or, *he* was classified, along with the other members of his team.

"I'm in the Air Force — in pararescue. A medic. Got into a little scrape during a rescue operation and my leg took the brunt of it all. Nothing big, but annoying nevertheless. Had to take a forced leave and here I am."

She leaned her chin into the heel of her hand and stared at him with her sapphire eyes. "What does pararescue do? I haven't really heard of them."

He put his hand over his heart. "That just kills me, honey. A knife, right through the heart. Mostly, we're doctors and nurses trained in combat rescue. We go in when our troops are shot the hell up, stabilize them enough to allow them to travel, and then cover them while we run to the helicopter hoping we don't get shot." He gave her a little grin. "I was too slow."

"That's your job?"

The smile faded and he nodded. "They're wounded soldiers. Our men. We're not going to leave them behind or leave them for the enemy to get. We sometimes have a couple of escort helicopters who try to keep the enemy off us. More often than not it's a hot zone, so we know ahead of time there's going to be bullets coming at us. When we have soldiers down, they need care immediately and some have to be flown to Germany or other places to be operated on, although a few of the docs have had to do that kind of thing right there in order to save a leg, an arm or a life."

"You aren't anything like I thought you'd be."

"What did you think?" He was curious. He noted a couple a few tables from theirs arguing, but very quietly. She was upset, insisting that she wanted to "tell" the cops, and he shook his head adamantly and said he didn't want to get involved. They really didn't know enough to "tell" anyone. He wanted her to shut up and change the subject.

"You look tough. Your body could be a bodybuilder's although you have definition. You don't have the large bulk; still, you're in very good shape. There's a look about you that says not to mess with you."

He gave her a faint smile, allowing his gaze to drift past the arguing couple and touch on others. He recognized the three from the bed-and-breakfast who had been in the hallway. The two men were talking about the best place in San Diego to surf, while the woman looked bored. A trio of men in suits with briefcases sat at another table. They'd been at the bed-and-breakfast working in one of the rooms designed for just that purpose.

"That's implying you think medics can't be tough. We have to be. We're doing fieldwork with bullets flying around us. We're sometimes packing the wounded out by ourselves. Running with them while carrying blood and fluids in bags to helicopters and leaping in as they're already in flight."

"That sounds so crazy. I never thought about the men and women who rescue the soldiers when they're wounded. In my mind, I guess I equated rescues with Rangers and SEALS, teams like that."

"I'm trying not to be insulted." He gave her his full attention. *"We* rescue *them."*

The sun shone down on her hair, turning the streaks of colors wheat, caramel and a silvery snow. She even had a little gold mixed in. Her hair color was as intriguing as her eye color. He loved both, but he thought her eyes were just a fraction ahead in the race. The more he looked into them, the less he thought she wore contacts.

She gave him a smile that melted his insides and told him it wasn't a good idea for him to fall too hard for her because one smile like that and she'd get her way in all things. He'd never hear the end of that shit from his brothers or fellow teammates.

"I wasn't intending to insult you, it's just, I never actually thought about it. Medics seemed to be held out of harm's way, at least in the movies. They come in after all the fighting is over."

Malichai shrugged. "I never thought about how we're portrayed in movies, nor does it matter to us. It's about the soldiers and getting them home in one piece and alive if at all possible."

He indicated the three businessmen. "I saw those three at the bed-and-breakfast as well as the two men and woman at that table. They were arguing in the hall and they still seem to be arguing. Are they always like that?"

"The three businessmen came in the day before you. They all work for the same company, Lanterns International, but each came in from a different country. One is from Texas, one is from Hong Kong and the third is from India. They apparently meet in person every six months. They're waiting for a fourth and fifth member, one from Switzerland and the last from Japan. They've met here before. The company is called Lantern International because it's all about bringing together ideas to spread peace and understanding among people of various countries. People with opposing beliefs and politics."

"That seems like a very unattainable goal," Malichai stated.

She drew back a little. "But surely you can see all the unrest in the world. Maybe if people weren't so busy judging one another and tried to be more understanding . . ." She trailed off with a little frown on her face.

Without thinking, he reached across the table and rubbed the pad of his fingers over her lips as if he could erase her frown. "I didn't say it wasn't an admirable idea, only that it seems unattainable, which it does. There are peace talks going on all the time, and no one seems to get anywhere."

Her lips were every bit as soft as they looked. Full, curved like a bow, they gave a man too many fantasies. She didn't move for a moment, but her eyes went an even deeper shade of blue, taking on that jeweled tone he'd first noticed. Then she pulled back slightly, and he dropped his hand as if just realizing what he was doing.

"Those talks don't work because every country is out for itself, to strike the best deal. Their idea is *people* getting together.

They're planning a huge conference in a couple of weeks, at least that's what Marie told me. It's been in the works for several years. I haven't been keeping up, but I do know that's why the five of them have flown in this time. The San Diego Convention Center isn't that far from here, and the convention's sold out."

"Well, I hope they're successful. I've pulled enough of our young men, dead or dying, without arms or legs, sometimes both . . ." He pressed his fingers to the corners of his eyes, thinking of Tim and Jerry. They were too close. Good men, both, one gone and the other with a very long road ahead of him.

She put her hand on his arm. "Don't think about it, Malichai. Whatever happened to your leg, whatever is making you sad, don't think about it." She looked around the patio. "Half the customers staying at the B and B are attending the conference. You know the three in suits already. The couple at the table across from you are staying on the first floor. This is their first time with us, according to Marie. Bryon and Anna Cooper have been here a week and are staying another week. Both are very nice. They leave good tips and are extremely polite."

The waiter brought their food out and put

it in front of them. Malichai had thought his stomach was going to go into a full mutiny if he didn't eat soon, so he tried not to look like a starved man when he picked up his hamburger and took a bite. It was delicious, or maybe he was just that hungry, but it could have been the best burger he'd ever eaten.

Amaryllis laughed softly. "You have this look on your face of absolute ecstasy."

He scowled at her, lowering the hamburger to his chest, but not relinquishing it for a moment. "Woman. You can't use that word. I would only look like that if I was having sex. The right kind of sex." He knew it was inappropriate, but he couldn't help himself. He was a little shocked that she would equate eating food with ecstasy.

She laughed again. "I can't help how you look. Maybe you get the same look on your face when you're having sex. Do you like food that much?"

"As much as sex?" He took another bite and chewed thoughtfully, pretending to weigh the two in his mind. "You need to eat to keep up your strength for sex, so food is important, and you may as well enjoy it. Nonny is an amazing cook."

"Is she attractive?"

Was there just a little hint of jealousy in

her voice? He hoped so. "I would say men would always find her attractive. She is eighty, but the woman is a legend in the swamp. Stayed true to one man her entire life though, even long after she lost him."

She nodded. "I see. Well, on with it. Which wins, sex or food?"

"Depends on who's cooking and who I'm having sex with."

"That's cheating. Totally cheating."

Malichai grinned at her. "You didn't state the rules, so I slipped right through the loophole." He indicated the two men and one woman he knew were staying at the bed-and-breakfast. He had to find something safer than sex to talk about with her. "Who are they?"

She rolled her eyes. "Tania and Tommy Leven are brother and sister. Billy Leven is their cousin. They are difficult. We always have one or two, but it isn't a big deal." She took a bite of her own hamburger. She hadn't gotten the double burger like he had, so hers was a much more delicate bite.

"What's difficult about them?"

She shrugged. "Nothing big. The usual kind of thing. They don't want their rooms cleaned, but they pile wet towels on the floor in the hall. Then they ask for new ones but won't let me clean their bathrooms.

They insist on room service when we don't offer it. They're always calling down for me to bring them coffee. I've told them a million times they can get coffee on the corner, or use the coffee maker in their room, but that isn't good enough. Nothing big, and those things aren't uncommon, but when I'm working like a crazy person, it can be annoying."

He could understand that. "The women in my family would probably hit them over the head." Cayenne, Trap's wife, would bundle them up in a silken cocoon and hang them from a tree, but he couldn't say that.

"I shouldn't complain about them. They were really nice to Jacy. They even brought her back a coloring book and crayons when she was upset one day and they heard her crying. Tania said she has a younger sister, a girl about ten years younger than her, but she adores her. She hated the fact that Jacy was upset, so even though they have annoying ways, they can be sweet. Everyone else heard her crying as well, I know because Bryon and Anna Cooper inquired about her the next day and so did one of the men from Lantern International, but only Tania thought to do something for Jacy."

Malichai had nearly finished off his burger and was working through his fries, trying not to eye hers. She hadn't touched one. In fact, she was the slowest eater he'd ever seen. She chewed each bite a hundred times or more.

"Tell me about your friend's little girls. You said he had five daughters. I've never seen actual triplets."

He felt the instant stillness in his body. None of the team members talked much about the girls. They protected them, just as they protected Pepper, Wyatt's wife. The triplets had been slated to be terminated by one of Whitney's followers, who had been head of a laboratory until Malichai's team killed him.

"I don't know that much about kids, but they're pretty damn cute. Probably wouldn't know what to do with one, but they make you want to have children. They smile at you and you just kind of melt." He held her eyes across the table. "You want kids?"

She nodded and pushed the little woven basket containing half her burger and all of her fries toward him. "I'm saving room for lasagna and sourdough bread." She indicated the basket. "I sit on the beach and watch the kids play in the sand or make castles. Jacy definitely melts my heart. Yeah, I'd like to have children someday."

Malichai watched the couple, Bryon and

Anna, get up together. Bryon slung his arm around his wife's shoulders, and they took the stairs heading down to the beach. The day was beautiful, clear, feeling to Malichai as if he could see all the way to the other side of the ocean. The waves rolled in gently to the sandy beach, where dozens of bright umbrellas were set up and families played or read or just enjoyed the late afternoon sun.

There was peace in being there. Or maybe it was just spending time with Amaryllis. It wasn't like he spent time with a lot of women. He usually picked one up in a bar, spent a few hours with her and was gone. His life was about service to his country, being with his teammates and building a fortress out in the middle of the Louisiana swamp in the hopes that they could protect themselves from any attack on them.

GhostWalkers were different. Experiments. Already, they had a few enemies in the White House, men and women who believed they were too dangerous to allow them to live. There were four teams of GhostWalkers. The first team had problems with brain bleeds and other major issues, but they still went out and did the work deemed necessary for their country.

All of them had gone through rigorous

special forces training and then some. The first team had joined with the second squad out in the wilds of Montana and were building a fortress there to protect their families. Team three was in San Francisco, putting together their stronghold, and his team was in Louisiana doing the same.

"Never thought I'd be sitting in a place like this, talking to a woman like you," Malichai said. He picked up the burger she'd carefully cut in half and took a bite.

"Like me?"

"So damn beautiful I can barely breathe." He couldn't believe the words in his brain came out of his mouth. "Clearly I can't censor either."

She looked pleased and a little embarrassed. "Thank you, that's a very sweet thing to say."

He winced. "Don't do that 'sweet' thing. Women start viewing a man as sweet and he has zero chance with her."

"Zero chance?" she echoed. "Barring sweet, you'd like a chance with me?"

"That's right." He finished off the burger. "Thanks for sharing."

"You're never going to be able to eat dinner, and the lasagna is so good. It's one of the house specialties."

"I'll eat it. Nonny always says I have a hole

in my leg and the food falls out. My woman is going to have a very difficult time keeping up with my appetites." He grinned at her.

Amaryllis shook her head. "You're awful."

"But now you're so much more interested. I can tell."

She laughed, just as he knew she would. "You're awful," she repeated, "and we should get going. Are you taking those fries?"

"No, the birds can have them." He indicated the gulls that walked on the sand and the wooden patio waiting for them to leave. "I want the lasagna, remember?"

Malichai stood when she did and held out his hand to her. She took it without hesitation, which pleased him. She started toward the stairs that led to the beach, the same direction the couple from the bed-and-breakfast had taken. As they walked back toward the B and B, he moved closer to her and drew her hand to his chest, pressing her palm against his heart for a moment.

He felt her look, but he kept walking, observing around him, not her. It felt right just walking with her. Being with her. That was a new experience for him as well. It was the simplest thing, just strolling together, neither feeling the need to break their silence. They got all the way to the bed-and-breakfast before she stopped and pulled her hand from his.

"What is it, honey?" He slid his fingers around the nape of her neck, but his thumb dared to slide over her exquisite cheekbone.

"I just want you to know, I like your sweet."

She leaned into him and pressed a kiss to his jaw, just a brief touch of her lips against that inevitable shadow that darkened the lower half of his face. His heart felt as though it had stopped in his chest while his entire body absorbed the feel of those lips on his skin. That fast, she turned away from him and was gone down the hall, disappearing into the part of the house that was off-limits to guests. He stared after her for a longer time than necessary and was grateful none of his fellow GhostWalkers were around. They would never have allowed him to hear the end of it.

Malichai headed to his room. This time he met two men coming out of their room. They were new at the B and B, arrivals sometime that day. He took his phone out of his pocket on the pretense of reading text messages. It wasn't like he didn't have plenty to read. Mostly they were from his brothers telling him he was going to get a beating if he didn't answer soon. They wanted to know if he was all right.

Instead of answering, he snapped several pictures discreetly, as he'd done for every visitor he'd run into. It was a necessary evil. He'd even turned in Amaryllis's picture without saying a word about what he suspected at times — that she was physically and psychically enhanced, just as he was. If she really was, that meant Whitney had sent her on a mission, or she had escaped his compound and was on the run.

She didn't appear to be on the run and she had been working over a year at the bed-and-breakfast. That long ago, he'd never even considered a vacation in sunny California. It didn't make sense that there was some big conspiracy involving him.

He noted that the two newcomers watched him as he came down the hall to his room. They parted, forcing him to walk between them, and still stared at him as he closed the door. He supposed some men might find him intimidating. Although, more likely, they were sent to kill him. That was definitely more in his wheelhouse. Great, now he was getting paranoid about all the other guests.

At least none of them were flirting too much with Amaryllis. That would get under his skin, and he wasn't a good enough man for others to give him that kind of itch that could only be scratched the bayou way. He wasn't a jealous man, so feeling that way — a little murderous and ready to fight — was another new experience for him.

He lay down on the bed and eased his leg up. Stretching it out hurt, but taking his weight off it definitely felt better than walking around on it. His thigh protested, as did his hip and calf. GhostWalkers healed faster than normal, and although he seemed to be fairly healed on the outside, the leg just didn't want to get back to normal. He was swimming the way he was supposed to, but that was the only time his leg felt halfway decent.

Rubin, a psychic surgeon, had healed it from the inside out. Joe, a psychic healer, had worked on him numerous times. An orthopedic surgeon had performed a miraculous surgery on him. He'd gone through physical therapy. He'd always healed very fast, and with his enhancements, his ability to do so had more than tripled.

The physical therapist had told him no strenuous workouts. He was expected to walk on the injured leg, but not push it — to stop when the pain level rose and to keep those walks short, no running — which was a joke for a man like him. They wanted him swimming in the ocean every day. He was an excellent swimmer — a bullet in the water — and they thought that would help to strengthen the leg without the weight of his body on it. Walking in the sand every day was supposed to help. With all the therapy, psychic healing and surgeries, his leg should have been in excellent condition, but it hurt like hell.

Lying on a bed with an aching leg made him feel like a whiner. He was used to action and without Amaryllis to distract him, he felt a little like he was going out of his mind. Amaryllis, his little puzzle. His mind turned back to her eagerly. He wanted to remember every detail, especially the way her face lit up when she laughed.

She had moved through the sand easily, he would have to say fluidly, like water flowing across the surface, not at all bogged down by the granules of sand. GhostWalkers sensed one another. Most of the time they recognized one another just by the energy fields projected around them. If she was a GhostWalker, one of her talents had to be to shield herself, and that talent was rare.

Suppose she was one of Whitney's experiments. He'd have to conclude that he'd stumbled across one of the women who had escaped from one of the many compounds scattered throughout the world and that she'd successfully managed to stay under Whitney's radar. If that was true, she would view him as a threat, not someone she found "sweet."

He sighed. He wasn't good at the woman thing, but he wanted to be. He was already missing her. Already eager to see her again. He was very glad the dishwasher needed a part that had to be sent away for. It was extra work for Amaryllis, but it meant, as the resident dishwasher, he got to spend time with her.

His phone kept pinging, annoying him to no end. He pulled it out of his pocket and glared at the screen. Ezekiel was blowing his phone up, now using numerous profanities, demanding his response. The last message said he would be using Trap's plane to come and find him. Shit. That wasn't good, and Zeke would really do it too.

"It's about damn time," his oldest brother greeted him.

"What's the problem?"

"You disappeared."

His body relaxed. He hadn't even realized he'd been tense. His brother was as tough as nails, mean as a snake, but he was a worrier. "As I recall, Zeke, your wife was instrumental in picking my vacation spot. She knows exactly where I am."

"You could have had Mordichai go with you, or Rubin. Someone."

"You think I need someone to hold my hand?"

There was a small silence. "I think I nearly lost my brother on that last mission, Malichai. That's what I think. I came too damn close to losing you. We don't know if that leg is going to recover and —"

Malichai cut him off. "It's going to recover. I did my walk in the sand, swam in the ocean and didn't overdo it, just like I promised. I'm fine. Everything is good here. I'm snapping pictures of the other guests at the B and B and sending them for facial recognition and all that bullshit. I don't think any other vacationer does that sort of thing. Don't worry so much."

Ezekiel sighed. "I just don't like you so far from home when you're vulnerable, Malichai. If Whitney gets wind you're there, you could be in trouble. We have all kinds of enemies, not just Whitney. There's an entire faction of fanatics who'd like to eliminate every one of us. What about Cheng in China? He's still around. And we've got the coalition of bankers or whatever they are. It isn't like we're not surrounded on every front by enemies."

Malichai decided it wasn't a good time to bring up Amaryllis and the fact that he was a little apprehensive she might be one of Whitney's girls. One word about her, even if he didn't voice his suspicions, and Ezekiel would be on that plane, just as he'd threatened to do earlier.

"You get me, Malichai? Don't treat this as a joke, or act like it's me being paranoid. The danger to you is very real. You're fucked-up right now. We both know that leg won't hold if you need to run."

Malichai knew he didn't have a prayer that the leg would hold if he needed to run.

"I'm alive, Zeke," he said quietly, gently. He loved his brother. Ezekiel had fought for everything they had when they were young, clothes, food, even toothbrushes. What he couldn't buy with the money he earned in various ways, he stole for Malichai and Mordichai. He fought off two-legged predators and other kids wanting their territory. "I'm alive and I'm on vacation for the first time in my life. I've got a beach out my front door, good food and good company."

There was another silence. "Good company?" Ezekiel ventured.

Malichai wouldn't go there. That was dangerous territory. "Yeah, there're these five men, each from a different country, with a cool idea for peaceful talks —"

Ezekiel broke in, just the way Malichai knew he would. "That's good, Kai, but you do exactly what the doc said. Don't deviate. You want that leg to heal."

"Roger that."

"And next time I text you, answer me."

Malichai wasn't going to promise that, not even when his brother called him by his half-forgotten childhood nickname. "Good-bye, brother."

"Catch you later," Ezekiel returned.

Malichai rolled over to see his alarm clock. They would be serving in the dining room now. All that lasagna that was smelling so good his stomach was reacting with protests, angry with him because he was starving it. The aroma of that casserole, especially after he'd watched Amaryllis make it that morning, was driving him to get up. His stomach didn't care whether or not he'd just eaten or if his leg was going to work. His stomach didn't even care about his leg — it was all about the food.

Amaryllis looked up the moment he entered the dining room and she smiled directly at him. That was worth anything, even a lecture from his brother. She lit up the room — for him. He took his plate and went to the end of the line. The two men who had stared at him like a pair of idiots were at the front of the line being served by her. Another man was behind the two, another newcomer he didn't recognize. A trio of women stood directly in front of him and one of them turned to say hello and she just stared. Then she smiled big.

Malichai had his gaze fixed on Amaryllis, but he still saw the entire room. She dished up a very large square of the lasagna and indicated that the next station held salads and bread. The two men moved on. The woman kept smiling at him and started to get chatty.

"Malichai," Amaryllis called to him. She sounded anxious.

He immediately left the line and went to her. "What is it, honey?"

"I didn't bring enough lasagna out to serve a first round. Would you please grab another one for me? Don't forget to use gloves and heating pads."

"No problem." He put the plate down and strode out, doing his best to look as if his leg wasn't on fire and he believed her. She had enough to serve everyone. She hadn't liked the woman flirting with him. That put him in a good mood.

Once in the kitchen, it took him a few

minutes to find the other casseroles. Amaryllis was using the oven as a warmer. He took one out, resisting the urge to cut out a square for his own dinner and eat it right there. He sauntered back in, being casual about it. She'd managed to serve nearly everyone in line. The ladies who had been just ahead of him were in front of her. The flirtatious one gave him a big smile. Amaryllis dropped the square of lasagna on her plate.

Malichai smiled at her, his focus on Amaryllis. "Do you want this entire thing on the buffet table? I can cut the squares for you."

"Would you, hon?" she asked. "You really are the best, Malichai."

He knew what she was doing, and he was perfectly all right with it. She'd told the ladies to back off, he was taken.

"You eating?"

"As soon as I'm finished with this round."

"Same table?" He indicated the one where she'd been reading when he'd first laid eyes on her — when he'd first been intrigued and considered that she might be enhanced, a GhostWalker like he was.

She nodded. "That's the one."

Malichai cut the lasagna into large squares, took a good portion and added green salad and bread to his plate before walking to her little table and seating himself there to wait for her.

4

Something woke him, setting him on full alert. A sound. A whisper of conspiracy? A scratch at his door. Someone moving in his bedroom. Malichai stayed very still and allowed his enhanced senses freedom. He'd been careful to rein it in, to act normal. Now, he used every advantage that he had. He listened with ears that used his cat DNA, as well as that of a moth. Yeah, he had moth in him. Bizarre, but true. He figured his heightened sense of smell was the reason he was particularly susceptible to Amaryllis. She gave off waves of pheromones, ones he could detect, even when he was running. He had elephant in him as well, and he could find water even if it was twenty-five feet below the ground. Penguin allowed him to be a bullet in the water and to stay under for long periods of time.

He slid the knife into his hand. It fit perfectly, a part of him. He waited for the attack, breathing evenly, keeping up the pretense of sleep. He had a lot of practice at it. Missions, all over the world, catching naps anywhere he could, surrounded by the enemy.

He inhaled and knew instantly he wasn't alone in the room. One of the two men who had been staying there nearly as long as he had. Burnell Strathom had a bad habit of trying to provoke him. He would deliberately walk close to Malichai in the hallway and bump him hard with his shoulder. His partner, Jay Carpenter, would close in from the other side and try a squeeze play on him. They'd done it several times over the last week.

Malichai and Amaryllis often went out together to the little café and then walked along the beach, just holding hands and talking. He was always content, always at peace, when he was with her. The two men sometimes followed, although there was no way to call them on it. They stayed well back and seemed to just walk aimlessly. Amaryllis had commented on their presence, noting that it seemed they were always heading in the same direction. Malichai made a joke of it and said he thought maybe they were afraid of getting lost.

He swam in the early mornings, before

anyone else was up, and one or the other shadowed him. They didn't come close, but he spotted them watching him. It was annoying, especially since they weren't very good at following him. He sometimes would walk aimlessly around the block and deliberately lose them so he could be sitting in the foyer of the B and B drinking coffee when they rushed in, just to watch them panic.

Burnell came toward the bed, the soles of his shoes whispering along the floorboards. He was not very good at whatever he thought he was doing.

"You've got one chance to pull back, Burnell," Malichai warned. "You come at me and I'm going to stick this knife through your throat and out your spine. It isn't polite to interrupt a man's sleep."

There was silence. Burnell sighed softly. "I need to talk to you."

"There's always breakfast."

"Can't do that. You're always with her."

Malichai stiffened. He was always with Amaryllis. She was the "her" Burnell was referring to. He sat up slowly, his cat DNA giving him excellent night vision. "Go sit in the chair across the room. You make one wrong move and you're a dead man."

Burnell did as he was told, but it cost him

in pride. Malichai didn't care. The man had broken into his room and interrupted his sleep.

"Where's your partner?"

"He's in the hallway. Watching the door."

Malichai shook his head. The dumbass was probably standing right where the security cameras could get a good photograph of him for the cops if Burnell made a move on Malichai. "So, conspiracy charges if you managed to kill me and you both get caught," he observed. "Are you armed with a gun?"

"No."

"What about your partner?"

"Jay? No, he's not either."

"Just tell me why you've been following me." He sounded as exasperated as he felt.

"We want to hire you," Burnell confided.

It was the last thing Malichai expected. Keeping his bad leg stretched out on the mattress, he lowered his good one to the floor. "Keep talking."

"There's this man."

"I don't want to hear 'this man.' Give me a name."

"Craig Williams."

"The one here at the B and B?"

"Yes, he followed us here. At least we think he may have, we don't know that for certain. We think he's going to try to kill us."

Malichai couldn't decide if it was bullshit or not. It was possible Burnell was good at spinning tales whenever he was caught in someone's room. "Why would he want to kill you?"

"I don't know. We don't know him." Burnell's voice rose to a dramatic pitch and he made an effort to get it under control. "We decided to get the biggest, toughest man at the B and B to persuade him to leave."

"You aren't making any sense, Burnell. Zero sense. Every time we meet in the hallway, you deliberately try to pick a fight with me. If you're so worried about this man, pick a fight with him and get him thrown out."

"I've never actually been in a fight, Malichai. I was always the biggest in the classroom and everyone was afraid of me. I wanted to know if you could defend yourself. Jay said not to worry, that you could, but I didn't want to take chances that you were like me."

Malichai didn't like Burnell sounding ashamed because he wasn't a fighter. "First, it's a good thing not to fight, Burnell. On the other hand, it isn't smart to try to deliberately pick a fight with a stranger, someone you know nothing about. And you don't break into their room. Those are the kinds of things that can quickly escalate out of control and someone ends up dead. When I put someone down, it's usually in a permanent way." He figured that was safe enough to tell him since he was a soldier. Soldiers often had to kill.

Burnell shuddered. "I don't know this man, but he's been following us since he saw us at the beach and we're both certain he intends to kill us."

"You must have some idea of a reason this man would want to kill you." At first, Malichai thought Burnell was lying. Then he began to think he was just paranoid. Now, a little bit of uneasiness was beginning to creep in.

Burnell shook his head. "We don't know him."

Malichai sighed. "Call in your partner."

"What if Craig is creeping around out there and sets fire to your room or something?"

"Call your partner in, Burnell. And just so we're on the same page, the man you're talking about is about five-ten, light brown hair, brown eyes, dresses in sport jacket and jeans? That's the one you're calling Craig Williams?"

Burnell nodded several times. "That's him." He got up, opened Malichai's door and beckoned to his partner.

While he whispered to Jay, Malichai texted his brother, asking for all the information they had already gathered on Burnell, Jay and the third man, Craig Williams. Malichai had gotten his name from Marie. She'd told him he came from Georgia. Craig had been there nearly as long as Burnell and Jay, arriving the day after they'd checked in. Malichai was beginning to feel as if he were playing a hypothetical Clue game.

Jay seated himself next to Burnell. "Thanks for listening to us. I told Burnell breaking into your room in the dead of night wasn't the best approach, but he insisted it was the safest."

"It wasn't," Malichai said. "You're lucky I didn't call the cops or slit your throat. Either could have happened. Speaking of cops, why haven't you called them?"

The two men looked at each other and both shook their heads. "We're life partners," Jay explained. "That means a lot of time no one takes what we say seriously. We own a very respectable art gallery in Los Angeles, but we still get those looks, as if we're not quite bright. Or something is wrong with us. We don't have any proof against this man."

Jay was easier to deal with. He spoke directly and logically to Malichai, without Burnell's drama.

"I didn't agree with Burnell's plan to enlist your aid, but at least you're listening to us and not dismissing what we have to say because of who we are."

"Jay" — Malichai leaned toward them — "no one would dismiss this because of who you are. It just doesn't make a lot of sense. You've never met this man in your life?"

Both men shook their heads.

"Have you had threats? Against you? Against the gallery?"

More head shakes. Malichai drummed his fingers on his thigh, searching his brain for anything that could tie Williams, from Georgia, to Jay and Burnell from Southern California. "When did you first notice him?"

"We were with Anna and Bryon Cooper, at the beach. We'd spent a good portion of the day together and were walking back to the B and B together," Jay said. "Anna spotted this little shop, a magic shop. It looked very old chic. Nostalgic. Very cool. We all went in together. We wandered around the shop and found so many cool magic tricks from other eras, but no one ever came out from behind the curtain to take our money.

122

We could have robbed the place."

Burnell nodded. "The store is set back from the street in this little alley between the building next door and a stamp shop. Have you seen the alley?"

Malichai had. Artists often set up their wares there and sold to tourists. Many of them seemed to be making a lot of money. He'd seen the outside of the magic shop, but he'd never gone in.

"We went behind the counter where this curtain was hung in the doorway," Burnell took up the story. "Anna started to call out because we could hear a bunch of people talking. It sounded like some kind of meeting, so we decided to leave. I figured they'd just forgotten to put the closed sign on the door. It was late. But then we heard something about killing the maximum amount of people. That's what the man was saying. The maximum amount of people." He said the last almost defiantly, looking at Jay. "He repeated those words and they were very clear."

A chill went down Malichai's spine. "Who said that?"

"I don't know," Burnell admitted. "I didn't see anyone. We were afraid to pull the curtain aside. It was scary."

"They didn't say that," Jay objected.

"Anna and Burnell thought that was said, but Bryon and I didn't hear that at all. It was more like, we have to make a clean sweep across the board. I thought they were playing a game of some kind. You know, a board game."

"It isn't like there are that many murder board games where they have to *kill* the *maximum* amount of people, Jay."

Malichai held up his hand to stop any arguments. "Where does Craig Williams come into all of this?"

"We left the shop fast," Jay said. "Anna was very upset and wanted to go to the cops. Bryon told her no, that she didn't hear what she thought she'd heard. We hurried out to the main street and Craig was standing there, just watching us. There was something very scary about him. He just stared at us like someone out of one of those horror films."

"He followed us back to the B and B," Burnell added.

"He didn't follow us back," Jay objected. "Burnell, you can't exaggerate. We didn't see him again until we met him in the hall. He just stares at us."

Malichai had encountered Craig's stare. There was nothing against the law about staring. "When was that, the day and time?"

It was easy enough to have Amaryllis double-check when Craig had arrived.

"A week earlier," Burnell answered vaguely.

Malichai knew it had been the day before he had fixed Marie's dishwasher.

"You didn't go back to the magic shop, did you?" he asked the two men.

Jay shook his head. "Of course not. Bryon and I made it very clear it wouldn't be a smart move. We wanted to just drop it."

Burnell hung his head. Malichai waited. The other man remained stubbornly silent. Malichai sighed. "Just tell me. If I'm going to help, I need all the facts."

Burnell shot a quick glance at his partner. "Anna and I did go back to the shop. Just a quick visit. We wanted to see who worked there. An older man, with darker skin and a few wrinkles, like he'd been in the sun a lot, was there. He was very fit though. He kept pointing things out to us, and seemed very grateful when we purchased a few items."

"Burnell." Jay sounded horrified. "What were you thinking?"

"We didn't like the way you and Bryon acted like we couldn't have heard what we know we heard," Burnell said defiantly. "They were going to kill the maximum amount of people. I heard that. Anna heard it. Then creeper man showed up and he just stared at us."

"For all you know, he could have some sort of staring disability," Jay said.

Malichai nearly choked. "It isn't going to do any good to argue amongst ourselves. Burnell, don't break into anyone's room. I'll look into this, but you have to just go about your business and forget Craig no matter how much he stares. Don't let him get to you."

"He could be a serial killer," Burnell pointed out. "He might plan to murder every single person in this B and B." He shuddered at the thought and then glared at Jay. "It could happen."

"It could," Jay conceded. "But it's unlikely."

"Give me a couple of days to do some investigating," Malichai said. "I'll get back to you as soon as I know anything."

"We're leaving in another week," Burnell said.

"I'll get back to you before that." Because on the off chance that they'd really overhead something, whether or not Williams was involved, he wanted to make certain he investigated every possibility. Or he really was that lost on what vacations were supposed to be.

The two men thanked him and left his room. Malichai padded barefoot across the room in order to inspect the lock. It was a really bad lock, easily picked, but in this case, he hadn't locked it. Just in case Amaryllis decided to visit him. That would teach him to be so careless.

He fired off more data to Ezekiel. The name of the magic shop. He needed to know who owned it. What they looked like. How long they'd owned it.

Ezekiel came back with a thumbs-up and a question of his own. Malichai had sent him a picture of a woman. So far no one had identified her. Was she still at the bed-and-breakfast? How long had she been there? What was her name? Could he lift a fingerprint?

His heart thudded once very hard in protest. He had known. Amaryllis had to be one of Whitney's escaped girls. What was he going to do about her?

His first week of vacation was over. It had gone by fast when Malichai had been certain it would drag on forever. Now, he was contemplating extending his leave. He could. He certainly had it coming, and his leg wasn't healing as rapidly as everyone had anticipated. He could always use that as an excuse, although Joe Spagnola, his team leader, would more than likely insist he come home to have the doctors check him out if he admitted how much the damn thing hurt. Still, he looked forward to waking up every morning. He couldn't wait to start his day — all because of Amaryllis.

He got up at five and went "walking" every morning. For him, that meant, running-jogging-walking. He'd been running nearly every day for the last ten years or more, and just stopping seemed impossible. Then he went swimming, the best part of his protocol. That was the only thing that felt halfway decent. The leg felt great in the water, with no weight on it.

He liked San Diego, although the weather was far different than in his beloved swamp. He couldn't help but wonder if Amaryllis would be comfortable in the swamp. Some people had a lot of trouble with the humid heat.

In the mornings, when he went through the house — and it was always quiet — he detoured into the kitchen, where she was continuously cooking. Today she had the day off and Marie insisted Amaryllis actually take the time off, which she hadn't since Malichai had been there.

He dressed and went down the long hallway, his footsteps whispering on the tiled floor. He liked when it was so peaceful and still, before all the guests rose and he could hear the sounds of conversations coming from every direction, sometimes making it difficult to block out the noise.

He paused for a moment, thinking about the times he'd woken with that feeling of conspiracy so strong in him. Was he as paranoid as Burnell? Had he dreamt the whispers? Was he finally losing his mind? He knew it happened to soldiers, especially ones like him.

"Good morning, Malichai," Marie greeted cheerfully when he stood in the doorway, draping himself against the doorjamb. "You're up early."

"I'm used to getting up at the crack of dawn," he admitted. "I like the peace of it. The colors in the sky as the sun comes up. It's especially beautiful in the swamp," he added.

"I'd like to see that someday." Marie whisked the eggs to pour over the other ingredients for her egg casseroles. She made several of them for the guests.

"You say the word and we'll have you and Jacy for a visit. You'd love Nonny, and the girls would love to meet Jacy. We can show you all the most beautiful spots and feed you good Cajun food."

"I'd like that. You've been such a joy around here, Malichai. Amaryllis and I will miss you when you're gone."

"Amaryllis," he repeated, grateful for the opening. "How long have you known her now?"

"Just a little over a year. I met her in a grocery store. It was the best day ever. I was desperate for someone to work with me. I'd hired person after person, but they never actually wanted to work. She just pitches in and does everything. She learns fast too. Jacy began to get sick and I couldn't manage the B and B and her illness. I thought I'd have to close and then I found Amaryllis. She's been such a help to me as well as being a real friend."

"She's beautiful," Malichai said.

Marie nodded. "That she is."

"Someday, I'm going to take her away with me," he warned, shocking himself.

She turned slowly to look at him. "I was afraid of that, but I want her happy, Malichai. You've only known her a week. You need to give it more time."

He nodded. "I've been thinking about that. I know the place is always booked up, but I can sleep anywhere. If you don't have room, I can find another place. I've got quite a bit of leave racked up and since my leg isn't healing as fast as they'd like . . ." Deliberately, he played the sympathy card.

"Wait. Your leg?"

He didn't smirk, although she'd bought right into it. He knew she would. Marie was a very compassionate lady. "I'm pararescue. My last mission was to bring some boys home and we ran into a little trouble. Got my leg shot up. Nothing too serious."

"Malichai, you should have told me. You've been in my kitchen, doing dishes every night, standing. I feel terrible."

"My choice, Marie. I wanted to help out. I'd feel useless sitting on the beach. I just don't know how to do that kind of thing. I've enjoyed helping out, not to mention, I was able to spend time with Amaryllis."

"She's really wonderful."

"Has she mentioned her parents to you? She never talks about them."

Marie shook her head. "No, she doesn't talk about her past at all, and I respect that. I hope you do too. When she wants you to know, she'll tell you."

He didn't think that was true. He thought Amaryllis would run before she'd admit she was one of Dr. Whitney's experiments.

"What can you tell me about that little magic shop in the alley? Do you know the owner?"

Marie's eyes lit up. "I know most of the shop owners around me. We all try to help one another out. I have all the brochures and advertisements for each of the shops close to me, both sides of that alley and down the block. Miss Crystal owns the store. She's about eighty, but very spry, you'd never know that was her age. She has a little apartment in the back of the store. We have tea sometimes after the season's over."

"What do you know about her?"

"Her husband was a magician, a very popular one for a time. Unfortunately, she lost him some years ago to cancer. They both loved the business and amassed all kinds of magic collections through the years. They never had children and she often lamented to me about not having anyone to take over the store. She said she was afraid the memories would die out with the memorabilia. I suggested selling but she said she just couldn't. She wouldn't have anything to live for if she did that. Is there a reason you're asking?"

He shook his head. "It just seems like a very interesting shop. I wondered if it was at all popular with tourists."

"Miss Crystal says it is, but she just might want it to be. She loves that store and all the memories she has of her days with her husband." Sorrow crept into Marie's voice.

Malichai felt guilty asking her questions about the magic shop. Burnell was most likely mistaken about what he'd heard. Anna too. They'd probably talked back and forth, convincing each other that someone wanted to kill the maximum number of people. Now, he was harassing Marie and making her sad.

"I'd better go for my jog and swim. That's my therapy. I'm supposed to meet Amaryllis for breakfast this morning and then she's taking me to the beach to teach me how to enjoy the ocean properly."

Marie laughed. "She's not leading you to your doom, Malichai. You'll like it."

"I don't know, Marie, she keeps talking about surfer boy. I don't know if I'm ready to meet someone she refers to as 'surfer boy' and then laughs that amazing laugh of hers."

"I can't wait to hear all about it." Marie made a shooing motion with her hand and Malichai took the hint, walking down the dark hallway to the front door.

The day was going to be another beautiful one. He went straight down to the sand and began a brisk walk, getting a feel for the grains beneath his feet. Next a slow jog. His leg did seem as if it might be getting stronger. The doctors had agreed walking in sand and swimming would be good for him. They were certain both would help strengthen the muscles.

When he was running in the sand, he wasn't convinced the muscles were his problem. Sometimes, when he tuned in to his leg, trying to feel the issues, it felt as if the bones had tiny fractures, little cracks that ran along like fault lines refusing to knit back together. When he thought that way, he would panic and have to stop, bend over and breathe deeply. Then he'd remind himself it hadn't been that long since he'd been shot multiple times. It wasn't the first time he'd been shot in that leg, although the first time he'd healed without a problem. Was having already been shot in that same leg causing some problem this time?

Amaryllis came up behind him, not making a sound, another reason for him to think she was a GhostWalker. With his head down, breathing deeply, he took her into his lungs before he actually saw her. She also moved through the sand easily, whether she walked, jogged or ran. She never stumbled or complained about how difficult it was. Running in sand was always a workout, yet she didn't raise a sweat.

Amaryllis put her hand on his back. "Are

you okay?"

"Little panic attack, nothing serious." He answered her honestly. He tried to be as honest as he could with her. "Sometimes, I worry that my leg isn't going to heal properly, and they'll pull me. I'm a soldier. I don't know any other life. My family is my team. I know that sounds crazy, but I can feel these cracks like spiderwebs spreading out over my bones."

She didn't laugh at him or try to argue. "Really? You should have told me. Come sit down on one of the lounge chairs." She pointed to the chairs laid out along the beach. "No one is up this early."

He straightened and looked out to the ocean, a smile forming. "Babe. Seriously? Who are all those nuts?"

"Surfers. They aren't going to care if we use a lounge chair. They wouldn't know what to do with one." She took his hand and tugged.

It was the first time she'd taken his hand instead of the other way around. He was good with that and willing to follow her anywhere. She led him to a woven, brightly colored lounge chair and had him sit, stretching out his legs.

"Don't make fun of me," she said. "I've always been able to 'feel' what's going on inside a person. Their muscles or bones. Most people don't believe me, but I can."

"Don't know why they wouldn't believe you. It's a known fact that some people are born gifted. Do your worst."

He felt her gaze on his face. He couldn't stop himself from looking at her. All that made him want to do was kiss her. He framed her face with both hands. "Don't look so scared, honey. I believe anything you want to tell me because you've always been honest with me."

Her gaze skittered away from his. He wanted to comfort her and tell her it didn't matter if she'd escaped from Whitney's hellish experiments. Good for her. He couldn't do that because he wasn't supposed to know about Whitney's experiments. He was a soldier on vacation.

She indicated for him to pull up his loose track pants. He did so, reluctant for her to see his leg, getting them just above his knee. The shots had ripped into him from the side, tearing up his leg as if trying to open a zipper into muscle and bone. The scars were raw and ugly, going all the way up to his hip.

Amaryllis gasped when she saw the raw, shiny wounds. "Malichai. How did you survive this?"

He shrugged. "I was bleeding pretty bad and slapped field dressings on the worst of the wounds to slow them down. My brother Rubin carried me to the helicopter. He worked on me the entire time. I was lucky the doctors were there with blood and whatever else they needed to keep me alive until they could land. Ezekiel, my oldest brother, operated on me. He was able to keep me from bleeding out until we got the orthopedic surgeon. Even then, it was a bit of a fight."

He downplayed it but had the feeling she knew that was what he was doing. If Rubin hadn't been a psychic surgeon, he would have been dead. Had they not had his blood on hand, he wouldn't have made it. There were a million things that could have gone wrong for him. He'd been lucky.

Her hand hovered over his leg and he immediately felt warmth that quickly turned to a raw blazing heat. More than once he'd experienced this same kind of thing when Joe helped him. He watched her face, not her hand. At once he could see her eyes, the difference. Those blue, blue eyes that turned inward. He'd only seen that once before, with Joe. Amaryllis was a psychic healer, and they were very rare. If Whitney knew she had that gift, she would have had no option but to escape if she didn't want to spend the rest of her life being taken apart or in his breeding program.

His leg suddenly felt on fire, as if flames licked up his bone from his calf to his hip. It was a flash-fire. Hot and fast burning. It took every ounce of discipline he had not to react, to not drag his leg away, out from under that terrible heat.

She suddenly pulled her palm away from his leg and sat abruptly on the lounger as if her legs had given out. It took a few minutes with Amaryllis first staring down at her hands and rocking back and forth, breathing deeply and then looking out to the ocean and the surfers there.

Malichai waited patiently for the verdict. When she turned to look at him, he didn't like what he saw on her face. He rubbed his hand down the leg. The fire had slowly subsided, but he still felt the aftereffects.

"I'm pretty fucked, aren't I?" He tried to be realistic.

"I think it can be fixed, but, Malichai, something chewed that bone up. It's still doing damage. Either there was something chemical in the bullets that hit you, or you reacted very poorly with those field dressings you used. You could have been highly allergic to one of the compounds used.

Whatever it is, it's trying to eat through your bone."

He rested the back of his head against the lounger. "Can you fix it? I don't think a doctor can. If they could have, they already would have. I've had three operations already." He forced his voice to be matter of fact when inside he was screaming. He couldn't lose his leg.

He had to contact Joe fast. Even if Amaryllis thought she could fix it, why hadn't it worked when Joe had worked on him? But even more so, Rubin? Rubin's gift was so powerful, they literally hid him from everyone. There could be no whisper of what he was capable of or every faction would be after him. There would be no way to protect him. Rubin had worked on him on more than one occasion. Why hadn't it worked? Now, he was past worry and on to terrified.

"I discovered that weird little ability I just showed you when I was around fourteen and one of the girls was very sick."

"Girls?" He ventured the question cautiously, mostly because if he didn't and she realized what she'd just said, she would wonder why he hadn't asked.

There was the briefest of hesitations. "I'm sorry, didn't I tell you? I grew up in an orphanage. My parents abandoned me

139

when I was first born. Those of us who weren't perfect babies grew up and went to school there."

"I had no idea orphanages still raised children. I suppose they must. Was it difficult? Or did you like it?" He didn't bother to keep the curiosity out of his voice.

"I liked it. Two of the girls didn't. They felt . . . less because of it. There were six of us raised there, although not really together. I was lucky and spent a lot of time in the kitchen with the cook. It was fun and I picked up things fast. In that respect, I was able to excel in school and just about anything I chose to do."

"Are you still in touch with the other girls?"

For the first time she looked at him directly, her gaze moving over his face, a touch of suspicion in her eyes. "Not really, why?"

He shrugged. "They'd be your family. I never go more than a couple of days before I check in with Ezekiel or Rubin, with any of my brothers."

"You didn't have a sister?"

He shook his head and rubbed his aching leg. She immediately began to massage the cramping muscles. Her hands felt warm — they felt magic. The cramping stopped almost immediately.

"You have a gift, Amaryllis. My leg aches quite a bit and for the first time in a long while it feels better."

She hesitated. "Malichai, I can try to fix the damage that's being done to your leg, but I've never really tried anything that severe. I think you should call your doctor and get them to do an MRI, something that will reveal the damage to the bone. If you don't do something soon, there's a possibility something could go really wrong."

He knew that. Subconsciously, he knew it before he'd ever agreed to take a vacation. He supposed he'd really come there to think about his future and what he'd do if he lost his leg. He'd allowed himself to be distracted because the last thing he wanted to do was face his reality. The leg had started off fine during all the physical therapy, feeling strong and sound and little by little it had begun to ache. And then hurt. His gut had begun to give him that alarm that always told him when something was really wrong.

When he was a boy, he'd worried about losing a limb. Every time he'd gotten a cut and an infection, that had been his biggest worry, although he'd never shared it with his brothers. The worry had carried over into his career when he was carrying out

141

the wounded with their many losses of limbs. At first, when his leg just ached, he'd told himself it was his old paranoia; now, with Amaryllis clearly concerned, he was more worried than ever.

"The docs have done everything they know how to do," he admitted. "I don't have any more options."

She remained sitting very still, her hand on his leg gently rubbing up and down the ragged scar tissue, a soothing gesture that was comforting.

"Can you do something?" He had to be careful, not act like he knew too much about the kind of gift she had.

She hesitated. "I don't honestly know, Malichai. I don't have a lot of practice and I'm not very good at toning it down. It feels like a lot of power, almost too much. Okay. Too much. If I do something wrong and damage the bone further . . ." She trailed off.

"You think I could lose my leg." He had to say it out loud to someone. It seemed ridiculous there on the beach with the ocean rolling in the background.

Amaryllis bit her lip and then nodded. "I don't know. Maybe, but I don't want to carry that responsibility. I'll have to think about it, maybe practice on something first.

There's so much heat . . ." She trailed off, looking up as a tall, gangly man with a surfboard tucked under his arm came bounding up to them like a shaggy collie.

"Amaryllis. Dude. You should be ridin' the waves. They're perfect today."

His blond hair looked darker slicked back, the salt water still dripping.

"Malichai, this is my friend Dozer. Dozer, this is Malichai."

Dozer shoved out his fist to do a bump. "Gnarly scars, man. I saw some on a man who had a shark take him down, but they weren't even close to that. Cool."

Malichai resisted pulling down the material of his pants. He wasn't five.

Dozer beamed at him, his teeth gleaming almost as white as his hair. "What's the good word?"

"Nice morning," Malichai observed, uncertain what one said to Dozer. Amaryllis, from the way she introduced Dozer, had made it clear he was her friend. "Everything good?"

Dozer frowned. "Had some whack job in full diving gear grab my ankle and pull me off my board just now. It was on purpose too. I don't understand these tourists anymore. There's a big ocean out there. Why get upset because a few of us are riding the waves?"

Malichai sat up straighter, exchanging a long look with Amaryllis. "Is Dozer given to fantasy? Because if someone pulled him off his board and —" He broke off.

"Right here, dude, and no, I'm not given to fantasy. Some asshole in full scuba gear came off the shelf underwater right at me."

"You're telling us a diver caught your ankle and deliberately jerked you off your surfboard? What else did he do once he had you off the board?" Amaryllis demanded.

"I kicked him in the head before he got me off," Dozer admitted. "At first, I thought he was a shark, then I got a good look at him. I've heard of divers messing with surfers, but he could have drowned me. He came at me a second time, like maybe he was going to try to take me under, but I punched him, right in his face mask. Three of my buddies swam over to make sure I was all right and he dove deep and was gone."

Malichai didn't like it. First, he'd read Anna's lips and she wanted to tell the cops she'd overheard something worrisome. Then there was the artsy couple, one believing he'd overheard — with Anna — a group wanting to kill the maximum amount of

144

people. Now, Dozer. "You hear anything recently, or see anything that bothered you, Dozer?"

Amaryllis slipped her hand in Malichai's, threading her fingers through his and squeezing down gratefully. She liked that he didn't just dismiss what Dozer was saying. He couldn't. In spite of Dozer acting far younger than his age, he was more than a good swimmer. He practically lived in the ocean. If he said someone yanked him off his board and acted as if he was trying to drown him, it was most likely true.

Dozer shrugged, leaning on the surf board he'd stuck in the sand. "I hear lots of things that bother me, but I went to see Miss Crystal the other morning. She hadn't opened her magic shop on time. She's kinda getting up there in age, you know. Just checkin' on her. Man answers the door. Says Miss Crystal is gone for a few days, that she's off vacationing with her son. I said she didn't have a son. The man says he made a mistake, that she's vacationing with some-one she *regards* as her son and she'll be back in a couple of weeks. I told him I was going to call the cops and have them do a well check. She doesn't like to be away from her store. Guy was a liar and total asshole, but he's the only one I can think of other than the diver."

"Be careful," Malichai warned. "Weird things seem to be happening around here."

Dozer nodded, caught up his surfboard and made his way down the beach.

Malichai watched him go. "That's going to teach me not to make snap judgments on anyone. I wouldn't have thought he even knew what a well check was."

"What are we going to do about Miss Crystal, Malichai?" Amaryllis asked.

"We don't know anything is wrong yet," he answered. "But I'm getting a little worried. Early this morning, around three, some visitors came to my room."

Instantly her face changed. "Let me guess, that would be Linda, Lorrie and Lexie. The sinful, divine sisters. They tell enough stories about how they share their men." She rolled her eyes and moved very subtly away from him. At the same time, she tried to slip her hand from his.

Malichai laughed as he tightened his fingers around hers. "The sinful, divine sharing sisters. I see. No, they didn't come visit me, which is just as well. I wouldn't like having to throw women out of my room, and I'd have to. I'm taken. This woman right here is everything I'm ever going to need. And I'm not into sharing. At.

All. Man or woman. Just so you know. I would hope you wouldn't be either."

She drew in her breath and relaxed a little beside him. She didn't protest or agree with his assessment of being taken. "Who came to your room at three in the morning?"

"Burnell and Jay. They wanted my help. I guess I must look like a hit man or bodyguard to them. They were afraid of another one of the guests, he's in room fourteen. Craig Williams."

"Our southern gentleman. He is always unfailingly polite. A very nice man."

"Apparently he stares at Burnell and Jay."

"Oh, for heaven's sake. He's a really nice man."

"Has he been here before?"

"No, this is his first time. He's meeting a couple of old school friends here for a reunion of sorts."

"You seem to know a lot about him." Malichai didn't like the suddenly cold feeling sweeping over him.

"I clean his room, remember? We talk sometimes."

"I see." The swamp was looking better and better to take his woman to. He might ask Cayenne to wrap her in silk, and drape more all over the walls to make it impossible to escape.

Amaryllis burst out laughing. "You don't see anything. You should, but you don't. I'm not looking at Craig Williams. I'm looking at you. I shouldn't be, but I am. Now, tell me what you plan to do to figure out whether Miss Crystal is alive and well."

"Dozer did say he asked for a well check. I think it wouldn't do any harm to have Marie call them as well, but let's wait a day on that. Two callers, and the cops might very well decide she's a priority. Tomorrow I'll pay a visit to the magic shop and inquire about my good friend, Miss Crystal."

"I'll go with you," she offered immediately.

Malichai brought her hand up to his mouth and gently bit down on her fingertips. "I'm potentially setting myself up. After I make the inquiries, I'm going to go swimming in the ocean without scuba or snorkeling gear. I'll make certain to let whoever answers the door know that's where I'm heading next. If they make their try for me, we'll know something is off and we need to bring in the cops."

"If they make a try for you?" she echoed. "You're setting yourself up as bait."

He nodded. "I told you, vacations aren't my thing. If Miss Crystal is being held somewhere, or is dead, I want to know. I'm not letting her suffer, thinking no one is looking for her. Maybe if enough people ask, they'll have to produce her."

"I don't know if I like this plan."

"I'm good in the water, babe. You just think about trying to fix my leg. In the meantime, we have to eat breakfast because I'm starving, and then we're going to see that movie you've been wanting to see. And tonight, we're on the roof again. I like being on the roof."

Mostly, he was going to take the day to sort through everything Burnell, Jay and Dozer had told him. He was also going to send out for more information on everyone staying at the bed-and-breakfast. In the back of his head, the whisper of conspiracy was getting louder.

5

Malichai rolled over and stared up at the stars. Amaryllis lay beside him on a blanket. The roof was flat and closed in on all four sides by a low redwood planter filled with green, lacy plants. The flat space was accessed through the attic. The roof jutted out over the porch at the front of the building. Few knew that one could hide right there in plain sight and look out over the beach and the rolling waves. The view was incredible.

"I've never smiled so much in my life," he confessed, knowing he was probably giving away too much, but he didn't care if he left himself vulnerable. He liked Amaryllis — a hell of a lot. He needed to quit dancing around the issue and just come out and tell her he was very serious and wanted her to go home with him when he went.

Doing the dishes, listening to her exchange banter with Jacy and Marie and including him in their circle as they teased one another made him feel part of her. He knew he was getting the genuine Amaryllis, just as he was giving her the real Malichai.

"You don't smile very often?" She turned her head to look at him.

He kept looking at the stars, knowing he shouldn't give her any more, but he couldn't stop himself. For him, this was real. This woman. His chance. The more he was in her company, the more he was certain she was the one.

"I'm not a man given to smiles, mostly I save them for Wyatt's little girls and Nonny."

"That's so crazy." She rubbed the pad of her finger over his lips. "You have a beautiful smile. I noticed the first time I ever saw you laugh. Why wouldn't you want to smile?"

He resisted pulling her finger into his mouth. "I guess I didn't have a lot to smile about after my drug-addicted mother thought that renting out her little sons to men for sex for drug money was a good idea."

"Oh my God." Amaryllis sat up straight, looking horrified. Her eyes shone with unshed tears. "Seriously? She seriously did that? Malichai."

"I have an older brother. Ezekiel. He's not all that much older, but he took Mordichai

151

and me and hit the streets with us. We learned to steal food, pick pockets, do all kinds of very bad things." He flashed a small grin at her. "Ezekiel used his fists to protect us and the territory we claimed. Eventually, he taught us to fight and then made us get schooling. He found two other boys that knew nothing about the streets and brought them in. They're still with us."

She lay back down, blinking up at the stars. He could see the little teardrops that looked almost like diamonds on the ends of her lashes.

"That's just horrible. I don't know what I thought — or hoped. Maybe that all mothers were like Marie. She'd do anything for Jacy. She would have done anything for her husband. I think he felt the same, yet he died. Life sometimes doesn't make any sense to me."

He rolled to his side, propped himself up on his elbow and reached across her to curl his fingers around the nape of her neck and sweep his thumb from her high cheekbone to the corner of her mouth.

"Amaryllis, the last thing I wanted to do was make you sad. I remember being scared, but after a while, I wasn't scared anymore. I got strong. I learned survival skills. Those skills allow me to do the work I do. I can save other men, good men like Marie's husband, men who belong home with people who love them. Their wives. Their husbands. Their children. What those lessons taught me so long ago gives me the skills I need now."

He watched her throat work as she swallowed, nodding as she did so. "Your injury isn't a small one, Malichai. You hide it very well, but I could see when you were standing too long, like when you did dishes, that it really bothers you. Now, I've seen it and I know it's bad. Please don't tell me it's all right, because I know that it isn't. What really happened to you?"

"I seem to be doing all the talking, honey, and I'm not used to it." He bunched her hair in his fist and ran thick strands through his fingers. She remained silent, just looking at him with those sapphire eyes that seemed to look right through him.

"I told you, we were getting some very courageous soldiers off a mountain. We'd destroyed most of the enemy's weapons, the ones capable of taking out helicopters, or at least we thought we did. As we were trying to load the wounded, we came under fire. More fighters had arrived, and they were manning a few of the guns that hadn't been destroyed. The hell they unloaded on us was murderous. We were exposed and they had enough ammunition to take down the mountain, or at least it felt that way. It was bad. It happens all the time."

Malichai rolled back over and stared up at the stars again. They were beautiful. Bright. A field of diamonds overhead. He needed that kind of beauty in the world after witnessing so much ugliness. To his shock, she slipped her hand into his, threading her fingers through his as if she were weaving them together, and then she leaned into him, her soft body nearly blanketing his. She didn't speak, she just waited.

He felt like a fool talking about it. He didn't want to. He was no hero and he knew it would come off to her that way. Or bragging. He wasn't bragging. He didn't want to even think about it. He had no choice. In order for the wounded to be brought to the helicopter rendezvous safely, he'd had to clear those bunkers and get rid of the weapons.

"I charged straight into the gunfire." He'd used his enhanced speed, going low and then high. "The bombardment of gunfire was horrendous, never stopping, and I felt bullets whipping around me, some so close they ripped my clothing and in a few cases skin."

He touched his arm without thinking. "Sometimes I can still hear that sound. It was like continuous thunder rolling right over top of me. Worse." He shook his head. "It was bad."

"Keep going."

If anyone else had asked him, he would have told them to go to hell. "I tossed grenade after grenade into the bunker while the enemy continued to fire at me until the grenades exploded. Some of the enemy must have split up, spread out and went to the other bunkers we thought we'd destroyed in the middle of the night. Or they brought weapons and ammunition with them. Who knows? In any case, they began firing at me too."

She sat up and turned around to face him, tucking her legs tailor-fashion, but still holding his hand. Her eyes shone like twin jewels, never leaving his face.

"The smell of blood and death is difficult to get out of one's nose. The images of blood and shrapnel and what's done to a human being are equally as bad to purge. I had to go into that mess because the firepower coming from the second bunker was a steady stream. I used the still-intact mortar gun and immediately engaged the enemy. I was lucky because Rubin was there with his rifle and he's damn good. He picked off a couple of them."

He fell silent, rubbing his thigh without thinking.

"Malichai?" She said his name gently. "Tell me what happened."

He shrugged. "Everything went quiet and I stepped out to check the bunkers, to make certain they were clear so the wounded could be loaded into the helicopter." He shook his head, remembering the silence. The smell of gunpowder, of blood. Even of death. The wind was blowing, he remembered it on his face.

He almost hadn't heard the sound of the machine gun as it spat out angry bullets, all with his name on them. "I don't know how many times I was hit, but it felt like a dozen, maybe more. All up and down my leg, from my calf to my thigh. I knew I was a dead man. I went to the ground. The bones in my leg were shattered. There was so much blood. I had field dressings with me, and I slapped them on as fast as I could in order to try to stop the bleeding."

He couldn't tell her what those field dressings were or that second-generation Zenith had saved his life.

"The bone was broken. Shattered. In so many places."

She knew. There was no hiding it from her, not after she had used her ability of psychic healing. She hadn't yet learned to control it, but she definitely had the power.

"Yeah, it wasn't the best of news for me. I was down, but the field dressings helped stop the bleeding and Rubin was taking out anything that moved. He kept shooting while I dragged myself across the distance to the bunker and tossed grenades in until my arm didn't want to work anymore."

He didn't tell her the ground was nothing but rock covered in snow and bullets hit all around him. Or that it was the strength in his arms that allowed him to drag himself, leaving a trail of blood behind him, basically pointing to his position, even though the clothes he wore and his special enhancements would have made him impossible to see.

Amaryllis was horrified. "You attacked them, even as wounded as you were?"

"I didn't think I had a whole hell of a lot to lose. The way I was bleeding, I was a dead man anyway. I had to give the helicopter a chance to take those boys home." To him, the logic made sense. "In any case, Rubin was picking them off, so I just hucked a few grenades and it was almost over. I still had to make it back to the

157

helicopter and it seemed a million miles away. Rubin came after me, rifle slung over his shoulder. He hauled my butt up the side of that mountain to the clearing, and I'm a heavy man."

She was silent for a very long time. Staring at him. Those eyes drifting over his face and down his chest, then back up to his face. "That's incredible, Malichai. What you did, what both of you did, was incredible."

"One of the other soldiers had done something similar before me. He was wounded, but he'd gotten the others undercover and kept them going until help arrived. By that, I mean for days, under heavy fire."

"And you're going back to that?" She looked appalled at the idea.

He reached up and found her hair again, that silken mass that appealed to him, the way her eyes and mouth did. He could look at her face for the rest of his life.

"I'm a soldier, honey. Of course I'm going back."

"You're not." She started to protest and then shook her head. "I'm sorry. I don't know why I'm arguing with you. I think you're extraordinary, not just because of the rescue, but the way you are with Jacy, with everyone. You always show respect to everyone. You're quiet about it and never look for someone to notice what you do. You're just so ready to pitch in and help out. I watched you, afraid you had another motive, but you're genuine."

"Babe. Come on," he said gently. He curled his palm around the nape of her neck. "You're my other motive. Would I help Marie out without you being around? Absolutely, I would, but I want you to see that guy, the one willing to help his woman out no matter what the problem is. I've been all over the world and I've never met anyone like you. I never thought I'd meet a woman like you."

Amaryllis didn't want him to go any further. He was so amazing. So extraordinary. He looked at her as if she was. He did so much for everyone around him. Complete strangers. Men he knew nothing about. He sacrificed himself. His body. His life. He risked everything. In spite of the worst childhood, he still managed to be connected to people in a positive way.

What was she? An assassin. A woman who worked alone. She'd trained alone. Grown up alone, even among the other girls. They'd been separated and kept that way for the most part. Until Marie and Jacy, she had no close bonds. When she planned her escape, she'd planned it alone. She hadn't gone back to ensure the other girls had gotten away. She hadn't taken the gunfire to make certain the other women had the time to get out. She'd known all along she'd convince only two of them to come with her. Once out of the compound, the plan was to separate and make a run for freedom. Each would be on her own.

She hadn't even told them about her plan to escape until she had her chance, because she didn't fully trust anyone. When the time came, she'd laid it out for them, knowing she was risking someone telling Whitney or, worse, Owen. She'd reasoned — and still believed — that had she told them earlier, the two who wanted to curry favor with Whitney would have told him immediately. One would have been indecisive and delayed any escape while the other two would have come with her. She'd studied them all carefully before she'd made her choices.

She closed her eyes, more ashamed than ever. She knew what she was. She knew the DNA Whitney had spliced into her. She had ruthless traits. He'd created her to be utterly ruthless until she was in a family unit and then she was utterly loyal to those she considered family. She wasn't worthy of a man like Malichai, who sacrificed everything for his fellow man.

She wanted him with every breath she took. She'd never been so attracted. She didn't see other men the way she saw him and when he told her the way he'd gotten hurt in that matter-of-fact way, everything feminine in her responded. She knew she could be loyal to him — that she would be. She also knew she wouldn't do that to him. He needed someone special . . .

"Stop shaking your head." Malichai regarded Amaryllis with a small smile, reaching out to tuck a stray strand of thick silky hair behind her ear. He loved her hair. "You're an amazing woman, although I can see you don't think so. And we have a lot more in common than you think."

"I don't understand what's so special about me." She pulled back slightly.

He held on to her. "You talk about me helping out Marie and Jacy. You give so much every single day and you don't have to. You could work your eight hours and leave her. Instead, you take as much off her plate as you can manage. That's extraordinary, Amaryllis. You're kind and compassionate and you know what kind of mother you want to be."

Amaryllis started to protest, but he put a finger to her mouth. "Honey, listen to me. I

161

know I live in Louisiana and you probably get hit on every time a single man comes to the B and B, but I'm not talking a two-week fling here. I don't have flings. I don't even have one-night stands. I'm going to be honest, and you're not going to like it much, but if I want sex, I pick up a woman in a bar, we fuck and then we part ways. I don't go out on dates and I don't think about the women I pick up ever again. Most of the time, I couldn't tell you what they look like. I'm not proud of it, but it's the truth."

"You're telling me this, why?"

"Because I could close my eyes right now and describe every detail of your face and body. The way you move. The way you laugh. I could tell you what kinds of things you like, what you don't like."

"No you can't."

He smiled again, because he could see it on her face that she was so certain. "You're a planner. You love Marie and Jacy and regard them as family. You like to cook but love to bake. You like old movies, mostly romantic ones, but prefer action if they have romance in them. Your favorite thing to do is read — again, romance. See the theme here?" His smile widened to a grin. "You get annoyed by pushy people, but you handle it. Love the beach and swimming in the ocean. You're fast too in the water. You like to look at the stars and you know all the constellations. Every single thing I like, you like. Mostly, you like me."

She couldn't help but laugh, and he wanted her to. He was revealing a lot about his own feelings toward her.

"I pay attention to detail because you count. You matter."

"How would you know all that so soon after we met?"

She was regarding him with suspicion again, and he didn't blame her. It was too fast. He was acting out of character, telling her things he'd never tell anyone, skating along the lines of saying too much when he was classified. He'd kept it simple, but she could piece where the rescue had taken place, maybe even when. She was intelligent. Still, he wanted this woman for his own. He questioned whether or not she was a GhostWalker with the ability to shield her energy, but he knew she couldn't possibly be there to hurt him. Whitney would never put one of his women undercover for over a year on the off chance that he would pick that particular bed-and-breakfast for his vacation.

Did it matter to him if she was enhanced? If she was one of Whitney's experiments?

No. Every team member had married a woman enhanced by Whitney. He liked to pair them, and Malichai knew that every time he inhaled Amaryllis into his lungs, he was a little more lost. Her intoxicating scent wasn't what had him tied up in knots. That was all Amaryllis's personality. Her character.

"You can't know, Malichai. Not this fast. There are things about me you don't know, things that aren't so great."

He gave her a reassuring smile. "Everyone has traits both good and bad. I do. You can't know that I'm the one, honey, because you're younger and haven't been all over the world. You haven't met what feels like a million women and none intrigued you. Amaryllis, I don't have reactions to women like I have to you. I look at you and want you with every cell in my body. I think about you every minute. I was having nightmares, now I have erotic dreams."

"They'll go away." Even as she denied it, he could see her neck and face flush with color. Her breathing turned a little ragged. Her breasts rose up and down with each labored breath. Even her nipples were peaked into two tight little buds. The night air wasn't that cold.

"You have every right to your opinion, and

I have another week to change your mind. I'd rather persuade you now, and reap the benefits, but I'm willing to do the necessary work for however long it takes."

She shook her head. "I don't get you, Malichai. You're risking scaring me off by telling me all this, you know that, don't you?"

"I like to be fair, and you're not someone who backs away from a fight. It's important to me that you know I have intentions, but it isn't just to get you in my bed." He grinned at her, his thumb sliding over her lips. "Well, okay, I'll be honest. I have intentions of getting you in my bed as soon as possible."

Beneath the pad of his thumb, her lips formed a smile. He felt that movement, the soft slide of silk along his nerve endings. It was a small, subtle movement, but it triggered an explosion of heat in him.

"You might actually have a chance of getting me in bed," she replied. "You've got charm on your side and I can see I'm a little too susceptible to that in you."

"Because I'm such a badass."

"Because you're so sweet."

He groaned. "You just can't use that word, Amaryllis. Seriously. If my brothers were here and heard you call me 'sweet,' I'd never hear the end of it. I'd have to shoot them, I'd be in jail and then you'd be coming to visit me, wearing something sexy, and I'd get in fights with the other inmates. It would be bad."

She laughed, just the way he knew she would. Soft. The notes scattering around him like a symphony playing in the night. The sound settled into him, finding its way inside. He wanted to hear that sound every day. It drowned out the sound of machine-gun fire. Mortar fire. The screams of the wounded and dying.

His palm settled around the nape of her neck and he exerted a little pressure, giving her every out, giving her time to pull away. She didn't. She bent her head down toward his. Up close, her face was even more beautiful than he'd realized, her skin flawless other than one crescent-shaped scar up by her left eye. It was tiny, like a little moon. Her lashes were long and thick, and they fluttered right before they lowered.

Then his mouth was on hers and his mind shut down. The taste of her, the heat, took him like a wildfire spreading through his body. It seemed she poured liquid fire down his throat to find his veins. His heart pounded. He found himself kissing her like a starved man, feeding off her. Wanting, even needing, more from her. It was never going to be enough. Never. Her taste was addicting, but it was that firestorm rushing through him, an experience he'd never had, that he knew he wanted for the rest of his life.

He pulled her down on top of his chest, his arms closing around her, so that she sprawled over him like a blanket, her lips like warm silk on his. Her mouth was a flame of scorching heat that just seemed to grow hotter and hotter as it spread through him and settled in his groin.

He knew if he didn't stop soon, he wasn't going to be able to. There was no halfway with her kisses. She simply gave herself to him — wholly surrendered to him. It was pure luxury, pure sin. A promise.

Malichai forced himself to pull away. He framed her face with both hands, looking into her eyes. A man could get lost there and he was certain it had happened to him. There wasn't a way out and he didn't want one.

"You kiss like sin, woman."

"Is that good or bad?"

"Did it feel bad?"

She shook her head. He tucked stray strands of her hair behind her ear, his heart still pounding, but his mood far lighter. She wasn't running from him, and that was all that mattered. Her small frown had him trying to erase it with his finger.

"What is it?"

"Lights. To the front of the house. Police lights." She rolled off him with that grace he had come to expect but that still bothered him. She was that little bit *too* graceful. When she got to her feet, she was already on the move. There was no awkward pause or being off-balance. She was always on the correct foot to lead off, so she just moved from one position to the next so easily.

He rolled over and watched her walk to the edge of the roof. She didn't fear heights. She had perfect balance. She knew about him, at least something about him; he needed to take the opportunity to ask her questions. He didn't want to, because more and more, he was becoming convinced that she was one of Whitney's orphan girls and he didn't want her to have to lie to him. That would hurt. He would understand, but it would still hurt.

"Malichai. The cops are here. I have to go down to Marie." There was wariness in her voice.

He was up immediately. She seemed on the verge of flight, as if those cops might be there for her. "I'll go down with you."

168

"It's after midnight, why would they come at this hour?" She sounded scared.

Malichai put his arm around her and pulled her in close as they made their way to the door leading back inside. The steps were narrow, so he moved in front of her, leading the way down from the attic, his larger frame protecting her. She slipped her fingers into his back pocket as they stepped into the hall, keeping a connection between them.

"We'll find out. There's no use in speculating."

She didn't move up beside him, and he didn't insist. They went down the next flight of stairs to the main floor. Marie stood at the front door with two men in suits and an officer in a uniform. She turned toward them, relief immediate on her face.

"Oh, good. Malichai. Amaryllis. Something terrible has happened to two of our guests."

"I'm Detective Duncan," the taller of the two men in suits said. "This is Detective Brady. We have a few questions, if you don't mind."

Malichai could see that Marie was very distraught. He swept his arm around her. "Why don't you come in, gentlemen. I'm Malichai Fortunes. This is Amaryllis."

He kept his body angled slightly to provide cover for the woman he considered his. Amaryllis was strangely nervous around the cops. Even if she was one of Whitney's orphans, she shouldn't have to worry — unless she didn't have the proper paperwork. He hadn't thought of that. And he had refused to send her name to his team. They had her photograph and Ezekiel had asked for more information on her, which meant she wasn't in the facial recognition program.

He stepped back from the door and allowed all three men into the building. Marie immediately led the way down the hall to her private sitting room.

"Please sit down," she invited. "Can I get you anything? Coffee? Tea? I do have a coffee cake if you'd like something with it."

Both detectives asked for coffee. The officer asked for both. No one took milk or sugar. Amaryllis jumped up to go fill the orders. Marie almost protested but then she settled in her chair.

"Where do you fit in?" Duncan asked, turning toward Malichai.

Malichai shrugged. "I'm actually here on vacation, a forced leave. Took a hit in my leg during a mission and was sent to relax somewhere. I'm dating Amaryllis and I do the dishes for them and help out however I can."

Duncan's eyebrow nearly went through his scalp. "You're on vacation but you're working for the owner?"

Malichai shook his head, wanting to be very clear. "No money exchanges hands. We're friends. She needs help, I help her. It's that simple. I can give you my unit and commander. They'll verify I'm here at the moment on forced leave."

Malichai spotted Amaryllis with a tray and he immediately went to her and took it from her. "You okay, baby?" he asked softly.

She took a deep breath and nodded. He didn't believe her for a second, but he was willing to let it slide because there was no other choice. After the cops left, he was going to have to ask some hard questions. He didn't want to. He wanted to spend time with her like a normal man with a woman he enjoyed being around.

He watched her settle into one of the chairs across from the detectives as he gave each man his coffee order. The chair was the only one large enough to hold both of them. He sank into the space beside her and instantly she snuggled closer to him — as if for protection. He had that distinct impression and hoped the cops didn't get the same one.

"Which guests?" Marie asked, one hand going defensively to her throat. "And did you say it was an accident?"

"Anna and Bryon Cooper."

Amaryllis shook her head and caught at Malichai's wrist. She was trembling. Marie let out a small cry, cut off in midstream.

"That can't be. They were here for dinner. They always walk on the beach before retiring for the night and they went out as they've done every night," Marie said. "Amaryllis, you talked to them right before they left."

The detectives turned their gazes to Amaryllis and noted the way she was holding on to Malichai as if her life depended on it.

"I didn't catch your last name," Duncan said, leaning a little toward Amaryllis.

"It's Johnson. Amaryllis Johnson."

"What do you do here?"

"Whatever Marie needs me to do. I do a lot of housekeeping. Dishes. Cooking. That sort of thing."

"How long have you worked here?"

"About a year."

"Tell me everything you remember about Anna and Bryon. Especially tonight. What went on tonight? Were they upset about anything? What did they say or do?"

Malichai didn't watch Duncan; instead, he turned his attention to Detective Brady, who had his phone out. Recording. Taking photographs. Making certain they were who they said they were. Whatever had happened to Anna and Bryon Cooper hadn't been an accident.

He shifted his weight slightly in the chair so that his much larger body protected Amaryllis from being easily seen by Detective Brady.

"They didn't seem upset. Anna was laughing at something Bryon said. She usually was. She found him hilarious. All of us did. He was very popular with all the guests."

"Was she? Was Anna popular with all the guests?" Duncan persisted.

"Anna was much more reserved, and Bryon seemed protective of her. They were having a conversation about a bikini she'd purchased at one of the local shops. Bryon loved the bikini and wanted her to wear it on the beach tomorrow. She said no, it was for private swimming pools. He kept leering at her and chasing her around the hall. She was laughing so hard." Amaryllis looked up to meet the detective's eyes. "Did something really happen to her? To them? They were really nice."

Malichai swept his arm around her and pulled her beneath the shelter of his shoulder. Tears swam in her eyes and her lips trembled. She looked like she was about to plead with Duncan to save Anna and Bryon. "Baby," he whispered softly, knowing what was coming.

"I'm sorry, yes. Their bodies were found on the beach. It looks as if it was a murder-suicide. He killed her and then shot himself."

Amaryllis went rigid and then shook her head. "Absolutely not. No way did Bryon kill Anna. He absolutely would never do that."

"I agree," Marie said staunchly. "They were so in love and Bryon doted on Anna. He would no more kill her than I'd kill Jacy. That's not right."

"You only knew them for a week," Duncan pointed out. "He could have hidden a dark side from you. Maybe she looked at some man wrong and he was very jealous."

"He wanted her to wear a tiny bikini on the beach," Amaryllis contradicted him. "That's not jealousy. He was very confident in the way Anna felt about him. I'm telling you, he would *never* kill Anna."

The two detectives exchanged a look.

Malichai was almost certain neither believed the murder-suicide theory. Someone had murdered the couple and then tried to make it look like a murder-suicide. Easy enough when the couple were tourists, and no one really knew their personalities or what went on in their private business.

"What else do you know about tonight, Ms. Johnson?" Duncan asked. "Did Anna or Bryon say anything to you personally?"

Amaryllis sighed, exasperated that Duncan didn't appear to be listening to her evaluation of Anna and Bryon. "Anna was laughing over the swimsuit and she asked me if I wore a bikini to the beach. She said she didn't wear revealing clothes very often, but since they were on vacation, she was going to surprise Bryon and wear it. She had a cover-up."

She paused and when Malichai looked down at her, her eyes were swimming with tears, transforming them into twin jewels. Everything protective in him welled up so strong, he almost pulled her into his lap. He wanted to catch her up in his arms and carry her out of the room.

"She planned to wear it tomorrow for him." Her voice hitched and she pressed trembling fingers to her lips.

"I'd like to see their room," Detective

Brady said to Marie. "Perhaps you would show me while Detective Duncan interviews Ms. Johnson."

"Of course," Marie said, standing.

Amaryllis gripped Malichai's wrist and burrowed closer to his side. He knew she wasn't aware she'd done so. "I hate this. I hate this so much. They were sweet, both of them. Marie's business is finally paying off just when she needs it to. People will shy away once they hear about this. She's wonderful and deserving. I think Anna was as well."

"What about Bryon?" Duncan persisted.

Amaryllis frowned. Malichai took her hand and pressed her palm deep into the muscle of his thigh, his thumb sliding back and forth across the top, on her bare skin. Her fingers trembled against his warmth, and he pushed her palm deeper to assure her he wasn't going to allow anything to happen to her.

"I didn't know him as well, although, like I said, he was hilarious. He often went running in the mornings and Anna would come into the dining room. I always sit at a little table after the guests have eaten. Malichai sits with me and we eat our breakfast. Anna would come in, sometimes Marie and Jacy, and we'd just talk about things together."

"What kinds of things?" Duncan persisted.

"Her job. She and Bryon owned a very successful but small business, a small press. They did ads, brochures, little booklets, anything people wanted printed. They also did T-shirts and trophies. That sort of thing. She loved the people that came in, and so did Bryon. She talked mainly about him, how good he was with people, how charming he could be. She said she loved him so much because he never failed to help people."

Amaryllis turned her head to look up at Malichai. "We had that in common. I admitted to her that I felt that way about Malichai because he is the best man I've ever met. Working here, and living around the beach, believe me, I've met quite a few men."

Malichai brushed a kiss on top of her head. "Thanks, Amaryllis. I'm not certain it's true, but I love the fact that you think I'm a good man." He loved her all the more for that. Amaryllis was very sparing when talking about her feelings. She had just admitted that she cared a great deal for him. He had a chance with her after all.

"How do you think Bryon felt about Anna?"

"He loved her," Malichai said. "It showed

in the way he looked at her and all the things he did for her. The way he touched her. A man can tell, and Bryon loved Anna."

Amaryllis nodded and then pressed her face into Malichai's side.

"There's something else," Malichai said. "It's thin, I'll warn you of that. Very thin. Last week, when Amaryllis and I went to lunch at the café just up the block, we were sitting outside, and Anna and Bryon were sitting at a table straight across from me. There were several tables between us, but no people. I could see both of them clearly. They were holding hands, but they were arguing. Anna was very upset about something she'd overheard, and she wanted to go to the police. Bryon didn't think she'd heard correctly, and they didn't know who'd been speaking anyway."

"You heard them talking?" Duncan asked.

Malichai shook his head. He didn't look at Amaryllis. "I read lips."

Duncan went silent, eyeing him carefully. "I will need the name of your unit and commander."

"Of course, no problem." Malichai wanted to smile over that. He was so classified, he wondered if anyone would admit he was actually alive.

"What did Anna hear?"

"At that time, all I saw was that she wanted to tell someone — the police — and Bryon insisted she hadn't heard enough to give them the heads-up on anything."

"You're right. That's pretty thin," Duncan said, disappointment in his voice.

"True, but then I got a late-night visit from another couple here. They were with Anna and Bryon Cooper at the beach and on their way back to the bed-and-breakfast when they discovered a little magic shop that's just down the alleyway."

"I'm aware of it."

"According to Burnell and Jay, the four of them went in and wandered around, but no one was there to help them purchase anything. Anna and Burnell went to the counter to call out and they heard talking in the back behind the curtain. It sounded to Burnell and Anna as if one of those speaking in the back said something about killing the maximum amount of people. He repeated that phrase to me."

The detective leaned in closer. "This was at the magic shop."

Malichai nodded. "Then earlier today, Amaryllis and I ran into a local surfer named Dozer. He was upset, which I understand is unusual for him."

"I'm acquainted with Dozer."

"He knows the owner of the magic shop and he saw she hadn't opened at her usual time and was concerned. A man answered her door and told him that Miss Crystal was vacationing with her son. Dozer pointed out she had no son and the man backtracked, saying she was vacationing with someone she regarded as a son. Then, when Dozer was surfing, a man in scuba gear tried to pull him off his surfboard before he caught a wave and, according to Dozer, tried to drown him. Dozer fought back. Now, he didn't put those two things together, but he'd threatened the man at the magic shop with calling law enforcement and asking for a well check on Miss Crystal."

"Maybe not so thin," Duncan said. "I need the name of the other couple you spoke with. They're staying here at Marie's?"

Malichai nodded. He continued to slide little caresses over the back of Amaryllis's hand. Something in the way Duncan said Marie's name caught his interest. "Do you know Marie Stubbins?" Marie hadn't indicated she knew him.

"I knew Carl, her husband. He was a good man. When they got married, I was already in the service, finishing up my time. I went

180

straight into the police academy, but I talked to Carl often and he talked about Marie. Hard times, that loss." He looked directly at Malichai. "I'll need those names now."

Malichai gave them to him, feeling a little guilty, but Burnell and Jay needed to stay safe. If Anna and Bryon had been killed because they overheard something they shouldn't have, then it was better that they told everything they knew to the police, so there would be no reason to kill them.

Marie and Brady came down the hall, Duncan and the officer joined them, and Marie showed the three policemen out. Malichai and Amaryllis waited for her to return. Marie wrapped her arms around Amaryllis and held her tight.

"I can't believe this happened to them. Poor Anna and Bryon. I know Bryon didn't kill her. I just wish I could have said the right thing to convince them that Bryon would never kill Anna."

Malichai hugged Marie to him, trying to comfort her. "I don't think either of the detectives believed he killed his wife and then himself. I don't think they believed it before they even came here. Maybe the crime scene appeared too staged. I don't know. Watching them closely, I could see that neither thought that Bryon killed Anna.

You just confirmed that belief."

"Thank heaven," Marie said. "Those poor people deserve better than having their families believe something that horrible. Can you imagine how Bryon's parents would feel, having their child accused of something like that? And Anna's parents believing it? No, the detectives need to figure this out fast."

"They will, Marie," Amaryllis said. "They seem very confident."

Malichai waited again while Amaryllis walked with Marie to her room, all the while murmuring reassurances. He needed a few reassurances himself, specifically that his woman wasn't going to take off on him. She was that little bit too nervous. He'd looked at her a few times and she'd refused to meet his eyes.

They needed to talk, and he needed to bring in a couple of his teammates in order to ensure he didn't lose his woman. She wasn't going to like it when he admitted who and what he was — or that he knew she was one of Whitney's orphans.

6

Amaryllis caught Marie in a hug before she closed her door, holding on to her tightly. She closed her eyes, inhaling her scent, wanting to imprint every detail of her onto her brain. She wished she dared go in to Jacy and do the same, but Marie would get suspicious. Tears burned behind her eyes, but she forced them away. Marie hugged her back, just as hard.

"I love you," Amaryllis whispered. It was the first time in her life she'd ever said the words, ever meant them. Marie was mother, sister and friend all rolled into one. Leaving her was the hardest thing she'd ever do in her life.

Marie had taught her about love. About life. About families. She'd taught her compassion and how to be a better person. She was the one who made her think about the girls she'd escaped with and whether or not they ever made it out — whether the soldiers had chased after them, giving Amaryllis time to get away. She'd lain in bed for months wondering if they'd been captured, wondering what kind of person she was that she hadn't gone back to check. All because of Marie. Now it was too late, they were long gone.

Only two of the girls had left with her in the end. The others had never realized just what Whitney was doing to them or what he intended. Amaryllis feared for them. Whitney admired and sought intelligence. Those remaining didn't think logically, nor did they realize the danger they were in. The two girls who escaped were more like Amaryllis. Silver and Coral were both quick on making decisions and had been trained as assassins, as she had been. They were loners as well but had formed some sort of loose friendship that had never included her. Part of that had been her fault. She'd preferred solitude. Peace. A good book.

"I love you too," Marie whispered, hugging her hard. "I don't know how I would have gotten through this last year without you."

That made Amaryllis feel guilty, not good. She had to leave. She'd never gotten her paperwork done. To get the necessary forgeries, she needed money, and instead of saving her paychecks, she'd turned the money back into the bed-and-breakfast, helping to redecorate and open each new room so they could take in more guests. They still had other rooms they could renovate. They just needed the money. Marie's money went to Jacy's medical care.

"You would have found a way," Amaryllis whispered. "You can move mountains, Marie. Without you, I would have drowned."

Marie pulled back, frowning, her eyes moving over Amaryllis's face. She clutched her arms even tighter. "You aren't planning . . ."

Amaryllis couldn't bear for her to say the words aloud. She hugged her again and then turned away, back toward the hall. To her consternation, Malichai was still there. He stood as still as a statue, blending into the shadows. He had a way of disappearing, making himself so still and quiet it was as if no one could see or hear him. His energy was so low she couldn't detect him.

She'd been taken from an orphanage as an infant by Dr. Peter Whitney, a genius billionaire. He had laboratories set up all over the United States and ultimately in other countries as well. She'd been raised from the time she could barely walk to fight. There were hundreds of visits to the hospital. Thousands of vials of blood taken. Her life had been one of strict discipline and learning. School and warfare. And then came the rumor of the breeding program. Amaryllis was *not* okay with that, especially once she caught Owen Starks's eye. He was the worst as far as she was concerned, and she decided to get out. Sometimes, she just knew — like now. No matter how much she wanted to stay, she had to get out of there before it was too late.

She did her best to pretend not to see Malichai as he stepped out of the shadows, but he cut her off and took her arm as she turned toward the room she claimed as her own.

"We need to talk."

The ominous words men never liked to hear and there he was, saying them to Amaryllis. She might have laughed if he didn't sound and look so serious. Her stomach plummeted. She blinked at him and then looked down at the fingers curling around her arm. "I really need to get some sleep, Malichai. We can talk in the morning."

"Who do you think you're kidding, baby?" he asked. "By morning you'll be gone. Let's talk before you do your disappearing act."

She closed her eyes and shook her head,

but she didn't lie to him. She couldn't do that to him. Her heart accelerated, worried now that she might not be able to leave so easily. He could change her mind. One look. One word. His touch. She was so susceptible to him. How could she explain to him what she was? A killing machine. A woman who had never even checked on the two others who had escaped with her, while he had gone back for complete strangers and gotten his body shot up. He would never look at her again.

And how did he know she had planned to leave? How could he know her so well after only a week? Had she given herself away in other ways as well? She'd grown complacent there in the bed-and-breakfast. She'd felt too safe for too long.

Amaryllis walked beside Malichai down the hall to his room. She stayed tucked into his side, right under his shoulder. She loved being there. It felt right. So right. She wrapped her arm around his waist, although it was an indulgence and she knew she shouldn't have. Her body brushed his with every step he took, and she wanted that for the rest of her life. A partner. Malichai. The thought came unbidden and out of nowhere, scaring her. Still, she stayed tight against him until she was in his room.

She took the armchair closest to the window and curled up in it, pulling her legs up and tucking them under her, making herself smaller. Malichai didn't bother with the lights. It didn't matter to her. She could easily see in the dark. He paced across the room and when he turned back toward her, she caught the predatory sheen in his eyes and a chill went down her spine.

"I'm a GhostWalker," he announced without preamble.

It was the last thing she expected him to say and it was akin to a physical blow. She hunched, better to absorb it. Slowly, she uncurled her legs, putting her feet to the floor, every bit the predator he was, ready to unleash her power when it was needed. Inside, she was crumbling. Falling apart. Shocked, dizzy with grief. Malichai. Her Malichai, the enemy.

"I'm not going to give you an explanation because I know you know what that is. You know because you're one of Whitney's orphans. I can only surmise you managed to escape on your own."

He fell silent, his hand going up as if that would stop her from launching herself at him. The only thing stopping her was her inability to breathe properly. But the moment she got that under control . . .

"If you're waiting for me to say something, it isn't going to happen." She went very still. There was none of the warmth that normally showed in her expression when she looked at him. She watched him, wholly focused on him, revealing the cat, letting him see she wasn't without her own physical aids.

Malichai went doggedly on. "I really am on vacation. It was entirely a coincidence for me to be here. At first, I worried that you were sent after me for some reason. I was weaker than normal and if Whitney was looking to get one of his soldiers back, it would be a perfect time."

He shrugged and began to pace across the floor, restless energy building in him until his energy felt as if he might explode. She actually felt the pounding ache in his leg, but there was nothing she could do about it, no matter how much she longed to, no matter how strong that pull was to help him.

"Amaryllis . . . I have to find the right words. Make you believe me, so you don't leave me, but I'm not that man. I'm not good with words." He sighed, pushed his hand through his hair and resumed his restless pacing. Now he was limping a little. "I'm required to take photographs of anyone I encounter, anyone that gets close to me.

189

My team watches over me, but I found myself protecting you even from them." He stole a glance at her, clearly trying to read her expression. "I wasn't positive about you then, but I still had to protect you."

There was sincerity in his voice. If he was lying to her, then he was the best actor in the world. He was just . . . too good. Too amazing. Too everything. She sat there, shaking her head. Not even realizing she was doing it. She bit down hard on her bottom lip, wishing she was good enough for this man.

She glanced down at the book he had lying in plain sight on his end table. *Toxic Game.* Her stomach did a slow flip. Her heart actually stuttered. She didn't believe for a minute that it was his favorite book or that he'd read the dog-eared copy before he'd teased her about it, but he'd sent away for it and read it because she liked it. What man did that?

"Malichai." She said his name softly, wanting to cry. There was no hope for them. None. She had to go. He had to get out of there. The cops would find out she didn't exist, and Whitney had ears and eyes everywhere. He wouldn't be safe. She hadn't thought about that — that Malichai wouldn't be safe. She had to persuade him to go. If she couldn't . . . she would have no choice but to stay and protect him. That leg was so messed up. How had everything gotten to this point so fast? That was Whitney. He could ruin lives so quickly, so easily, and never think anything of it.

"The more time we spent together the more I was certain you were one of Whitney's orphans, but you have a powerful shield. That's rare, you know. Only a very few GhostWalkers have that talent. And your healing ability . . . if Whitney found out about that one, he'd take you apart just to learn how it works. Is that why you ran? He found out you were a psychic healer?"

If she hadn't been falling for him before, she would be now. The compassion in his voice. The understanding on his face. In the year she had been at Marie's bed-and-breakfast, she had watched all kinds of men come through, and just as she'd studied the guards, she'd carefully observed the various men. None of them had appealed to her the way Malichai did. He was simply extraordinary.

She couldn't take her eyes off of him. He was so honest. She nodded slowly. "Yes. It was an accident. I never would have allowed him to see, especially once I knew about his idiot breeding program. A couple of the other girls were eager to show Whitney the things they could do, and I couldn't stop them. Nothing I said made them stop."

She dropped her head into her hands and rubbed her suddenly throbbing temples. Those girls. They just wouldn't hear that Whitney didn't love them and have their best interests at heart. They were so certain if they just did everything he wanted, he would give them the world someday. Amaryllis had no idea what he promised them, but they always sold the other girls out by telling Whitney everything they said or did.

"How did he find out about your healing gift? Was it the time you were fourteen?"

She shook her head. That voice of his. Who could possibly resist it? She sighed and forced herself to look at him. Just because those girls were ninnies didn't mean she should have left them there, although she still had no idea what else she could have done. What would Malichai have done? He was probably strong enough to carry them out on his shoulders.

"One of the girls cut herself with a knife. It was really deep, and she was bleeding too much, too fast. I didn't think, I just . . . stopped it. She told him. She told him everything. I knew immediately I was going to have to escape the minute I saw the way he was looking at me. He hadn't even called me in to ask me a single question yet. It was just that look on his face." She pressed her hand to her stomach, remembering. "The moment he knew I could heal, everything changed. He wanted my babies — that became the most important thing in the world to him. And there was a soldier who just wouldn't leave me alone. The moment he found out I was being put into that program, he asked Whitney to pair me with him."

Her eyes met Malichai's there in the dark and a chill went down her spine. Her sweet Malichai had a dark side to him. A very lethal side. There was no getting around it. He didn't like the idea of another man insisting Whitney give her to him. He didn't move at all. He was so still he seemed part of the shadows, but his eyes were as cold as ice yet alive with ice-cold flames. She'd never seen anything so frightening or so charismatic in her life.

"That wasn't going to happen. I asked if the girls wanted out, but I waited until the last possible moment because I knew there were two girls always fawning on Whitney, currying his favor by ratting on us. Two went with me. We went over the fence and split up. I have no idea if they got away clean. I didn't have time to create an identity. The cops will realize I don't exist, and once I'm put in their system, Whitney will know where I am."

"You should have told me. You know about me. You had to have suspected all along what I was." He began pacing again, as if he couldn't keep all of his restless energy cooped up one minute longer, or he wanted to shake her — she couldn't decide which.

She shrugged. "I liked you. I liked spending time with you. I hoped you didn't guess I was one as well so I could stay here. It's the first real home I've had. Marie and Jacy feel like family to me, but I can't stay, not when the cops will be all over the fact that Amaryllis Johnson doesn't exist." She took a deep breath. "And, Malichai, sit down. Every step you take is hurting that leg worse. Your bone is going to disintegrate if you keep it up. I think the pressure you're putting on it is causing more of those tiny fractures. Like stress fractures people can get when they run on concrete."

He turned his head and looked straight at her. Right into her eyes. Those cat eyes staring at her in the dark. "I'm in love with you, Amaryllis, and I don't want to lose you. If you give me permission, I can have my team get your identity fixed and in place so that the first time the police search for you and can't find you will appear to be an error in their system."

Her heart nearly stopped and then began beating overtime. There was a strange roaring in her ears. She almost didn't hear anything after he declared he loved her. No one had ever said those words to her. Not one single person. She almost couldn't breathe. She even felt a little dizzy. Malichai had actually said he loved her. Her. The woman who had escaped Whitney and left behind two other girls. She didn't know where the other three were.

She burst into tears. She wasn't a crier. You couldn't cry if you were one of Whitney's orphans; that earned you all kinds of really bad punishments. She couldn't stop though. She found herself with her hands over her face, sobbing. All because he loved her. He couldn't love her. He just couldn't.

"Baby, stop."

Malichai's voice, as always, was so gentle when he spoke to her. That brush of velvet over her skin, in her mind. Now she recognized it as something else — emotion. Love. She hadn't known what it was. What it felt like. He had given her that as well, and she couldn't accept it.

"I can't. You can't love me. You just can't, Malichai. You're so good and I'm . . . *not*. I'm just not."

"Amaryllis."

He said her name and there was a hint of laughter in his voice. Male amusement, although she knew he was trying to hide it. She glared up at him through her tears. She was spilling her guts, telling him the very worst of her, and he found that funny?

"Babe, there is nothing in your life you could possibly have done that is worse than anything I've ever done. I'm a fucking soldier. I'm a GhostWalker. What the hell do you think that means I do?"

"I left those girls. I *left* them. You would never have left them. You know you wouldn't have. You're all about loyalty. I'm not. I'm only loyal to a few people. The rest, I don't think about. I don't worry about. It's just my little circle. I have jackal in me. *Jackal.* Do you know what that means?" She nearly spat it at him, wanting him to see that those hideous traits in her were never going to go away. They were in her DNA. Deep. And she'd pass them on to her children. She had even worse than that, but she wasn't even going there.

"Why do you think that's a bad thing? Jackals mate for life. The young return as adults and help raise the juveniles year after year, forming a tight group. They defend their territory and each other. GhostWalkers do that same thing, Amaryllis. There's nothing wrong with that. They run like the wind. We're all made up of many things. Whitney fed you a line of crap to make you think less of yourself because he controlled all of you that way. He couldn't let any of you think you were extraordinary. God help him if the women rose up knowing they were strong and smart and beautiful inside and out. Fuck him and whatever he told you. There's not a damn thing wrong with you."

He bent down and brushed at her tears with his lips, and then tipped her face up to his. Her heart wouldn't stop pounding. She looked up at his face. She loved his face. Loved his eyes, even though at that moment he looked a little watery. He brushed more kisses over her cheeks, eyes and lips.

"Stop crying, baby, and let's talk about this. I love you exactly the way you are. Those women made their choice when they listened to Whitney and went running to him for every little thing. I'm in love with you and I want you to come with me when I leave here. My people can fix your identity, but they'll know about you, Amaryllis, and they have to eventually anyway."

She pushed her forehead into the heel of her hand. "How do you know no one will betray you, Malichai? The more people who know, the more likely that is."

Malichai moved away from her, pacing again, taking most of the warmth of the room with him. "My entire team is enhanced. We've banded together because we have enemies on every side of us. We know that and we prepare always for a fight. Wyatt's little girls were scheduled to be terminated, designated failures. We took them and we protect them. His wife escaped that same lab. Trap's wife was also scheduled for termination. She's with us now. My brother's wife was sent out with a virus that would kill her if she didn't get the antidote. I could go on and on. Whitney uses us and sends his supersoldiers against us every now and then to test us, or them, who knows what's in his head, but he fights against the faction in the White House that wants all of us terminated. And then, there's the enemies we've made by the missions we've taken on."

"You paint such an enticing picture, Malichai." There was humor in her voice.

He turned back to her, those eyes of his once again gleaming in the darkness. "I want you to know up front, what I'm offering you isn't rosy. I'm not going to lie about what you're getting into. Some days it feels like we have to fight every minute for a decent chance with our families. Other times we have months of peace, and we all know it's a luxury. There's my leg. Realistically, I could lose it. I'm worth too much money to sideline me, so they'll fix me up with some kind of fancy bionic one, but I know some people have an aversion to body parts that aren't natural."

She pointed to the chair opposite hers. "Sit down, Malichai. I mean it. And don't insult me. I am not one of those people, and you're not going to lose your leg." He was exasperating. He just kept up that pacing as if he couldn't make himself stop. She wanted to yank him into the chair herself.

"If you don't stick around and save it, I might," he pointed out.

She clenched her teeth. "You are an exasperating man. You could tell your brother and he'd have a team of doctors here tomorrow."

He stopped moving then and when he did, her heart stopped with his movement. He turned his head slowly to look at her and the bottom dropped out of her stomach. Her heart began to pound. He knew. He'd known all along. She wasn't certain. She had a gift but she had no idea how to use it. It was undeveloped.

"What good will a team of doctors do, Amaryllis? You know they can't save that bone. If I know it, you know it."

She hadn't known it, not really. She had instincts. She could have called up energy and power to heal but she didn't really know what she was doing. She wanted to stay with him more than she wanted to run and hide from Whitney, but now this . . . What if she failed him on top of everything else? She would be responsible for him losing his leg. She didn't know anything about healing. Nothing at all. She really didn't. He didn't understand that.

She sighed and looked down at her hands. "It's such a risk, and I just can't ever go back there. I'll never have a child with that disgusting soldier Whitney wants to pair me with. And Whitney will never get his hands on any child I have."

"Have your children with me, Amaryllis. I can keep you safe. I can keep our children safe. My team is building a stronghold in the middle of the swamp. It's unbelievable. We can visit Marie and Jacy and have them out to visit us. I've already talked to Lily and asked her to look into getting Jacy any surgeries she needs for free. Also, to pay off Marie's hospital bills. It didn't sit well with me that she had those bills at all. I had some money in the bank just sitting there. Marie and Jacy need it far more than I do."

Amaryllis looked up at him, her breath catching in her throat. She knew that feeling welling up inside of her was love. It was soft and tender. It was alien to her. Completely foreign. She'd felt something close to it for Jacy and Marie, but not this overwhelming emotion that threatened to choke her. He was making it impossible for her to leave him. Impossible for her to stay. No one could measure up to him. No one could ever be worthy of him.

"You're so compassionate. That's a wonderful, generous thing to do."

"Stay with me, Amaryllis. I know it will be scary, but I swear to you, I won't let Whitney, or anyone else, take you from me."

She studied his face. "You're asking for a very huge leap of faith. Whitney is a very vindictive man. I already had an escape plan and the moment I needed to put it into use, I didn't hesitate. He didn't have a chance to know I was even planning it. If he got his hands on me a second time, he would never give me another opportunity."

"You have one ready for here as well."

"Of course. And, Malichai, I am perfectly capable of defending myself." She needed him to know that. And that she would. She wouldn't hesitate. She had more than one animal in her DNA. She had been trained to fight since she was a toddler. Whitney may have recently decided to put her in his breeding program, but prior to that, she'd been a soldier, just like Malichai, maybe a lone one, an assassin, but she'd gone out on missions and used deadly force to defend herself.

There was warning in her voice as well as a need for him to know there was more to her than the side she'd shown to him. She was afraid he might not like that side of her. He might prefer that she not be a woman who would fight with any kind of weapon to defend her family and herself from any kind of attack.

"Baby, do you think I don't want you capable of defending yourself, our children, or even our home? The woman I admire most in the world is Nonny, Wyatt's grand-mother. She raised her children and then her grandsons in that swamp. Mostly alone. When you go into her house, the first thing that hits you is the feeling of home. Even if you've never felt it before, you know it when you're in her home. She's a beautiful person, kind and compassionate. Intelligent and filled with wisdom. Her shotgun is inches from her hand most of the time. I admire that trait in her. She doesn't look to others to get her out of trouble."

"You're a very protective man." He was. Everything about him screamed it. Proclaimed it. No one could look at him without seeing it.

Malichai nodded and sank down into the chair. She could see pain etched into the lines of his face. That leg was on fire and was about to give out on him, but he didn't want to let on.

"Yes, there's no question about it. And I gave my married friends a bad time and said my woman was going to be in the kitchen and bedroom, nowhere else. But I knew all along that my woman was going to have Nonny's traits. You have them in abundance, Amaryllis, everything I admire most."

Amaryllis stood up and went to him. She had feline traits, allowing her muscles to move beneath her skin, causing her to be graceful, fluid and silent in the dark, and she padded across the room to him. Tiny beads of sweat trickled down his face and he wiped them away. He looked a little shocked to find them there. It wasn't that hot in the room.

He looked up at her. "Can you get the window, babe?"

Instead of going to the window, she laid her palm on his forehead, frowning. "Malichai, you're burning up."

Amaryllis crouched down to push up the denim material on his leg. She surrounded his calf with both hands. "Your leg is hot to the touch. You have an infection. Most likely it's a bone infection. Can you make it to the bed?"

She couldn't keep the anxiety from her voice. Without waiting for an answer, she wrapped her arm around him and almost heaved him out of the chair. She was much stronger than she looked, enhanced, like he was, with her GhostWalker DNA.

"It's probably not a good thing if that soldier comes looking for you, Amaryllis. If I didn't kill him, you'd do it."

Malichai was stalling. She knew it but she didn't call him on it. Sweat beaded on his body and she was furious with herself for being focused on their conversation. On the fact that he'd said he loved her. On her need to run. On his leg. On everything but that he was in severe trouble. He swayed for a moment, the foot in the air, his arm around her waist, his weight slightly on her, but none on that hurt leg.

"He's tough, Malichai. I honestly don't know if I could kill him. I think Whitney did something to make it impossible for me to use all my weapons against him. I've tried before and failed, but I'd do my best. One of us would die." She stated the truth.

Malichai put his foot on the floor and shifted his weight onto it. His entire body shuddered with pain. He didn't make a sound but took his weight off it immediately.

"Shit, baby, I'm sorry, that's not going to work."

"It's all right. I'm strong. We can get to the bed. Seriously, honey. I was worried something was wrong this morning when I examined you. I wish I knew more about healing," she admitted to him. She wanted him to know she wasn't qualified to help him. "I've never been trained as a psychic healer, but I do know GhostWalkers heal so much faster than anyone else and your leg should have been so much better than it was."

With her support, Malichai managed to hop across the room to the bed and nearly fell onto the mattress. She could see it was a relief for him to lie down. She wondered if all the pacing he'd done was because he'd been in such pain. She hurried to get a cool cloth for his face.

"Here, honey, let me cool you down with this. Drink some water, you don't want to get dehydrated on top of everything else." He was burning up. When had the fever started? Why hadn't she noticed?

"I'm trying to impress you, Amaryllis, convince you I can be this badass husband that can keep you safe, and I'm literally falling down on the job."

She forced herself to smile at his attempt at humor in a situation that had her heart pounding in terror. She would have rather faced Whitney's supersoldiers trying to recapture her than this situation. If she called the regular doctors, they wouldn't be able to do anything. She wasn't certain what to do.

She sent him a brief, tight smile. "Where's your phone?"

"Why? You're not calling my brother."

Amaryllis looked down at his face. He looked petulant, an expression she never thought she'd see on his face. He wasn't making any sense. He was going to lose his leg from an infection and wasn't going to call his brother and a team with some of the best doctors in the world to come and save his leg as well as life? That defied all sanity. They had a psychic healer as well.

She brushed back his damp hair gently

and looked at his eyes again. They were glazed with fever. He wasn't making any sense because he wasn't really aware of what he was saying or doing. She had to take control of the situation.

"I want to talk to him, honey. Just let me have your phone. I want his advice."

Malichai crossed his arms and shook his head. "I don't. You call him, Amaryllis, and he'll have a platoon here along with every GhostWalker unit we have. He's a master of overkill when it comes to his brothers and their safety. I'm trying to get you to stay with me. He'll ask you questions and then he'll scare you off."

"I don't scare so easily."

"You were going to leave me."

Her hands dropped to his belt buckle and his hands immediately covered hers.

"What the hell are you doing?"

"Not what you're hoping for, but we need these off. Where is your phone, Malichai, and quit stalling." She poured firmness into her voice, using the tone Marie used on Jacy when she meant business.

Malichai hesitated only for a moment but then complied. "My phone's in the back pocket of my jeans."

He was lying on the thing and didn't want to move. Amaryllis felt bad moving him, but it didn't matter, she had no choice, she shifted his body, pulling his jeans from him and sliding them over his hips and down his leg. She settled him carefully back onto the mattress and just pulled up the sheet as he was still so hot. He lay back against the pillows and closed his eyes.

She retrieved the phone and looked at him with one eyebrow raised. "Honey, I need your passcode. I know this is hard for you, but you need to concentrate for me."

He opened his eyes briefly and looked at her and then at his phone. He gave her the code and then closed his eyes again, frowning, clearly not fully comprehending what was going on around him.

Amaryllis immediately punched in the code, and then found his brother's number and hit that as well. She knew it was late, but he had to answer, and he did, very abruptly.

"It's late. What's wrong?"

She put her hand on Malichai's chest, more for her own reassurance than for Malichai's. He seemed to be drifting in and out.

She wasn't certain where to start. What to say. What Ezekiel would believe. She was feeling desperate. They needed help and they needed it immediately. "My name is Amaryllis. I'm here with Malichai. I need your help. That bone in his leg has been deteriorating at a rapid rate. There are little fragments spreading everywhere like a spiderweb. I examined it this morning and could see the bone was going to begin to fail completely. I'm not an experienced healer, but I do have the gift. If you know someone else, another healer like me that could talk me through it, I might be able to save the bone, but it has to be fast. He's developed an infection. His temperature is spiking, and he can't put weight on the leg at all. He's kind of drifting in and out so sometimes is responsive and other times not so much."

She took a breath. "I have absolutely no experience. None. Zero. I don't know what I'm doing. I'm willing to take him to the naval hospital, but he doesn't want to go. I don't think the bone has much time, by the look of it." Now she was just chattering like some ninny because she was so afraid of whatever this man might ask her to do. He was so far away. "He really needs help. He does and I don't know what I'm doing." That last was a plea.

There was a long silence. She knew what that meant. Ezekiel was looking for something from Malichai that would tell him the call was real and that his brother wasn't a prisoner or being used to set the team up in some way. There had to be a code they used between them.

She tried again. "He told me about all of you, including Nonny and Pepper and the three little ones. He's not unconscious but he's not very alert either. I don't know how much he's taking in. I don't know what you're looking for, but . . . *please* believe me when I tell you I need help."

"Is he with you now?"

"Yes."

"You say he's not unconscious. I need to hear his voice."

She wasn't certain how she could get Malichai to talk. She put the phone on speakerphone and put it close to Malichai's mouth. "Honey, can you hear me? Your brother is on the phone. He wants to hear your voice. Can you please say something to him? For me? Will you do that?"

She thought she might weep a million tears. She'd learned not to cry, but maybe she'd just stored up all those tears for just the right situation because she wanted to put her arms around Malichai and just give in to that need to weep. She felt helpless and she had never wanted to be that woman again.

Malichai seemed to rally when he heard

the tears in her voice. "I'm all right, baby," he whispered. His hand came up to stroke her hair. "Zeke, you there?"

"I'm here, bro."

"Amaryllis is my Bellisia. I need you to get her a clean ID. Amaryllis Johnson."

"Honey, we need to talk to your brother about your leg, not my identification," Amaryllis interrupted. It was so like him.

Malichai ignored her, his eyes closed, his fingers threading her hair, bunching it, holding it to his face. "If anything happens to me, you get her out of this mess. Cops will be looking into her, so get that ID fast."

Amaryllis took the cell off speakerphone. "Listen to me. He doesn't even know what he's saying. He's running a high fever. Don't worry about the identity thing. This is more important. Find me a healer. You don't have to give names, just have him talk me through this. I know that's the big worry. Whitney and everyone else in the world want the psychic healers, so no one can know who they are. I don't care who they are. I just want him better."

"I'll call back in a few minutes. I've got your photograph. You go by Amaryllis. What's the surname you gave to the cops?"

"Amaryllis Johnson. Please get a healer to call me."

"About that. Do you think a trained healer could actually heal that bone? Or would it take one even above you? A psychic surgeon?"

She was stunned. She wasn't certain there was really such a thing. She had heard a whisper of it but only when Whitney had speculated that it was possible, and he was always looking for such a talent.

"If there is such a person, I would get them here as fast as possible. A psychic surgeon might be the only one who can save Malichai's leg. I'm not certain how long they have, but the infection came on so fast it terrifies me. In the meantime, have a psychic healer talk me through getting him stable enough for a surgeon, psychic or otherwise to save his leg. I'm telling you, at this point, I think it isn't only his leg at risk. Right now, the possibility is there that his life is as well."

"A healer can turn that around in a matter of hours."

She was aware of that, but she also had never dealt with anything this enormous before. "It's Malichai," she whispered.

There was another silence. "He's my brother," Ezekiel said back.

For that one small moment of silence between them, she felt they touched each other across the distance. They connected. They understood what it was to love Malichai Fortunes.

"I'll call back very quickly. And we'll have a plane in the air immediately."

The relief was so tremendous, again the ridiculous, useless tears threatened. They didn't fall because she was trained not to let them, but she felt them burning behind her eyes.

"Thank you," she whispered, but he was already gone.

She put the phone down beside Malichai and then put her head on his chest just for a moment because she needed to take a breath. To think. To try to stop the fear pounding through her brain.

"I didn't tell you how I feel about you, Malichai. You're always so wonderfully direct. You had the courage to tell me you were a GhostWalker and that you knew I was one of Whitney's orphans . . ."

"GhostWalker," he murmured without opening his eyes. His hand landed on the back of her head, his fingers tangling in her hair again. "You're a GhostWalker."

The words weren't entirely distinct, but he said them like he meant them. A declaration he wanted her to understand. To him it made a difference and it did to her as well.

She wasn't just a frightened little girl no one wanted. She was a GhostWalker. They might have flaws, but they had unbelievable enhancements and they had formed family units and were fiercely loyal to one another.

"Yes, honey, that I was a GhostWalker like you. You had the courage to tell me you loved me . . ."

"I do love you. So much, baby. Can't think of a life without you."

Her heart beat so hard at what she was going to say. At what she was going to do. That leap of faith she'd never taken in her life. She closed her eyes tight, squeezing them shut like a little child, inside, holding herself still, while her blood pounded wildly through her veins.

"I love you when I've never loved anyone else like this. With everything in me, so much it truly terrifies me." She lifted her head inches off his chest and found herself looking into his glittering golden eyes.

7

Those eyes of his. Malichai Fortunes had the most unusual, beautiful golden eyes. They could be amber, or whiskey colored, or like now, a glittering gold that shone through the dark like a cat's predatory eyes. They focused wholly on her. Instead of feeling frightened by his nonblinking stare, she returned it steadily.

"You don't have to say that to me, Amaryllis."

His voice was low, burning with passion or fever, she couldn't decide which. Only that he was so ill and yet all he thought of was her. Never himself. Malichai was the most unselfish person in the world. She wanted to be like him. She wanted to be a woman who deserved to be his partner.

"I know I don't, Malichai." She lifted her chin and looked him straight in the eye, gathering her courage. He was courageous in everything he did. Everything he said. "I told you I loved you because I do. Absolutely I do. Every minute I spend in your company, I find I love you more."

A slow smile curved his mouth and he lay back against the pillows. "I knew you'd fall for me, woman. It's the way I wash dishes, isn't it?"

"Yes, I can't lie about that." His eyes were already closing, scaring her. She wanted him talking to her, staying alert.

The phone rang again. She snatched it up the moment she saw it was from Ezekiel. He didn't bother with a greeting. "Can you map out the cracks? That will help. You look at them now and draw them out? That will help show him what you're seeing. He's getting there as fast as possible. We'll be on a plane in about fifteen minutes and I'll be bringing a psychic surgeon with us."

Relief swept through her so that her legs shook so much she had to sink completely down onto the bed beside Malichai. "Yes, I can do that." She had no idea if she could, but she'd try. She was fairly good at drawing.

Ezekiel ended the call just as abruptly as he'd started it. She was beginning to see a pattern and was glad she wasn't a woman who took offense easily. Amaryllis sat on the bed, pushed the sheet from Malichai's leg and wrapped both hands around his calf. It was very hot to the touch. She could feel his muscles so defined and developed beneath the skin, but that didn't stop the deterioration of the bone beneath.

When she looked up, his gaze was fixed on her face. Watching her. Looking for her to give him a sign everything was okay. Everything was not okay. Her world had crumpled around her. Her sweet Malichai. He'd turned her inside out with his frank confession. He moved her with everything he said or did. Everything he was. He had to live. He had to be saved.

She was terrified for him. Absolutely terrified. She had no idea what to do, how to wield all that power that was inside of her. She felt the power rising the moment she touched his damaged leg, the way it did when she was around anyone hurt. There was only Amaryllis Johnson, who didn't know anything about healing to do it, and she needed to quit stalling and get on with it.

She focused her sight on his calf and allowed her vision to expand out of the narrow confines of what her mind told her she could see. At once, her hands, now hovering around Malichai's leg, grew warm. Then hot. She could see the glow coming from her palms, a reddish orange light that caused her eyes to swim with tears. She had excellent night vision, thanks to the large cat DNA. She also had the DNA of birds of prey, which further enhanced her sight. She had to get past that and tap into sight beyond even that.

There was fear in her mind. Chaos even. Malichai meant too much to her and she was very afraid for him — very afraid of hurting him — of damaging his leg even further. She needed to quiet her mind and let all fear drop away, a difficult feat when terror for him was nearly paralyzing.

Amaryllis found she was hyperventilating. She wasn't actually even healing him and yet she was already screwing up.

"Baby, breathe, you got this," Malichai said gently. "You were born to do this."

She knew she was. She knew it absolutely. She felt the heat. The power, the rising need to heal, but this was Malichai, the most important person in the world to her and she didn't have a clue what she was doing. She gave a little shake of her head.

"Look at me, Amaryllis," Malichai insisted.

She raised her gaze to his. His gold eyes captivated her. She felt as if she just fell into that deep, mysterious well and would drown in all that gold.

"Breathe with me. In and out. Feel your breath moving through your lungs. Concentrate on that. Don't think about anything else until your mind is calm."

Of course she knew how to center herself. It was one of the most basic things taught to them when they were children. Still, it felt different, like caring, when she followed Malichai's lead. It didn't matter to him that he was feverish, that he could barely understand what was happening to him or what was going on around him, she'd needed him and he'd found a way to come through for her. She *had* to come through for him — and she would.

She immediately focused on the air moving in and out of his lungs. He breathed slowly and evenly, but deeply, filling his lungs and letting it out slowly. Once she was breathing with him and concentrating on that, the chaos in her mind quieted.

With new determination, she looked at his leg, her palms once again hovering a scant quarter of an inch above it. She was able to let go of fear for him and just become a healing light. Immediately she focused on that. The lantern. What it looked like, what it felt like, how the light slowly turned away from her and into him.

Her vision changed subtly, became almost opaque, as if she were seeing through a dense, cloudy veil. Behind the veil was a map in the form of pure heat. Lines were bright red, so many of them, cracks in the bone running in every direction, with tiny bubbles of liquid boiling up through those cracks. It looked like she'd stumbled onto a volcano, with the magma spreading out under the ground in all directions, looking for veins to the surface.

She mapped out every single spiderweb crack she could see and then blinked rapidly to clear her vision. Sinking back onto her heels, she looked around his room. "I need something to draw on."

She should have found that first, but she'd been so worried that she couldn't do it. "Malichai, honey, I need paper and a pen."

She was already at the small desk under the window, looking back at him for confirmation. She detested going through his things without his permission, but she really didn't know how much he was comprehending.

He didn't respond and she found what she was looking for in one of the drawers, snapped on the light over the desk and drew a map of his bone, numbering every crack. She wanted the healer to see what they would be working with. She was as careful and as accurate as possible. Using Malichai's phone, she snapped a picture of it and then sent it to Ezekiel with the text stating it was of his bone, a three-dimensional drawing numbering every crack and the infection seeping out of it. It was the best she could do. Now it was a matter of waiting.

She went back to the bed and once more used a cool, wet cloth to try to get Malichai's temperature to come down. He didn't open his eyes, but she knew he was aware of her presence because he kept reaching for her. She put lip balm on his dry lips and tried to shush him when he so obviously wanted to talk to her.

"Honey, just conserve your strength. I think your brother is taking care of things very fast for us. It won't be long, and I'll work on your leg and then they'll be here to really help you. Just try to ride it out until then."

"I have things that have to be said."

Her heart clenched hard in her chest. Did he think he was going to die? She didn't want to hear the things he thought necessary if that was the case. "You can say them after I work on you. Right now, it's imperative you stay as strong as possible."

"If something happens to me, Amaryllis, you promise me you'll go back with Zeke and the others to Nonny. You'll be safe there."

Why would she want to go there without him to be reminded every single day she'd lost him? There was no way she was going to promise him something like that. No way.

He waited for her answer and when none came, when there was only silence and the cold cloth moving over his forehead, he caught her wrist. "Baby, this is serious. Sooner or later, Whitney is bound to find you. Even after Zeke gets you the perfect ID, something could trip you up. A random photo of you taken by some tourist at the wrong time."

His voice was so low, barely a thread of sound, but each note thrummed through her body, touching her soul. Mattering to her because she mattered so much to him.

"Nothing is going to happen to you, Malichai. I'm going to heal your leg and then by tomorrow your brother will be here with some big shot healer that really knows what he's doing and he's going to save the day."

Malichai still didn't open his eyes, but his hand unerringly found hers and he wrapped his fingers around it, pulling it from his forehead to bring it to his mouth. "You're going to save the day. You always do." He kissed her fingers.

His lips felt hot and dry. His breath hot. But the gesture was so sweet her stomach did that slow roll that sent butterflies winging their way through her entire body.

She was desperate to change the subject. If he insisted on talking, she didn't want to talk about him dying, or her leaving. "Do you really think Anna and Burnell overheard those people in the magic shop talking about killing the maximum amount of people?"

He was silent for a moment. She listened to his breathing. It was a little scary when it was so shallow. She wanted to snatch up the phone and tell Ezekiel to get a move on. To *hurry.*

"I think any time you think something like that is said, it warrants investigation. Now that someone has murdered Anna and Bryon, I would say chances are very good that something isn't right in that magic shop."

"That really makes me worry for Miss Crystal."

His lashes fluttered. "Stay away from there, Amaryllis."

"You were going to set yourself up as bait. I could do it. I'm very fast in the water and

I've had comparable training in hand-to-hand combat if someone comes at me underwater."

He did open his eyes then. All that gold glittered and gleamed dangerously now behind a haze of fever. "Don't you dare."

She wanted to smile at the absolute dictate. Her sweet Malichai thought that would stop her. Nothing stopped her when she thought something was right. In this case, she wasn't certain.

The phone buzzed and she snatched it up to look at the message splashed across the screen.

Plane in air headed your way. Mordichai, Rubin and I are on board. Joe, our team leader and healer, is looking over your drawing now and will be contacting you under ten. Malichai needs liquids. Hydration. Do you have IV set up?

No on IV, no access. Yes on liquids. Will wait for call.

It was amazing the relief she felt knowing they were on the way when just a couple of hours earlier that would have panicked her. She got an arm behind his back and helped him half sit so she could hold a water bottle to his mouth.

"Drink, honey. Zeke's on the way with Mordichai, who I presume is your brother, and Rubin, who you told me was with you when you saved those men on that mission. They'll be here soon. Someone named Joe is going to call me and guide me through helping you."

He drank some of the water, but most ran down to his chest. He lay back without commenting. She closed her eyes and pressed the cold bottle of water to her forehead. Every minute that ticked by seemed like an hour.

The phone rang in some program she wasn't familiar with, but she answered it and immediately realized it was one much like FaceTime, but probably a secure one. Even though she wanted this more than anything, she felt all the color draining from her face. Her hand trembled as she answered.

On his side, the picture was shadowy, but she could make him out, just not his facial features that clearly. Just as she didn't want Whitney to know about her, neither did the man who at the moment was her lifeline. She was just grateful that he was willing to do this for her.

"Amaryllis here." Her heart pounded. She

had zero confidence in herself when it came to using this particular gift. One had to learn. To practice. Especially before attempting on a human being.

"Your diagram was particularly helpful. Are you ready? Ezekiel and the others have been conferenced in, but they will stay absolutely silent."

"They told you I have never done this, right?" She wanted him to know.

"Yes, but you can follow my instructions. I'll be with you every step of the way." Joe's voice was calm and steady, but more than anything filled with confidence. "Your instincts will kick in."

She started to protest but Malichai unexpectedly reached out and enveloped her hand with his. Just his touch gave her a level of composure she hadn't had before. Deliberately she looked at him, let her gaze drift over his face, taking in his tough features. She leaned into him and brushed his lips with hers. Her stomach did a slow somersault.

"I'm counting on you talking me through this," she said aloud to the healer. She forced a smile at Malichai and whispered to him, "We've got this, don't worry."

"I know you do, baby," he murmured.

She hoped so for his sake. She could live

with him having one leg, but she knew he would still continue to be sent on missions whether he had one leg or two — and he'd go. She brushed one more kiss on his lips and then she moved down to his calf once more.

She laid her hands right over his skin, not quite touching, but she could feel the hairs there rising up to meet the energy emanating from her palms. Once again, she expanded her vision outside normal human sight. It was easier now, she was familiar with the way it felt, and she didn't fight it. Her eyes went opaque again, that dense cloudiness, a foggy barrier between her and the outside world.

Her stomach lurched as her vision moved through his skin and muscle until she could see the bone. It was much clearer to her this time. The entire bone, from thigh to calf, was riddled with tiny spiderwebbing cracks. At first the cracks appeared a dull pink behind a gray veil, but then they became clearer and clearer, turning into a deep crimson. She took her time, breathing in and out, making herself conscious of doing so. With each breath, she focused on the scorching heat rising in her, seeking an outlet, seeking the stench of illness.

Immediately, her body tuned itself to his.

She felt that too, the way every cell in her body reached for the cells in his. Merged with them. Those tiny spidery lines dissecting his bone, weakening it, glittered and danced like tiny flames, ran through the crevasses. She saw the droplets of infection seeping out, looking like veins of yellow.

Her heat rushed over those small streams. Steam rose, obscuring her vision. She nearly jerked away.

"No, no, you're perfect right where you are. Don't be afraid. You're doing everything correctly. Let your body heal his."

The voice steadied her. It was soft, gentle even. Encouraging. Even admiring. So calm. She didn't understand how the other healer could be so calm in the face of such a huge disaster. She wanted him there. To do this himself. He was experienced. She was . . .

"The power you have is enormous," the voice continued, as if she weren't crumbling in the way Malichai's bone was.

That steadied her even more. Even she could feel her power. It was impossible not to. She told herself she was born for this. She'd been born with that gift. She was supposed to use it for good. Malichai was not only good — he was the best. The best part of her. She kept her hands moving very slowly up his leg, watching the steam rise as the scorching heat boiled away those long yellow tracks, all that infection seeping out of the spiderwebbing.

It was exhilarating, terrifying and exhausting. Her body seemed to be burning out the infection, cauterizing the tracks, so the infection couldn't return and then processing it through her own cells. She felt ill. Dizzy. She wanted to vomit. Fever made her grow hot and turned her hair damp, matting it to her head. She felt very weak, her body swaying and her legs threatening to give out on her.

"You have to fight it, Amaryllis," the healer said. "You have more work to do. Your assessment of the bone was correct. If you don't fix it, it will continue to deteriorate. I don't believe a surgeon would be able to stop the bone from continuing on its downward spiral."

She didn't believe, even with her working on the infection, that even a surgeon could save his leg. Alarm spread through her. "His brother said a psychic surgeon was coming."

"He's on the way. You get rid of the infection and as soon as he gets there, he'll do the rest, but that infection has to be taken out now. Concentrate. You're going to have to fix that bone now, or he's going to lose it."

"Don't tell her that," Malichai snapped, shocking her. He sounded unexpectedly strong. His voice almost growled. There was menace in it, as if he would leap off the bed and attack the unseen man on the phone.

Amaryllis put her hand on his chest to ensure he didn't try to sit up or move. "Honey," she cautioned, not knowing how to calm him. He was clearly very agitated.

His hands surrounded hers. His eyes were glazed with fever, but they looked directly into hers. "Amaryllis, this isn't on you. If it doesn't work, or you're too tired, it is what it is. This isn't on you."

"He's right," the healer said immediately. "I misspoke, Amaryllis. I didn't mean to imply you were in any way responsible. Sometimes when I work on something, I can get it, other times not. I know that. We all do. I've never actually talked someone else through the process."

"It's all right," Amaryllis said. Just that brief respite from concentrating, from using vision that turned inward rather than outward, gave her renewed energy. She leaned down and brushed her lips across Malichai's. "I got a little scared, honey. It's bound to happen, but I'm doing this and it's making me feel as if I'm doing something valuable. He's really helping me, and I appreciate it so much."

Malichai didn't let go of her hand for a moment, staring into her eyes, searching. "You good, Amaryllis? Really?"

"I am." She poured confidence into her voice.

He slowly, almost reluctantly, released her hand and she moved back down to position herself once more by his leg. Taking a deep breath, she glanced at the man on the screen.

"I'm ready. Tell me what to do."

He sighed. "I'm not there. I can't feel my way. That's what you have to do. Judging by the energy coming out from under your palms, you're extremely powerful. Start with your palms hovering about an inch from his skin. If the cracks don't come wholly into focus for you, drop your hands lower until you can see those lines perfectly clear. Those are breaks. Start from the bottom of the bone and work your way up. Don't let your palms touch his skin or you'll burn him. It will be very uncomfortable for you, Amaryllis. I can't stress that enough. Once you start up a break, you have to keep going no matter how difficult it is. When you reach the top, that's when you can take a breath and let yourself relax for a moment."

Once more, before Amaryllis could do anything, Malichai caught her arm. He was very strong. Extremely so, and he pulled her away from his leg and back up closer to his head. Once he had her there, he wrapped his arm around her waist, locking her to the side of the bed.

"What do you mean, it's uncomfortable for her? Why?" Malichai asked.

"Honey," Amaryllis said, trying to extricate herself without actually fighting him. He was stronger because she had pushed the infection from his body. He was no longer feeling those effects. She was tired from using her gift when she wasn't used to it. Her body felt as if she'd run a marathon. She wanted to lie down and rest. "It doesn't really matter why it would be uncomfortable, I'm doing it because it has to be done. You have to let go of me."

"Stop squirming. You can't get away from me and you know it," Malichai said. He used a calm, fierce voice, as if he were immovable. "Joe, explain this to me. Why?"

"It doesn't matter why. I'm doing it." Now it was a matter of pride. Not only was the mysterious healer, Joe, listening, but his brothers and friends on the plane were as well.

Amaryllis was certain the worst way she could handle the situation was to allow it to become a matter of pride, and she was falling into that trap. She needed to find a way to make Malichai understand. This wasn't about his brothers, or Joe. This wasn't about her or her ability to heal. This was about Malichai and what he needed. He was willing to sacrifice himself in the way he always did, for everyone else, but she wasn't willing to allow him to do that.

Malichai ignored her. "Is she safe doing this?"

"Malichai." That was Ezekiel, warning plain in his voice.

"You're not supposed to make a sound, Zeke," Malichai snapped. "I have every right to protect my woman. Tell me why it's painful for her."

"He said 'uncomfortable,'" Amaryllis pointed out.

"You meant 'painful,' didn't you, Joe?" Malichai asked, ignoring her.

"Yes," Joe capitulated, knowing Malichai, knowing he would never give in until he got the information he wanted. "For a brief time, the healer transfers the infection, or in this case the fractures in your bone, to his or her bones. We feel the pain the patient feels. It is momentary, but it can be severe and if you're not ready for it, mistakes can be made during the healing process."

"Hell no, you're not doing this," Malichai hissed, his face a mask of fury. His arm tightened around her waist as if he could tie her to him. "I should have been told this from the beginning. That meant that the infection in my leg went through your body. Joe, could she have any of that left in her?"

"No, like I said, it's momentary."

"You're positive?"

Amaryllis knew there was no arguing with him. That way, she had no chance of winning. She had to think of something completely different, something he would understand, respect and be unable to get around.

"I'm as sure as possible, Malichai. To my knowledge, it's never happened."

Amaryllis put a knee on the bed and he immediately loosened his arm enough that she could crawl onto it. She framed Malichai's face with both hands and pressed her forehead to his, uncaring that it was possible that Joe could see her, and maybe even those in the plane. The only thing that mattered to her was convincing Malichai.

"Don't do this, Malichai. I would always, always respect what you do when it comes to your work. I won't like it, because you're going to be in danger, but I know it's something you're driven to do. You told me you wanted a woman in your life like Nonny. Would she back away from saving her man's leg because of a little pain? She wouldn't. I can't either, honey. You know you can't ask that of me. You can't demand it. I need to do this. It isn't a want. It's a need. This is who I am."

"Damn it, Amaryllis. Do you have any idea what it feels like knowing I'm causing you pain?"

She used the pads of her fingers to stroke velvet caresses along his cheekbones and jaw the way he did to hers. His face. She had come to love just looking at his face. There was such strength there. She knew, whenever she looked at him, that he was someone to count on. She wanted to be that someone for him.

"You aren't causing me pain. You would never cause me pain, Malichai. You aren't that man and you never will be that man. You have an injury and I'm a healer. I'm fortunate in that there's a generous healer willing to teach me when I need it most. I would help anyone through an injury like this, because like you, when others need you, you go. When someone needs me to do this, I'm driven to aid them."

She brushed kisses over his eyes and then

down his nose to his mouth. "This is *you,* Malichai. The most important person in my world. This is you. More than any other I need to do this because you're injured. If pain is a by-product of what I do, then I gladly accept it in order to heal someone. Never for one moment think it has anything to do with you."

For a moment she thought tears swam close to the surface of his eyes, but he blinked and then he was kissing her. If there was fire in her, there was equally as much in him and he transferred it all to her. She tasted love for the first time in her life. Nothing had ever tasted so good. The sensation settled deep and wrapped her in him, wrapped her in such warmth and happiness she felt safe and secure at the worst possible moment. That was all Malichai. That was *her* Malichai.

She lifted her head, once again framed his face with her hands and looked into his strange, golden eyes. "Are we good?"

"We're always going to be good, baby." He hesitated briefly. She could see the visible struggle in him as he warred with himself. "It's a go."

"Thank you." She said it simply and then slid back off the bed to go stand by his calf, once more positioning the phone so the faceless healer could see what she was doing. "We're ready. Thanks for being so patient. We're new at this."

"You're both doing fine." There was even more respect in his voice. "Tell me when you're in."

She didn't reply but let go of her outside vision. Each time she did so, she was amazed at how much faster and more efficiently she managed to get to the place she needed to be. Her "inward" vision cleared much faster as well. She had to experiment a little to find the best place to position her hands. She chose one of the shortest cracks in order to test the amount of pain she would feel before she could take a good breath.

The crack was jagged, and it ran just to the side of his knee in a zigzag pattern. Glowing a deep red, she saw it was deeper in spots than others.

"I didn't realize the depths of the cracks would be different."

"Yes, I should have warned you. You'll have to stick with it until it's completely closed up," the healer explained. "Obviously, the deeper the crack, the more intense it is to heal it. You have very good energy, so you have the power to do it, but expect even varying amounts of discomfort with each of those fractures."

There were so many cracks running up Malichai's leg it was a little intimidating. She didn't waste time, but she did think fleetingly that she should have texted Marie to tell her she couldn't make breakfast. She doubted she'd be finished in time, or if she was, she wouldn't be in any shape to do it. If she got close to the time, she'd have to have Malichai text.

Her hands grew hot and then the fracture lit up bright, hot crimson. She felt her cells reaching for his. It was intimate, their bodies merging on a molecular level. Instantly she felt a jolt of bright hot pain and forced herself to relax into it. He'd been living with far worse, doing dishes, walking with her on the beach, running errands for the bed-and-breakfast. Love welled up and nearly overwhelmed her. Malichai. He was such a gift.

It took time, and she was meticulous, filling in the fissures until the bone looked completely sealed and she could move upward. Sometimes it was difficult, other times easy, but always, always, it was painful. The longer ones, reaching up the side of his thigh, seemed to be the worst, branching out in every direction, trying to wrap around the bone to places hard to get, but she was meticulous. She had learned patience in a hard school, so she was very steady, ignoring the pain once it settled into her body.

Light crept through the window, spotlighting the man lying on the bed by the time she was certain she had gotten to every fracture. She made one last sweep, just because she wasn't going to take any chances that the fractures and infection could begin all over again before the psychic surgeon got there.

Taking a long, deep breath, she pulled herself back from the merge with him. The moment she did, she landed on the floor, her legs nothing but ragged noodles.

"Amaryllis?" The healer called out her name anxiously.

"I'm okay, but I don't think I'm going to fix breakfast for everyone this morning," she said and curled up on the floor.

"We've landed," Ezekiel announced. "We'll be there in a half hour."

"Good." She wanted someone to take over. If she had a blanket, she'd just pull it over her and go to sleep right where she was.

"Baby, climb onto the bed. At least lie here with me. If you don't get up here, I'm going to pick you up and put you up here," Malichai threatened.

"Text Marie and tell her I can't do breakfast this morning." She was too tired even to give in to his threats. "Thanks, Joe, someday I hope to meet you and thank you in person. I couldn't have done this without you."

"Yes, you could have, but hopefully I helped to give you confidence. Malichai, you need to rest. Don't do anything until someone else works on you. We don't know why that bone isn't standing up but we can't take any chances with it," Joe said. "Rubin's worked on you once. I did several times and now Amaryllis. It should be enough, but I have this gut feeling. Stay put until Rubin assesses that bone and determines what the problem is. And that, my good friend, is an order."

"Will do," Malichai promised.

Malichai's voice was definitely stronger, while she was feeling as if she couldn't move. She didn't want to move and never wanted to move again. But she was also feeling more satisfied than she'd ever felt. She'd done it. She'd driven out the infection that was threatening his life and maybe she'd even mended the bone enough to keep the leg stable until the reputed psychic surgeon could get there.

"Baby, come up here with me. The others will be here soon. I don't want them to find you on the floor. If you don't, I swear, I'm coming to get you."

Amaryllis had to make a supreme effort to move. Everything hurt. Every bone in her body. Every muscle. Still, she forced herself to ease her body onto the mattress beside him. He wasn't nearly as hot as he had been, and she was grateful for that. His arm went around her waist and he dragged her back into him until her butt was snuggled in the cradle of his hips.

She knew it was only a few minutes later before several men slipped into the room. She should have been up and ready to defend Malichai, but there was no tension in his body and no strength in hers, so she lay passively, but as alert as possible as they surrounded the bed. Two men went straight to Malichai's side of the bed, while one pulled down the shade at the window and the other locked and stood in front of the door.

"Zeke," Malichai greeted. "You got here fast."

"What did you think I was going to do?" There was gruff affection in the voice. Ezekiel put his hand on Malichai's forehead in the way a father might check for a temperature in his child.

The gesture choked Amaryllis up. She was

uncomfortable with Malichai curled around her so intimately with so many strangers in the room and she shifted position as if to get up. All that did was draw Ezekiel's attention.

"You must be Amaryllis. Thank you for saving my brother's life. Just stay there. I know it must have been tough on you. You rest while Rubin does the rest."

Rubin. The true miracle worker. She looked at the man. He looked striking. Handsome. Dark hair, dark lashes. If she didn't have excellent night vision, she wouldn't have been able to see him in the blacked-out room. She had a feeling that might have been deliberate, but she couldn't help staring. This man had a skill probably only one or two other people on earth had.

He didn't waste time asking questions. Or even speaking at all. He simply crooked his finger at Malichai and Malichai rolled over to lay straight. Amaryllis sat up so she could see better. Rubin spread his palms above the leg and moved upward from the ankle to the hip slowly. There was no expression on his face, but Amaryllis suddenly felt a heaviness in her chest. The pressure was so severe she pushed with both hands against it.

There was no light bursting beneath his

palms. Nothing to indicate he was working, but that pressure she felt told her he was. Just as her body took the brunt of the healing process, his had to be doing so as well. She admired his efficiency, but she wished she dared ask him questions and that she could see what he was doing. It was impossible not to be curious. She could push out infections and bind together a broken bone, but she couldn't actually perform a surgery on a person. She might hold an artery together for a short length of time, but he could repair it, he could do what surgeons couldn't when it came to actually putting together a human body.

She understood, probably better than the GhostWalkers, why Rubin's ability had to be kept a secret from Whitney and the rest of the world. She also understood that just by giving her that knowledge, she was being included in their circle, accepted into their family because of Malichai, and if she ever tried to betray them, she would be hunted by every GhostWalker alive and they would never stop until she was dead. That was the code they lived by. And she would live by it too. She would protect this man and his gift as well.

Another hour passed. She chewed on her bottom lip. No one moved. No one fidgeted.

She didn't like that so much time slipped by. That meant, in spite of all the work she'd done, there was so much more to do. Had she missed some fractures? What was really wrong with Malichai's bone that it continued to have those small fractures erupt around the original bullet wounds? It didn't make sense. She tried to puzzle it out. A few times she felt eyes on her and found the man standing in front of the door watching her.

That was Trap, the owner of the plane. The genius. The one Malichai'd said had Asperger's and wasn't always nice to everyone but was a good friend. Mordichai, his brother, stood in front of the window, making certain no one could catch a glimpse of Rubin working, not that she thought they would have a clue what he was doing.

Eventually Rubin straightened and lifted a hand to his neck to ease his sore muscles. "This is certainly interesting, Malichai." He looked around, saw the armchair and immediately went to it and sank down. There was weariness in his voice.

Immediately, Mordichai went to his brother and gripped his shoulder. "You okay?"

"I'm good. Not so sure about Rubin."

"Introduce us to your lady," Trap said.

"She kicked ass for you."

Amaryllis thought that was a good thing. Trap might accept her into the circle after hearing and watching on the phone while she tried her best to heal Malichai's leg. She was more interested in Rubin's assessment of Malichai's injury but before she could say so, she realized they were deliberately giving him time to recover.

"Amaryllis, these are my brothers, Ezekiel, Mordichai, Trap and Rubin." Malichai indicated each one. "This is my woman, Amaryllis." Malichai took her hand and pressed a kiss to her knuckles.

She tried not to pull her hand away, but the gesture had embarrassed her a little. The darkness helped, although she knew they could see every bit as well as she could.

"Nice job you did," Rubin said. "Especially for a first time and given the mess his bone had to have been. Just seeing it again after you worked on it, I realized how close we came to losing him. You saved his life whether you know it or not."

"What is going on with his leg?" Ezekiel asked.

"I'm not certain what is causing the continual damage, but if I had to take a guess, I'd say it had something to do with the second-generation Zenith. The damage originates around the wounds where Malichai slapped on the field dressings. Of course, they were the worst wounds."

Rubin ran his fingers through his hair. "I need to sleep. All of you do. Malichai. You and Amaryllis need sleep, as much as possible. I want you treating that leg with care. You walk, and slowly, not jog or run. You swim as often as possible. In the water you're exercising it but it isn't weight bearing. I'll check it daily to make certain you aren't overdoing it. Stay off it when you can. No more standing around. When you sit, put the leg up."

"Roger that," Malichai said.

"We have to get out of here before anyone sees us in this room," Ezekiel said.

Just like that, they were gone. Like ghosts. Amaryllis slid down and Malichai curled around her. She had a hundred questions, but her eyes were already closing, and she fell asleep before she could ask any of them.

8

Malichai flashed what he hoped was a charming smile at the older woman working behind the counter at the magic shop. "I'm actually looking for a good friend of mine. She owns the shop. Miss Crystal? I'm only in town for a few days and we had an appointment to meet, but she didn't show."

A flash of annoyance crossed the older woman's face. "She isn't here."

Your charm clearly isn't working. Mordichai's amused voice slipped into his head.

Malichai gave the mental equivalent of flipping his brother off. He leaned on the counter and gave the woman another smile. "I'm sorry, I didn't catch your name."

"Tess." She gave it abruptly. "Why?"

"Just being polite," Malichai said and gave her another smile, this one not so charming. "Where is Miss Crystal? She's never broken an appointment with me yet."

"I have no idea. She asked me to cover for

her and I'm doing it. If you're not going to buy anything, you might move along." She had a slight southern accent, but she certainly didn't have southern manners.

Malichai's eyebrow shot up. "I doubt Miss Crystal is aware of how rude you are to her friends and customers. If I didn't have to go swimming this morning as part of my physical therapy, I'd be going to the cops to ask them to do a well check. You'd have to come up with answers then." He turned and stormed out, making certain to limp heavily, before she could respond.

As part of your physical therapy? Mordichai sounded very amused. *You might have overplayed that one, bro.*

I wanted her to know I was injured, and it's true.

Limping like a three-legged dog wasn't enough?

Malichai couldn't help the small grin as he made his way down the steps of the magic shop and limped through the alley, ignoring the other stores.

She's watching you, Mordichai reported. *A man joined her. Getting photographs now. Will run them through facial recognition. Now they've been joined by a third man. You've gained quite an audience. Don't overdo your performance.*

I think I've done this before, and my acting has always been praised for outstanding realism.

Mordichai groaned. *I knew that one stupid article that was planted in the college paper was going to come back to bite me in the ass. You didn't actually act in that play, Malichai. It was a setup.*

So you say and you've always been jealous of my ability to impress the audiences with my skills. Malichai rounded the corner and almost ran directly into Amaryllis. She'd been sound asleep when he'd left that morning.

She glared at him, stopping directly in front of him. He was grateful he'd gotten around the corner and out of sight of the three people watching him. The late morning sun turned her hair into a blaze of icy gold. He couldn't help smoothing the strands with his hands, feeling all that silk. Soothing her.

"You did it, didn't you? You set yourself up without me to have your back."

"Babe. I'm working here. Don't rain on my parade. My brothers are in town and they agreed you needed sleep after working on my leg."

"That healer said you needed to rest the leg, not walk around on it just hours after

249

we worked on it."

He took her elbow and turned her toward the beach. "First, *you* did the work too. Just because someone else did work after you doesn't negate the fact that you need to rest. Second, you should still be in bed."

And I'm going to kill Zeke. He was supposed to be watching her. Where the hell is he? He could have used a warning that she was close. Amaryllis could have blown everything.

"I woke up and you weren't there," she said. "Seriously, Malichai. You could undo all the work that was done last night."

"The leg is strong. Stronger than it's ever been. It will hold. You can't be here, honey. I mean it. I have to see if they'll try to attack me in the water the way someone did Dozer."

"Dozer is a little crazy, Malichai." She threw her hands into the air. "You shouldn't be running around on that leg. I'm serious. I can swim just as fast in the water as you can. If someone needs to be a target, I can do it. You should have waited for me. I would have set myself up."

"You've got enough work to do at the B and B for Marie and Jacy, babe. I can do this much. It's no big thing."

"Malichai, just think about what you

could be doing to that leg." She shook her head, looking more anxious than ever.

He took her face gently between his hands. "You know Rubin worked on my leg. He wants me swimming in the ocean. He thinks that will be what strengthens my leg. I hope he's right. I won't be running or even jogging. I'm not going to overdo it. I'm just going to swim."

She took a deep breath and then forced herself to nod when she clearly didn't want to give in. "Tell me what's happening." She didn't like it, but she accepted what he said and was willing to go along with it.

"Miss Crystal wasn't in the shop. The woman who was in there was very rude and didn't like me asking questions. If she was hired to watch the store in the owner's absence, there would be no reason for her to be rude to one of Miss Crystal's friends. And to have two men join her at the door and watch me walk off says something even more sinister."

"You could be absolutely right. But setting yourself up to be killed underwater where no one can see you or help you is ludicrous. I can go into the water with you. You know I'm a really good swimmer, probably as good as you."

"No, you're going to go back to the bed-

and-breakfast and watch over Marie and Jacy. I don't like the fact that Anna and Bryon were murdered, and Burnell and Jay feel threatened. That's too close to Marie and Jacy."

She glanced up at him, a shadow crossing her face. "Do you really think there could be a danger to them?"

"I think it's a good possibility if Anna and Bryon were really murdered — and I think they were. I don't know what's going on, but we need to get to the bottom of it. I'd feel better if you were there to watch over them. Rubin should be somewhere close by if you need backup. He needed sleep, and unlike you, I imagine he's actually getting it. Ezekiel is probably making himself and everyone else crazy by inspecting every inch of the bed-and-breakfast to see if someone has the place wired."

"It sounds as if your people have every-thing well in hand."

They stood together on the sidewalk just in front of the long expanse of sand. Already the lounge chairs were filling up as people claimed their spots for the day. The water glittered as if diamonds were scattered across the surface. Waves raced toward the beach, folding over to form foamy crests several yards from shore. It was an idyllic scene. Beautiful and peaceful. One would never consider murder might have taken place on that white sand or near the serenity of the ocean.

"Marie needs you, Amaryllis," Malichai said gently. He framed her face again and bent his head toward hers. "I need to know you've got this. I can't be worried about them and still go into the sea knowing I might be attacked."

"Your brothers . . ."

"Marie doesn't know them. She knows you. If you say run, she'll run. No hesitation. You know that. I'm enhanced. I can stay underwater far longer than Dozer can. I don't feel the cold the way others do. Once I'm in the water, my weight is off my leg. I'm going to be far more worried about you, Marie and Jacy than myself."

He brushed kisses over each of her eyes, her nose and finally her mouth. He was very fond of her mouth. She parted her lips and he was kissing her, bringing her body tight against his. Immediately she swept him away into another world where he only had to feel. Everything else dropped away but Amaryllis and how her body felt against his. How her mouth was hot and seductive, putting all kinds of erotic images in his head.

"Looks like you two know each other very well."

They broke apart, laughing, turning to face the man who stood there grinning at them. Craig Williams was dressed in board shorts and a tee that said "Hittin' the Waves Today." His hair was slightly a mess and his dark glasses were reflective.

Malichai nodded, giving Craig a slightly sheepish grin in return. "Amaryllis is my fiancée. So, yeah, we know each other very well."

"You're very professional, Amaryllis," Craig said. "I couldn't tell. I thought maybe you were friends, but it isn't like you're all over each other."

"We try to show restraint in front of the guests," Malichai answered for her, again giving Craig a small smile of camaraderie, as if sharing that it wasn't always that easy. "Do you visit San Diego often?"

Craig shook his head. "First time. I met a few people online and have become good friends with them over the last year or so. We're meeting in person for the first time here in San Diego at a convention."

"The convention to exchange ideas for world peace?" Amaryllis asked.

Craig nodded. "That's the one. I've been an avid participant in the forums. It's been shocking to see the number of countries represented and the amount of people willing to try to come up with ideas. The discussions are always respectful, although they have gotten heated occasionally, but the monitors seem to always get everyone back to the same page — respecting points of view and actually listening."

Malichai hadn't really thought too much about the convention being held at the San Diego Convention Center, but it was a huge facility, capable of housing thousands of people. He couldn't help thinking of the phrase "maximum number of people killed." If one wanted to kill a lot of people, the convention for ideas on world peace would be a good place to start. He glanced down at Amaryllis. She was looking up at him and he could see on her face that she was thinking the same thing he was.

"Are any of your friends staying at the bed-and-breakfast?" Malichai asked.

Craig shook his head. "They're scattered around in various hotels. There are very few rooms anywhere with the convention so close." He winked at Amaryllis. "I can see he's not in town for world peace."

He held out his hand to Malichai. "I'm Craig Williams."

"Malichai Fortunes. You've met Amaryllis."

"I have." His expression changed. "There's a rumor going around that the couple in one of the rooms carried out a murder-suicide pact right there. If that was true, the cops would be all over the place, but there is one room with tape across the door."

Amaryllis nodded. "Unfortunately, the couple was found dead elsewhere, but we don't have many details on what happened or how they died."

That much was true and Malichai was proud of how she handled it. Very matter-of-factly, but her voice was tinged with sadness.

"I didn't get the chance to meet them," Craig said. "I normally meet people online. I spend most of my time on a computer. This is my first real foray into a live event." He looked toward the water. "What are you two up to this morning?"

"I have to get back to help Marie," Amaryllis said.

"I'm going for a swim this morning." Malichai made a face. "Took a little bit of a hit and need some physical therapy. Promised, since I insisted on visiting Amaryllis, that I'd swim. Apparently, that's good for my leg."

"A little bit of a hit?" Craig echoed.

"He's in the service," Amaryllis answered, rolling her eyes. "He was shot. Several times. He wasn't supposed to come and see me, but he never listens."

Craig's eyes widened in shock. "You got shot? With a gun?"

"A machine gun, actually," Amaryllis clarified when Malichai didn't answer.

Malichai sent her a quelling look. She wrapped her arm around his waist and gazed up at him adoringly. He had no idea if she was acting or if she meant it.

"He doesn't like me talking about it because he's so modest, but he saved a lot of lives."

"Go to work," Malichai ordered gruffly. He bent his head, kissed her upturned mouth and then gave her a little push in the direction of the bed-and-breakfast.

Laughing, Amaryllis waved at the two men and sauntered off, her hips swaying. Malichai sighed. "That woman."

"She's beautiful. And nice. I don't leave my house that much. I work from home on a computer and most of the time, my friends do as well. She's easy to talk to."

That explained the awkward stares Craig gave Burnell and Jay. He probably had no idea how to talk to real human beings, face-to-face.

"Amaryllis is very easy to talk to," Malichai conceded. He began to inch toward the edge of the sidewalk. To his consternation, Craig moved with him. "I'm going to have to get this swim done." He kept walking, determinedly stepping onto the sand.

Craig followed him. "I don't swim. I don't even know how."

Malichai picked up the pace. He was fairly certain Craig was going to follow him right down to the water's edge so he could see Malichai's "wound." If that was the case, he might as well get it over with. He had to strip off his track pants. He wore board shorts under them, but he wasn't walking around that way, revealing to the world the raw, shiny wounds in his leg.

He didn't answer but found a lounge chair up closer to the water and casually tugged down the track pants. He heard Craig's swift inhale and caught sight of the very real horror on the man's face.

"Wow. You really did get shot. More than once."

"Yeah. I did," Malichai said.

"Looks recent."

"A few weeks ago. Had a couple of operations." Make that several. Lots of blood transfusions. He'd nearly died on the helicopter ride, but he'd been lucky that Rubin had been with him. If not, no one could have saved him. Then Ezekiel and the rest of the team refused to give up on him once he was taken off the helicopter and brought to their makeshift hospital before being transferred to Germany. It was a long road back and he was still traveling it.

"So, they think swimming will strengthen the leg? It's pretty weak?" Craig persisted. He took out his cell phone. "Do you mind if I take a picture for my friends to see? They aren't going to believe this."

"Yeah, I do mind," Malichai said. He didn't care if anyone thought he was rude. Craig might not have any idea how to interact with real human beings, but it was time he learned. "I would prefer that we don't talk about it again. In fact, I would prefer that you don't mention it at the B and B."

"Oh, yeah. Of course not." Craig hastily put his phone away. "I'm sorry. I just got carried away. That's just cool. Well. I'm sorry." He turned toward the street, still muttering apologies as he hurried away.

You okay, bro? Mordichai asked.

Malichai took a deep breath and let it out. Was he? He hadn't expected to have such a visceral reaction. He should have found the entire thing humorous. He knew there were a lot of men like Craig who rarely left their homes. They lived virtual lives, playing games, having online friends, working on their computers and really living on them. They seemed to lose touch with reality. He really should give the man kudos for actually taking the step to leave his house and meet a few of the people he had talked to, probably for years, face-to-face.

Malichai had been shot more than once. This wasn't his first time. He'd gone on countless missions. None of them had been easy or pretty. This time the wounds had been different. He didn't know why, and he didn't want to look too closely at it. He was alive. His leg was intact. He'd found Amaryllis. That was all in the plus column. He wasn't going to look at the negative side.

He tossed his track pants on the lounge chair and made his way to the water's edge. The water was cool, maybe mid to high sixties. It didn't matter to him, but he wondered if it would be unusual for a man to go swimming in deeper water without a wet suit. None of the surfers wore them.

Going in now, Mordichai.

We're on you. Take your time heading out, Malichai. It was Ezekiel who answered him.

Ezekiel had been hovering ever since that first notice he got from Rubin that Malichai had been shot and was slipping away. Zeke had been fierce in his fight to save his brother. Once Malichai had been brought out of Afghanistan, Ezekiel hadn't left his brother's side for days. Then operation after operation, he had insisted on being in the operating room, double-checking everything, making the surgeons and anesthesiologists crazy. He pretty much could make Malichai crazy as well, but he was used to his older brother hovering when they were sick. He'd been doing it all their lives.

Thought you were staying at the B and B looking after Amaryllis. Malichai didn't know how to feel about having his woman with only Rubin there. *Anna and Bryon Cooper were murdered, Zeke.*

I agree, Malichai. But Amaryllis has assured me that she is perfectly capable of looking after the women, and she personally asked me to look after you.

That was a bullshit excuse if he ever heard one. Ezekiel would never leave a primary target unless he wanted to — and he wanted to. He wanted to hover some more, forever acting like the big brother. What would be the point of calling him on it?

I can handle myself in the water, Zeke. I

don't have to depend on my leg.

Just so you know, dipshit, I'm not fucking losing my brother to whatever bullshit is happening here.

Three swear words in one sentence. That had to be a record. He wasn't about to touch that. *Roger that.*

Amaryllis's cover is solid. The cops can dig away to their heart's content and they'll find her complete history. She's engaged to you, by the way. Mordichai changed the subject for both of his brothers. *I thought that was a particularly nice touch. You won't even have to ask her. She already said yes.*

Malichai struck out for the waves, cutting smoothly through the water. *Nice. Now I just have to find the perfect ring and get it on her finger. I already introduced her as my fiancée to Craig and she didn't object.*

That's the way it should be, Mordichai said. *Just tell the woman how it is and no arguments. Marital bliss.*

I can't say it's always bliss, Ezekiel chimed in. *But it's worth it. You do actually have to put a little work into it, Mordichai.*

Mordichai gave a little snort of derision. *You're whipped. Bellisia has you totally whipped, and everyone knows it. I'm beginning to think I'm the last hope for the Fortunes brothers. I've seen how Malichai gives his woman those goofy-assed drowned-calf ador-ing looks. He's going to be just like you, Zeke. You gave him such a poor example. Now that woman's going to walk on him, and it will be all your fault.*

Malichai enjoyed the feeling of his body cutting through the water. He swam slowly at first, warming up his muscles, but his body needed the workout. Every muscle stretched, began to respond more quickly as he loosened up. He dove under a wave and swam even faster, cutting through the water like a rocket and then easing up as he surfaced.

Slow it down, Ezekiel advised. *You don't want anyone watching to get suspicious that you're more than you seem in the water. You're supposed to be injured.*

Did you get names of those three at the magic shop? Malichai had gone to inquire after Miss Crystal at the first opportunity, afraid if he waited, the detectives, Duncan and Brady, would get there before him. They seemed to be very methodical cops, the type that didn't miss even a small detail. That had been why he'd been apprehensive about Amaryllis not having her identity in place.

Not yet. We're working on it. Your girl seems very competent. Is she real competent at . . .

um . . . everything?

Mordichai, I'm not talking to you about Amaryllis. You're such a fucking perv. The water felt amazing now, his body almost humming every time he dove beneath the surface and let himself actually work his muscles. He felt warm. Alive. Whole again.

I have to live vicariously.

Malichai nearly choked. *I'm underwater, you moron. Don't make me laugh.*

He surfaced some distance from the few surfers who had gone out that morning. The waves weren't high at all. Mostly those out were the younger and inexperienced. He angled farther away from them, heading toward a long, sweeping bend. At the same time, he swam farther out to sea. Each time that he could, he dove under a wave and swam a little faster and held his breath a little longer. He often swam in Louisiana. The entire team did to stay in practice, so his lungs responded to his demands.

His leg did begin to ache a little when he pushed himself to really hit the speeds he wanted to go in open water. He was certain if anyone was going to attack him, it would be around the same place that Dozer had been grabbed. Malichai didn't have a surfboard, but when he returned after swimming awhile, he would swim deliberately slow right through that exact spot. Most of the surfers would be gone.

You're going too far, Ezekiel cautioned. *You're going to tire yourself out.*

Malichai would have protested that he was old enough to decide for himself what was too far, too fast, or too anything, but he heard the underlying worry in his older brother's voice. He owed everything to Zeke. Malichai knew he had to give his brother this, whether the entire ordeal of being shot by machine gun had gotten to him or not. The injuries had definitely gotten to Zeke.

Coming back in now, Malichai assured. *I've slowed down and should be in the right spot for the attack in another five.*

I'm watching from a distance and haven't spotted a diver in the water, Mordichai reported, all business now that Malichai might really be in danger.

Malichai took his time, feeling his muscles contract and stretch. He concentrated now on sound underwater. He had excellent hearing thanks to the physical enhancements Whitney had given him — without his consent. Still, at times those enhancements came in handy. The fact that those enhancements made him different enough to scare people in high places didn't matter when they saved his life.

He and his team would never be like other soldiers. He would always be classified. No government wanted to admit to experiments on children, especially if those children were sometimes given cancer or other diseases in the name of science, or even terminated because they were deemed too dangerous. The GhostWalkers had learned that although they were soldiers and identified themselves that way, they couldn't allow others to know what they really were. That meant they stuck together, formed their own families for protection. They lived close to one another and relied on each other rather than those above them who were directing their missions.

He heard a peculiar noise as he swam toward shore, much like something scraping against rock. It was near the same place where Dozer had been attacked. A small shelf rose from the ocean floor, rock crusted with sea life. A man in a wet suit complete with scuba gear shot off the rock right toward him as he swam past.

Malichai allowed the diver to get up on him. He came in from behind, attempting to circle Malichai's neck in a choke hold. They wanted it to appear to be a simple drowning. Not murder. No one wanted an investigation, not after the deaths of Anna and Bryon Cooper. Malichai caught his arms and rolled, throwing the attacker off him.

They faced each other under the water, Malichai without a breathing apparatus. The diver was confident he could keep Malichai beneath the surface and he would drown trying to get up to the air. Malichai dove at the diver, a burst of speed like an attacking shark, going straight for the belly. At the last possible moment, he rolled over the man and ripped the hose connecting the tank to the mouthpiece. Bubbles rushed to the surface.

Hurry. You can take him now. If Mordichai didn't get there fast, the diver would try to get away. *He's armed with a knife. There's one strapped to his leg. I can remove it if you need me to.*

No, I'm right behind him.

Mordichai came out of nowhere, right behind the diver, stripping the knife from him and catching his arms to drag them behind his back. He wasn't alone. Trap dropped a loop around the man, tying him up fast. They dragged him farther away from the area where there were swimmers or surfers, all the while pressing air to his mouth, allowing him to take a breath every now and then.

Malichai continued a leisurely swim back to shore. He rose out of the water, his gaze sweeping the sand and lounge chairs. Over by the tree Billy Leven was talking to Craig Williams. They were gesturing toward the cordoned-off area where forensics was sifting through the fine grains of sand for any evidence that might help uncover who had killed Anna and Bryon Cooper.

As he dried himself off, still continuing his sweep, he spotted the older woman he'd spoken to earlier. She was with an older man. Both sat in chairs under a brightly colored umbrella, a small table between them. They seemed to be in a highly animated conversation.

Have the cops done a well check on Miss Crystal? Malichai sent the query to Rubin. He was supposed to be watching Amaryllis, Marie and Jacy. The well check had been requested from Amaryllis, giving the police a reason for entering her apartment and shop, asking questions. They didn't need to wait.

Yes. Four people were in the apartment. One claimed to be Miss Crystal's cousin. She is an older female, about sixty-five. Graying hair. She said Miss Crystal had asked them to stay in her apartment and run the magic shop until her return. Supposedly Miss Crystal is on a cruise to the Mediterranean. She gave the ship's name and was confident the police could call the ship and the captain would confirm that she was on board.

Malichai thought that over. Was it possible that Miss Crystal really was alive and Anna and Burnell had misinterpreted what they thought they overheard? He pulled on his track pants, aware several people in the lounge chairs around him had noticed the raw, shiny scars crawling up his leg like a long zipper. Nothing made sense. Especially now that a diver had actually tried to drown him. Without a doubt the magic shop was tied in to the attacks on him and Dozer and most likely even the murders of Anna and Bryon. But how? And why?

He pulled on his T-shirt, wrapped the towel around his neck and set off in the general direction of the bed-and-breakfast. He angled across the wide expanse of sand and then, at the last moment, hesitated as if wondering if he should go right in, changed his mind and headed toward the little café where most of those staying at Marie's got their caffeine fixes during the day.

Once out of sight of the first beach, he picked up the pace and hurried around a second and then third corner. Twice he backtracked to make certain he wasn't being followed. He ended up in the small garage just off a house his brother Ezekiel had found to rent. That was like Zeke. He always found the perfect place for any occasion that might come up.

Mordichai let him into the darkened room. They had a hood over the diver's face. Ezekiel glanced up but didn't say anything to Malichai. Instead, he turned back to the diver.

"I take that hood off your face, you're a dead man. Do you understand me?"

The head bobbed up and down. The diver's breathing was harsh and ragged.

"Why did you try to drown Dozer and then Malichai? I'm warning you, I'm not going to ask again. You don't tell me what I want to know, the hood comes off, we do this the hard way and then you die. You got that?"

The head bobbed again. "I got orders. I do what I'm told."

"Who gave you the orders?"

"I don't know. I have a business. I'm an independent contractor and I don't meet with clients. I just get the money up front and I carry out the order. If the order isn't carried out, then I keep going until it's done. That surfer should have been an easy target, but he wasn't. They hardly paid much of anything for him. When I missed, I just returned the money. They were pissed as hell."

"They?" Ezekiel pounced on that.

"Well, yeah. There are at least two of them. They type out the orders and send them over the computer. It's encrypted, but I can tell it isn't always the same man. They use different phrasing."

Someone doing business the way this man did would pay attention to something like that. He hadn't hesitated either, searching for a reason. He readily gave one. Malichai was certain he was telling the truth.

"Why did they want the surfer and then the soldier drowned?"

The prisoner shrugged. "I don't ask. Usually it's some husband or wife wanting the other killed, so they don't have to share everything if they're getting a divorce. I try to arrange accidents if possible. Makes it easier all the way around."

Malichai was a little sickened by the easy way the diver spoke of killing others. Malichai was a soldier. He was also a medic. It bothered him when he had to take a life, and he did it often. It was never done easily. He shook his head and looked at Mordichai. His brother was watching the prisoner very closely.

Ezekiel was close to the prisoner, and that meant they all had eyes on him just in case. Trap was standing just to the left of him. Mordichai to the right. Malichai had remained near the door to block the exit as well.

"Your name is Henry Shevfield? You live here in San Diego?" They'd gotten his name and identity from his prints.

The man nodded.

"You're married with three kids?"

The prisoner stiffened. "Leave my wife and kids out of this. They have no idea what I do for a living."

"I'm sure they don't," Ezekiel said. "Was this the first time you dealt with these people?"

"No. They've used my services a few times over the last couple of years."

Malichai stiffened and straightened from where he'd been draped against the door. A couple of years? Big things took planning. A lot of planning.

"When you say 'a couple of years,' is that two? Three? Just how many and what were those jobs?" Ezekiel persisted.

"Maybe two and a half. Yeah. That's about right. The first job was some hotshot that worked for the San Diego Unified Port

272

District. He was holding up something big and they needed him out of the way. That one was easy enough to arrange and he died in an accident. Drove a sports car way too fast. It was tragic."

"And the next?" Ezekiel prompted.

"Woman worked for the board of directors at the San Diego Convention Center. She was a little more difficult. You'd think a suit would get out more often, but she worked mostly from home. I had to arrange a home accident. Those are much more dangerous because you can't control the environment."

He spoke so matter-of-factly that Malichai winced. Henry Shevfield thought very little about arranging accidents or killing other human beings for his own personal gain.

"This woman you killed, was she married? Did she have children?"

"Well, yes, but I don't see how that's pertinent. It's not my business to look at those things. I just take the contract, do the job and we're done."

Ezekiel moved away from the prisoner, as if he didn't quite trust himself. "Keep going. I'd like to know what other jobs you've done for these men."

"A couple of maintenance workers. Both

273

jobs were recent. In the last couple of months. One was an old guy. He 'fell' down some stairs and broke his neck. The other was younger, and he stepped off the curb right in front of a car. Lived for a few hours."

"Where did the maintenance men work?"

Henry shrugged his shoulders, a casual roll that annoyed the hell out of Malichai. This man was clearly bored with the conversation, as if the people he killed didn't matter at all to him.

"They were part of some big group that has contracts with the San Diego Unified Port District. Seriously, none of that can matter. It was a while ago."

"It matters or I wouldn't be asking you these questions," Ezekiel said. "I suggest you shut the hell up and just answer when I ask you to. You've already got me so pissed off I want to stick a knife through your fucking throat."

Malichai's head jerked up. He was truly shocked. Ezekiel just wasn't like that. He kept a cool head. He was a doctor, a surgeon. A damn good one too. He didn't just swear. This man was really getting to him. As prisoners they had to interrogate, Henry Shevfield seemed easy. He just answered, certain, because he was wearing a hood, that they would let him go. He didn't mind answering because there was no proof to back up any allegations they might make against him to the authorities. Besides, the jobs had been completed.

Henry pressed his lips together tightly. He had to have heard the danger in Ezekiel's voice.

"The recent killings, Anna and Bryon Cooper, tourists staying at the bed-and-breakfast. Did you have anything to do with those killings?"

"No way. Sloppy job." He sounded contemptuous. "The cops already are suspicious, I could tell when I was watching them examining the crime scene. Whoever wanted it done should have asked me."

There was a long silence, as if Ezekiel were trying to pull himself together. When he did speak, his voice was under control. "Any other jobs asked of you by these two customers?" he pressed.

Henry hesitated for the first time and Ezekiel exploded into action, backhanding the prisoner so hard, the chair went flying backward, proving his control had been a sham. There was no way for Henry to stop his fall and he landed hard on the cement floor of the garage. Trap and Mordichai righted the chair and prisoner while Ezekiel paced across the garage, trying to get rid of the adrenaline pounding through his veins — a direct reaction to Henry's sociopathic behavior.

Do you want me to take over? Malichai asked tentatively. He didn't want Ezekiel to think he thought his brother was losing it and couldn't finish the interview.

No, I'm all right. It's just that he's so casual about killing a woman with a family, or shoving an older man down the stairs as if that man were trash. People like this man . . .

I get it, Malichai assured. And he did. They saw so many good soldiers die. Sometimes, when they went on a rescue, it seemed like they saw nothing but body parts or dead soldiers. They go to a beautiful place like San Diego and some man runs around killing for hire. He wanted to take a shot or two with his fists at the prisoner as well.

Thanks for the offer.

That surprised Malichai. His brother had never been one to express affection or the small niceties. Bellisia, his wife, must be having a positive effect on him. Malichai wasn't going to mention that either.

"Let's try this again," Ezekiel said very patiently. "I'm sure you realize I am an experienced interrogator and I am not going to be happy anytime you think about lying to me. It isn't a good idea. Just continue to tell the truth and you'll be fine. If not, you're a dead man and you'll never get out of this room."

The head bobbing went on once again.

"Do you have another contract with these same people?"

"Yes." Henry mumbled his answer, sounding completely dejected.

"Who is the contract for?"

Henry shrugged. "It's not exactly that kind of contract. This is more like a diversion. At least they used that word once. I'm to kill three people in a 'messy' way and start their bed-and-breakfast on fire. The more people are panicked, the better."

Malichai straightened again, this time stalking silently toward the prisoner. "Bed-and-breakfast" was a red flag. The way Henry said "three people" bothered the hell out of him.

"Random three people or specific three people?" Ezekiel persisted.

"Three females. The B and B owner, her kid and the main worker there. Do them in a nasty way that brings a million cops and detectives and then once everyone's inside, start one hell of a fire. Pull in the rest of them. Like I say, a diversion of some kind."

"A kid?" Ezekiel echoed. "As in a little

girl? You don't mind killing a child?"

"It's just business. I don't pick them. Someone else is responsible for that."

As he answered Ezekiel, Henry had been loosening his bonds. He ripped off the hood and leapt at Ezekiel at the same time. Ezekiel seemed to be waiting for him. As the man's body slammed hard into Zeke's, the knife Malichai's brother was holding low, blade up, went right into the prisoner. It sank in and, almost on reflex, Ezekiel twisted it. He stepped back as he pulled the blade free.

Henry went to his knees and then fell facedown. He lay there without a sound.

"Guess I should have checked those ties after he was on the ground," Ezekiel said.

"Hope that made you feel better," Malichai said. "We needed to get a lot more out of him. I noticed you just happened to have a tarp and plastic down to cover the cement."

Ezekiel shrugged. "It sucks trying to get blood out of cement. It was a precaution."

"I'll just bet it was," Malichai said. Had he done the same thing, Ezekiel would lecture him for a week. "How are you going to explain to the cops what went on here?"

"Military investigation suddenly running into a civilian one. I'll report the dead guy to Joe and he'll have to give the news to Major General," Ezekiel said.

"I'll leave you to it. I need to get back to Amaryllis." He was definitely running like a chicken, but he wasn't going to answer any of Ezekiel's questions about his woman and why he hadn't reported right away that she was one of Whitney's orphans.

Ezekiel hissed something derogatory about his parents, but since they weren't the nicest of people, and they shared them, Malichai didn't mind. It didn't even slow him down. He got out of the danger zone and back into the street, trying not to laugh at his brother's annoyance.

9

"I just don't understand what's going on," Lorrie Montclair said, shivering, moving her body close to Malichai as if for protection. "Lexie wanted to leave, but Linda and I said that wouldn't be right. And the murder didn't occur here."

"It could have," Lexie said stubbornly. "It could have, right, Mr. Fortunes?" She batted her eyelashes at him.

Before he could answer, Linda jumped into the conversation. "Lexie, honey, what about Marie losing all that money? It's not like she could get anyone else in at this late date. Isn't that right, Mr. Fortunes?"

"Call me Malichai," he said, trying not to grit his teeth. He felt like he wanted to scream. He'd rather be skinned alive than talk to the trio of sisters. Talking to the Montclair women was a little like attending a Ping-Pong tournament.

"Please sit with us tonight," Lorrie added,

looking up at him with what, he was certain, she thought was a vulnerable, frightened face.

Malichai saw a wolf in lamb's clothing. His woman needed protection from these three. Most likely, he did as well.

"I'm so frightened. So is Lexie. We need to know what's going on."

He looked helplessly up at Amaryllis as she stood behind the counter, serving the main course to everyone — the main course she'd prepared. The food was always made with the best ingredients and whatever else she put into it that made the dishes taste amazing.

Amaryllis hid a smile, but it was impossible to hide the lights dancing in her eyes. She was having just a little too much fun at his expense. "Actually, Malichai, I think Lorrie has a very good idea. If you sit with them, you can explain everything to them and alleviate their worries." She flashed another reassuring smile at the three women. "Malichai did speak at length with the detectives, so he can answer any of your questions," she added.

He sent her a look that promised retaliation but obediently took his plate and followed the three women to the tables. He noticed the talk was rather subdued as he moved through the dining room to get to the table the sisters considered "theirs." They'd taken over that particular table almost immediately and glared at anyone who dared to try to sit there. It was empty and the women put their plates down, Lorrie scooting her chair as close to Malichai's as she could without sitting in his lap.

"Are you dating Amaryllis?" Linda asked abruptly.

"She's my fiancée," he said, feeling a little desperate, but more than happy to claim his woman for protection.

"What?" Lorrie pulled back in her chair, glaring at Amaryllis, who was busy talking to Tania and Tommy Leven.

Malichai tried not to fixate on Amaryllis's smile. She had a beautiful smile. He wished he was there right next to her, or even out in the jungle with a million ants and termites crawling all over him — anywhere but at the table with the three sisters who looked like they would prefer to eat him rather than the delicious barbecued honeyed ribs and grilled corn on the cob.

"You're *engaged*?" Lexie demanded. "I had no idea. None of us did."

"Why would you know?" Malichai asked, picking up a rib, uncertain if one cut it up in polite company. He didn't think the women were all that polite. They seemed more interested in whether or not he was free than their fear of the recent events with Anna and Bryon.

"Well, you're so interesting," Lorrie said. "Absolutely the most interesting man we've run across since we've been here."

"Fascinating," Lexie added, leaning her chin into the heel of her hand and gazing at him.

He was unsure how he was supposed to respond to that so he muttered something that might or might not have been bullshit but was supposed to pass for "thank you." He bit into the rib and chewed. It tasted amazing. He was definitely marrying Amaryllis. She could cook for him for the rest of his life. He wasn't about to share with Ezekiel or Mordichai that she was such a good cook. They'd be over every day.

"Are you even paying attention?" Linda demanded.

Actually, no, but he would now so he'd never have to hear that strident, shriek note again. "I'm sorry." Malichai wasn't above using his injuries to get him out of trouble with the three barracuda sisters. "I'm recovering from an injury and the meds sometimes make me wander a little bit."

"An injury?" Linda echoed.

"I'm in the service. I've been in for several years and I've done quite a few tours overseas. A few months ago, I was shot several times and my leg's been operated on repeatedly. That's why Amaryllis and I haven't seen much of each other lately."

The three women exchanged a look he barely caught, but for some reason, it bothered him. He had silent exchanges with his brothers all the time, but found when other siblings did so, he was uncomfortable with it.

"What?" he asked, not wanting them to think he wasn't paying attention now. He continued to eat the ribs, wishing he'd taken a lot more. They were that good.

"It makes sense now. We're actually from this area. We own a house just up the road. We rent it out whenever there's a convention, especially one like Comic-Con. We make bank on the rentals and we usually stay with a friend. She's got company so we booked here. We've seen Amaryllis a lot around the neighborhood, but never you."

He shrugged. He'd found the less he explained, the fewer mistakes were made. Let them think what they wanted. They were coming to believe him if they hadn't before.

"Do a lot of people rent out their homes

during a large convention?" It would go along with the reason his brother had located one in the neighborhood and was able to rent it so quickly.

Linda shrugged. "If they're smart, they do. We make so much money, especially because we usually can stay at our friends' house rent-free." She took a bite of a rib, holding it delicately between her fingers. "Oh my God, you have to try these," she said to her sisters. "They're amazing."

Malichai couldn't have agreed with her more.

"This is our first murder-suicide," Lexie ventured as she picked up one of the ribs. "*Ever.* I liked Anne. I especially liked Bryon. He didn't seem the type to kill anyone, let alone Anne. Did you ever talk to them?"

She sounded sad. For the first time, Malichai genuinely felt sorry for her. He did for all three of them when he looked at their faces. They might be a little man-crazy, but they definitely felt the deaths of the couple, a large contrast to Henry Shevfield and his contract business.

"I did. I thought they were a very nice couple. I don't necessarily buy the entire murder-suicide verdict floating around. I prefer to wait and see what the medical examiner's office rules it. There's no reason

285

to jump to conclusions."

He kept eating and didn't notice the sudden silence around the table immediately. When he finally did, he looked up. Each of the three women were staring at him, eyes wide, mouths slightly open, the ribs in their fingers.

"What?" He lowered his last rib, reluctant to finish it off.

"If Bryon didn't kill Anna, who did? Because it was murder. Either Bryon did it or someone had to have murdered *both* of them," Lorrie whispered, looking around the dining room suspiciously, as if she might spot the killer right in the room with them.

"You don't really have to worry," Malichai said. "I don't know anything more than you do. I just thought they were a nice couple. So don't start worrying when there's no reason to."

"You don't know that. There could be a serial killer on the loose. Maybe this nutjob likes blond women. Anna was blond, so are we." Lexie looked around the room again. "There's an entire smorgasbord right in this room for a serial killer if he's looking for blondes to off."

"It's probably his ex-wife that started the entire thing. He hates her but can't kill her," Lorrie contributed. "So, he substitutes every blond woman about her age."

"Oh, for heaven's sake," Linda burst out. "You have to stop. Malichai, before they decide to write the book of the century on serial killers offing blondes, can you tell us anything about what's happening? The investigation? Did you talk to the cops?"

She knew he had. Amaryllis had told all three of the women that he had spoken at great length to the detectives the night before. She was trying to divert her sisters from their odd path of feeding each other fantasy horror stories.

He nodded slowly. "I did. The night they came to inform Marie that the Coopers were dead, I was with Amaryllis and we saw the flashing lights of the cop car and went down to let them in. Marie was there as well. They wanted to see the bedroom and cordon it off so no one could go inside."

"Looking for evidence," Lorrie whispered. "In case the serial killer had been in their room."

It was all Malichai could do not to roll his eyes. He lifted his gaze to Amaryllis, conveying to her with one look that he was considering murder, but whether it was hers or Lorrie's he was uncertain.

Linda glared at her sister. "It makes sense that they would want to make certain no one would go in their room. Did they tell you anything at all? Do they believe Bryon would really kill Anna?"

"I have no idea what they believe, Linda, they played their cards very close to their chest. Mostly the detectives asked questions about them. I think they wanted to know if the couple ever fought in front of us. I said no, because I never heard them fight. Did you hear them fight? Did Anna ever tell you Bryon was abusing her?"

The three women exchanged another long look. Again, it was Linda who answered. "No, she always said wonderful things about him. I really hate that it was her. She was such a nice person."

Again, Malichai felt sorry for them. Genuine sadness loomed over the table. He looked across the room to Amaryllis again. His woman. She put another tray of ribs on the long counter and then, using tongs, heaped several onto a plate, got her own food and took both plates to the small table where they always ate together.

"Do you think we're safe?" Linda asked.

"Absolutely, you should be safe," he said. What else could he say?

Something big was lurking under the surface, but he had no idea what. It most likely had something to do with the Ideas for Peace conference at the San Diego Convention Center. It was a guess, but several of Henry's victims could be tied back to the center itself. He was uneasy, very concerned that some faction had decided to hit the peace convention to make a statement and disrupt any real ideas that might be kicked around by the various planned panels.

"Do you plan on attending the convention?" he asked.

"We volunteer to work them," Lexie said. "That way we get in free. This one, we went back and forth about, but we're on the list. We'll do it."

"Boring," Lorrie said. "No movie stars. I love Comic-Con."

"Everyone loves it," Linda said. "This might be interesting. Informative."

"Political," Lorrie said with some disgust. "You know how much I hate politics. No one can agree on anything, so what's the point of it all?"

"To change that," Linda said. "Maybe get a climate of tolerance so everyone is willing to discuss issues rather than call each other names."

Lorrie rolled her eyes. "I find people who don't think the same way I do ridiculous. They're morons and can't see logic. How can you talk to that?"

Linda met Malichai's eyes and shrugged as if to say, "See what I deal with?" He gave her a faint grin. He'd met more than his share of Lorries.

He knew without turning around that Amaryllis was close. Her scent reached him first, that delicate fragrance that seemed to put him instantly into a heightened sense of awareness. Every nerve ending. Every cell in his body. He inhaled deeply, letting her settle into his lungs so he could carry her throughout his body.

"Hey, babe." Amaryllis bent down, her lips whispering along his neck.

Malichai wanted to cover that brief touch with his palm and hold it to him. He made himself sit very still, knowing all three women at the table were watching.

"I hope you've reassured everyone." Amaryllis flashed a smile at the other women. "I'm afraid I need him at my table now. We have so much business to discuss." Her long lashes swept down and then back up.

She was saving him. That was what she was doing. She didn't have business she needed to go over, and she wouldn't discuss the murders in the dining room where they could be overheard. This was about saving him from the three sisters she'd allowed to steal him out from under her. He'd never been more grateful in his life. He picked up his plate and silverware, standing as he did so.

"Thank you, ladies, for the good conversation. I hope you know you're safe," he added as he started away from the table.

Amaryllis tucked her hand into the crook of his elbow, slowing him down. "Thanks for looking after my man for me while I worked."

"Thanks for lending him to us," Linda said.

Lorrie and Lexie looked pouty, and neither said a word as they walked away.

Malichai looked down at the top of Amaryllis's head. Her hair was that silvery platinum blond that shone like a waterfall. His breath caught in his throat. What if someone was targeting blondes?

"Malichai?" Amaryllis looked up at him, her blue eyes like twin jewels. "What is it?"

He placed his plate very precisely onto the table and looked around the room, noting each person, pushing them into his brain so he would remember them. "Just something crazy the loony sisters came up with, excluding Linda. She's not nearly as loony as the other two."

"What did they come up with?"

"They were speculating that the killer is a serial killer after blondes. Anna's hair was nearly the same color as yours."

She slipped into the little chair facing the room. He always moved his chair to the side where the wall was. No one could come up behind him and he could see anything coming at him.

"You know that's crazy. Anna is the only woman reported dead. And they killed Bryon as well. He had dark hair. Honey, really, those women are just determined to scare themselves."

He nodded. He did know it was crazy. Ezekiel had interrogated a hit man who had confirmed that he had targeted several people connected to the San Diego Convention Center. This wasn't about a serial killer. This was about something altogether different. He just wanted his woman tucked safely away somewhere — like in another state.

"Your friends haven't been in. I thought they might come for the food."

That was blatant fishing. She wanted to know what had happened after she went back to the bed-and-breakfast. He couldn't blame her, but he couldn't tell her yet either. "Tonight, on the roof," he said.

She nodded. "What do you think of the ribs?" She pushed over the plate she'd heaped ribs on for him.

"I'm so in love with you, baby, we need to get married immediately. You don't just cook in the kitchen and bake, you actually grill."

She burst out laughing. "You're going to marry me because I can grill?"

"Sex first. I'm marrying you for the sex, baby. After that, for your awesome culinary abilities."

"You don't know if I'm good in bed or not, Malichai. I'm beginning to think the loony tunes have rubbed off on you."

Deliberately, his gaze drifted over her body and then moved back up to her face. "Babe."

She raised her eyebrow and picked up her corn on the cob. "That supposed to mean something to me?"

"I'll show you what it means tonight."

She blinked her feathery lashes at him and then started laughing. "You're so insane, I don't know when you're serious and when you're not."

"There's two things I never joke about, Amaryllis." He leaned toward her, looking her in the eyes so she knew he meant what he said. "I don't joke about sex, not when it comes to you. I'm absolutely serious about it. And there's never joking about marriage.

That's a sacred, serious topic."

She went very still, her long lashes sweeping down to cover her expression. He just laid it out on the table for her. He expected sex and marriage.

"I'm not a patient man when it comes to those things. I just discovered that about myself. I thought I could be, but I'm not. I want you wearing my ring. I want you in my bed. And I want it now, not some time in the future."

She regarded him as she chewed her corn, her gaze steady on his face. "Malichai." She swallowed the corn, those blue eyes finding the way inside him. "The fiancée thing wasn't true. We used it to get us out of trouble."

"You agreed, that's what I heard."

"I certainly did not. You didn't ask properly."

"If I'd asked properly you would have said no."

"Exactly," she confirmed. "I barely know you."

"So why would I ever be dumb enough to ask you when you've already agreed to be my fiancée? That would be stupid on my part and I assure you, you're getting an intelligent man."

"It's hardly intelligent to want to marry

someone you've known for a week."

"We're past the week."

She burst out laughing. He loved that laugh. It was crazy how much he loved to hear her laugh. He watched her face, the way it lit up, the way her eyes gleamed like sapphires.

"You're really serious, aren't you?"

"Yep. No going back now. It's off to the swamp we go. I'll build you a house you'll love, one all our own where we can raise our children and protect them from anything that might come along."

She sent him a small smile. "How could I possibly leave Marie?"

"You know already that I've arranged for Marie's debts to be paid and for money to go into a fund for Jacy's doctor bills. She'll be able to hire within the Navy community. We'll reach out to the wives and girlfriends and see if any of them want jobs first. We can even find a general manager, so it frees Marie up to travel with Jacy if she wants to. The bed-and-breakfast makes money. It's never been a problem. It's the amount of debt she's accumulated from hospital bills."

"How do you do all those things so fast?"

"I haven't gotten the workers for her yet. I haven't even had a moment to talk to her about it. And, Amaryllis, this doesn't hinge on whether or not you go with me. As soon as I got to know Marie, I knew I was going to take the load off her shoulders. There are GhostWalkers attached to the Navy. They instantly wanted to help. They'll go up the chain of command and figure out how best to get her the workers she needs. The right ones."

She was silent for a long time and then she looked down at her hands. "I wish I could find them. The two others that escaped when I did. Silver and Coral. They were nice girls. Strong. Smart. They would have loved it here and they would have loved Marie and Jacy. I think, given the chance, they would be perfect to run this place."

Malichai studied her face. No matter how much he reassured her, she was always going to feel responsible for the other women. They were grown, and they'd taken their chances just as she had. Most likely they were grateful to her, whether they'd succeeded or not in their escape.

"I can have the other GhostWalker teams try to find them, if you want. They'll have to do so very carefully so as not to alert Whitney that anyone is looking," Malichai offered.

She raised her incredibly blue eyes to his face and there was a look of wonder, of near adoration, which he didn't deserve but any man would want. "You would really do that for me, wouldn't you?"

"Anything in the world that I'm capable of giving you, Amaryllis," he assured.

She shook her head. "It's better if we leave them alone. Otherwise Whitney might lock on to them. He's so good at finding us."

"If you change your mind . . ."

"I know you don't like me to say so, Malichai, but you're so incredibly sweet. It's very hard to resist a man like you."

"Are you trying to resist me?"

She nodded slowly. "And you make it very, very difficult. I want to be with you, but it's so dangerous, Malichai. Whitney is so determined to get all of us back and if he finds out I'm with you, he'll send an army to try to get me. You have those little girls to protect. The wives of your friends. It isn't fair to them."

He stroked his fingers over the back of her hand. She had her palm curled around the edge of the table, gripping so hard, her knuckles turned white.

"Baby, we have a real stronghold out in the swamp because Whitney wants every single one of the women back. And the children. No matter what, we would have to protect them. It will be easier for us to protect you and the children if we live there, but if you insist on staying in San Diego, I'll find a way to protect us here."

She stared at him for a long time, her gaze moving over his face, studying his expression. The look in his eyes. She swallowed and shook her head as if she couldn't quite believe him. "You're serious. You would stay here with me knowing we were completely exposed."

"If the woman I love is here, then I'm here as well. I can guarantee that the moment Whitney knows you're here, he'll find a way to send me off somewhere on a mission to leave you alone. If that happens, I would want you to go to the compound in Louisiana. You would be protected there while I go wherever I'm sent."

She took a deep breath and shook her head again. "You're so . . . unexpected. I had no idea a man could be like you. The ones I've met have been terrible human beings."

"I don't think they were always terrible, Amaryllis. I think Whitney experimented on them in the same way he did me. The men he's got for his own private army are soldiers who failed the psych evals. They had some psychic abilities, but their psychological evaluations, for whatever reasons, red-flagged them and kicked them out of the GhostWalker program. Whitney talked them into his 'supersoldier' program. Unfortunately, he experiments on them, in much the same way he experimented on the female orphans he took from various institutions. They are flawed and of no use to him as soldiers, so he considers them useful only as experiments and fodder for testing against us."

"Those men are extremely aggressive and belligerent. They fight each other at the drop of a hat. When they fight, the others gather around and egg them on. I've seen the fight go so far that one of them dies. No one ever seems to feel bad about it either." A little shiver went through her and she wrapped her arms around her middle. "I don't ever want to have a child with a man like that."

"You aren't going to," Malichai affirmed.

"I tried to talk to Whitney once about it. I pointed out how deficient these men were, and did he really want to pass those traits on to his future soldiers. Whitney wanted to debate the point that his soldiers were lacking good traits. I knew immediately that there was no talking to him. He's continually researching, due to his mistakes trying to better his soldiers. He doesn't care if the women have flaws and he detests that the earlier teams have them. He's made up his mind that the newer teams won't, and that justifies anything he has to do to ensure those soldiers get the best of everything. That's when I made up my mind I'd get out of there. I hadn't yet been selected for his breeding program, but I knew it was only a matter of time. I planned my escape meticulously, because I knew if I didn't make it out the first time, I'd never have another chance."

He sat back in his chair. "I like that about you, Amaryllis. The fact that you don't just jump into things. You think them over."

She pounced on that. "Which is why I'm taking my time, not rushing into anything. You might think about doing the same. That way neither of us makes a mistake."

His gut tightened. She still didn't understand. He leaned toward her, his gaze wholly focused on her. "Baby, you aren't hearing me when I talk to you. I've been all over the world. In just about every country. I've looked for you. I've actively looked for you. I didn't think you actually existed. There is no way, after finding you, that I'm going to wait to tell you how I feel. I know the real thing because I saw so many others who weren't. You're right for me. You're always going to be right for me. Now, or ten years from now. It won't matter. We fit. I told you this already."

"You're making it very hard to resist. And you told me when you had a very high fever."

The door to the dining room was flung open so hard it slammed into the wall with a loud bang. Most of the diners had cleared out. The three Montclair sisters were still seated at their table, and they turned toward the door with loud shrieks. Burnell and Jay nearly flipped their table over. Craig Williams sat with a woman Malichai recognized as a guest who had come in the day before. She was part of the peace group meeting there at the bed-and-breakfast. Her name was Stefani Charles and she was from Finland.

Malichai turned his gaze toward the door and the man filling the frame. He was big. Pumped up. Malichai was a big man with roped, defined muscles on his upper body and thighs. He was naturally muscular, and his lifestyle had added to his frame. Enhancement of his DNA had also contributed. The man standing in the doorway, looking around the dining room with a furious expression on his face, was clearly a bodybuilder, but his enhancement wasn't the work he did with weights, it was with steroids.

"You know him?" Malichai asked, his voice low.

Amaryllis shook her head. "I've never seen him before. But he's the type Whitney would send after me."

"Lorrie! Get your ass over here!" The man roared the order. "I'm going to beat your dumb ass until you're black and blue and can't stand up."

Lorrie gave a little squawk and jumped up, nearly knocking over her chair. She looked genuinely frightened. Linda stood up slowly and put a hand on her sister's arm, pushing her gently behind her.

"You and Lorrie haven't been together for months, Tag. You know that. She has a restraining order against you. You can't come in here."

"Shut up, bitch. This isn't your concern. Lorrie, if you don't want anyone else to get hurt, get over here."

"I've called the cops, Tag," Lexie said. She stood too, stepping close to Linda to protect her sister from the huge man who had taken a couple of steps into the room, clenching his fists threateningly. She held up her cell phone. "They'll be here any moment."

Marie came in behind him. "Sir, I'm going to have to ask you to leave right now."

Tag swung around and took a threatening step toward Marie. "Shut the fuck up, bitch, or you're going to get hurt."

Malichai was immediately on his feet, Amaryllis moving to the right some distance from him. "That's enough," Malichai said, his voice low. "You can stop threatening the women. Marie is the owner and she's asked you to leave the premises. Lorrie has a restraining order against you, and the police have been called."

"Lorrie!" He spat the name. "You call her Lorrie? Are you fucking him, Lorrie? Is that why you left? Him?" He gestured at Malichai contemptuously.

"I left you because you beat me up every few days."

"All you had to do was stop being such a lazy bitch," Tag said.

He ignored Marie now that he had a real target. He didn't walk around the tables, he simply walked a straight line toward Lorrie, shoving or kicking tables and chairs out of his way. Diners got up hastily, moving out of his way, rushing toward the walls to stand there, phones out, recording his menacing progress.

Malichai stepped smoothly in front of Linda and Lexie. To his shock, Craig, Burnell and Jay also joined him. Malichai silently applauded them, but they were going to be in his way when the fight started, and there was no doubt in his mind that one or more of them was going to get hurt.

"Step back behind me," he said softly to them. "Keep Lorrie behind you and Linda. I need fighting room."

The three men moved quickly out of harm's way, but they did what he said, standing directly in front of the Montclair sisters, forming another line of defense. The few diners left in the room continued to press against the wall silently, trying to be as small as possible and not call attention to themselves.

"That's so you, Lorrie, probably blowing all of them so they'll come to your rescue when your real man comes to take your worthless ass home."

"If you feel that way about her, Tag, why don't you leave her alone?" Linda demanded.

Amaryllis had made her way around the room, signaling to Marie to keep back, and then she kept moving, her eyes on her target. Those eyes of hers, two bright blue jewels, had gone feral, predatory. Her eyes nearly glowed, turning silvery as she approached, coming in on Tag's left side.

Tag was almost to Malichai, his eyes burning with anger. He was used to being the biggest, baddest guy in the room. He didn't like that Malichai showed no fear or respect for him. He caught sight of Amaryllis closing in on his left.

"Another bitch, needing a lesson in manners," he snapped, and took one step toward her, swinging his fist.

Amaryllis ducked and kicked him in the belly, putting her entire body weight behind the kick. Tag grunted hard and doubled over for a moment, folding in on himself. When he straightened, there was fury in his gaze.

Fire exploded through Malichai. He moved almost before he thought. He caught Tag's shoulder, swung him around and smashed a fist into his face, using his enhanced strength without thinking about it. Bone crushed beneath his fist, the jaw and cheekbone shattering, even turning to powder in two places. Tag dropped like a stone just as the police burst into the room, weapons drawn.

Malichai stepped back, hands in the air. Amaryllis raised her hands and everyone behind them did the same. Tag was known to the local cops and they ignored those with their hands in the air, intent on securing him before he could fight them.

"He needs medical attention," one said, looking up at Malichai.

"She kicked him," Craig offered helpfully, pointing to Amaryllis. "Right in the gut. You should have seen it. He folded over like he was bent in half. Amaryllis, my hat is off to you. That was a thing of beauty."

The diners clapped their appreciation.

"I don't think her kick destroyed his face," the cop said. "He's having trouble breathing properly. Too much blood going down his throat."

Malichai tried to look innocent as Craig stepped up, in spite of the police surrounding Tag, so he could get a better look. Craig nodded in satisfaction.

"He was threatening everyone, but particularly Lorrie. Marie asked him to leave and Linda said there was a restraining order out against him, but he kept coming like he was going to kill her. It was brutal. We were prepared to try to stop him, but you see how big he is. Malichai hit him with one punch. That was all. To save Lorrie. It was self-defense for all of us."

The cop turned his head to look at Malichai, a frown on his face. "What did you hit him with?"

"His fist," Craig answered before Malichai could. "We all saw him."

"We have recordings. Video," one of the diners called out helpfully.

Malichai nodded and showed the cops his knuckles. "I just hit him with one punch. He's a big man and I didn't want him getting to Lorrie. He was threatening to beat her. He threatened all the women. He swung at Amaryllis. Maybe the adrenaline was rushing, I don't know. More likely, whatever he was on, and he was higher than a kite, might have weakened his bones. I think his jaw broke when I hit him."

"All of you stay right here in this room. I want to get your statements," one of the cops said and directed the medical people into the room to take care of Tag, who was continuously groaning, the sound coming out more like that of an animal in distress.

Amaryllis slipped under Malichai's shoulder, fitting tight, her arm circling his waist. "He was really jacked up on something. I know all the bodybuilders that work out around here. None of them act like that."

One by one each occupant of the dining room gave their account of what had happened. Amaryllis was fearful Malichai would be arrested, but he knew, even if he was, Ezekiel would be there immediately, and a call would come in from Major General Tennessee Milton and he would be walking away a free man. Of course he might be ordered home and he'd have to leave, but he resolved that he wouldn't leave without Amaryllis.

In the end, everyone in the dining room told similar stories, all included that they were afraid, not only for Lorrie but for all the women and even themselves. They maintained that both Amaryllis and Malichai had defended themselves as well as everyone else in the room.

They all slumped gratefully in seats around the largest table and Amaryllis and Marie brought out celebratory ice cream.

"I've never seen such a big man," Burnell said. "And so mean. He didn't have to be so mean to you, Lorrie."

She'd been crying and her makeup made little tracks down her face. Lexie and Linda were trying to wipe it off. Stefani pulled makeup wipes from her purse and offered them to the three women.

"Thank you," Lorrie said tearfully. "Thanks, all of you, so much for standing up for me. He won't stop. I've done everything the police have told me to do, but he won't stop."

"He gave her a broken arm," Lexie said.

"In two places," Linda added. "He knocked out two teeth. Broke her jaw once.

Gave her black eyes several times and a cut lip multiple times. He broke her ribs twice. She got away from him twice, but he'd always find her and drag her back. Then she came home to us and we got the restraining order against him. We knew he was still looking so we rented out the main house and couch surfed with friends for a few months. I don't know how he keeps finding her, but every few weeks, he calls on a number she just got, letting her know he's coming for her."

"He's going to have a very long stay in the hospital," Malichai said. "And probably several surgeries. Hopefully, by the time he is out from under his now-major medical problems, he'll forget all about you."

"I never thought I'd say I wanted a man to forget about me," Lorrie said, "but I totally do. I want him to forget he ever knew my name." She reached over and patted Burnell's hand. "You risked your life for me. All of you." Tears welled up again and spilled over. "I can't believe you did that for me. You don't even know me and I'm not always a nice person."

"Lorrie, stop crying," Linda said. "You're making your face all red and splotchy. Eat your ice cream."

"There's hot fudge to put on it, just use

the dipper," Marie added. She'd put a big pot filled with hot fudge in the middle of the table along with a bowl of chopped walnuts and two bowls of fresh whipped cream.

Amaryllis didn't hesitate. She scooped up hot fudge with the dipper three times. "I don't know what's wrong with the rest of you, but I'm not taking a chance she takes this away from us."

"Put like that," Lexie said and poured fudge over her ice cream and then passed the dipper to Stefani. "I love your accent. Where are you from?"

"Finland," Stefani said readily. "I am here for the peace convention, to represent my country. I'm meeting the others for the first time in person. We've worked hard to put this convention together. None of us had any idea that it would be so large we would have to have a place like the San Diego Convention Center."

"We're working the convention as volunteers," Lexie said proudly, forgetting just a few hours earlier she wasn't all that excited to do so.

"It's such a good thing," Craig said. "That's why I came. I'm attending it with a few friends I met online. I'm actually speaking on one of the panels."

"Really? Which one?" Stefani asked.

"My friends and I thought up a couple of cool ideas for games to promote a peaceful solution at the end of the day to make things work between people that don't believe the same ways." Enthusiasm edged into his voice. "They're the kind of games we like, very action packed and with lots of shooting, but at the end of the game, only the peaceful solutions the teams think of will help."

Malichai thought maybe the game sounded a little conflicted, but he hadn't heard the full presentation and it was an ideas convention, so any ideas were welcome. They would be thrown out to those attending to expand on and hopefully improve on. In any case, Craig had come out of his shell and interacted with those at the B and B in order to go to the convention.

"That sounds so cool, Craig," Lexie said, looking up at him and batting her lashes. "Do you want some of the hot fudge for your ice cream?"

He nodded and she scooped the dipper into the melted fudge and then poured it into his bowl. She smiled full-on at him. "Tell me when."

Craig looked as if he might faint at her attention. "That's perfect, Lexie." He hesitated before he said her name, half expecting her to protest.

Malichai smiled at Amaryllis and reached under the table for her hand. He pressed her palm to his thigh, his thumb sliding over the back of her hand. "I'll help clean up tonight. I have a surprise for you."

"I can clean up," Marie stated firmly. "You go have fun."

Malichai shook his head. "We wouldn't be able to have fun knowing we left you with the cleanup. It will go fast with the three of us doing it together."

"That sounds so dirty," Burnell said, winking at Jay. "The three of you doing it together."

"We got it," Malichai said, trying not to laugh.

Amaryllis and Marie exchanged a long look. Both were also attempting to keep a straight face.

Malichai gave them a fierce look. In an overloud whisper, he reprimanded them. "No laughing. That will only encourage him."

10

The stars were out in full force, so much so that the sky, in places, looked almost milky. Malichai stretched out on the thick futon mattress he'd gotten from Marie earlier. He had two pillows and a blanket, just in case his woman got cold. More likely she would have cold feet now that she'd had time to think about the things he'd told her. She had to know he was going to ask her to marry him. Well, not ask. He was already her fiancé.

He found himself smiling as he gazed at the stars. Amaryllis turned over onto her stomach, propping herself up on her elbows so she could look down at his face. "You're smirking."

"It's a smile, not a smirk." He might be smirking. He was already her fiancé and didn't have to actually ask her the big question. That was definitely worth a smirk.

"It's a smirk. But the futon mattress is

313

wonderful, so I'm letting the smirk go. Tell me what happened after I left this morning. It was really difficult to leave, by the way. If I'm ever in trouble for anything, that's a pass right there."

He scowled at her. "You can't negotiate that on the fly. That's an entire discussion."

"No, I think it's one of those things that just makes sense. If I do something really difficult that I don't want to do, I should get a pass the next time I screw up."

"Does it work both ways?"

"That would depend."

"Depend?" He turned toward her, one arm curling around her waist and dragging her body in close to his. Tightly. She felt warm and soft and all his. "What does that mean?"

"You can't say you don't like taking out the garbage, but if you do it, you get a pass."

"I *don't* like taking out the garbage. At. All. It smells, and the women are all about saving the damn environment, and that means sorting crap. So yeah, I take that out, I get a pass."

She started laughing. He was watching her face carefully and he saw it first in the curve of her lower lip, and then her lips parted, and the smile climbed to her eyes, lighting them a deep blue. Her face lit up and she

314

was laughing, throwing her head back, uncaring about anything else but the two of them and their ridiculous conversation.

He shifted his weight, curled his hand around the nape of her neck and brought her head down to his. The moment his mouth made contact with hers his world transformed. Fire licked at his skin. Electricity danced through his veins. Heat rushed to his groin, settled there and grew into a firestorm that fast. He pulled her tighter against him, his mouth commanding hers.

The hand at her waist slid up her back, finding bare skin beneath her top. The night was warm and as usual, she wore a tank top and the yoga pants she preferred for comfort at the end of a long day. He used the pads of his fingers to stroke long caresses over her skin while he devoured her. The more he kissed her, the more he was addicted to her taste. To her fire. He wanted more. He even needed it.

Reluctantly, he let her raise her head, both needing more air than he could give them. He kept his palm curled around her nape, his eyes looking into hers. Drowning there in her. "Baby, you know you're not getting away from me tonight."

"I'm not?"

That little twinge of amusement was back

in her voice, and those eyes of hers were lit like twin sapphires.

"You're not." He pressed a kiss to her forehead and reached with his other hand to find the little jeweler's box beneath the futon mattress. "Got this for you." He didn't know how other men did this sort of thing, but she might as well know he was awkward when it came to expressing himself when it counted. He might think poetry, but he wasn't about to say it out loud.

She looked at the box as if it might bite her.

"It's not a snake, babe."

Her gaze lifted to his. She didn't lift the lid.

"Babe. Seriously. It isn't going to bite you."

"It might." She took a deep breath and pushed the lid up. The ring was nestled in the velvet box, a glowing natural star sapphire to match her eyes, surrounded by small diamonds all set in a platinum band. Her breath caught in her throat.

Malichai found himself relaxing. She liked it. There was no question, he could see it on her face. She wanted that ring. He'd chosen the right stones and setting. He'd talked to the jeweler early in the week, looked at designs, stones and bands. He'd paid an enormous amount of money to get to the front of the line to have the ring made.

"Tell me what this is, Malichai." She flicked him a glance and then her gaze went right back to the ring.

"You're my fiancée. You need a ring on your finger. That's the one. Marie got me the right size, so it should fit."

"I'm your fiancée?"

He was beginning to get tense again. He took the box out of her hand, pulled the ring out and put it on her finger. "Yes." He said it firmly. "Apparently everybody in San Diego and the entire state of Louisiana knows but you."

He caught the hem of her tank and pulled it over her head. She wasn't wearing a bra and her breasts spilled out. He took advantage, cupping them in his palms and leaning in to cover her left nipple with his mouth, pulling her breast in deep while he kneaded the right one. She was soft, full and her skin tasted of exotic strawberries. He feasted, moving his body over top of hers, pinning her under him while he used the heat of his mouth, his tongue and his teeth to devour her. He tugged and rolled her right nipple and kneaded her breast, until he heard her soft little moan and her body moved beneath his.

He kissed his way over the top curve of her breasts, leaving his mark everywhere. Scraping with his teeth, nipping, soothing with his tongue, claiming every inch of her breasts for his own. Making certain there was no mistake whose mark was on her. It was primitive, but he felt more than primal. He felt almost feral. He didn't even care if it was the animal DNA in him or the man, his body was hard, hot and in urgent need. He wanted her more than he wanted to breathe.

Then his mouth was on her right breast and he used his teeth and tongue to drive her up, needing her wanting him with the same intensity he wanted her. He wasn't taking any chances with rejection. Not now, not ever. She was his woman. He knew that with absolute certainty. Her hips bucked and he swept his hands down her body, stripping the yoga pants from her, taking her panties with the stretchy material down her legs. He had to give up her breasts to take them all the way off.

He'd been smart enough to be prepared, already removing his boots and not bothering with a belt. He knew he was going to seduce her any way he could. Kisses seemed to work with her, and he always lost himself when he kissed her. She took him to another world where there was feeling. Pure feeling. No demons crept in. Nothing but sheer pleasure.

He kissed his way down the valley between her breasts so he could nibble on the underside curves, leaving his mark there as well. He explored her rib cage, taking his time, easily pinning her smaller body beneath his so he could find every inch of her with his teeth and tongue, with his mouth so he could continue to get that exotic flavor he craved. He spent time on her belly button, kissed his way down her belly to the blond curls that lay tight there like a little landing strip. He appreciated that. He made certain to find each color, the gold, the silver and platinum.

He reached down, caught his shirt and ripped it over his head, tossing it to one side. He wanted to be skin to skin, although right at that precise moment, all he could think about was feasting on her, gathering that taste of hers on his tongue. He gripped her thighs and pulled them apart, so he could wedge his broad shoulders between them.

"Malichai." She said his name. A little breathless. Ragged.

He loved the sounds she made. She wasn't

319

quiet, but she wasn't loud. Just soft moans and the occasional shattered cry of his name.

"I'm right here, Amaryllis. I'll take care of you. It's going to be good, I promise you." He was already nuzzling the inside of her thighs, the shadow along his jaw like sandpaper, arousing the nerve endings in her body even more.

He took one taste, just a long sweep with his tongue, and his entire body reacted. Dark desire slid down his spine. She flung out one hand and gripped the edge of the futon mattress, the other settled in his hair, fisted there, as if she might deny him what he wanted. He tightened his hold on her bottom, lifted her hips easily to him and settled his mouth over her.

Amaryllis's breath left her lungs in a rush of heat. It was all she could do not to scream. She was unprepared for the way it felt to have Malichai's mouth on her, his tongue and teeth. The assault on her scattered senses sent her almost into a panic. Nothing had ever felt so good, yet at the same time, it was a takeover. A complete, absolute takeover.

Malichai held her still easily, his strength enormous. There was no letup in him. He drove her closer and closer to something huge. She could feel the tension coiling in her tighter and tighter, the pressure unrelenting. Fear slid through her, creeping down her spine and spreading through her, adding to the nerve endings that were screaming with arousal. Whatever was waiting, crouching there, swelling out of control, growing so large it was like some dark wave — a tsunami — threatening to engulf her, take her over . . .

Then it hit, moving through her, swamping her senses, drowning her in pleasure, spreading through her body like a wild, out-of-control sweeping entity. Alive. Fierce. Pounding through her. Taking her mind and throwing it into complete chaos. She didn't know if her eyes were open or closed, but the stars were brighter than ever, bursting behind her eyelids while rockets went off. Little bursts of color scattered across her vision.

Then he was stripping, and she caught a glimpse of his body. He looked chiseled. Hard as a rock. His chest and abdomen nothing but sheer muscle. His cock impressive and a little intimidating.

He stroked his hand from her throat, down her breasts to the little curls on top of her mound. She pulsed with need, desperate for him to be in her, even while she was

321

a little frightened that he wasn't going to fit.

"Shh, sweetheart. It's going to be all right, baby."

His voice was like black velvet, sliding over her skin, caressing her, setting off another round of sparks as his fingers slid into her. She couldn't help responding, riding them, her needs overcoming any sense of embarrassment. Any inhibition. He tore at the condom package with his teeth and quickly rolled it over his heavy erection.

Amaryllis had no idea she was making any sounds at all. She heard them now, those soft little whimpers that meant anything and everything from fear to desperation. She felt the broad flared head at her entrance. Hot. Slick. Velvet and firm at the same time. Large. Lodging in her. His gaze burned into her, branding her, claiming her. She loved the way he looked at her. So focused. So completely hers. There was nothing else in his world at that moment, only her.

He didn't surge into her but rather invaded gently, persistently, when her tight muscles tried to refuse him entry. Her breath caught. She was somewhere between real pleasure and real pain. She couldn't figure out which it was, but she knew she didn't want him to stop.

"Relax for me, baby," he encouraged. His hand stroked her belly with that patient gentleness she was coming to associate with him.

She made an effort to do as he instructed, and he slipped in a couple more inches. It felt scary and wonderful. The burn was exquisite — it was also terrifying and painful. She felt a part of him. The cool night air teased at her body like fingers sliding over her skin. Above her was his face, that beloved face, his eyes looking down at her with a mixture of lust and something else, an emotion she had never believed in, but now was beginning to accept might actually exist — in this man.

Amaryllis felt overwhelmed with a sudden rising emotion she could only identify as love, and that scared her to death. She had never expected to feel so much for another human being. For a moment, he leaned down to kiss her. When he did, he surged forward. She felt that bite of pain and then he was fully in her, buried deep, stealing her breath and her heart.

"Kiss me back, baby," he whispered against her lips. "You're freaking out for no reason at all. You're safe with me."

"Am I?" She needed the reassurance because having him in her body, letting him take her heart and soul, was terrifying. "You have to be real, Malichai."

"I'm more real than you can imagine, Amaryllis."

She didn't have to imagine anything, not with his body buried so deep in hers. Not with his mouth taking control of hers. She couldn't help but give herself to him. He began to move as he lifted his head, at first gently. Flashes of fire spread through her with every thrust of his hips. She couldn't breathe with the flames reaching to her lungs and licking over her skin.

He seized her hips and she felt every one of his fingers gripping her tightly. He thrust faster. Harder. Deeper. It felt as if streaks of lightning raced through her body, spreading flames everywhere. Every hard jolt sent her breasts swaying, a sexy thrill that added to the sensual sensation.

He lifted her bottom, holding her still while he plunged into her. Again and again. Over and over. The breath rushed out of her lungs, leaving them empty and burning raw. Everything in her seemed to center in one place, the tension building and building. Winding tighter and tighter. Coiling deep. She couldn't breathe. Couldn't scream. Couldn't think.

There was only Malichai in her world.

Malichai's body moving in hers, creating that fiery friction that scored through her until she was nearly sobbing his name. Her fingers found the mattress, digging deep to hold on to some sort of reality. Streaks of fire raced from her sex to her breasts, dozens of bright hot arrows, shooting through her body. All the while her center just coiled tighter and tighter until she thought she might go insane.

She felt his cock expanding, pushing at her tight sheath. She could feel his heart beat as he stretched her impossibly. It was so sexy, just like his face, those sensual lines carved deep. He kept moving in her, an impressive piston, surging so deep that each thrust robbed her of her ability to think straight.

"Let go for me, baby," he coaxed. "Just let go. I'm right here. Let go for me."

She had to, there was no other choice. It was terrifying, like the highest roller-coaster ride she could imagine, where that drop might be the very end of her, or the greatest thrill of her life. She fought for a breath, and looking into his eyes, let her body take over completely.

The tsunami was far bigger than the last one he'd induced, rushing over her like that tidal wave that refused to be held back. One swell followed the next, each one larger, stronger, much more powerful, her body rippling with pleasure. Colors sparkled behind her eyes and she felt herself being flung out somewhere else, floating in a sea of sheer indulgence. Sensual. Sexy. Perfect.

She took him with her, clamping down on his cock like a vise, the friction exquisite, demanding everything from him. Every last drop. She wanted it all, everything he had, and he gave it to her. She felt the hot splash of his seed, inside that glove, that was how tight the fit, the stretch in her muscles he created. She cried out as he emptied himself into her, as her body responded to the fierce jerking and pulsing of his with more hot, passionate shocks.

He lay over top of her, fighting for breath, his face pressed against her throat. She could feel his harsh breathing, matching her own ragged desperation. It seemed like forever before he kissed her throat and then pulled slowly out of her with clear reluctance. She hissed as another exquisite wave rushed over her. Any little movement seemed to trigger an orgasm, not that she was complaining, but it was rather shocking.

Amaryllis stretched, her eyes on him as he tied a knot in the condom and set it aside before turning back to her. She lay looking up at the stars, her body still rippling occasionally, sending little shock waves through her. Malichai remained on his stomach, his arm around her hips, pillowing his head on her belly. His thick, dark hair teased her stomach, adding to the sensations moving through her body, until all she could feel was bliss. Sheer bliss. She hadn't known a body could feel that way and continue to feel it even afterward.

Her fingers idly slid through his hair, massaging his scalp. "Malichai, do you really want me to marry you? As in the real thing? A forever kind of thing?"

No one had ever really wanted her, not for herself, her own sake. Whitney had wanted to conduct his experiments on her, even as a child. She didn't have a sisterhood, because Whitney had separated the girls, afraid they would be loyal to one another, not to him. He was a monster. There was no being loyal to him. He might have been her only parent figure, but she had known, early on, that something was very wrong with him. Some of the other girls hadn't figured it out for a long time and she felt bad for them. They had needed a parent. She might have needed one, but she had come to the conclusion, very early, that Whitney was not that person.

Malichai lifted his head and pressed kisses over her belly. So many. Each found its way inside her. His lips were warm and soft, yet so firm, sliding over her skin like living flames. His teeth nipped, stinging deliciously, and then his tongue stroked, easing that little ache that seemed to trigger more explosions inside her.

"Forever is what I'm asking of you, Amaryllis. I want you to come home with me, marry me, stay with me no matter what happens. To do that, you're going to have to trust me." He rested his chin on her belly, his eyes that peculiar shade of Florentine gold. When his eyes were that color, his gaze seemed to burn his name right into her bones, branding her his.

"I trust you." She thought she did . . . She did . . . It was difficult.

"You're getting there," he said. "I expect, after Whitney, trusting anyone would be hard, but trusting a man you barely know would be next to impossible."

"Not impossible. I watched you all the time, Malichai." She had. Every move he made. Every word he'd said. If there was a stalker, it wasn't Malichai. It had been her. From the moment he'd offered to fix the dishwasher, inserting himself into Marie's and Jacy's lives, she'd observed him, needing to protect her friends from possible trouble.

She knew how he moved. How he turned his head. What he looked like when he took a breath. His smile. God. His smile. How could anyone resist his smile? It came slowly and then lit those golden eyes. Sometimes his eyes seemed to be the color of whiskey, then a deeper amber, and finally, finally, her favorite, that Florentine gold. She loved that burn as the flames licked over her skin and went bone deep. That was when she felt the closest to him.

"Are you beginning to think I'm trustworthy?"

He smiled at her and her heart seemed to melt while her stomach did that slow somersault that always made her go damp and needy. Her hand found his hair as he lay his cheek on her belly again. She liked the feel of the scratchy shadow on his jaw. It was sexy. Sensual. A burn that was real and had that same effect of setting off a reaction in her body. This time, she wanted to touch him. Explore his body. Only she couldn't move. She was too exhausted. She liked just lying there feeling sated and happy.

"Amaryllis?" He turned his head to nip her firm skin.

She jumped and then laughed. She'd never had anyone to share an evening like this with. Both lay naked under the stars, the cool night breeze fanning their overheated bodies. Talking quietly together. Was that what couples did? Was it small things that wove those relationships tighter? Made them stronger? She didn't know, but she loved being with Malichai just like this. Talking softly to him. Getting his reassurance. Giving him the same.

"I trusted you with my body, Malichai. And I'm letting you steal my heart, so I'd have to say you're in there. I definitely have reached a point where I trust you."

"Enough to go home with me?" he pressed.

"I said I would. As long as I'm not leaving Marie and Jacy in a bad way, I'll go."

"And you'll marry me?"

She found herself laughing just for the sheer joy of being with him. "I said I would."

"You didn't sound like you meant it."

"I meant it. You just want to hear me say it over and over."

"That too."

They both laughed. She liked the way they sounded together. Almost as if they were creating music together.

"And you really do want children, Amaryllis? I know we sort of talked about this, but it wasn't like you knew I was asking because it mattered to me."

She stilled. She loved Jacy, but she wasn't Jacy's mother. "You know I never had a mother, Malichai."

"I didn't either. Or at least mine didn't count. But I want children. Maybe a dozen."

She burst out laughing again. "You do not."

"Okay, I led with that so you wouldn't think three or four was a huge number."

"Are you trying to make me throw you off the roof?"

"I'm trying to tell you I want a family with you. I want to be close to my brothers and their children so we're the best aunt and uncle that ever lived. I want to raise the children strong, so my daughters are like you, always thinking, always using their brains, and when they have to use self-defense, hands, feet or weapons, they don't hesitate. You didn't hesitate. I loved that."

Again, he turned his head, so she felt the brush of the bristly shadow on his jaw and then the sweep of his lips before his teeth teased at the skin of her belly. "My little warrior woman. You really can do it all. Cook. Give me children. And fight. You're damned amazing."

She laughed, trying not to move her legs restlessly. That burning had gone through her skin to burrow deep. The smoldering fire seemed to be building into something much stronger. "Roll over, Malichai." Desperation was beginning to set in.

He did so immediately. "Sorry, baby. Was I too heavy?"

Malichai lay on his back. He turned his head toward Amaryllis, drinking in the sight of her. She didn't answer him but instead scooted down until she lay in the position he'd been in — her head on his belly, her arm across his thighs, one hand on his hips, in close to his groin. He tried not to feel her fingers as she began to idly trace along his hip bone and then the muscles of his abdomen. Every time she traced around one, the muscles rippled, as if they found her fingers as sensual as he did.

"You don't mind that I can fight?"

Her breath was warm on his skin. Every word sent an intriguing puff of air along his abdomen, so close to his groin. His cock stirred. There was no stopping it. He felt the broad head nudge along her throat as if asking for entrance. Her breasts pushed tight against his thigh, her nipples two hard peaks.

"Why would I mind? You'll need to be able

to fight. Sooner or later, enemies will come. I like knowing I can have confidence in my partner, that she'll be right there with me when we defend our home, our children and our extended family."

It was a little difficult to talk when she turned her face into his belly, nuzzling him, her tongue tracing his muscles the way a paintbrush might. He stayed very still, but his cock didn't. It just kept growing. Getting longer. Thicker. Harder. His heavy sac tightened. He hadn't thought it possible so soon, but he was already feeling heat spreading through him. That relentless ache building. His cock pushed against the underside of her chin.

Amaryllis tilted her head just a scant inch or two and her warm breath seemed to engulf him. Malichai closed his eyes. He enjoyed every second, yet at the same time, he wanted to take control, catch her hair in his hand and push his cock deep into her mouth. He forced himself to be patient.

Her fingers moved from his belly to his balls, sliding over them, shaping them, stroking, a whisper of touch that left behind flickering points of flames dancing over his sac, feeding the heat inside. Then she was cupping his balls, rolling with equal gentleness. Her body shifted and his breath left his lungs in a rush he couldn't control. Her tongue licked up and over each of the balls, and then her lips sipped delicately. Tasting him.

She lifted her head. "You're like velvet, did you know that?"

He didn't. "No, baby." He dropped his hand to her head because he couldn't help himself. He needed more. Much more, but he wanted her to have her exploration, if that was what she was doing. It had to come from her. He wasn't going to take anything she didn't offer him. No matter how much he wanted or needed her mouth, he refused to give in to the urgent demands of his body. Or push her head down over him where he needed her mouth to the point he might not survive if she didn't give him that immediately. "I didn't know."

"Well, that's how you feel. Just like velvet. And your skin tastes good. Sort of wild and masculine, like a rare, exotic flavor that was created just for me."

Before he could reply, she turned her head and licked along the base of his shaft. Her tongue felt just like the velvet she claimed his balls were. She curled it and teased around the very base, over and over, lapping, stroking, even flicking. The sensations were amazing. All the while, her fingers were sliding over his balls, stroking those long caresses that threatened to drive him insane.

"You really do taste good, Malichai."

"I'm glad you think so, Amaryllis, because what you're doing is hot as hell."

She licked up his shaft as if it were ice cream. "I can see you feel that way. I love how responsive you are to me. I don't have to ask if you like something."

He found himself smiling. "Yeah, my cock is letting you know, baby. Keep it up."

She already was, the tip of her tongue sliding under the crown, finding that little vee that had his cock pulsing, jerking hotly, his heart beating furiously along the heavy vein. She licked over the broad head, finding the little drops leaking, telling her she was doing everything he loved. She spent time, lapping them up and then, without warning, her mouth engulfed the entire crown.

His hips bucked. He had to fight for a single breath of air. She might just kill him. Her mouth was hot and moist. She looked hot as hell with her lips stretched around his cock. She'd rolled all the way onto her belly, her legs in between his, her upper body lying on his thighs. She sucked hard and then her tongue lashed and curled, slid up and down and around the sensitive head of his cock. There was no rhythm to what she was doing, no way to guess what was coming next. She simply did whatever she wanted in her exploration.

Then her mouth was off him and she lapped at him, over his balls, up his shaft, under and over the crown. This time she took him deeper, taking in a little more of him. Her fist curled around the base of his shaft while her mouth once more drove him to the point where he thought his head would explode.

When she took her mouth off him again, he growled. Her gaze jumped to his face and he swore there was a hint of laughter in her eyes.

"Do you know how sexy it feels to have you in my mouth? You're so heavy on my tongue. And hot. Scorching hot. I love your taste and texture. I could do this all night. What would you think about that?"

The idea of lying in bed with her, her mouth around his cock, feeding it to her, feeling her sucking while they just lay together . . . She was conjuring up erotic images with her talk of taste and texture and wanting to suck on his cock all night. Hell. He growled again because he couldn't actually find words to say.

"Is there something you want, honey?" She sounded innocent. A little too innocent.

"I want your mouth right back where it was." He didn't mind in the least letting her know what he wanted. He fisted her hair and pulled her toward his cock. "Suck hard, baby, and do that thing with your tongue. It drives me crazy."

She laughed as he all but pushed her head down over his cock, forcing his way into her mouth. The vibration ran up his shaft and teased the sensitive crown. He loved looking at her lips stretched so wide around him. She hollowed her cheeks and sucked hard. The sensation was exquisite. Perfection. Just as the vision was.

"That's it, baby, use your fist. Tighter. Pump up and down." She was fast at learning because she listened, and it mattered to her that he was loving what she was doing to him.

Her tongue moved on him again and he couldn't help but use his hips to inch farther into that hot, tight tunnel. He was careful, but he couldn't stop the movement, rocking into her, pulling back just enough to let her breathe and then pushing in again. He didn't try to go too deep, but he felt that suction, drawing his balls up. The slide of her tight fist with one hand while she continuously caressed his sac with the other brought chaos to his brain.

"Baby, you have to stop," he tried to warn her. "I'm going to blow big, and your first time you don't want to swallow. Most women don't like it."

She didn't let up and he was already so far gone there was no stopping. His seed boiled up and rocketed out like a volcano. His cock jerked over and over. Hot seed sprayed into that hot cavern. He felt her mouth moving. Felt her throat working. His cock just kept trying to find more to give her before it finally lay peacefully on her tongue.

Amaryllis's long lashes lifted, and he found himself looking into those blue-flamed eyes. He realized he was still gripping her hair tightly in his hands. She smiled around his cock. He pulled out slowly, savoring the sensation as he dragged over her tongue.

"Baby, you didn't have to do that."

"I wanted to," Amaryllis stated. She sat up and looked around.

He snagged the water bottle and handed it to her. "That was indescribable, but if you want to repeat that at any time, I'm more than willing."

She smiled at him, her blue eyes dancing. "It was rather fun. I really do like the way you feel and taste, Malichai. And respond."

He was good with that because he was addicted to her taste and scent. To her body. Every part of her body.

"Are you okay?"

"I felt like you got to explore. It was only fair that I had a turn," she explained.

"Anytime, baby." He held out his hand and she passed him the water bottle. "We need to get back inside before it gets much later. You need to get some sleep. I'd like you to sleep in my room tonight. With me."

She moistened her lips with her tongue. "I don't know, Malichai. I've never really slept with anyone before. This sleeping together might not be such a good idea."

"We're getting married, remember? You're going to snuggle up next to me every night after we're married. That's kind of non-negotiable."

"Is it?" She knelt up on the futon mattress, her hands going up to push back her hair. "That was never disclosed before I agreed to marry you. I feel like that could negate all business transactions."

She was beautiful, the moonlight shining down on her like a spotlight, highlighting her soft skin and the curve of her breasts. He tackled her, taking her back down to the mattress.

"It's a hostile takeover, then, baby."

Her laughter spilled over, bright and filled with light. Even her eyes danced at him, sending his stomach on a roller-coaster ride. He held her down easily, his larger body blanketing hers. She raised her head off the mattress so she could brush kisses over his chest.

"Is that even in the rule book? I feel like you're making new policies up to benefit yourself."

"And your point is?" He took advantage, feasting on her breasts, ignoring all the little squeals and writhing she did.

"My point is, you're cheating."

"Have you ever heard the expression 'All's fair in love and war'? Because this is love, and if you don't marry me, it's also going to be war."

"Hmm." She pretended to think it over, but she cradled his head to her breast and let him have his way.

He used his tongue and teeth and then his fingers, taking full advantage. He loved the feel and shape of her, just as she loved his cock. Those full curves took his mark easily, and when his hand slid to the junction between her legs, he found she was once again slick. He loved that her breasts were so sensitive she would immediately get ready for him.

He lifted his head and looked down at her. "What's the verdict?"

"I forgot the question." She laughed, the sound rueful and joyous at the same time.

"I want you sleeping in my bed with me."

"I'll get in your bed, but I don't know about sleeping. I swear I'll try, though."

He was definitely falling in love with her. "Hot bath first. Let's get moving." He stood and began to put items on the tray and then gather their clothes.

"We can't go naked, Malichai," she protested, laughing all over again.

"We can't? Who are we going to run into? Just wrap the blanket around you. I'll take the sheet. Be daring, baby."

"You're not kidding, are you?"

"No. I don't see what the big deal is. You have my ring on your finger and it's no one's damn business what we do or where we do it. Just put the blanket around you and we'll hurry to the room. The only one I'd worry about is Jacy, and she's in bed asleep. Everyone else pretty much knows about sex, and if they don't, it's time they did."

Amaryllis caught up the blanket and wrapped it closely around her. He took the sheet and wrapped it around his hips, making a sarong out of it. She rolled her eyes.

341

"That's cheating."

"How is this cheating? I need my hands free to carry the tray." He strode to the door leading back into the house.

"You planned that all along. I can't get away with that because women aren't supposed to show their breasts."

"Which, by the way, few men find reasonable. I wouldn't mind if every woman in the world decided to show her breasts. It would make for a very nice world."

She had to jam the corner of the blanket into her mouth to muffle her laughter as she shuffled down the hall on bare feet. He loved watching her. The way her eyes lit up. The way she looked wrapped in the ridiculous blanket, tight across her little ass and drooping around her shoulders, leaving them bare, with just that hair of hers falling down her back. The shuffle was probably the cutest thing ever, but he wasn't a man who used words like "cute" or "adorable," so he didn't say them aloud.

Once in his room, he went through the door leading to the bathroom he shared with Craig Williams. Craig was meticulously clean and Malichai appreciated that about him. He locked that side of the bathroom and ran his woman — his fiancée — a bath. She leaned against the door, watching him, those blue eyes fixed on his face. The laughter had faded and she looked very serious.

"What is it, baby?" He kept his voice gentle, afraid she might be considering reneging on her word now that the beauty of the orgasms had faded. He might have to handle the next few minutes with extreme care.

"You are an amazing man, Malichai, and I can't believe you chose me. When did you know? Because you seem to have been set on this path from the very beginning."

This could be dangerous ground since Whitney was known for pairing couples. "I knew when I first laid eyes on you. I observed the way you were with Marie and Jacy — the way you worked, letting Marie have so much extra time with her daughter even though it meant you worked long hours. I couldn't help but see how protective you were of them, and I wanted that for myself, for my children, for Wyatt's children and Trap's. For all of them living in the compound near us. I know that sounds selfish, but hell, baby, you're like this fresh summer breeze that can move mountains when you go from breeze to hurricane force winds. Not to mention, I find you damned sexy. Who wouldn't want that?"

She gave him a small smile. "From time to time, I'm going to have to ask you that question again. I hope you don't mind. It's just that I think you're this extraordinary man and having you choose me — maybe fall in love with me — want me as the mother of your children . . ." She shook her head. "That's almost too incredible to believe."

"That's Whitney feeding you bullshit, baby." He crossed the short distance between them and pulled her into his arms, uncaring that the blanket fell to the ground. He kissed her. Hard. Meaning it. Wanting her to feel everything he felt for her. He'd gone from physical attraction to love in a very short time for a very good reason, and she was in his arms, her mouth moving under his.

11

Malichai lay in bed, staring up at the ceiling, Amaryllis cuddled close to his body. He hadn't been a man who ever slept with a woman close. Or at all. It wasn't his thing, until right then. He needed her close to him. When she'd gotten up and said she was going back to her room, he hadn't been able to stand the idea of the two of them apart.

But still . . . there was something nagging at him. It just wouldn't leave him alone. His brain refused to shut down, alarms whispering, looping through his mind over and over. The warnings weren't loud, just a soft background noise that refused to be quiet. Something was wrong. Something was off and he needed to figure it out. He knew it wasn't immediate, no one was threatening them, but once he felt this kind of warning, he knew it was only a matter of time before trouble was on his doorstep. He also needed to tell Amaryllis what they had learned from interrogating Henry Shevfield. He wasn't looking forward to that conversation.

"Malichai?" Amaryllis's voice was soft, a barely there sound, as if instinctively, she was aware of the need for silence. "Can't you sleep?"

He stroked a caress over her hair, trying not to get lost in the feel of silk. Her head was against his bare chest and the slide of silk over his skin sent hot blood rushing to his groin. He'd been enjoying the sensation, liking that his woman, even in her sleep, could arouse his body the way she did, but there was that whisper in his mind that something wasn't right. Something was off. Maybe he just needed to have that difficult talk with her he didn't want to have. He knew better, but it was one more thing . . .

"I can go back to my room," she offered. "You're not used to sleeping with anyone." There was a hint of satisfaction in her voice.

"Go back to sleep, baby. I think I'm just going to take a quick walk around the house and make certain everything is quiet." She wasn't getting out of sleeping with him, no matter how hard she tried.

She wrapped her arm around his hips. "Talk to me, honey. What's got you uneasy?"

"I don't know. That's the problem. Something's nagging at me —" He broke off, because what was it? Something silly, really. "How did Tag know Lorrie was here? Those women were actually very smart covering their tracks the way they did. They gave up their place, renting it out so they don't lose anything, and couch surfed, so they didn't leave a trail. This was the first time they paid for a place to stay. Maybe he had someone watching for credit card activity, but that seems a little over his head."

Amaryllis sat up slowly. She stayed close to him, fitting her body against his hip. "No, they actually paid cash. Marie told me because it's extremely unusual. They paid for a month's stay for the three of them."

He heard the sudden concern in her voice and it spurred his alarm even more. "So, if they paid cash, did one of their friends give them up to Tag? If so, why?"

"What are you thinking, Malichai? Are they in more danger? What?"

"I'm thinking I don't like anything I don't have answers for, that's all. I didn't mean to alarm you, babe. I'll just take a look around, maybe contact my brothers and see what they've seen watching the place. Fortunately, no one knows they're close by."

"You really think something's wrong, don't you?" she challenged. "You still haven't told me what happened when you went swimming. You've been avoiding talking about it."

He sighed. He'd known he was going to have to tell her and she was going to freak out on him. Instinctively, he reached down and pulled her up and over him so he could roll over and pin her beneath him. Immediately, suspicion etched a little frown into her face.

"So, it's bad."

"Yes. I think so. Very bad. Dozer got something right. Diver tried to kill me. We got him in our trap and took him to a place Zeke rented to talk to him."

She made a face. "I can imagine."

"Zeke can be intimidating without having to touch anyone," Malichai assured. "I didn't get anywhere near the jerk and it was a good thing. He was a local. A hit man. He didn't do Anna and Bryon, but he happily told us of several others he'd done for the same people, all over the last two years. He was also contracted to create a diversion for those same people by killing the owner of a bed-and-breakfast, her daughter and her manager. Then after the cops were inside, he was to burn the place to the ground, drawing all the cops and fire engines there."

He felt the breath leave her body. Her face went white there in the darkness, so she looked almost transparent.

"You're talking about here. Us. Marie, Jacy and me. He's supposed to kill us and burn this beautiful place down."

"And he didn't even so much as flinch talking about killing a child when he's married and has children of his own," Malichai said.

"You should have told me right away."

"There's no immediate threat. We're setting up a sting."

"You can't know there's no threat."

"He's dead. He was stupid and made a try for Zeke. Rubin is going to be arrested on suspicion of killing Anna and Bryon, and then released because he didn't do it, but there will be a write-up in the paper portraying his past as being murky. Whoever these people are that hired Henry Shevfield will need another local fast. We're hoping they'll contact him, especially because he's staying here."

"They won't fall for that. It's too easy."

"Sometimes, easy is best." He brushed kisses in her hair and then dribbled more down the side of her face.

"Stop trying to change the subject."

Malichai rolled her over fast, so she was on top again, his mouth on hers, creating fire, igniting a storm between them. He felt it in his belly, hot and wild, in his groin, rising like the tide. She tried to sit up and he wrapped his arm around her waist and pulled her down over top of him again. She landed, chest to chest, her breasts pushing against his bare skin. He loved the feel of her. He could lie there all day with her body sprawled out, arms and legs on either side of him, surrounding him with her heat. Her softness.

She lifted her head, her blue eyes colliding with his. There was laughter there. "How easily you distract me."

"Clearly I haven't distracted you properly." His mouth took hers again, his palm curling around the nape of her neck. He loved kissing her and he took his time. A slow assault on her senses. On his. Building the fire until it poured down their throats into their bellies. Until it spread like a wildfire out of control through their veins. Until he could almost — almost — ignore that warning that had ratcheted up a notch and nagged at the back of his mind.

He broke the kiss and once again found himself staring into her eyes. "I love kissing you." He rubbed the bare cheeks of her ass. He loved that as much as, or more than, staring into her eyes.

"I know you do. The feeling's mutual."

She shifted her weight and casually reached for her tank top. "Babe, I can tell when you're uneasy. You're a soldier. You think something isn't right, we don't ignore that."

"Are you feeling it at all?"

She shook her head. "I feel you. Your mouth. Your cock. I'm a little sore, but in this wonderful, delicious way. I'm still wrapped up in us. But if something's wrong, honey, we need to find out what it is in order to protect everyone at this inn. Marie can't afford to lose the place, not even with you helping her so much. And she does love it."

Amaryllis pulled her tank top over her head, covering her breasts, much to his dismay. She rolled to the very edge of his bed and nabbed her yoga pants. He was a little in love with those pants, especially when, like now, he knew she wasn't wearing anything beneath them. The stretchy material clung to her curves lovingly, drawing attention to the shape of her bottom and her slender legs.

Malichai slid to the opposite side of the bed and reached for his clothes, no longer fighting the nagging whisper that something wasn't right — wasn't adding up. He had to block out everything and just hear it. That was how he'd stayed alive for years. Now he had Amaryllis to look out for. And the bed-and-breakfast. He told himself it wasn't immediate, but it was still a warning. He had to get past what she did to his body and listen to the warning system that was always set to alert him to possible threats.

Malichai pulled his clothes on slowly, sorting through the dozens of questions in his head. It always came back to two. How had Tag found Lorrie? Why was that answer so important?

"Do you want me to make us some coffee?" Amaryllis asked.

Malichai glanced at his watch. He loved Amaryllis's coffee. Everything she did was done with the utmost care for detail. Part of the reason her food was so delicious was because she cared about the person eating it. "Will Marie be up? Who's working on breakfast?"

"That would be me. I have to start work in another hour. Marie has the day off, remember? She's taking Jacy to a couple of appointments and then they're going to catch a show. Marie always likes to end the day with something very fun for Jacy, especially if they have numerous doctor appointments."

"Smart woman. Coffee would be great, baby. I'm going to walk around and see if I can figure out what's going on that's bugging me."

"I'll do the same. I'll try to puzzle out how Tag could have found Lorrie. You know, Malichai, we can't always rule out coincidence. It does happen. It's that unexpected thing that you don't count on that trips you up sometimes. Tag might have been at the beach and seen her. Maybe one of his friends did."

Malichai wanted to know what unexpected things had tripped Amaryllis up before she'd found her way to Marie, but he decided it was best to let that go for another time. She'd talk to him in time and if not, he'd coax it out of her when she was more comfortable sharing. Like him, she compartmentalized her life. He couldn't blame her when he did the same thing.

"I'm not a big believer in coincidence. Lorrie and Lexie seem like they might have fluff where their brains are supposed to be, but Linda is always thinking. She wouldn't have allowed either of her sisters to go somewhere Tag or his friends might go. Lorrie was really afraid of him. Had she continued their relationship, I'm afraid he might have killed her. He doesn't seem to realize she isn't his possession. Linda saw that as well."

Amaryllis nodded, watching as he pulled on his jeans. "What are you thinking, then, Malichai, because there must be something nagging at you."

He dragged on socks and then his boots before looking up at her. "I don't know. But my weird warning system has never let me down. If it's going off — and it is — something's not quite right and we need to figure it out. Make a pot of coffee and I'll join you as soon as I finish walking around the place." He glanced at the little device sitting on the bedside table, the jammer that was kept active when he was in the room. He reached over and shut it down, shoved it inside his pocket, making a mental note to sweep his room when they came back again. So far, his room had been bug-free, but he wasn't taking any chances, now that he knew for certain something big was going on involving the bed-and-breakfast and the magic shop.

Amaryllis stood up as he came around the bed, still shoving weapons into the hidden loops in his clothing. She came right up to him and put her slender arms around his neck. He loved that, the way her body leaned into his. The way she held him, clearly proprietorial.

"I am giving you up under protest. I like

being with you and if something is wrong, don't go into action without me. Think of it as me having to stay in practice."

She could make his heart jump, and she often did. Right now, it was doing weird little somersaults. As long as his brothers didn't know, he was okay with that. He wasn't okay with the razzing he'd get if they ever found out how gone he was over Amaryllis. Or maybe he was — she was definitely worth it.

"I'm not expecting action. I'm looking for answers," he assured. "I'm getting worried that you might be a little bloodthirsty."

She laughed and his entire body tightened. "Not bloodthirsty. I just like action. I get restless sometimes if I'm cooped up too long."

"What do you do then?"

"I run along the rooftops as fast as I can, jumping from one to the next."

He closed his eyes briefly. A couple of the buildings were a good distance apart. "I think I'm going to have to make love to you a few times a day and keep you tired out. That seems the safest bet."

She laughed again, turning her face up to his for another kiss. He obliged her because there was no resisting Amaryllis, especially if she wanted kisses. Her mouth tasted like that addicting exotic strawberry, reminding him of her skin. Then he wanted to taste her skin, and that reminded him of her sex. Instantly he needed his mouth between her legs. It was a fascinating cycle that he wanted to explore and keep on exploring.

Amaryllis pulled back first. "We have to stop if you're going to figure out what's bugging you," she whispered into his ear, immediately blowing it by teasing his earlobe with her tongue and teeth.

The moment she did that, the flush of dark desire skittered through him, making him very aware of her body so close to his. She wore nothing beneath her yoga pants, and he wore nothing beneath his jeans. Already his hands were turning her body back to the bed, pressing her down with one hand to her back so that she was bent over the bed.

He yanked down her yoga pants with his free hand and then, keeping her in place, opened his jeans. He was so hard, just circling his shaft with his fist sent an explosion of pleasure bursting through him.

"God, baby, tell me you're ready for me." He gently pushed her legs wider with his boot, and then slipped his hand between her legs to find her hot and slick. His heart pounded hard in time to the pulsing and throbbing in his cock.

He didn't wait. He needed to be in her and he pressed the broad head to her entrance. Fire seemed to engulf him. So scorching hot as he pushed deep. She felt like a silken sheath, tight beyond belief, wrapping him in a fiery fist. He threw back his head and let pleasure take him. He just held there for long moments, breathing deeply, absorbing the feeling. Then he began to move, pushing through tight, reluctant folds, forcing his way until he was so deep, he didn't know where she began and he left off.

Moving in her was heaven, or what he thought heaven should be. This. Lust and love coming together to create something indescribably beautiful. He gripped her hips, using them to pull back in order to increase the fiery friction as he surged into her. The breath hissed out between his teeth. Fire raced up his spine.

"You're so tight, Amaryllis. You're squeezing me like a vise. And hot. Scorching. Paradise can't feel as good as you."

She gripped the comforter in her fists and pushed back with her hips, her little cries soft, but each one punctuated the movement of his cock as he drove into her. The firestorm surrounded him, flames rolling over his cock, into it, threading through him, burning him clean. It was some kind of ecstasy, that tight grip her sheath had on him, the friction almost unbearable. And then he felt the rising of his seed, climbing, climbing, boiling and seething, needing the explosion.

"Now, baby, come with me now."

She did. Her sheath clamped down so hard he thought he might shatter, but that exquisite friction was there, sliding over him, pumping, massaging, kneading, pulling and, finally, squeezing down on him. Milking him. So hot. Scorching. Searing him through his thick cock as it grew and pushed back, stretching her channel as she tried to clamp down. He erupted, the hot seed coating the walls of her sheath triggering more and more orgasms. He felt each one.

He bent over her, fighting for air, when he realized why she felt so hot. Why he felt every squeeze of her muscles so intimately. He'd gone without a glove. He hadn't protected her. Malichai dropped his head on her back with a groan.

"Damn it, baby, I didn't wear a glove. I'm clean, I swear I am. I would have gotten that confirmed before I ever went without one. Are you on birth control?" She was a virgin. He doubted it. She'd been one of Whitney's experiments. Maybe she didn't even know about birth control. "I wouldn't mind if you got pregnant, Amaryllis, other than I'd prefer to have some time with you alone, but we'd make it work."

"I'm on birth control," she said. "The minute I got away, I went to a clinic. I was afraid he would haul me back and throw me in with Owen Starks."

He stiffened. "Owen Starks?" He repeated the name. "When did you meet Owen Starks?"

"He was one of Whitney's top guards. Whitney never went anywhere without him for a while. I think he showed up when I was about seventeen. He was good-looking and some of the girls would flirt with him. At the time, we were training as soldiers. Hand-to-hand combat. Weapons training. There were always new weapons. Bomb making and taking them apart. Any gifts we had we worked on to use in the field. Starks became one of the main trainers."

Very slowly, keeping a hand on her back, Malichai pulled out of her. Her body gave him up reluctantly, still clamping down, still holding on, so as he slowly dragged his cock from her, the action sent flames licking up his spine and caused more explosions to go off in her body. He felt every one of them. She made a little sound, catching her breath, while he cleaned off with his T-shirt and then cleaned between her legs.

"Tell me more about Starks." It was an order. He'd been a GhostWalker too long and was used to being obeyed. His voice was harsher than he intended.

She pulled up her yoga pants and turned to face him, half sitting on the bed. "Is it important? Do you know him?"

"I know him. I want the information, Amaryllis, anything you can tell me about him and what you were to him in the time you've known him. He was declared dead about six years ago. Supposedly he was killed in action, but there was a lot of controversy around his career in the military. Quite a few believed he killed some of those he served with. It shouldn't surprise me that Whitney would take a man like Starks to work for him, but it still does. He tried for the program and failed."

She sat all the way up on the bed and pulled her legs up tailor-fashion. She often did that, even in the dining room, he'd noticed.

"Starks didn't seem to pay attention to the girls, although, like I said, they flirted outrageously with him. When it came to training, he was very strict. We learned to listen first time out with him. I didn't like him at all. I don't know why. The feeling was so strong, I would have to label it an aversion. I thought he was unnecessarily cruel, especially to the girls who flirted with him. Almost every single training session with him, someone ended up in tears. Often they carried these horrendous bruises."

"And you?" He kept his eyes on her face, wanting to read her every expression.

"I didn't talk much. I was quiet and I worked hard to learn everything. I practiced with anyone who would practice with me. There were a couple of the guys who were decent. Starks didn't pay much attention because I did the work and didn't flirt. He noticed I was good, but that was about it. The better I was, the harsher he got, but I didn't care because it made me better. I knew not to challenge his ego."

Malichai kept his gaze fixed on her face. There was so much more, and she was try-ing to sound matter-of-fact when there was so much pent-up emotion, she could barely contain it.

"Douglas Hines, one of the trainers, was nice. He worked with me most of the time. Over the years, I liked partnering with him because he was fast, and I had to be faster if I wasn't going to get hit. Sometimes we practiced with rubber knives. In the beginning he'd raise welts all over me where he could slip through my guard, but eventually, he couldn't do that anymore."

She rubbed her chin and then stroked three fingers over her throat. Both were nervous gestures. "That was important to tell you. I'm not just rambling. One day Starks came outside where we were working with those practice knives. The rubber ones. I loved those workouts."

There were tears in her voice and he wanted to comfort her. He made himself stay where he was. He needed to know everything about Starks she could give him.

"He was angry with Douglas and told him that training with rubber knives was for pussies and I would never learn anything unless I felt the blade go in. He pulled out his knife and indicated Douglas do the same. They went at it, and it wasn't a training session anymore. Starks meant to kill him. Douglas knew it too. Starks was the head man in the yard, and there was no one to protest."

"Starks always did have to be the best at everything. He liked to show off." Malichai didn't like where this was going. The fact that Amaryllis hadn't flirted with him, had acted as if she barely acknowledged him, would have driven Starks crazy. He had a deep need to be noticed, to always be the one everyone feared or admired. Once his attention was centered on Amaryllis, he would have begun to really see her. Seeing her meant wanting her.

"When he slipped past Douglas's guard and sank that knife in, I could see he'd gone for the kill. I tried to fend him off and he hit me hard. I tried to go for the kill myself. I have a poison I can use, but I couldn't deliver it. I don't know why. When he hit me, I blacked out."

That was the first time Malichai had heard about a poison, but it didn't surprise him. Bellisia could deliver a poisonous bite, as could Cayenne and Pepper.

"When I woke up, Douglas was dying, his blood running all over him, the ground and me where I lay next to him. Starks was sitting about six feet from us, just watching Douglas die with me next to him. I tried to help Douglas, and I called for help. A couple of the girls came, but none of the guards approached. They were all afraid of Starks."

Malichai's gut tightened into hard knots. He knew Amaryllis. He'd made it a point to observe her. She was extremely protective. She was fierce. And she was a warrior. He wanted to reach out to her, to stop that young girl from making a terrible mistake, but she'd already made it, he saw it on her face.

"Douglas died in my arms, his blood all over me. I got up, dusted off my knees, which was ridiculous, considering I was covered in blood and dirt from where I'd fallen when Starks hit me, and I walked over to where Starks was just sitting there watching as if he was at a movie theater. I kicked him right in the face. He wasn't expecting it and he went over backward."

Starks should have been expecting it, Malichai would have been. The man had been watching her, but he hadn't really figured her out. His ego was probably too big to allow him to see her for what she was.

"I followed him, kicking and punching. I think I was a little insane. I tried again and again to kill him, to use the poison on him, but I couldn't deliver the venom. The other guards eventually pulled me off of him. I think they did it to protect me, but I fought them too. In the end, Whitney came out to see what the commotion was about, and he sedated me. After that, my life was a little bit of a nightmare."

Malichai could well imagine. The other guards would never make the mistake of laughing or even smirking at Starks, but he would always know they saw a girl beat the crap out of him.

Amaryllis rubbed the pad of her thumb across her forehead, back and forth, a soothing gesture, but he found it mesmerizing. "There was a photograph. Someone took it with a cell. No one was supposed to have a cell, especially in the yards around us, but one of the guards must have snuck it in."

Malichai groaned. "Seriously? What did he do with it? Did he want to get you killed?" He wanted to find the guard and teach him a lesson. Again, it was far too late. The damage was already done.

"The photograph apparently was printed out and taped to Starks's locker. I never saw the picture, but it was of me kicking the crap out of him. He was on the ground with his hands up, trying to keep me from kicking his teeth down his throat. He tried to make a joke of it, saying he thought it was funny and he didn't want to hurt me, but no one believed him."

Because it wasn't true. Malichai might have found it funny to have a girl beat him up, but Starks never would. Never. And he'd never forget. Starks would be fixated on her, completely obsessed. He would want her to know he was superior to her and he would set out to prove it.

"Your life became somewhat of a night-mare?" he prompted.

She shrugged. "When we trained, if he was there, he singled me out and I always ended up hurt. Always. He was careful of my face, but certainly not the rest of me. I was always the example. He would pull me out of the lineup and instantly the yard would go eerily quiet because everyone knew he was going to hurt me."

"Did you fight back?" He knew she had. Amaryllis didn't have it in her to surrender to a man like Starks.

"Every time. That made him very happy and very angry at the same time."

"Whitney decided he wanted you for his breeding program?"

"I'm certain it was Starks's idea until Whitney found out about my ability to heal. Prior to that, Starks was very insistent. He began telling me Whitney was going to pair us. He'd whisper it to me when we were training. I completed every mission Whitney sent me on, but it didn't matter how good I was in the field, Starks had Whitney's ear and he thought it would be a fitting revenge. Then I healed that cut and the girl told on me. So, I knew I had no choice but to escape. And I did it right out from under

Starks's nose too."

"All right, baby." Malichai sighed. They were definitely in trouble. "Starks is going to be an enemy who will never stop until he's dead. I think you know that. When I knew him, he always had to have his petty revenge against the smallest perceived infraction, I can imagine how he would feel about you besting him over and over."

"I had no choice, Malichai."

Her lashes lifted and she gave him that blue-eyed look that tore at his heart. He couldn't imagine thinking he had her and then losing her. Starks would be insane with the need to find her, especially if Whitney really had paired them.

"I'm well aware of that, Amaryllis. Do you know if Whitney paired you?"

She made a face. "He tried. It didn't work. I was so repulsed by Starks after what he'd done to Douglas, no amount of pheromones was going to work. Whitney found that fascinating, but that was one more strike against me as far as Starks was concerned."

"Sometimes Whitney only paired the man so that he was obsessed. Do you know if he included Starks or was it just on your side?"

"Starks was so fixated on me that I don't think Whitney really needed to do it on his side, but I'm positive he did anyway. Starks was crazy."

She gave her assessment matter-of-factly, but Malichai could see the little telltale nervous gestures. She was afraid of Starks, and he knew she should be. The man was capable of anything, and his ego was enormous. He was arrogant and felt superior to everyone. Malichai couldn't imagine how he would get along with Whitney, who was a megalomaniac in his opinion, yet he'd managed for years. How?

"Babe, tell me about the relationship between Whitney and Starks. You said he became Whitney's head guard. I imagine he traveled with Whitney as well."

She nodded. "They would often leave, which was a relief for everyone. No one knew who was worse, Whitney or Starks."

"Did you observe them together?"

"All the time. Whitney rarely went anywhere without Starks."

"Did Starks defer to Whitney? Was he subservient in any way?"

She shook her head. "Absolutely not. He never appeared to be like some of the other guards. His head was always up. He was alert. He took the job seriously and acted as if he thought Whitney was worth guarding. That in itself was extremely rare. I can't see Starks putting his life on the line for anyone, yet he clearly would have for Whitney."

Malichai knew Starks wasn't a team player. He would never have helped out a fellow GhostWalker. He'd been cut from the program for psychological reasons. Whitney had been the one to cut him. And yet he'd ended up working for Whitney, as had many others Whitney had deemed unfit to be GhostWalkers.

"He's going to keep looking for you, Amaryllis. Once we get married and we're back home, you'll have to be prepared for Starks to make his try for you."

She took a deep breath and let it out. He could see she was worried. "I know he will, Malichai. I've been careful here. I told Marie that an ex-boyfriend was stalking me and I had to be careful and she helped me as much as she could to hide who I was. I made up my last name and date of birth because I wasn't certain when I was born. My paperwork wasn't that good, that's why I was so afraid when I knew the police would look closely at it. I'm sure Marie thought when Tag came in that he was the one after me."

"You don't have to worry about your paperwork now. That's been taken care of. Because we're getting married and you're coming home with me, and you're a Ghost-

Walker, you'll be valued as an asset by the government and protected at all times."

"Great. I'm an asset."

His smile was slow in coming because he was so worried about Starks being after her, but it found its way all the same. "You're definitely an asset. At least to me. The government might think you are as well. No matter what, they have to protect you. No foreign government can get their hands on you. You're really a national secret."

She laughed. "I'm something. I'd better get downstairs, Malichai. I still have a job to do. And just in case those people have hired someone other than your friend to do us all in, I've got weapons stashed from one end of this house to the other. I don't take chances either. I'm not so easy to kill."

He was very certain she was telling the truth.

"You can do your walk-through and hopefully figure out what's bothering you."

"You don't feel a threat at all?" Malichai asked. "Anything to raise your radar?"

She shook her head. "No. I just feel you. Maybe you short-circuited my warning system, in which case, there's no more . . . um . . . sex . . . until we're somewhere where we don't need a warning system."

"We're always going to need one," he protested.

She shrugged. "Well, I'm sorry then. No more sex for you." She stood up and acted as if she was going to walk right past him.

Malichai reached out and caught her, pulling her into his body and closing his arms around her, locking her to him. "I'm afraid that's a total no-go. Sex is going to be right up there with breathing, baby, so you'll have to learn to keep the radar system in place."

"I think you've permanently damaged it," she said, looking up at him.

He kissed her. There was no looking down at that upturned mouth and not kissing her. His warning system might work fine, but his ability to stop kissing her was put to the test. He loved the way she tasted. The fire in her mouth. The passion that matched his. When he was finally able to come to his senses, he rested his forehead against hers.

"Listen, baby. Generally, when I have this vague feeling, it means a threat is headed my way, not that it's here. It means it's close. I just can't shake the feeling, so I want you to be extra cautious. If you have to leave the house, let me know. Or let one of my brothers know."

"I figured if you took the time out to have sex and then a long talk about Starks, the threat couldn't be imminent," she said. "I wish I felt it too, Malichai."

He shrugged and straightened, reluctant to leave her, but knowing he really needed to do a walk-through before everyone else was up. "Promise me, Amaryllis. Had I known that Starks had gotten anywhere near you, let alone the things you've told me, I wouldn't have let you out of my sight."

A small frown crossed her face. She did that little nervous thing, stroking the pads of her fingers down her throat as if it ached. He stiffened.

"Babe. Starks. Did he choke you?" If he had, the man was dead. Malichai was going to hunt him down and kill him. He didn't care if that meant going directly after Whitney and starting an all-out war with him. Half of those in the White House would support the hunt. The other half would probably sanction Malichai's death.

She studied his face. "Honey, I don't want to discuss Starks anymore. He gives me nightmares. Let's just say, he made me so afraid I found the courage to leave and I did it in a smart enough way that I had a good start and could get out in front of them when they came hunting me."

Yeah, the bastard had choked her. Malichai pushed down anger and forced himself to nod. Amaryllis was far too perceptive. Just as he was able to read her, she was able to read him. She knew, if she admitted what Starks had done, Malichai would go hunting. He didn't need her confirmation. He'd gone on two missions with Starks. One had been enough to know his character. Two had shown all of them that Starks would put a bullet in their heads if it in any way benefited him. The man was certifiable.

Malichai followed Amaryllis out of the room. The hallways were dimly lit. Just enough light spilled from the ceiling to allow anyone to see where they were going. The lights weren't so bright that if doors were opened it would disturb guests sleeping in the rooms. She headed toward the kitchen while he turned to make his way down the long hall.

There were twelve mini-suites on the first floor. He knew the layouts and the names of each of those staying in those rooms. He caught the muffled sounds of snores coming from several of the rooms. That was to be expected. He was looking for something that might jar. A single note, anything that would make the knots in his gut either relax or tighten more.

He was a GhostWalker, so he moved like a wraith down the long, snaking hallway. It wasn't straight, so he couldn't see all the way to the end. The dim light cast enough shadows that he was able to disappear into them. Someone was stirring in the dolphin room.

Marie had decorated each of the downstairs rooms with sea animals to make it easier to identify guests and where they were staying. The dolphin room was Tania Leven's. She was already up, moving around. Malichai could hear her talking quietly to someone else — a male. He slid deeper into the shadows beside her room in an effort to identify the male voice speaking with her at four in the morning.

It wasn't as if, on a vacation, she couldn't hook up with someone, it was done all the time. It was just that Tania was surrounded by family, all men, and everywhere she went, she had her brother or cousin with her. Malichai had never noticed her flirting either.

The door swung open and Tommy Leven stood there, looking back inside. "See you at breakfast, honey," he said.

"Thanks for staying with me," Tania said. She sounded as if she'd been crying.

Tommy shrugged and closed the door quietly. He stood there for a moment looking at the door and then he went on past

Malichai, back toward his room. Malichai leaned against the wall, trying to puzzle out why Tania would be so upset that her brother had to spend most of the night talking to her. She always seemed a very steady woman.

He was about to move on down the hall when the door to the orca room opened. It was the one right beside the dolphin room, the one rented to Linda, Lorrie, and Lexie Montclair. Linda looked out into the hall, toward Tommy's room, and then crept out and knocked softly on Tania's door. Malichai frowned. He'd never seen the women talking to each other.

Tania opened her door slightly and then, seeing who it was, cracked it wider. Fresh tears instantly began to track down her face. The two women stood there looking at each other and then Tania hiccupped.

"I'm so sorry," she whispered. "Linda, I was careless. That was all. Careless. It wasn't on purpose. You have to know that."

She sounded so contrite, Malichai felt sorry for her and he didn't even know what she'd done. Linda stepped closer to the door and Tania backed inside to allow the other woman entry. Linda put her arms around Tania and held her while Tania began to sob quietly.

"You're going to give yourself a headache. It's over. Tag's not going to hurt her now. Were you jealous? Why would you ever think I'd want to be with a man like that?"

"He kept asking for you, not Lorrie. It was always, 'Do you know this woman, Linda Montclair?' I thought he was your ex and he wanted you back."

Linda reached behind her and closed the door, but as she did so, he could see she caught at Tania's hair, turning her face so she could find her mouth with hers.

Linda and Tania? What the hell was going on? And Tania had contacted Tag and brought him to the bed-and-breakfast because he'd been asking around for Linda? He probably realized Linda ran the show. She would be the one hiding her sister from him. But Tania and Linda? Linda was from San Diego. Tania was from North Carolina, at least that was what was on her driver's license. They couldn't have just struck up the relationship. How had they met? How long had they been together?

Malichai waited a few more minutes, listening carefully, but there was no more conversation. None. He sighed and continued down the hallway until he was at the stairs leading to the second floor. There were two sets of staircases, one on either end of the first floor. There was also a lift a wheelchair could use from the foyer where the front desk was, so three ways to access the top floor.

He went up the stairs and stood in the wide hallway for a moment, just listening, allowing his enhanced senses to scan for him. The five men from the various countries represented at the Ideas for Peace conference were each staying in one of the five suites on the second floor. Stefani Charles, representing Finland, was also on that floor. Three more of the rooms had been reserved for representatives of other countries. The remaining vacant two rooms on that floor were reserved for attendees of the conference. Those people would be coming in that morning or afternoon. The Ideas for Peace conference had turned out to be a huge draw, and the local motels, hotels and B and B places had all benefited.

Malichai walked up and down the hallway, but as far as he could see, nothing seemed out of place. His alarm kept nagging at him, but there weren't any whispers, no voices talking conspiracy. Just his gut telling him something wasn't right. It was possibly left over from Tag's sudden appearance, but that didn't feel right to him.

He turned to start back down the hall

when the door to suite Atlantis opened and Billy Leven came out. He wore gloves, very dark ones, as he gripped the doorknob to make certain he had closed it properly. He tugged twice and then sauntered down the hall as if he didn't have a care in the world. Suite Atlantis was the room Amaryllis had prepared for a representative of Egypt who had been coming in that night but was delayed until the next afternoon.

Malichai stared at the closed door. The Levens were up to something. Billy seemed a good old boy, a man who was perpetually cheerful and yet, at the same time, stayed to himself. Tania seemed a sweet woman, but she was having an affair with a woman she acted as if she didn't know. Tommy? What was he up to?

Malichai waited for Billy to make his way down the stairs and then he followed at a more leisurely pace, not wanting to draw the eye to him. Billy didn't go straight to his room but followed the aroma of freshly brewed coffee and bacon to the kitchen.

Malichai heard Amaryllis's laughter before he came up behind the man from North Carolina. He was using all his charm on her. Billy had one hip against the doorjamb as he casually draped himself there to observe Amaryllis putting the last touches on her trays of breakfast casserole.

"You're going to have to show me how to make that before I head home," Billy said. "One of the best breakfasts I've ever had."

"It's Marie's recipe," Amaryllis volunteered. She looked past Billy to Malichai. "Hi, honey," she greeted softly. "Looking for coffee?"

"I'm always looking for coffee," Malichai said and nodded at Billy as the man moved in order for him to get by. "I see you found my girl and you're giving me a run for my money this morning with the compliments."

"All sincere," Billy said. "You're a lucky man."

"I am that," Malichai agreed, inhaling the aroma of coffee as he took the cup from Amaryllis. "And she makes the best coffee as well."

"You're a soldier, Malichai," Billy said. "What do you think about all this Ideas for Peace nonsense?"

Malichai shrugged noncommittally. "I think nations have tried to talk peace for centuries and it never actually happens, so while I think it's commendable, do I believe anything will come of it? Unfortunately, no."

Billy nodded several times, as if Malichai was only confirming what he believed. "Thanks for the coffee, little darlin'," he said to Amaryllis and went off, whistling off-key down the hall back toward his room.

12

"I think we need to explore the very real possibility that an unknown faction of terrorists may try to bomb the Ideas for Peace conference," Ezekiel said. "We don't have a lot of evidence. The police have done a well check on Miss Crystal from the magic shop and spoken with a woman they believe is her from the cruise ship. Her passport and ID have checked out. That's a dead end for now, until she returns."

"That doesn't negate what Anna and Burnell thought they overheard," Malichai pointed out. "If we just ignore it, and it turns out they were talking about the maximum number of people they could kill, the convention center would be the place to do it."

"Exactly," Ezekiel agreed. "I've got this nagging feeling. Malichai's got it. Mordichai's got it as well. In the past, whenever the three of us had that same feeling, something was very wrong. And we have the hit man going around over a two-year period doing in people all connected to the convention center."

"How did Miss Crystal pay for her cruise?" Malichai asked.

"She 'won' the trip," Ezekiel said. "She did enter every contest known to man, according to all of her friends, so it is a possibility that she actually won a legit contest."

Rubin was silent as he studied the board Ezekiel had made. He didn't have the radar they did, but he was very good at puzzles. Right now, Malichai could see he was moving those names around like chess pieces on a board. They needed new insights, because he was fresh out of them. What would be the reasoning of targeting the peace conference? Malichai had told the truth to Billy when he said he doubted the conference would come up with anything that would change the world and the way it thought. Nations could talk to one another, but in the end, it all seemed to come down to who could gain what.

"Are there any politicians or world leaders of significance going?" Mordichai asked.

Ezekiel shook his head. "They were deliberately not invited. This conference is for the people and it's all about ideas. Things to contribute to change the way people of various nations think about one another, their customs, religion and governments. Simply put, to shift world opinion in every nation toward tolerance."

"It's a very lofty idea," Mordichai said.

"True, and it isn't going to solve the world's problems, but they're hoping they can just shift the tolerance level so people can come together first before igniting into terrorism and hatred," Ezekiel said. "We're not about judging whether something works or not. We don't have to agree or disagree. We're soldiers and we protect people and those unable to protect themselves."

Malichai shook his head, trying to puzzle it out. Politics aside, he needed to look at the bigger picture. There would be no reason to try to destroy the conference . . .

Thinking aloud sometimes helped him. "We're trying to find a reason. Suppose Anna and Burnell overheard the one thing that holds true. Whoever is behind this wants the largest body count possible. It doesn't matter if they think the conference is a threat or not. They simply want the notoriety of killing as many people as possible. It doesn't even matter if they're Americans, just simply a body count."

"They could get that at a football game,"

Mordichai said.

Rubin shook his head. "Not like this. These are buildings. If the exits were blocked, thousands could be trapped inside. Have you seen what happens at Comic-Con? It's insane."

There was a brief silence while the Fortunes brothers exchanged amused glances.

"Rubin? You've been to Comic-Con? You actually know what that is?" Ezekiel asked, trying to keep a straight face and failing.

"Get any autographs?" Mordichai teased.

"He does like Harley Quinn," Malichai told them. "He would stand in line for a couple of hours to get her autograph."

Rubin scowled at them. "I just said I wouldn't mind a girlfriend like her, not that I'd stand in line anywhere to get an autograph. For that matter, if I really wanted one, I'd just bypass her security and wait for her in her living room."

"You do realize she's a fictional character," Ezekiel said. "An actress played her."

Rubin gave them all the finger, the standard answer when they were at their worst with one another. "I'm just saying, that many people filling up that big of a convention center, that would take out more than a football stadium."

"We might have to return to the subject

384

of whether or not you attended one or more of those events," Ezekiel said, "but you're right, the San Diego Convention Center is enormous and holds thousands. I'll see about getting us in there and taking a look at security."

"What about Henry Shevfield and his attack on Malichai? All the people he killed had something to do with the convention center. And this big diversion he's supposed to run, we didn't get the exact timing of that." Mordichai didn't look at Ezekiel when he pointed that out.

"Joe contacted Major General," Ezekiel said. "Joe said to keep Shevfield's death under wraps for the moment and then the body will turn up. Rubin will go undercover as a suspected hit man. He'll be questioned and released and then set up at the bed-and-breakfast. We'll hope he gets contacted. They won't have a lot of time to choose who they're going to use to create their diversion and he'll already be in place."

Malichai knew that wasn't Major General's idea. Ezekiel had already told Malichai that was the plan. He must have informed Joe and Joe sold the plan to Major General.

"How much have you let the detectives in on?" Malichai asked.

"Not much yet. We didn't have a lot to

give them. Nothing on who murdered Anna and Bryon Cooper. It wasn't Shevfield. Looking at his work, he had to be telling the truth. If he had created that scenario, there would have been nothing for the detectives to question. As it was, they had Bryon shooting himself with the wrong gun hand," Ezekiel said.

"When is the rest of the team arriving?" Malichai asked.

"They're on the way. The potential for this is big and we're only leaving a skeleton crew behind to protect Pepper and the kids, although a few of the other teams are offering to cover for us," Ezekiel continued.

"I'd like to have a couple of our people staying at Marie's," Malichai said. "Unfortunately, it isn't as if we can boot anyone from their room. I can double up with Amaryllis, which leaves my room free."

"I thought we could take this to Marie, see if she'd let us get Jacy to safety, maybe even her. In the meantime, she might be able to get creative. There're two rooms she doesn't use for guests because they don't have bathrooms that even are shared. She was planning on adding them but hasn't had the time. There's the attic room, hot as hell, and there's the basement," Ezekiel said. "I've looked at the blueprints. We can get some of our people inside the basement for certain and the two rooms without shared bathrooms. They'll have to use Amaryllis's private one. If we get the cops to release the Coopers' room, that will be another room we'll have available."

Malichai didn't doubt that everything Ezekiel said was there. The bed-and-breakfast was enormous. At one time it had been a small apartment building. Then it had been renovated to look on the outside like an old Victorian mansion. The owner had poured hundreds of thousands of dollars into it, making it into a vacation home for him and his extended family. He had been the one to create suites for his married children and their families. Marie and her husband had envisioned the bed-and-breakfast when it came up for sale.

"That's good, then. I don't like the idea of talking to Marie and Amaryllis at the inn. The only possible conclusion I can reach for Billy Leven to be in that room at that time in the morning was to plant a listening device. I planned on going with Amaryllis when she does the final walk-through to ensure the room is perfect. I can check for devices at that time. If we find one, we're going to have to find a way to inspect each of the other rooms."

"You're right, Malichai. But Billy Leven? What would he have to do with those in the magic shop? I'm certain those people are tied to this plot, but Leven? Where would he fit in?" Ezekiel asked.

"Money? People do all kinds of things for money," Mordichai said.

"It wouldn't make sense to contact someone in North Carolina. They would contact someone here in San Diego," Malichai pointed out. "Like they did with Shevfield."

Ezekiel shrugged. "We can speculate until the cows come home, but that doesn't mean we'll know what's going on. Malichai, you'll need to arrange it so we can talk with Marie and see if we can get some of the team members into the bed-and-breakfast. I'd particularly like to have Draden and Shylah stationed there. Shylah is lethal. She looks sweet, like the girl next door, but she will take you down so fast your head will spin. I'd also like Trap and Cayenne to be here as well."

"Is Trap allowing Cayenne to come? She's pretty pregnant, isn't she?" Mordichai asked.

Malichai snorted his derision. "I really fear for you, Mordichai. A woman is either pregnant or she isn't. She isn't more pregnant or less pregnant. Or 'pretty pregnant.' "

Mordichai flipped him off. "With Cayenne, who knows? She might be more or less."

"I have no idea when that woman got pregnant, so I don't have a clue how far along she is, and Trap isn't saying," Ezekiel said. "She doesn't look pregnant, but then Cayenne is built differently. I was surprised that Joe gave the okay for her to come on this one, especially since it involves being around the public so much."

"Cayenne definitely isn't comfortable being around people," Malichai said.

"I'm not either," Rubin said unexpectedly, as if he was defending Cayenne.

Malichai looked at him. There was no expression on Rubin's face, but he was uncomfortable with the direction of the conversation, that much was coming off of him in waves.

"Cayenne is very much loved, Rubin," he assured as gently as possible. "She's different, yes, but she's a part of our team and a part of us. She loves Trap and makes his life a thousand times better. The thing is, as lethal as she is, as extraordinary, she still needs protection during times like this. Just as we do when we're wounded or laid up. I'm shocked that not only Joe allowed her to travel but that Trap did. And I mean really shocked." And he was. Cayenne might not be showing because she was built differently, but she had to be pretty far along.

He had no idea where Rubin's sudden protective streak of Cayenne was coming from, but that well of darkness that sometimes shrouded both Rubin and Diego had settled over Rubin's shoulders like a cloak. He looked at Ezekiel. His older brother had taken Rubin and Diego under his wing when he'd found them living on the streets.

The brothers were from a very poor part of the Appalachian Mountains and as teens they'd made their way to the city, where the streets had threatened to swallow them. Ezekiel had protected them, and taught them how to live on the streets. They'd stayed with Ezekiel, Malichai and Mordichai, following them into the service.

"The bottom line is, Trap is here, Cayenne will be," Ezekiel said.

Rubin nodded. "Cayenne is not only dedicated completely to Trap, she is to our team."

That much was true. "And Nonny," Malichai said, hoping to lighten the mood. "Who wouldn't be dedicated to Nonny? I can't wait to get Amaryllis back to Louisiana and have her meet everyone there. Speaking of, do you think Zara will be coming with Gino?"

Ezekiel coughed behind his hand. "Yeah, that's not likely. Danger here means Zara is stashed somewhere safe. Gino doesn't like it if she stubs her toe. She's on some killer research project at the moment, and from what I understand, doesn't want to stop while the team is here. That's causing a bit of a controversy. She never goes against Gino. And I mean never. He wants her to do something, she just smiles that sweet smile of hers and does it."

He sounded so wistful, Malichai burst out laughing. "Is my sweet sister-in-law giving you trouble again, Zeke?" There was a taunting note in his voice he knew shouldn't be there because Amaryllis was going to give him nothing but trouble, but having little petite Bellisia stand up to the force that was Ezekiel made for great fun.

"I'm not certain Bellisia knows the word 'yes,' Malichai," Ezekiel said mournfully. "I've made a subliminal tape and play it for her at night, but so far it hasn't done any good."

Even Rubin laughed at that and Malichai realized his brother had deliberately turned the conversation into something that allowed them to laugh at Ezekiel. Zeke would do that for any of them. Bellisia was so tiny and yet she was a warrior through and through. Tough. Tenacious. Deadly.

Zara was sweet, gentle, kind and compassionate. She had been tortured and had never given up the GhostWalkers, but her feet had been damaged beyond the capabilities of any of the doctors to fix them. She could walk, but it was slow and careful most of the time. She was a strong woman and loyal to all of them. She would fight for them and with them if need be, but it was her brain that was her greatest gift. She was one of the leading researchers in artificial intelligence, something the government was very much interested in.

"What in the world did Gino do when his sweet, accommodating woman defied him and said she wanted to continue working instead of pulling back to the main house with the others?" Malichai asked, curious. He couldn't imagine doing anything if Amaryllis defied him. What could a man do? A woman had the right to make up her own mind — except that Gino didn't always think in modern terms.

"I don't know, but before we left, he was bringing her to the Fontenot home," Ezekiel said. "She doesn't talk to Bellisia about her marriage to Gino. Bellisia had been so opposed to the match that I think Zara's afraid if she tells her anything negative, it would be a betrayal of Gino. And before you ask, Bellisia tells me if I'm being a caveman, and then she announces it to the rest of you. She could use a little more of Zara's silence on marital matters."

Malichai laughed with the others. "I don't think you being a caveman is a marital matter, Zeke. We're used to it, but poor Bellisia thinks the sun rises and sets with you. It's probably a shocker every time you act like the Neanderthal we know you to be."

"I wish I had a club right now," Ezekiel murmured. "Get back to the bed-and-breakfast and set something up so I can talk with Marie as soon as possible."

Malichai nodded and got up to leave. The moment he did, the pressure he hadn't even noticed in his chest eased. The knots in his guts unraveled just a little bit. He hadn't realized he was uneasy being away from Amaryllis. He wanted to put it down to his being concerned that unknown danger lurked at the B and B, but he knew better than to try to deceive himself. It was Amaryllis. He just plain didn't like being away from her. He was going to be one of those men.

He knew better than to look too eager as

he left the house Ezekiel was renting. He'd never live it down if his brothers and teammates discovered he was forever wrapped around Amaryllis's little finger and would do anything for her, not after all the crap he'd given them — especially Zeke. He forced himself to saunter out into the bright sun. He shoved his dark glasses on his nose and picked up the pace, striding down the long sidewalk across the street from the ocean side.

Ezekiel had been lucky enough — or someone high up had aided him — in getting his team a house close to the bed-and-breakfast. As far as Malichai could see, more and more people were coming into San Diego from all parts of the country, and the world, for the convention. It was actually nice to see that so many people had ideas to contribute. Still, Malichai couldn't think about anything but how to protect those people. It wouldn't be easy in a place as big as the San Diego Convention Center.

Malichai pushed open the front door of the bed-and-breakfast and immediately felt the tension in the large house. He picked up the pace, hurrying down the hall toward the kitchen, where he knew Amaryllis would be cleaning and setting up for dinner. She'd been working all day and he'd helped her until he had to attend the meeting with Ezekiel and the others.

The sound of raised voices was loud as he made that sweep in the hall that took him from the suites to the kitchen and the beginnings of Marie's apartment.

Marie stood up against the door leading to her private living quarters, a large man towering over her. The man was tall with wide shoulders and a barrel chest. He had both hands curled into fists and stood so close to Marie that it would have been difficult to get a piece of paper between them.

Amaryllis stood on Marie's right, looking up at the man, not in the least intimidated, at least nothing showed on her face.

"Back up. I'm calling the cops if you don't step back away from her right now. It's not like she's hiding this man in one of the rooms," Amaryllis said. "We don't have a clue what you're talking about."

"Bitch, stay out of this," the man snarled, without taking his eyes from Marie. "This is the address he gave me," he continued, practically spitting in Marie's face as he spoke. "You know where he is. He owes me money and I'm going to collect it whether or not you tell me. If I don't collect it from him, I'll collect from you."

"That's a threat," Amaryllis said. "I've

recorded it and I can guarantee the police won't like you making that threat."

"I *am* the police, you bitch," the man sneered. "I don't think anyone's going to take your word over mine. Malichai Fortunes is in this house somewhere."

"I'm right behind you," Malichai said softly. He'd already texted his brother to ensure he would have backup. If he was arrested, he wanted to be bailed out immediately. The only reason he could see for making this kind of power play was to remove him from the inn. That made no sense this early. The convention was still a week away.

The big man swung around, sizing Malichai up immediately. "Turn around and put your hands behind your back," he ordered.

"I'll need to see a badge first," Malichai said. "I'm not taking your word for it that you're a cop, especially since you came in here and tried to intimidate these women."

"The women lied to me. I can arrest them for obstruction."

"Actually, you can't. Marie, as the owner of this establishment, isn't obliged to give out her guests' names to anyone. If anything, she has to protect them," Malichai said mildly.

The man produced his badge. His name

was John Mills. Malichai looked him over carefully. "I'm armed," he said. "And I have a concealed weapons permit. I'll place my weapons on the table and allow you to handcuff me." Deliberately, he was slow about it, removing two guns and assorted knives, none of which were illegal. No officer of the law would want him to remove his own weapons. If anything, that would provoke them to be afraid he might shoot them.

Zeke, you close?

Very. Rubin has him in his sights.

That made sense, Rubin could run like the wind when he had to. The moment Malichai had contacted them, he would have come flying out of the nearby house and sprinted down the sidewalk with Ezekiel, Trap and Mordichai, uncaring who might see them.

Amaryllis could take him. I don't believe for one second he's a cop. He wants something. Let's find out what it is.

I don't like you taking chances with your life. A thread of steel ran through his brother's voice. Through his mind. There was something close to that berserker rage Ezekiel only felt when it came to the protection of his brothers. He'd been that way as long as Malichai could remember. That rage could be lethal if it was allowed to slip loose.

It isn't a chance when the four of you are close. You'll need a car though.

Even as he spoke to his brother, his eyes were on Amaryllis's face. She shook her head slightly and then glanced at Marie.

This is insane. You know he plans on killing you, Ezekiel snapped.

This is our best chance to find out what he wants. And find out who we're up against. If this man went to the police academy, he flunked out. I took out my own weapons. Handled them right in front of him. I could have turned the gun on him and shot him or threw a knife and killed him that way. When he put the cuffs on, he didn't notice I made certain to flex my wrists, giving myself as much room as possible.

You're still in cuffs and he still wants you dead.

There was no arguing with Ezekiel, but there was satisfaction in knowing his brother would move heaven and earth to keep him safe.

"Let me kiss my girl good-bye," Malichai said in a reasonable tone and stepped around Mills before he could protest.

"Zeke is watching over me," he whispered against her lips and then took her mouth. Hard. Taking his time. Making it a luxury.

She had that addicting fire that sent his mind into a place it shouldn't go when someone wanted him dead.

"That's enough," Mills sputtered. He caught Malichai's arm.

"Where are you taking him, so I can bail him out?" Amaryllis demanded.

Marie glared at him. "I'll be filing a complaint against you personally and the department for this. It's an outrage the way you behaved, and we have video evidence of it. Social media will get you fired."

Mills ignored the two women and hurried Malichai away from them. Marie and Amaryllis followed, at a short distance. Malichai ignored Mills shoving him forward, his hand between Malichai's shoulder blades, his other on his upper arm. As if that would have stopped him.

"I can take him," Amaryllis said loud enough for Mills to hear.

He stiffened but kept walking, not turning around.

Malichai glanced over his shoulder at her and winked. "I know you can, baby. I'll be back in an hour or so. Looking forward to dinner. You know how I love my food."

Amaryllis didn't return his smile, and he was certain she wasn't going to continue cooking the dinner for the bed-and-breakfast. She would be following John Mills to get her man back. Like Malichai, she didn't believe for one moment that he was a cop.

"What the hell did she mean by that?" Mills demanded as he yanked open the passenger rear door to a dark SUV.

"Nice ride for a cop," Malichai observed. "She means she could kick your ass, and she could. You should never underestimate a woman just because she is one."

Mills shoved him into the car and slammed the door, sending one furious look toward the doorway of the bed-and-breakfast. Only Marie stood there. Amaryllis had already rushed to retrieve her car.

Malichai leaned his head back against the leather seat, ignoring Mills as he threw himself behind the wheel and pulled into traffic. Whoever these people were, whatever their ultimate goal, they weren't a real terrorist cell, maybe a fledging one, but they were amateurs. Kidnapping him was a stupid move. They knew next to nothing about him. Mills's face had not only been seen by the two women, but he'd allowed them to capture his image on their phones.

His gut knotted. Either that or they didn't care. They had some other reason for not caring. What could that be? Mills carried himself very upright. Military, if Malichai had to take a stab at his background. He would not only be military but be used to giving orders or carrying them out. Something wasn't right and Malichai just didn't have enough pieces of the puzzle to fit them all together.

He didn't make the mistake of looking out the back window to ensure his brother was following. He knew Ezekiel would be. He was totally confident he could take John Mills himself if he had to, but the fact that Zeke and the others remained close gave him that added coolness.

It didn't seem to occur to Mills that he might be followed. He drove through several backstreets, moving away from the ocean toward the industrial side of town where there was a series of storage units. Mills drove in, barely stopping to put a code in to open the gate. The heavy gate swung open and then closed behind them as Mills immediately made a right turn down a long row of units. A van was parked toward the end of the row. Malichai didn't like that. He knew the gate wouldn't slow Ezekiel down, they would just go over it and head for the rooftops, but still, if Malichai was transferred to the van and his team wasn't close . . .

Dark-colored van. Can't see the license plate, Zeke. Don't know if it's for my body or for me.

The SUV came to an abrupt halt, nearly throwing his head into the seat in front of him. Mills leapt from the vehicle, opened the door and yanked Malichai out. Malichai caught a glimpse of the older woman from the magic shop, the one who had been so rude to him. Before he could react, Mills kicked him hard in his damaged leg. He wore heavy, steel-toed boots and he kicked hard, driving through the injuries.

Instantly, Malichai's body reacted, so nauseated he nearly vomited as he went down hard. His head hit the asphalt, but that barely registered as Mills delivered two more vicious kicks to his leg, going for maximum impairment. He seemed to know exactly where Malichai had been shot and he used that knowledge to his advantage, kicking him again and again, clearly wanting to permanently damage his leg.

He reached down, caught Malichai under his shoulders and dragged him the few feet to the open door of the storage unit where the woman waited. There was another man with her. He looked to be about fifty and that man reached up, caught the door and slammed it down hard, closing them all inside. There was a light on, but it was fairly dim. Still, when Malichai could get beyond the nausea swirling in his gut, the bile rising in his throat and the pain hammering at his leg all the way to his hip, he could see the scars pitting the man's face.

"Mr. Fortunes," the man greeted. "As one soldier to another, I really am sorry we have to meet under such poor circumstances. I'm sure you can appreciate that it's a sign of respect that we are being so careful. A man who's sustained the kinds of wounds you have in combat is a very lethal human being."

The man spoke very precisely. The way he spoke suggested education. Malichai guessed that he had been an officer. Yeah, it was a great sign of respect to kick the shit out of his wounded leg so he couldn't defend himself. What an asshole. He stayed silent.

The handcuffs were somewhat loose and he worked at slipping them off without moving his shoulders. To cover what he was doing, he made a show of struggling into a sitting position. He kept an expressionless mask, but every movement of his body, as he tried to push himself so his back was to the wall of the unit, was excruciatingly painful.

His leg hurt so bad he feared Mills had those tiny fractures Amaryllis had worked on dissecting his bones all over again. He knew, without a shadow of a doubt, that Mills had undone the miracle Rubin had worked.

"What is it you want from me, Mr. . . . ?" Deliberately he called the man "mister," knowing if he was in charge and he'd been an officer, that would rankle.

"I'm Lieutenant Colonel Callendine. This is Major Salsberry." He indicated the older woman. I'm afraid you've stumbled onto one of our missions, Mr. Fortunes. You've met Sergeant Mills already." He drummed his fingers against his thigh. "I find it incredible that I can't find anything on you other than you do in fact exist and you are in the military. Understand, my orders come all the way from the White House, so I do have resources that should have uncovered everything about you, yet so far, they've been unable to do so."

Those sharp eyes moved over Malichai carefully, inspecting every inch of him. He couldn't fail to see the very real beads of sweat trickling down his forehead or running from his neck down his chest. Malichai tried to keep his breathing even, but it seemed impossible when every breath caused pain to explode through him.

Zeke, this is some kind of military operation. Man claims he's got orders from the White House. Who in the White House he hasn't said, but he doesn't know about our unit. Says his name's Lieutenant Colonel Callendine. Woman with him is Major Salsberry. Says the gorilla who just kicked the holy shit out of my leg is named Sergeant Mills. I've got the cuffs off. I just need a couple of minutes to catch my breath. I want to see if I can find out what the hell they're up to.

"If you really are who you say you are, why didn't you just come to me, soldier to soldier, and tell me to back off? Your man there scared the shit out of the owner of the bed-and-breakfast. Both the owner and the manager have video of him trying to intimidate them. If you're on some secret mission, why would he be dumb enough to have his face plastered all over social media? And why would you attack and injure a fellow soldier? That makes even less sense."

Callendine turned to look at Mills, his eyebrow raised as if seeking an answer.

"The woman, Amaryllis is her name, she gave off this vibe that said she was going to make trouble. I didn't want to hurt her, so I went for maximum intimidation. I planned on taking their phones, but Fortunes showed up."

Callendine nodded as if that was a perfectly acceptable explanation. It wasn't and it didn't make sense to Malichai. Nothing was adding up — unless these were the people planning on killing Marie, Jacy and Amaryllis and then burning down the bed-and-breakfast. Callendine spoke in a very sincere tone as if he was telling the truth. Malichai leaned his head back against the wall as if he was exhausted from fighting the pain. He was just plain pissed off at this point. He was more than positive that it was Callendine who planned on killing the women and Jacy.

Right now, Ezekiel would be contacting Major General for information regarding Callendine, Salsberry and Mills. Who they worked for and why they were in San Diego. Malichai didn't think it was possible they were working toward the same end, but it was possible someone in the White House had a very different agenda and had sent a team out. Whatever their mission was, they were far too comfortable using deadly force against civilians.

"We are looking for a colleague of ours who has disappeared," Callendine continued. "His name is Henry Shevfield. I'm certain you met him."

Malichai made a show of frowning and even glanced up and to his left in a manner many people used when trying to recall a specific person or event. *They're asking about Shevfield, Zeke.* He wanted his brother informed every step of the way just in case he didn't make it out alive.

"I'm sorry. I don't recall anyone by that name." He had gone through interrogation techniques. He'd been interrogated. He'd been tortured, and the evidence was on his body had anyone bothered to look. He could look and sound as if he was telling the truth even when he was lying his ass off. "When was I supposed to have run across him?"

Mills stirred as if he might kick the shit out of Malichai's leg all over again. Every cell in his body rebelled but he kept his face expressionless. He didn't want to encourage the bastard if he was into torture. He needed to get his heart rate down and slowly test how much of his leg he could count on when he needed to explode into action.

"The other day you visited the magic shop and spoke to the major," Callendine said patiently.

Malichai let his gaze shift to the older woman, a faint smile on his face. "Now, *that,*

I remember. She was rude as hell."

"You were lying," Callendine said. "You don't know Miss Crystal."

"Actually," Malichai contradicted, "I do. My fiancée works at the bed-and-breakfast. She's been there for the last year. She introduced me to Miss Crystal some time ago. It's true I don't get leave that often, but when I do, I come to see my girl. She's been helping Marie while Jacy's sick again and so she can't come with me. I'm gone a lot, so it was okay. Miss Crystal is a sweet old lady and a good friend to both women and Jacy."

Callendine glared at the major. "I thought you researched thoroughly."

The major ducked her head, clearly embarrassed that she hadn't uncovered Amaryllis's engagement.

"What branch of the service are you in?" Callendine demanded.

"Air Force," Malichai said.

Mills snickered outright. Malichai was careful not to allow his gaze to shift toward the man. He didn't want any of the three of them to see the sudden burning in his eyes. He was proud of his branch of the military. Very proud. He wasn't going to blow this entire thing in order to get into a pissing match with Mills, whom he already considered an idiot.

"I don't understand what's going on here, sir," he added, using the term of respect as if it was a habit and he wasn't aware of it. He knew Callendine would like that. "If you're running an operation, you should have told me to stand down. I was only looking for Miss Crystal. The major was rude, and that didn't seem right when she was working at the shop supposedly trying to sell to customers. Big red flag to me. It didn't occur to me not to ask questions."

Callendine shook his head. "Perhaps the major could have been a little more personable. She's used to deference."

"What about Anna and Bryon Cooper? Why did you have Mills kill them? He did, I'm certain of it. What kind of threat were they?"

"Why would you think Mills killed them?" Callendine asked.

"It was sloppy. He's military, not a professional. He didn't have a lot of time when the opportunity presented itself, so he improvised instead of waiting for a better time." It was all guesswork, but if Shevfield hadn't killed the couple, someone else did, and it was too big of a coincidence to think that there was another killer involved.

"He should have waited," Callendine

conceded. "The woman couldn't keep her mouth shut. She overheard things she shouldn't have. How much was impossible to say, but she was a threat to national security we couldn't afford."

"She wasn't a threat," Malichai protested. "No one listened to anything she said."

"Getting back to Shevfield. You went swimming that day you spoke with Major Salsberry."

Malichai nodded. He didn't make the mistake of running his hand down his thigh, but the temptation was there. He kept his hands firmly behind his back, shifting his shoulders every now and then as if to ease the strain being handcuffed caused. "My physical therapist advised me to swim in the ocean. I'd promised to continue. The doctors wouldn't release me to come to see Amaryllis unless I agreed to swim. I do so every morning."

"So a recent injury."

Now they were getting into things Malichai didn't want to talk about. Callendine could use that information to help whoever was financing his mission to find out information about Malichai and his unit — at least where he'd been.

Malichai stared at Callendine. Mills made a move toward him, but Callendine waved him off.

"I see," he said. "You must belong to a special unit. I assume wherever you got that injury, and from the photographs I saw, you were shot multiple times, you had to have been on a covert mission."

Malichai remained silent, not taking the bait. Callendine sighed. "Mr. Shevfield entered the water in full scuba gear. You weren't wearing even a partial wet suit and yet you swam for some time in what amounts to very cold water. You came out without a single problem. Shevfield did not return."

Malichai allowed himself to frown. "Are you in some way implying I had something to do with your man Shevfield not returning? It's a damn big ocean. Why would you think I even encountered him? I swam a good distance and then swam back like I do every morning. It was that simple."

"You stayed underwater for a long time, Mr. Fortunes. You were under observation."

"Then your observer would tell you I didn't encounter Shevfield."

"My observer was in touch with Shevfield and he was waiting for you. That was the last we heard of him."

"Then your observer ought to know where he is because I don't. And why would Shevfield be waiting for me? What the hell do I have to do with your mission?" Malichai inserted a note of belligerence into his voice. "Has it occurred to you that maybe your observer had something to do with Shevfield's disappearance and is trying to blame it on me? It wouldn't be the first time someone in a unit made someone else disappear because they didn't like them."

He kept an eye on Mills, judging the distance between them. He had the feeling Mills had been the observer Callendine kept referring to and Mills clearly had a bit of a temper. If he came at Malichai again, Malichai planned on taking him down hard.

"Stand down," Callendine hissed, clearly knowing Mills and that he would take great offense to Malichai's implication. "The pararescue squads go in where few venture, pulling our boys out when they're wounded. Is that what you do?"

"I am a doctor," Malichai admitted.

Callendine was going to keep up with the charade of interrogating him. Giving him a few things wouldn't get him any closer to what he wanted to know. His contacts at the White House hadn't mentioned the GhostWalkers or that very secret project. By telling Callendine he was a doctor, he appeared to be somewhat cooperating.

Those in pararescue weren't GhostWalkers. He was stalling, hoping Callendine would ease up and give him something that would allow Ezekiel to figure out who was directing the mission there and just what it was, because no self-respecting Army man would hire a local hit man to kill two women and a child and set an entire bed-and-breakfast filled with guests on fire.

"That means you're an officer as well." For just one moment, Callendine shifted his gaze toward first the major, and then Mills.

"Yes, sir, I am."

"You were wounded pulling our boys out of the line of fire, weren't you?"

"Sir, I would prefer not to answer that question."

"Because you were on a covert mission. Do you work for the CIA?"

"I am Air Force. Pararescue." It was time to at least admit that much.

Callendine looked triumphant.

"Are you CIA?" Malichai asked.

"I am Army. Just as proud of my branch as you are of yours."

He's claiming he's Army, Zeke. Someone higher up has to be directing him. The major clearly has worked with him before. I asked directly if he was CIA and he said no. I believe him. He had pride in his voice when he said he's Army.

"I need you to tell me who's giving you orders," Malichai said.

"You know I can't do that. I can only tell you the orders are coming directly from the White House."

"Not the president," Malichai guessed. The president would never consider a peace conference a problem. Who then? They weren't there to stop a bombing, not with a hit man employed.

Callendine heaved a sigh. "I know you believe you're doing the right thing, Dr. Fortunes. It is possible, but improbable, that you're telling the truth about why you're here. The fact that my contacts can't find out anything about you suggests that you're a member of a covert unit. The wounds you sustained also suggest the same thing. You have to understand, we can't take any chances that you are here to interfere with our mission."

Malichai knew immediately what he was going to say. Callendine was going to give the go-ahead to his attack dog.

You'd better come in for the party, Zeke. They plan on making me the main event.

Malichai's entire body tensed when it was the last thing he wanted or needed it to do.

414

He had to be relaxed, ready to move, ready to defend himself when the attack came — and it was coming. It was inevitable.

415

13

"I'm giving you one last chance to help yourself out, soldier," Callendine warned.

He's got a contingency of soldiers out here, Ezekiel said. *Can you handle things in there?*

Inwardly, Malichai cursed. He wasn't about to let that asshole Mills kick his leg again. He was going to have to fight them.

Do my best, I'm not going to lie. My leg is damaged again. I don't know how long it will hold up, so speed things up out there.

"I'm afraid I'll have to say the same to you," Malichai said, shifting his weight subtly. He was going to have to use enhanced speed and strength to get his ass off the ground when his leg refused to work properly.

Callendine smiled, but there was little humor in it. None in his eyes. This was a man who had tortured — and ordered torture — on more than one occasion. He didn't mind. He was the type of man who ordered the deaths of two women and a child as well as burning down an establishment with the guests, police and firefighters inside in order to create a diversion for himself.

"I've got a lot of respect for you, Dr. Fortunes, but I can't have you standing in the way of my mission." He stepped back and gestured at Mills.

As Mills sprang at him, Malichai leapt into the air and kicked the man hard with his good leg, putting every bit of strength he had behind it. The man's face imploded inward, disappearing into a mask of blood. At the same time, the door to the left flew open and Amaryllis was there, moving so fast she was a mere blur. She went for Major Salsberry, who had pulled out a weapon and was aiming it at Malichai's head.

The two women went down just inches from where Mills thrashed on the floor, blood pouring from his nose, mouth and eyes. Callendine backed up, his weapon in his hand, but he couldn't take the shot, as Malichai landed awkwardly on the one leg he'd kicked with, smashing into him, knocking him off-balance. When his bad leg touched down, pain spread through him like a burning torch, robbing him of breath. Of momentum. Of even his vision. Blackness swirled around him until everything went dim and he had to fight to stay conscious and in the present.

Amaryllis rolled away from the major and brought Callendine crashing to the cement floor with a scissor takedown, threading her legs through his and rolling again. Outside the storage unit, the sound of gunfire erupted. Callendine scrambled toward the door, yelling to the major. She crawled over Mills, putting his body between hers and Amaryllis.

Callendine aimed at Malichai and squeezed the trigger just as Mills reared up, throwing blind punches. He connected with Malichai just by chance. The blow glanced off his jaw and Malichai pitched sideways. The bullet from Callendine's gun took Mills through the throat.

Major Salsberry caught at Callendine, jerking him out of the unit and into the parking lot where both the SUV that Mills had used to bring Malichai and the van were waiting. She threw herself into the driver's seat of the SUV.

"Stay down," she hissed at Callendine as he joined her, his weapon out, ready to help his team as they fought off Malichai's people.

Callendine ignored her, watching as one

of the unknown soldiers came flying off the roof of the storage unit, wrapping his legs around one of Callendine's men's neck, clearly breaking it, and then leaping off to rush at the next one. Callendine had the superior force by the numbers, but they were going to go down. The men they were fighting were too fast, too accurate and they disappeared like ghosts. He roared the signal to retreat. That was all the time he had before the major had their vehicle racing away.

Amaryllis knelt beside Malichai, running her hands over his leg. "I should have killed that bitch," she whispered. "Who did this?"

Malichai closed his eyes, trying to absorb the pain into his body. He could hear the fight dying down outside as fast as it had begun. They had Mills's body, but little else to figure out what the hell was going on. Nothing made sense. Absolutely nothing. He gestured toward Mills. "He has the boots on. He kicks like a mule."

"Honey. This is bad." There were tears in her voice.

He opened his eyes to look at her. She was beautiful. So damn beautiful. "Thanks for following, baby," he said. He was exhausted, so tired he could barely move. "You saved my life." He laid his head back, uncaring if blood from Mills's body was spreading across the concrete floor. He couldn't move. Every breath seemed forced through his lungs. Raw. Burning.

"I don't like the way this feels, Malichai, but there's too much negative energy swirling around this place. I need to get you out of here, even if we just make it to the parking lot."

He wanted to try for her, but it seemed an impossible task. His leg. He wasn't certain he could feel it anymore, and did he really care?

"Malichai." She said his name sharply. "Look at me. I'm going to have to try to repair that tear. You're bleeding internally and I'm not losing you. Where is Rubin? He has to be close. I can keep you safe until he gets here."

His lashes fluttered and her face swam into his line of vision. "Sorry, baby." He thought he said the words. He tried to lift his hand to her face, to brush away her tears, but his arm weighed a ton.

"Malichai."

He recognized Ezekiel's voice. It was different. Filled with concern. With emotion. Then it was all Ezekiel. Ezekiel at his worst, his big brother, I'll-beat-you-within-an-inch-of-your-life-if-you-don't-obey-me voice. "Don't you fucking die on me."

Mordichai slid his arm around him, holding him. Rubin crowded close. But it was Amaryllis he focused on. Her face swam in and out of his consciousness. She knelt over him, her face a mask of absolute concentration.

"Rubin, I think he's bleeding internally," she said.

"I need his leg bare. Hurry. Please, hurry." The urgency in Rubin's voice must have triggered awareness in his brothers because no one asked him questions. No one voiced concerns over his intentions or suggested calling an ambulance. Trap produced a large knife, and without a word, simply sliced the denim up Malichai's leg, leaving it exposed. He knew they'd shredded the material because his leg felt cold, but he couldn't see it. All he could see was Amaryllis's face and that mask of absolute concentration as she stood beside Rubin, both bent over his leg.

Rubin was quiet and unruffled, like a calm, deep pool of blue icy water moving through him, settling in one spot, staying there and working unemotionally. He worked with complete confidence and at times even directed Amaryllis to something on the bone that only the two of them could see. Even while he directed her, he never stopped what he was doing.

Amaryllis was just the opposite of Rubin. He could feel emotion, even passion, in her every touch. Her hands slid over his thigh. Back and forth. Her breath hitched. He felt heat. Intense heat, so intense it felt as if a laser was focused deep inside his leg. It went from uncomfortable to a burning pain that refused to go away. He tried to move, hoping the laser would at least move spots, but it seemed to move with him.

Amaryllis's breath hissed out and her long lashes lifted. She seemed to glare at Ezekiel and Trap for a moment, and then once more she was wholly focused on him. He felt his brother grip his upper thigh between his large hands. Trap did the same with his calf, holding him immobile.

The laser stayed on that brutal spot for what seemed forever and then moved slightly and began the same concentrated, *intense* heat that had his heart pounding and his head swimming. He leaned back against Mordichai, wishing he could see him, but his vision had gone dark. Black almost. He closed his eyes and let them take over.

"Shit. Shit. Damn it, Zeke. He's slipping away," Mordichai said, panic in his voice.

"He lost too much blood. We have to get

him blood," Rubin said, as calm as ever. "I've got the artery holding, but, Zeke, you'll need to text the SEAL you know and have them get to us like yesterday with the supplies we need."

"I've already done it," Ezekiel replied, his voice grim. "They're on their way. We're lucky they were here in San Diego. Their home is in Montana."

Amaryllis could tell her energy was fading. The repairs to Malichai's bone were much more difficult and involved than the last time. She had managed to stop the worst of the spreading of fracturing but there was far more than last time. She couldn't imagine how Rubin must feel, with the tears that were threatening to take Malichai's life his responsibility.

She could barely kneel upright. Rubin still had to keep Malichai alive, while she could rest, which wasn't fair. Her job had been horrendous, but his had been so much more complex and life-threatening. He was working to keep Malichai's heart, lungs and kidneys going, pushing the blood through his body even when there wasn't enough pressure to do so.

"I can help with that," she whispered to Rubin.

"I'll need you later," he said softly. "Just

get as much rest as possible."

She closed her eyes, not wanting to look at any of them. She couldn't just sit there waiting. Watching. Hoping. She had to do something. She knelt up beside him and once again felt for his bone. The strange thing about his bone was the density of it. She had very dense bones. The density allowed her to swim so much faster beneath the water, and she imagined that was the reason Malichai could as well, but was it the reason for the weird fragmenting along those wounds? They should be long healed by now, yet the small hairline cracks continued to reoccur with any kind of stress. It made no sense. Just like this attack on Malichai made no sense.

She wiped at the tears running down her face, embarrassed to be crying in front of the men. She kept her eyes closed, let them only see internally, the opaque veil that allowed her to see into Malichai's injury. She took her time, meticulously repairing the smaller cracks now, making certain each jagged fissure was closed and knitted together.

Thoughts tumbled around her head, making her feel a little crazy. Had she hesitated before exposing herself to the enemy? She didn't know the answer to that, only that she had to save him. That Malichai had somehow become her world and she didn't want to live without him. There was no going back to an existence of no hope of a future. Malichai was her future.

She kept repairing the bone even when the SEALs showed up, two men with grim faces, scarred and yet beautiful at the same time. They registered somewhere in her mind even though she later didn't remember even looking at them. She was aware of them working on Malichai, setting up an IV and pushing fluids and blood into him.

Both Rubin and Amaryllis shared the exact moment when the turnaround came, when his body realized it was alive and needed to function on its own without Rubin keeping his heart and lungs working, without Rubin pushing blood through his body to his brain and vital organs. They looked at each other, sharing that triumph. She could see utter exhaustion etched into the lines of Rubin's face. He always looked so young. Right at that moment, not so much. He looked pale and drained, but he knew, as she did, that he had saved Malichai's life.

"Thank you," she said softly, for only him to hear. "You're a miracle." The others thought they knew he was; she actually knew. What he did . . . was impossible.

He gave her a faint smile and slumped down for a brief moment. She turned back to continue her work on Malichai's bone because she couldn't make herself quit. She couldn't. She blamed herself. She should have been working on his leg every single night. Not lying in her bed fantasizing about him. Dreaming of having a life with him.

"You have to stop now," Ezekiel's voice whispered in her ear.

He sounded so much like Malichai she felt tears burn in her eyes again. She shook her head and laid her hands over the top section of his fragmented bone. She wanted his body to be strong. No way would that bone hold up. She knew that. The bone still had numbers of tiny little fractures, tiny, barely there cracks that would get wider over time.

"Amaryllis, you have to listen to me. You aren't going to do Malichai any good if you hurt yourself. We'll get him back to the bed-and-breakfast, you can rest and then start again fresh."

She could barely hear the words. Ezekiel sounded far away. She felt his arms around her and then he was lifting her, carrying her away from Malichai. She struggled, terrified of being too far away, afraid she'd lose him if she wasn't there to see inside him, to see that every organ was working properly.

"We've got him. Rubin's with him too. You know Rubin isn't going to let go of him. You just rest. We'll get you back to his room and you can work on him again when you're rested," Ezekiel assured. "In the meantime, we'll look after all three of you until you're on your feet again."

He put her in the seat of a dark-colored car, snapping a seat belt in place, and then went around to the driver's side. "I suppose Malichai didn't have the chance to tell you we have a little bit of intel. Whoever these people are, they hired a hit man to kill you, Marie and Jacy and then set fire to the bed-and-breakfast."

She forced her eyes open to stare into his. Malichai had told her that and she'd left them unprotected in order to follow after him and the man who had taken him. She rubbed her throbbing temples. She'd honestly forgotten that very important piece of information. What was wrong with her? "I need to get back there. Marie and Jacy are completely unprotected."

"There's a specific time period before they make their move," Ezekiel assured. "Doing all that was actually to create a diversion from the real attack, which would be at a different location. We're going to set Rubin up as a hit man, although with what just occurred today, I doubt this crew will oblige us and remain at the magic shop."

"I doubt that as well. Who are they? What do they want?" On some level she knew he was engaging her in conversation in order to keep her from falling apart because she wasn't with Malichai.

"We think they're planning to bomb the San Diego Convention Center during the Ideas for Peace conference," Ezekiel said.

Amaryllis's entire body went still as it really sank in. "Thousands of innocent people could be in those buildings," she whispered. "Why?"

"We don't know the answer and we could be completely wrong. Other than what Anna and Burnell overheard or thought they overheard, we don't have any proof of anything going on. Callendine probably has some kind of government immunity. They'll pull him back and we'll never know why he was here. He's an American, on American soil. He's sworn to protect these people. It doesn't make sense that he would be the one leading a group of soldiers to bring down buildings on innocent people."

It didn't make sense to Amaryllis either. She knew with absolute certainty that Whitney wasn't in any way behind it. He was many things, most not good, but he was definitely a patriot and he would want Callendine stopped.

She swiveled in her seat. Behind them was a large gray van driven by one of the SEALs. "They're GhostWalkers, aren't they? Like you."

"And like you. You're a GhostWalker as well, Amaryllis."

She shrugged. "I'm the misfit, not the GhostWalker."

"Do you have any idea how rare a psychic healer actually is? I've only ever witnessed a couple of real psychic healers. Joe said you're very powerful."

"If I was that powerful, his bone would be healed."

"Joe worked on him as well," Ezekiel reminded her. "And so did Rubin. Rubin is as good as it gets. Better than any human surgeon. If it's impossible, he can do it."

She hugged herself, pressing her arms close to keep from shivering. She was freezing, as if every bit of heat and body temperature control had gone completely out the window. She hated the feeling of complete weakness that had descended over her. She could barely sit upright in the warm, padded seat. She threw a quick glance at Malichai's brother.

"He wants to marry me." She held up her hand with the ring weighing her finger down.

Ezekiel sent her a faint smile. "I'm well aware. He's very happy he found you."

She moistened her very dry lips. Everything felt dry. Her skin. Her hair. Her mouth. "He wants to take me back to Louisiana and have us live there near all of you."

He sent her a sharp glance. "Do you want to live there? We're setting up our homes there, close to one another where in an emergency we can gather into one of the fortresses we've created for our families to be safe. It's a good solution." He gestured toward all the cars on the road. "A place like this would be extremely difficult to protect."

"I've made a few friends here," she conceded. "Marie and Jacy are like family, but I would go wherever Malichai wanted to live. I'm not tied into anything. When you're running from Whitney, you don't dare make too many plans of settling down. If you stay too long in one place, he'll find you. If you move too often, you can attract attention. I was anonymous here. I used Marie's address and I made up a name for documents. I needed money to get a really good forgery, and have been saving toward that end."

"I love my brother," Ezekiel said. "And I want him happy. He seems to have found that with you. I don't know you, Amaryllis, but he seems to think you're very lethal, that you haven't showed him everything you can do. If you are what he suspects, you'll be an even bigger asset to us. On the other hand, if all you do is make my brother happy, you're more than welcome into our family, and we'll protect you from Whitney. We have the means to do that. Not to mention, the more of us there are, the less he'll be able to come at us."

She'd been expecting a warning. She wouldn't have blamed him if he'd threatened her. The last thing she'd expected was a welcome. "Thank you." What else was there to say? She knew she was always expecting rejection. Marie and Jacy had made her feel welcome, and she'd believed it completely after being with them for a good six months. Malichai had given her that same nonjudgmental acceptance. Now, Ezekiel had as well. She felt as if she'd found people with whom she actually fit. She belonged.

"I'm going to need your help with Marie, Amaryllis," Ezekiel went on as he turned toward the parking lot where guests of the bed-and-breakfast had parking spaces reserved.

"Oh my gosh, I forgot my car," she suddenly realized. "I just left it there. And there's a dead body in the storage unit. The cops will be swarming there."

"First, it's a military matter," Ezekiel said. "National security. Second, Trap's bringing your car back for you. And you wore gloves when you picked the lock. Trap had your back."

A little skitter of awareness went down her spine. She had no idea anyone was watching out for her and it felt good to hear. "Why do you need help with Marie?"

"I want to be up-front with her. Tell her what is happening and what we think is going to happen. We need some of our people there at the bed-and-breakfast. I've got a plan, but I want to remove Jacy. I don't want a child at risk. If Marie chooses to leave with her and go to Louisiana where they'll both be safe, I'm good with that. Of course the running of the place will fall on you."

"We have a few regulars who come in during the season for us. I know them. They'll be there daily to clean rooms and help in the kitchen. They've been coming in for the last month."

Ezekiel nodded as he parked the car in

her reserved space. "I'm going to help you walk if you think you can. If not, we're going in the back way and I can carry you."

"I just need fluids and a little rest, and I'll be fine. My body feels like sandpaper," Amaryllis admitted. She had a whopper of a headache, which came with dehydration, but she didn't tell him. She sent him a small grin. "We can test the theory that I can walk."

"My wife is going to love you," he stated and reached in to help her off the seat. "She looks like this little fragile pixie, but she's tough as nails."

Amaryllis heard the love in his voice and somehow, that made her like him even more. She especially liked that he looked after Malichai, and he didn't hide the fact that his brothers meant everything to him. Now she could see that same protection and love extended to his wife — and would be to her.

Her legs nearly buckled, and she had to hold on to him. Craig Williams stood a few feet from them beside a smooth little Mazda, and when he saw her nearly go down, he rushed over.

"What can I do to help? Should I call an ambulance?" He looked genuinely upset, although clearly curiosity was eating him up.

The van carrying Malichai pulled up to the back door of the bed-and-breakfast and Craig swiveled around, watching as several GhostWalkers exited the vehicle. One opened the back doors and reached in. Amaryllis held her breath. She hadn't wanted to leave Malichai, but she didn't have a choice. Now she stared into the van, her heart beating overtime.

The two men, twins it appeared, pulled out the gurney as if they knew exactly what they were doing. They were strong too. Malichai was a big man and heavy with muscle, but they handled the gurney as if it was an easy task. Blood and fluids were still going into Malichai as they carried him toward the back door. They moved fast, as if they did this sort of thing all the time.

Mordichai leapt from the front seat and rushed to open the door. Craig stared after them, his mouth wide open, and then he turned back to Amaryllis. Ezekiel lifted her into his arms and carried her right around the man to follow Malichai and the others inside. Craig abruptly closed his mouth and hurried after them.

Marie came halfway down the hall, saw Malichai on the gurney and, without a single word, led the way to his room, unlocking the door quickly to allow them in.

"Ma'am," one of the SEALs said as he moved past her with the gurney. "I'm Jack Norton. Thanks for helping us out."

"Ken, ma'am," his twin introduced himself as they gently placed Malichai in his bed and hung the equipment as high as possible on the bedpost. He was the more scarred of the two. He had very symmetrical scarring down his face and neck. Every bit of exposed skin showed those scars. "He'll be fine. Just wanted a little sympathy from his girl and went a little too far. Navy won this round." He winked at Marie.

Amaryllis thought he was one of the most charming men she'd ever been around. Once he started talking, it was easy to see past the scars to the man.

Marie fussed with Malichai's pillow before looking up at Amaryllis. "Are you certain he's going to be all right?"

"It's his leg," Amaryllis assured her. "He reinjured it, but with a little rest, he'll be fine. There's a little thing in the parking lot, with my car, their cars, whatever. Too many cars, you know how it goes, and not enough parking spaces. Do you think you could go with Ezekiel and straighten it out for me? Zeke is Malichai's older brother." She wanted to give Ezekiel his time alone with Marie.

She hoped if anyone was listening in, it would make sense that, even though Amaryllis was engaged to Malichai, his family weren't frequent visitors to San Diego.

"Of course," Marie said readily, clearly happy to do something to help out.

Ezekiel was all charm, taking the van keys from the Navy men and then gently putting his hand on Marie's back as he escorted her past Craig, who lingered in the hallway, staring into the room. Mordichai reached over and closed the door without looking at the man.

The moment the door was closed, Rubin shoved a bottle of water into Amaryllis's hand. "You need to drink that." He leaned back in the armchair and downed just about an entire bottle of water.

"I have to check his leg again," she protested. She took the bottle of water and then perched on the bed beside Malichai. Her hands felt hot, the healing energy already pushing out of her, needing to find the fragmenting along the bones, those tiny lines that would spread and widen until his bones would no longer hold up and he would lose his leg.

"You have to rest, Amaryllis," Rubin said

firmly. "You won't do him any good if you collapse. Drink the damn water and give yourself a few minutes."

She removed the cap and took a drink. The water seemed to soak into her parched throat. She crawled up on the bed beside Malichai, ignoring everyone, and lay next to him, intending to just take a minute to rest the way Rubin instructed. He was experienced and knew what he was talking about and he clearly regarded Malichai as a brother. Her eyelids drooped but she saw one of the twins go over to Rubin and set up an IV in order to give him fluids.

She jerked awake about an hour later, shocked that she'd been asleep. Rubin was already standing beside Malichai, his face a mask of concentration. She could see that he hadn't been the only one given fluids. While she'd been asleep, the two Ghost-Walkers from the other team had been busy giving fluids to her. She slid off the bed and knelt beside Malichai's leg, careful to keep out of Rubin's way.

Her attention refused to stay focused on the two men who were moving around the room, pulling shades, changing the bag of blood, checking Malichai's pulse and blood pressure. Her mind kept straying to his leg, to those horrendous wounds, to the damage

Mills had done to him. She'd had episodes in the past when someone was injured where she'd been unable to stay away from them, knowing she needed to help heal them. This was different. This was far more intense. Everything in her seemed completely focused on Malichai's injuries. She *had* to help him. She had no choice. The healer in her was becoming much stronger, much more demanding.

"Amaryllis, work on his calf," Rubin suggested, as if understanding or feeling the powerful energy amassing in her.

He didn't look at her. He was, like her, seeing a different way altogether. She could tell by his eyes, the way they were crystallized, his vision seemingly turned inward. It wasn't that at all. Vision expanded outward; she saw the injuries *through* skin and muscle. His entire leg was stretched out in front of her as if she were a surgeon and that bone was under a bright light and a magnifying lens. She saw every detail in sharp relief.

Amaryllis knew her talent was getting stronger with use. She'd never seen an injury so clearly. The tiny cracks had done just as they had before, moved through the bone like an invasive cancer, spreading out from the points where the bullets had struck and where Mills had landed the worst of his kicks. She could see the impact point and the spreading destruction. His bone was dense. Why was it so brittle and open for destruction?

That made her wonder about his other bones. Had they also suffered similar damage? She would have to remember to check. In the meantime, she had a lot of work to do. She started at the worst point, where the cracks radiated outward like a giant tree with many branches coming off of it. She was patient. She wanted her repairs to be stronger than ever so that if anyone did something similar to Malichai again, there wouldn't be a recurrence of this problem. Each jagged line was knitted back together with meticulous attention to detail.

Because the lines weren't even, she had to be extremely careful as she filled in those tiny cracks, to get all the way to the very bottom of each of them. Some of the cracks were extremely deep. The upper surface was deceptive in that the fissures could look shallow, just barely a faint line, but beneath that, on the next layer down, the crack extended at an angle, a much deeper gap. That would make the bone more unstable than ever.

The heat gathering inside her became a laser to work with. The pinpoint of light made it easier to see into the fissures, noting which ones were truly shallow and others that continued farther down at an angle. She had managed to work almost the entire calf when the energy suddenly just left her body. As it did, she found she couldn't kneel upright any longer. She actually slumped over, hitting her head on his hip.

Mordichai was there instantly, his arm around her, helping her to slide down beside Malichai and then half sit so Trap could push another bottle of water at her.

Ezekiel gripped Rubin by the shoulder. "You have to stop. You two have been at this for hours. Rubin. I mean it. Sit the fuck down." He poured command into his voice.

Rubin looked so pale she wanted to make him stop, even though she knew Malichai's bone was a disaster. And maybe there was no saving it. If Rubin couldn't do it, no one could. He stumbled once to the chair Ezekiel took him to, but his hands were steady as he drank from the water bottle and then he sent her a faint smile.

"How you holding up?"

She felt a real camaraderie with him. He knew what Malichai's leg was really like and what it was going to take to keep it from shattering. He also knew the drive a healer felt when they saw that kind of horrendous damage. She sent him a small smile. "I'm doing okay. It's strange, but I don't even feel time passing. Do you?"

He shook his head. "We were at it for hours though." He glanced across the room.

Amaryllis followed his gaze with her own. Ezekiel was seated in the armchair. His fingers drummed on the small table. There was a cup of coffee right beside his hand.

"I don't think either of you should keep these healing sessions quite so long," he said. "I don't want to risk your health. If you slow it down, Rubin, won't you still accomplish the same thing without such an obvious risk? Amaryllis?"

She didn't answer. She was too tired to do so, and she wasn't certain what she would have said. She didn't know if she could slow down. Her mind mapped out the injuries, and that powerful healing energy inside her insisted on working. She hadn't noticed the passage of time. She only saw the injury and needed to fix it. She thought that need was more of a compulsion than anything else. How could she stop herself if she wasn't even aware of time passing?

"The injury is quite severe," Rubin said. "Mills was wearing steel-toed boots and his kicks landed right on each of the spots where Malichai was shot. Even so, the bone should have held up. The exact same weird fracturing occurred. It doesn't make sense. Some other factor is at play here, and honestly, the only thing I can think of that's suspicious is the field dressing." He glanced at Trap, who remained a silent sentry, his back to the door.

"Can you repair the bone again?" Ezekiel asked. This time his voice was grim.

"We're trying. The damage to his artery was severe. Had I not been there, he would have been gone within a matter of a couple of minutes," Rubin said. "The bone" — he looked at Amaryllis — "I don't have an answer. We're trying."

Beside her, Malichai stirred, trying to pull himself into a sitting position. Instantly, Mordichai helped him. Malichai slipped his arm around Amaryllis.

"How does your leg feel?" Ezekiel asked his brother.

"Like it's on fire. Much hotter than the last time. She generates so much energy, it's brutal." He looked at Rubin. "You're icy cool. It's interesting to have both sensations at the same time on my bone."

It comforted her that Malichai was talking. He lay in the bed, his upper body propped up on pillows while his legs were stretched out in front of him. He had one arm around her and that didn't move, as if he feared he would lose her if he let go of her.

Amaryllis turned her face away from all of them. She just wanted to sleep. If she was able to get a little bit of time to sleep, then she could start again.

"Need a half hour or so," she murmured and turned her face into Malichai's rib cage, closing her eyes. The light in the room was dim, but everything was beginning to hurt, especially her eyes, as if she'd burned them. One leg ached until the ache became a pain so intense, she thought she might have to scream. She just wanted a few minutes to sleep.

Ezekiel picked up his coffee cup. "The magic shop has been deserted, which is no surprise. Nothing was left behind that was incriminating or a clue to what those people were up to, but clearly it isn't good."

"They walked right in here and took Malichai. They could have come in and shot Amaryllis, Marie and Malichai," Mordichai said, a bite to his voice. "But they took him with clear intentions to interrogate him."

There was no going to sleep now. Amaryllis wanted to hear every word. She couldn't pry her eyes open, so she just lay against Malichai's side and listened.

"Who are *they*? You get anywhere with that?" Rubin asked.

"Callendine is a lieutenant colonel in the Army. Major Roseland Salsberry worked with Callendine for several years and is very devoted to him, although they aren't romantically involved. Mills is under Callendine's command. Callendine, across the board, has commanded respect and admiration, both from his superiors and from his men. More than once I was told Callendine's men would follow him anywhere, straight into the jaws of hell," Ezekiel informed them.

"What's he doing here? Did I mess up an investigation of some kind?" Malichai asked. "Because even if I did, whatever they're up to can't be good."

Ezekiel put his coffee cup back on the small table and once more drummed his fingers. "No one seems to know what he's doing here. He — and the major — are supposedly on extended leave along with a number of their trusted unit. Joe is looking into it. He's discussing it with Major General.

"I've gotten Marie to agree to bring Jacy to Louisiana. I don't like any of this, and the two of them are civilians and in danger through no fault of their own," Ezekiel continued. "Trap's sent the jet back for our team, and Marie and Jacy can go back in his jet once they get here."

Malichai sent the man standing silently against the door a small smile. "Thanks, Trap."

Trap shrugged. "Wyatt's got those five little girls. Too many for me to stay home and guard." He sounded gruff.

Amaryllis didn't smile. She was beginning to believe that Trap wasn't nearly as antisocial as he pretended to be — at least not with those he claimed as his family.

"How close is Cayenne to giving birth?" Malichai asked Trap straight out.

Trap shrugged. "You know Cayenne. She'll give birth when she's ready and not before. You'll know soon enough."

"What does that mean?"

"She'll be on that plane. She doesn't like to be away from me, and she's gotten so she doesn't listen to a damn thing I say. Told her flying wasn't good for her. She's not showing at all so she thinks she can pretend she isn't pregnant."

"I just don't like the idea of her near combat when she's so close," Malichai said. "I have a bad feeling about this. If Callendine was telling the truth and orders came down for him to come here and carry out some mission, you and I both know someone at the White House wants to stamp out all GhostWalkers."

"They were here before you were. There's no way for them to have guessed you'd be coming," Ezekiel said. "This isn't about you."

"Amaryllis was here and she's a Ghost-Walker."

"You're just worried on her behalf, Malichai. Believe me, I understand the feeling. They had no way of knowing Amaryllis is a GhostWalker."

Amaryllis felt warm — very happy — when Ezekiel acknowledged that she was the same as they were. She'd never thought of herself as being a GhostWalker. She was part of the flawed group — a woman easily disposed of because she was so inferior. These men, elite soldiers, made her part of them with just a few words and the inclusive camaraderie she needed.

"Speculation on Callendine?" Malichai said.

"He is very committed to whatever his mission is, and so are his men," Mordichai said immediately. "When they took off, they carried their dead. The only body we have is Mills."

Ezekiel shook his head. "We don't have that either. Less than forty minutes ago, I got word that someone broke into the medical examiner's office and took the body. We know who Mills is. We have a clear identification, so the why of taking such a risk eludes me."

"Callendine hired a hit man," Malichai said. "Why would he do that? And what business did Mills have killing Anna and Bryon? This is so crazy."

Mordichai moved close to the bed, took Amaryllis's pulse and then tried to nudge her to sit so he could give her more water.

She tried to wave him away.

"You need it. You're badly dehydrated. Your lips are so cracked they're bleeding. If you don't drink this water, I'm hooking you up to an IV."

She didn't like that idea. She tried to open her eyes. They burned, refusing to cooperate. When she tried to move her head, it pounded, lashing at her. Mordichai was right, she was dehydrated.

"It's a good idea anyway, Mordichai," Malichai said. "No matter how much water you push into her that way, she's never going to catch up."

"She's awake," Amaryllis muttered, trying not to sound rebellious. "I can drink water."

No one seemed to pay attention to her. Mordichai was fast and very efficient, finding her vein without doing much more than looking at her arm. She couldn't summon up enough energy to protest. Malichai's arm pulled her tighter against him, making her feel safe and secure, so she just settled beside him and continued listening.

"I think we should go back to figuring the San Diego Convention Center is the target," Malichai said. "If Anna had to be silenced because she wanted to tell the cops, then she did, in fact, overhear something no one wanted her to repeat. Callendine, Salsberry and Mills were using the magic shop and Miss Crystal's apartment in the back of the store as their headquarters."

"They removed Miss Crystal by making her believe she'd won a trip on a cruise. They paid for everything," Ezekiel said. "So they didn't murder Miss Crystal. Why, when they so readily killed others over the last two years?"

"They needed her magic shop open," Amaryllis said without thinking. She didn't even open her eyes. "If they killed her, the shop would close. There was no one to take her place. She'd said so dozens of times. But if they just had her go away for a time, they would have the shop and be able to do anything they wanted from it."

Ezekiel nodded. "Thank you, Amaryllis. I

believe you're correct. They needed her alive more than they needed her dead."

"Callendine trusted someone to do the intel on Miss Crystal. He would never have been so sloppy as to say she was visiting a son. That was just idiocy not to say she was on a cruise," Malichai said.

"They practiced a script," Mordichai guessed. "Just like we rehearse a mission, over and over until we know exactly what we're going to do, they had to have rehearsed a script. My guess, in the script they first used, she was dead, they killed her, so they came up with various reasons why she wasn't there. Midstream, they sent her on a cruise and everyone got confused."

That was plausible. Amaryllis didn't like to think that the people she knew were so easily disposable to others, but it was obvious that they were to Callendine. He had hired a man to rid the world of Marie, Jacy and Amaryllis.

"Rubin, you can't go to the magic shop pretending to look for Shevfield because they aren't there. I'm going to have you arrested and put it in the papers that you're a suspect in Anna and Bryon Cooper's deaths. Callendine will look into you. He has to have someone at the police department or a hacker helping him. You will be suspected of being a hit man, but no one has ever been able to convict you. The police will have to release you because there is no evidence against you and you'll be staying here."

"Lovely," Amaryllis murmured. "Our reputation is growing."

"A thrill a minute, baby," Malichai assured. "People love that. The B and B will be more popular than ever."

Ezekiel ignored them. "Shevfield's body will be found so Callendine will have to use one of his men to create his diversion or contact the supposed hit man at the B and B. That puts Rubin right in an enticing situation. Callendine won't be able to resist the fact that you're exactly where you need to be to carry out his diversion."

"You don't think it's too big of an apple falling in his lap?" Malichai asked.

Ezekiel shrugged. "We have to take that chance. We don't have any other play. When Amaryllis is feeling better, she can unlock the attic. Trap and Cayenne want the basement. Cayenne will be more comfortable there. We've still got to go through the house and find any bugs. There weren't any in this room. We've gone over it several times. Even so, we've got a jammer in here, so when we need to talk, let's use this room."

"I thought you wanted to move us to

Amaryllis's room," Malichai said.

Ezekiel shook his head. "No, I'll put one of the men in there. Probably Gino. Draden and Shylah will take one of the two rooms Marie has been renovating. That will give us, including you and Amaryllis, eight here at the inn. Bellisia is joining me at the house I rented. Mordichai is already there and Joe will be coming in. So, we'll have three more of us within minutes of you."

"Only Wyatt and Diego home?" Malichai asked. "That's not good."

"Jack and Ken Norton have some of their team members on the way to Louisiana right now," Ezekiel said. "Everyone will be safe while we take care of whatever is going on here. Jack and Ken will back us up along with half of their team members here if we need to call on them. In addition, we have access to the base."

"I don't like the fact that Callendine is legitimately a soldier and was a good one at that," Malichai said.

"Decorated," Ezekiel supplied.

Malichai swore under his breath. "This has all the marks of a major clusterfuck, Zeke. If they're here on what is supposed to be legitimate business . . ."

"Hiring a hit man?"

"You know what I mean. Under orders.

451

And he's a decorated officer? His men?" Malichai shook his head. "We're under scrutiny already in the White House. They're looking for any excuse to terminate us."

Amaryllis gasped. Shocked. Whitney didn't mind terminating the girls. To him they were throwaways. He acted as if they should be happy to give their lives in service to their country through his experiments. But the soldiers? They were miracle workers on the battlefield. They ran covert missions and saved lives like no others. Someone wanted them terminated? How did that make any sense? She could see why they were building fortresses. It wasn't about Whitney. It was about any others who might consider them the enemy. Malichai had said that to her, but she hadn't really comprehended that someone in power, someone in the White House, maybe even the president of the country, might decide to give the order to have them killed.

"We can't let these people kill innocents, no matter who they are. They don't get a pass. That's why you let Mills walk out of here with you when you could have taken him. We don't operate that way and we never will."

Amaryllis decided she didn't mind connecting her life to Malichai's, not when his

GhostWalkers thought that way. They stood for the people she wanted to stand for. She wanted to be like they were and she was going to throw her lot in with them.

Once Malichai figured it out, that worked. She did surprise her parents, though, and it wasn't quite the way she wanted to because she was mad at them for trying to break them up.

14

Trap Dawkins glared at Malichai. "What were you told about trying to do exercise on that leg? Are you deliberately trying to make it worse?"

Trap was difficult at the best of times. He was an undisputed genius and owned so many patents Malichai had lost count. Draden and Wyatt were best at handling him, although all of the GhostWalkers on their team had gotten fairly good at being around him and not taking offense. Trap was very high-functioning Asperger's. His father had murdered his mother and siblings and then his uncles had taken his remaining aunt, the one who had raised him, and raped and murdered her. Trap had retreated even further into his mind and really, who could blame him?

He'd joined the military to learn to be strong, to make certain no one could ever take anyone from him again. He'd gotten that way, but he'd also developed habits of not speaking when he didn't want to and losing himself in his work for weeks on end. He was abrupt, rude and didn't give a damn if anyone liked him or not.

Malichai knew, under all of that roughness, Trap was dedicated to the men and women in their unit and family. And then he'd met Cayenne and fallen like a ton of bricks. She had never been out of a cage, not unless she was being experimented on or they were testing her abilities to defend herself against a team of supersoldiers. It was always a life-or-death test and at the end of the day, Cayenne was alive, and the team was dead. Eventually, the man who was running the laboratory had become so fearful of her, he had scheduled her for termination. Trap had been the man to set her free.

The last few days, when Trap had come with just a few of the team, he'd mostly remained silent, and stayed away from everyone, just doing his job, but now, he seemed to have strong opinions.

Malichai ignored Trap and concentrated on Cayenne. She was a little thing, deceptively so. Her hair was shiny black and if you looked closely, you could see the red hourglass running through the back of it when the silky strands settled a certain way.

"How are you, sweetheart?" he asked, because he liked her. They all did. She was elusive, but she was kind and sweet and loved Trap with everything in her.

She gave him a tentative smile. "Good. I'm so sorry about your leg, Malichai. We've all been very worried. Nonny sends her love and says to tell you she'll be cooking something very special when you get home."

"I really appreciate you coming, Cayenne, but I'm worried about your safety. You could give birth at any moment." It was a shot in the dark, but he was a doctor and he'd thought a lot about the possibility of when Cayenne could have gotten pregnant.

Trap was insane for her. He probably hadn't taken the time to protect her from pregnancies and she would know very little, if anything, about birth control with her background. If she'd gotten pregnant immediately, she would definitely be close to giving birth. When Malichai had asked Trap directly, he hadn't really given an answer.

"Any of us are capable of delivering a baby," Trap answered gruffly. "Stretch your leg all the way out. Zeke told me that your woman is a psychic healer." He glanced at Amaryllis, who was staying absolutely still, almost holding her breath.

Trap damn well knew Amaryllis was a psychic healer. He'd been there when she was with Rubin trying to save his leg. He was diverting attention from Cayenne and her pregnancy on purpose. Malichai wanted to strangle him. Malichai threaded his fingers through Amaryllis's to give her reassurance. Trap had shut down any other questions directed at Cayenne over the birth of their child so he just shrugged and moved on, answering for Cayenne's sake. "Yes, and she saved my leg a couple of times."

Amaryllis couldn't let Cayenne think that and Trap knew better. "Rubin really saved his life. And we both worked on the leg together," she corrected.

Cayenne sent her a small smile but didn't respond.

Trap ran his hands over the damaged leg from the top of Malichai's thigh to his ankle. "What did you find?" he asked Amaryllis.

"You know what she found, Trap," Malichai said. He didn't want to go through the entire thing again.

"I want her to tell me again," Trap said stubbornly. "It's important. I'm trying to figure out what the hell is going on and I can't get the visual in my head. It keeps happening over and over and fast now. I want Amaryllis to tell me. I don't want to hear it over a speaker while I'm on a plane. I want her to tell me."

That surprised Malichai. Trap rarely addressed anyone he didn't know.

Amaryllis answered without hesitation before Malichai could protest Trap's tone. "There were hundreds of little fissures running through the bone. The cracks widened fast. I had the feeling the field dressing Malichai used in order to stop the bleeding and get the necessary strength to get out of the situation caused some peculiarity in his bone, although that's only because I didn't find it anywhere else, and I expected to. There was just no other reasonable explanation. Rubin thought that same thing."

"I don't need to know what you thought, so much as what you actually saw. Did this same thing happen again when Mills kicked him?"

"Yes, but there was no chance that the bone was completely healed. Malichai told me the physical therapist wanted him walking daily as well as swimming. I didn't necessarily agree with that, but Malichai is impatient to be back on his feet one hundred percent. He doesn't mind working hard, but I think he actually needs to rest the leg."

She was watching Trap's hands as he inched his palms over the calf. Malichai felt heat sliding over his skin. It wasn't like when Amaryllis worked on him, which she had for the last two days. The energy she generated was so powerful that he always expected to see blisters on his skin, although the last time, it felt as if she'd been able to tone it down somewhat.

Amaryllis was often busy in the kitchen, and thankfully Mordichai and Ezekiel helped her, while Rubin spent his time in jail, and then was let go. He stayed to himself in his room as a rule. Gossip swept through the inn and reached Malichai through Burnell and Jay. They came to visit him and would happily tell him that Marie'd had to take Jacy to a hospital and there was a suspected *hit man* in their presence. They whispered the word "hit man" and yet emphasized it at the same time.

Craig came in and played chess with him occasionally and regaled him with tales of the other guests' reactions to the suspected hit man. He asked all kinds of questions about Malichai's injuries and how he got them and whether there was permanent damage, all of which Malichai fielded easily.

"I hate staying in bed when Amaryllis clearly needs help without Marie here."

"Everyone's here," Trap said. "She'll have plenty of help now. Draden and Shylah are a huge help in the kitchen. Shylah can actually cook — well — she can follow recipes according to Nonny, which most of the women can't."

Cayenne winced visibly and turned away from the bed. At once, Trap dropped his arm around her shoulders and pulled her to him. "Baby, you're too damned emotional. It's the fucking hormones. I don't give a damn if you ever learn to cook. You know I don't. I like you going to the lessons because you enjoy being around Nonny and the women, not because I want you to learn to cook. Stop being so damn sensitive."

Malichai winced. Trap clearly was showing his woman he loved her and it was obvious he really didn't care whether she could cook or not, but he sounded gruff, even a little mean when he swore at her.

Trap framed Cayenne's face with his hands, forcing her head up, and he took her mouth hard. Devouring her. Kissing her until neither of them seemed to breathe. Until her arms slid around his neck and she leaned her body completely into his, relaxing totally into him.

He lifted his head first. "You good, baby?"

Cayenne nodded. She didn't seem the

least embarrassed that there were witnesses to Trap's hungry kisses. Malichai couldn't help smiling at Amaryllis, who smiled back.

"Yes."

"I've got to make certain Malichai is healing. If I don't know what's going on with his leg, I can't boss him around adequately, and you know how pissed off that kind of thing makes me." He rubbed his chin on top of Cayenne's head and then turned back to Malichai. "It's official, you know, in case your brother didn't tell you. Mordichai finished his work in emergency care. He's been taking time off to do his clinicals, which is hysterical since he's been doing them for the last few years in the field. But he's officially a doc now. No one can give him a bad time."

That was just like Mordichai not to say a word. Anything to do with GhostWalkers was always so secretive. Malichai had known his brother had been going to school for several years, but they often interrupted him in order for him to go on regular missions. He'd gotten most of it out of the way, but he was persistent and continued even though it had taken much longer than normal.

"Trap, you never once admitted you had any healing ability," Malichai said. They all did in one capacity or another, but Trap had always insisted he didn't, that it was nonsense.

Trap abruptly pulled his hands off Malichai's leg. "I don't. I can 'see' sometimes, but I can't heal. I'm taking Cayenne downstairs. We don't want to be caught in here. But you stay off this leg and let the damn thing heal."

"Will do," Malichai said, uncertain if he meant it.

Amaryllis went to the door and looked out. They'd swept the other rooms for bugs and found several, all in the rooms of those attending the Ideas for Peace convention. The only other room to have one had been Malichai's. Malichai was fairly certain Callendine had paid someone to plant the bugs — most likely Billy. Malichai had destroyed the listening device and now, several times a day they swept the room just to be safe.

The hallway was dark, and Trap and Cayenne immediately disappeared into the shadows in the way the GhostWalkers did. Amaryllis watched down the hall to make certain no doors opened. The B and B was full, every room taken, and there was excitement over the upcoming convention. Often groups of guests congregated in the meeting room or front room to talk about the various ideas they had and what they were most looking forward to. Judging by the friendly way the strangers treated one another, no one would ever think a deadly threat could be hanging over their heads.

Amaryllis closed and locked the door, turned back to him and leaned against it. "I find it interesting that your GhostWalkers think nothing of visiting you in the dead of night, never thinking they might get seen by a guest."

"They rely on other senses to tell them if anyone is around, and they're used to working at night. Trap would have known if anyone was in the hallway."

"Some of the guests have a habit of sneaking down to the dining room and raiding the cookie stash there."

"Why are you way over there?" Malichai studied her face. She was nervous around the GhostWalker team members, and he couldn't blame her. Essentially, she had to rearrange her thinking from looking at them as supersoldiers — those belonging to Whitney's private army — and the GhostWalker teams serving their country.

Amaryllis continued to stay across the room from him. "I think all of you take too many chances, Malichai."

"All of you" meant him. She wasn't happy

that he'd been testing his leg already. She might not swear at him the way Trap did, but she was equally as upset, maybe more. He didn't want his woman to be the one looking out for him. He did have some pride, especially now that the others were there, and she could see all the various things they were capable of.

Trap and Wyatt were geniuses and they had more money than they knew what to do with. Draden had been some hotshot model before he was a GhostWalker. Women tended to fall at his feet and worship. Gino was an extremely dangerous man. It had been Malichai's observation that women had a tendency to think dangerous men were every bit as hot as a model.

What was he? His mother was an addict willing to sell her kids for drugs. He'd grown up on the streets, Ezekiel watching out for him. He was a doctor, but he wasn't gifted the way the others were. He was what he was — a soldier.

He'd never felt inferior before. Never. Not around any of them. But he hadn't been lying in a bed with a leg that wasn't worth shit while the woman he wanted most in the world to see him as someone worthwhile was surrounded by men who could do just about anything. Hell. She'd had to save his life, not just with her healing skills but by following him when he'd allowed himself to get kidnapped.

He'd been so arrogant, it hadn't occurred to him that Mills would kick the shit out of his injured leg. He should have. He'd exposed that injury to the enemy on purpose, using it as an excuse to go into the water so Shevfield could make his try. He'd been so damned smug. Now, seeing the men he admired most, the men he thought of as his family, he could barely stand being in bed, the one they all had to rally around because he couldn't take care of business himself. He wanted to be there for his woman, not have his family do it for him.

"We're soldiers, babe. All soldiers take chances. You certainly have. I know that Whitney's training exercises are often very lethal. You managed to escape and stay out of the sights of Whitney and any of his spies."

"Why are you doing this?" There was hurt in her voice. "Did you need your friend to tell you that you shouldn't try to exercise that leg yet because he's male? A hotshot doctor? I told you and you just ignored my advice."

He winced. He hadn't looked at it the way she might. "My working the leg or not working it has nothing to do with Trap. I listened to you. And I'll even admit, on some level I knew you were right. I just didn't want it to be true."

"Why?"

She hadn't moved. She remained pressing her body against the door, her large blue eyes reflecting the light from the lamp by the bed.

"Baby, come here," he insisted. He didn't want to sound like a self-pitying wimp, and he would if he had to explain to her that he was jealous of his friends.

"I need to know what's going on with you, Malichai. This isn't easy for me. I thought we'd go back to the swamp and meet your friends one at a time, in a casual setting. They're taking over my bed-and-breakfast. I'm not saying I'm not grateful for the help — I am — but they know more about what's going on than I do. These are my guests. My friends. I feel responsible for them. Before, you listened to me. You talked to me. We were a team. Now, I don't know what you're doing or thinking, and I feel very lost."

That was the last thing he wanted. "Please come here to me, Amaryllis. I'm feeling a little lost myself. I've never been in a relationship, and I've never had an injury that sidelined me at the worst possible time. There's something . . ." He couldn't put it into words, but something was really wrong with his leg. He could feel it. He knew the damage, whatever it was, wasn't going away anytime soon — if ever — and he needed to be one hundred percent to help his team against this new, very elusive threat. Maybe he was doing what he always did, working harder, trying to focus his attention on healing his injury faster by working it. Pushing himself to get stronger.

"What is it, Malichai? Talk to me."

"I'm afraid I'm going to lose you." He just blurted it out. He hadn't meant to say it. He hadn't even wanted to think it.

She tilted her head to one side and frowned. "Malichai, that doesn't make any sense at all. We're already together. I made a commitment to you. You have to talk to me and sort out what you're really feeling."

"Then come over here." He held out his hand. The anxiety in him was increasing, not decreasing. That part of him that always knew when something wasn't right. It was all-encompassing now, swamping him. The urge to move, to throw the covers back and get up and start taking care of every problem was so strong he actually turned in the bed to drop his feet toward the door.

The movement galvanized Amaryllis into action. "Don't you *dare,* Malichai." She leapt across the room, proving immediately that she was definitely a GhostWalker. She crossed the room in one single jump, landing beside the bed and putting a hand to his chest to deter him. "I think you need to learn to verbalize, Malichai."

That made him want to smile in spite of the churning in his gut, telling him something was off and danger was imminent. "I'm more of an action type."

"You have the most unusual eyes, almost golden. At night they shine back at me. Sometimes, when you're upset or worried, the shine becomes a glow and you look very dangerous." She frowned and leaned in to rub the pad of her finger across his lips. "Like now, Malichai. You look like a very lethal predator."

"Not to you, Amaryllis."

"I know that. Honey, why would you think that you would lose me? It has something to do with your team showing up, and don't try to tell me differently. You began to withdraw the moment they all began to call in saying they were here."

He shrugged, deciding truth was better than deception. "I'm going to look whiny and jealous, but better you see now that I can be that way than much later when we're married and we have a few dozen kids . . ."

"Stop." Laughing, she pushed at his hip so he moved over, and she could sit on the bed with him. "You're so crazy. Who in the world are you jealous of? Please don't say Trap. First, the man isn't exactly filled with scintillating conversation and he's very abrupt about his wife's pregnancy . . ."

He loved her laughter and let it soothe him, but he didn't want her to think Trap didn't pay attention to his wife. "Trap adores Cayenne." Still, he liked that she was annoyed with Trap. The man had money, was good-looking and had two good legs.

"He may adore her, honey, but to dismiss the fact that she might give birth any moment because there are doctors around is ludicrous. She's counting on him and he's thinking with some lofty part of his brain, not his heart. He needs to be her husband, not her doctor, who, by the way, has never actually delivered a baby out of his va-jay-jay so he needs to be just a little more thoughtful on the subject."

Malichai stared at her for a moment and then burst out laughing. "I'm falling more in love with you every minute. I do have to agree with you there. Trap thinks she can deliver a baby and just go right on fighting in the jungle. He might get a bit of a surprise with this one."

"So, stop worrying about me wanting to be with someone else, it's ludicrous."

"I don't stack up very well against men who have two legs and can take care of the enemy while I lie in bed twiddling my thumbs." He laid it out for her.

Amaryllis stared at him for a long time. Too long. His stomach dropped. She knelt up on the bed in front of him, framed his face with both hands and leaned in to brush her lips against his. Featherlight. The touch sent desire slipping into every cell in his body. Gently. A unique invasion. The sensation was so gentle, barely there, but every bit as impactful, craving building slowly but never stopping.

Then her teeth tugged at his lower lip. Her tongue slid along the seam of his mouth. He opened his mouth and she was there, pouring need and passion into him. Pouring something else that felt like love. He was so unfamiliar with that emotion that at first, he wasn't certain what it was that surrounded him and lifted him up. That he chased after. That he craved.

His arms went around her, locking her to him, and he took over the kiss. He was rougher than he intended, but she was driving him insane with need. With the possibility that she really would choose him no matter what.

"Lose the panties, Amaryllis." He kept kissing her, his hand in her hair, bunching it in his fist, making it difficult for her to comply, but it didn't matter. He had to keep kissing her. Her taste, the one that sent that emotion rocketing through his body, moving through him to center in his groin, drove him beyond all sanity. He wanted her with every breath he took. He needed her right then even more than that.

She struggled to obey him, dragging her jeans and panties down her legs all the while kissing him back. It should have been awkward and impossible, but somehow, they made it work, and then she was straddling his lap, lowering herself slowly over him.

His cock was on fire. Burning. Throbbing. It felt like a steel spike and she felt so tight as she sheathed him, inch by slow inch, that he thought his head might explode. She strangled him, a scorching-hot vise surrounding him with a silken fist.

Malichai threw back his head, wanting to roar with pleasure, but he stayed as silent as possible when she began to move at his urging. "That's it, baby, ride me." His hands guided her.

Amaryllis caught on fast, her muscles squeezing, biting down as she moved up and down his shaft, massaging and milking, the friction almost unbearable. He wasn't certain if it was pleasure he'd never known, or passion that bordered and rode that fine edge of pain because that silken fist was so tight. Whichever it was didn't matter, because he never wanted it to stop.

She threw back her head and picked up the pace so that his breath exploded out of his lungs in time with hers. She looked beautiful, exotic, so perfect there in the dark, her body surrounding his, his cock buried deep inside her. He loved knowing she was his woman. Some men needed many to make themselves feel like a man. He had always needed one. The only. Now that he had her, he knew why.

Every movement of her body sent little bolts of lightning forking through his entire being, so that flames rushed through his veins like a drug. His hips thrust hard, an automatic, nearly desperate response. He never wanted this to end. He let himself get lost in her, in all that fiery heat. He caught her hips and took over, using his strength to power her body to pound down over his. Each streak of that tight silken fist pounding up and down his shaft and over the sensitive crown nearly had him losing all control.

He held on grimly, forcing himself to look at his woman. To see her face, feel how close she was. She made little noises, a kind of soft moan that added to the need building so high in him. Everything about Amaryllis was perfection to him. Just looking at her, the way she threw her head back with abandon, the way she gave herself to him, total surrender, the way she moved her body over his, as if she could never get enough of his cock, and the expression of bliss on her face, all heightened his pleasure.

"You there, baby? You need to get there."

"I'm there." She panted the words, her breath as ragged as his.

He took her over the edge, took them both tumbling off into space somewhere, while the fire consumed them and the stars surrounded them. Her body gripped his so tightly, he thought he'd have the imprint of her sheath on his shaft, but it felt like nothing he'd ever experienced before. Pure fire enclosing him in a world of sensation. Searing him, branding him. Velvet stroked him. Silk gripped him. Her music surrounded him.

He held her to him, trying desperately to find air. Emotion overwhelmed him, rising out of nowhere, shocking him. He tightened his hold on her, locking her close, forcing her face against his chest so she couldn't look up at him. He knew his vulnerability to her was naked on his face. There was no way around it, not right then.

Amaryllis didn't fight him. She snuggled closer to him, her arms just as tight around him. She seemed to almost know before he did what he needed. Sometimes he was aware of the press of her lips against his skin. Other times it was the fan of her lashes against him, but she didn't lose patience, and just let him come down from the rush at his own pace.

When he could finally pull his thoughts together, he loosened his arms and reluctantly allowed her to slide off him. He found it amazing to be so connected to another human being, not just their bodies, sharing the same skin, but their minds and even hearts. He'd shied away from that thought from the beginning, but he had to face it. He was already all in. Completely.

Malichai searched his mind while she headed for the bathroom. She had alleviated that nagging fear — that she wouldn't want him now that he wasn't a hundred percent with a battle possibly looming. Why was his gut still churning and his radar going off so persistently? Something was wrong and it wasn't going away because his woman had just given him the best sex he'd ever had.

Amaryllis returned, dressed in capri yoga pants and a short tank top that hugged her breasts and left her midriff bare. When she moved, he could see the alluring underside of her breasts peeking out. He liked the sight of her. She looked around for somewhere to put her clothes and her gaze fell on his face. Instantly, she froze, her entire attention on him.

"What is it, Malichai? I thought we took care of your worries."

"I thought so too. My gut still says something is very, very wrong."

"I'll go check out the kitchen." She glanced at her watch. "It won't take any time to walk through the halls just to make certain everything is all right."

Malichai stiffened. "I'm not lying here in bed while you put yourself in danger. We don't even know how bad the leg is this time."

"I know how bad. I did my best, but those fractures in the bone are persistent. They keep returning. I don't know if they were already coming back before Mills kicked you, or if that brought them out again. The reason doesn't matter right this moment, it only matters that they're there. Rubin worked on you for hours. I did as well. Nothing can mess that up. He told you to rest the leg, Malichai, and you have to do what he says."

Rubin had avoided his eyes when he'd given him instructions on resting. "I'm not moving around, Amaryllis. Just lying right here." His voice held reluctance. He realized his entire body did. Something was wrong and he'd been looking outside himself for an external reason. Now, he realized, his radar was going off, warning him that the problem was with him. With his leg. His physical makeup.

"Malichai?" She put her clothes on top of his dresser. "What is it?"

She was growing very adept at reading him. He wasn't certain that was a good thing. He shoved both hands through his hair and looked at her. She was beautiful, ready for bed, ready to snuggle next to him. He wanted that closeness with her more than anything — other than losing his leg.

"I'm going to call Rubin in right now to examine my leg with you, but as much as I love that top, he doesn't get to see you looking like that. Only me. And I'm going to tell you up front that he's a good-looking man and if you look like you're going to trade up, I'm killing him."

She burst out laughing, the sound filling the room and pushing some of the sour notes from his knotted belly.

"I'll make certain I won't look like I'm trading up, so you won't have to go to all that trouble. Finding places for buried bodies is getting difficult these days."

"Thanks for that show of solidarity."

"Anything for you, honey." She whipped her little half shirt off and reached for her tee with deliberate slowness. Her firm breasts were high, calling to him immediately. She smirked as she pulled the T-shirt over her head, covering temptation.

"I can see that." His voice dripped with sarcasm.

She laughed again. "I'll just check the kitchen while you call in that healer."

"You're not checking the kitchen without backup," he said stubbornly.

"You just pointed out that I'm a Ghost-Walker. Do you always need backup? And it's my kitchen. I know every tiny inch of this house."

He'd hit her in her pride. "Fine, babe." He waved her toward the door. "I'll call Rubin in and you be back here in fifteen." He made a show of looking at his watch.

Trap, Amaryllis is heading to the kitchen and then to look around and make certain everything's tucked in tight. Can you shadow her? Not let her see you?

No problem. If not me, Cayenne will.

Malichai tried not to wince. Amaryllis had been right. Trap wasn't worried in the least about Cayenne's pregnancy. As far as he was concerned, it was a natural part of the cycle of life. Women had been giving birth since the dawn of time. He was one of those men who thought she should give birth, cut the cord herself, put the baby in a sling and hoe an entire field. Malichai couldn't afford the time to tell him differently, not right then. And Cayenne was a warrior through and through. Also, she could make herself incredibly small and crawl across a ceiling without being seen.

Going to call Rubin in tonight. I have a bad feeling about my leg.

Instantly Trap's attention was captured and Malichai knew there was no way Trap would be shadowing Amaryllis.

Bad feeling? About your leg? I'll come right up.

I want Amaryllis safe.

Trap stopped answering immediately, as was his way. Malichai cursed under his breath. He shouldn't have said anything at all. Rubin was a very strong psychic. He could bridge a telepathic gap even for those with little or no telepathic ability. Still, it was Ezekiel Malichai reached for. His older brother had always been the one they turned to when things weren't good. He needed Ezekiel there. He needed his brother just to be in the room with him.

Zeke, need you to ask Rubin to slip in and take a look at my leg.

Silence stretched for so long, at first Malichai didn't think they'd connected. Then his brother's voice slipped into his mind and with it, worry. *You mean right now, tonight? Are you all right?*

Just want his opinion, nothing big. Have any of you examined Cayenne? Do you know when she's supposed to give birth? Deliberately, he changed the subject.

Cayenne had slowly managed to invade their hearts. She was a fierce warrior and she went her own way. She knew little about life outside the cage she'd been raised in, but she was learning, mostly about Trap's world, his wants and needs. But she loved Nonny, Pepper and the five little girls who were Wyatt and Pepper's.

Do you honestly think Cayenne is going to let us examine her that way? She'd probably throw a web around us and hang us upside down for a while from a tree. Trap's been her doc.

Malichai groaned and repositioned his leg. It shouldn't be hurting the way it was. It alarmed him how much it hurt. If the bone was broken and not set, he could see having that ripping, persistent pain, but it wasn't broken. Something was happening that was bigger than anyone understood.

Both Rubin and Amaryllis had just spent hours working on it after Mills had kicked the shit out of it. They'd done a very meticulous psychic healing, closing every fracture, knitting them back together. His leg had been kicked, so sure, it was going to hurt. Mills was a big man. He might have delivered a kick strong enough to break the bone, but Malichai doubted it. Something was happening internally and whatever it was, that nagging alarm in his gut told him the consequences to him were going to be very bad.

Trap slipped inside. He looked around. "Your woman wasn't in the kitchen."

"She wanted to look around the place. I sometimes get these weird feelings, like I'm hearing whispers of conspiracy. I like to take a last walk through the halls just to see if I can get a better handle on whether or not I'm going crazy."

"What's the general consensus?" Trap crossed the room and flipped back the blanket covering Malichai's leg.

"So far, coming down on the side of crazy." Malichai rubbed the bridge of his nose. "When is Cayenne actually due, Trap? Give me a date. Or at least how far along she is in her pregnancy. She doesn't seem to show, so it's impossible to tell. It makes no sense that she doesn't show when she's so small."

Trap waved that assessment away dismissively. "She's got armor, silken armor, like a thin layer between her skin and the rest of her. Once she was stabbed and the tip of the knife nearly broke off. It didn't go in. That shield isn't going to allow her womb to push out. The baby has to be displacing her organs."

Malichai closed his eyes over the casual way Trap spoke. It was clear, to keep from panicking over Cayenne's pregnancy, Trap had distanced himself. It was a classic Trap maneuver. He allowed his brain to take over.

"You have to have an idea when she's due. Did she get regular checkups? Did she take prenatals? Wyatt must be out of his mind."

"Wyatt talks to her often and has her take the vitamins. He didn't want her coming on the trip, of course, but I'm not risking another Cayenne silence. I sent her away to safety when we were working on the hemorrhagic virus, and I'm not sure she's forgiven me yet. I needed to come to make certain you lived through this crap, so that meant she was coming too. I promised her, and I don't break my promises to her. I can't ever do that, Malichai. Not to her. Breaking trust with Cayenne would end us."

Again, Trap spoke without looking at him, casually, as if they were discussing the weather, but Malichai was totally shocked. The man *had* to come to ensure Malichai was all right. That choked him up. Trap didn't express emotion often. Malichai thought Trap tolerated him but wasn't very fond of him. This said something altogether different.

"Thanks, Trap. I don't know what the hell's going on, but I want my woman safe as well. It makes me feel better knowing you're here. I still want to know when Cayenne could go into labor."

Trap shrugged. "She's under a month out, but she's showing signs. At first I thought she might be carrying more than one, but she can't be because they would be totally squished in there. I couldn't get her to let me take a look. She's very resistant to any kind of exam. Too close to all the experi-

482

ments they did on her. Cayenne's capable of taking off if she feels too threatened. You all have to leave her be. Don't ask her too many questions."

"You're a doctor. Multiple births? Seriously, Trap? There could be complications."

"There *won't* be," Trap snapped. "There's no way there's two in there. You see her. She's too small."

"You're not thinking straight. How could you possibly know there won't be complications if it's a multiple birth when little is known about the pregnancy or the woman giving birth? Damn, Trap. Why did you think at first there was a possibility?"

Trap always considered odds. He wasn't someone to casually say or think multiple births. If he'd considered it, it was because the possibility was real. Malichai wanted to shake him.

"There can't be complications, Malichai." Trap ground the declaration out between his teeth. "I can't live without her. Do you understand? No Cayenne, no Trap. She can't leave and she can't die. So that means everything will go smoothly. She's fucking terrified. She's terrified of exams and too close to running off. You know her. We'll never find her if she goes. She thinks she can give birth by herself. I'm walking on eggshells with her. This all just has to go the way it's supposed to go."

Malichai took a deep breath before responding. Trap was right about Cayenne. She was capable of taking off on her own, and if she hid somewhere in the swamp, they wouldn't find her. She was terrified of examinations and with good reason. He could see why Trap was trying to walk a fine line with her.

Malichai nodded. "We'll make it happen." He didn't know how. What he did know was, Trap hadn't been casual about her pregnancy, he was trying to make certain she didn't panic and run.

Before Trap could answer, Rubin and Ezekiel slipped into the room and with them was Joe Spagnola, their team leader. Malichai wasn't shocked to see his older brother had come, but he was rather surprised and even more apprehensive to see Joe. Rubin and Joe came straight to the bed, nodded to Malichai and both held their hands inches from the leg.

"Looks like a bit of swelling," Rubin pointed out, hovering his palms over several nasty bruises already turning several shades of purple and blue. "What's it feel like, Malichai, and I need the truth, not some bullshit tough-guy response."

"At least you acknowledge that I'm a bullshit tough guy," Malichai said. His heart pounded and for the first time in a very long while there was no controlling fear. His mouth went dry. He glanced toward the door, needing her, understanding a little bit of what Trap felt when he said he needed Cayenne.

As if on cue, as if she was so connected to him, Amaryllis slipped into the room and without looking at the newcomers, came right to his side and took his hand. "You all right, honey?" She bent toward him and he leaned down to feel the silk of her lips brushing his.

His gut settled a little. "You going to stick with me if they have to cut it off?" He tried to make a joke, but his voice wasn't right.

Ezekiel glanced at him sharply. Trap did as well.

Amaryllis nodded. "Absolutely. I'm not that in love with your leg. Maybe if it was other body parts, I'd have to think about that." She squeezed his hand and then angled her body closer to watch Rubin. "Do you mind if I see as well? Maybe I screwed something up."

Malichai's heart contracted hard. She was hoping she missed something, willing to take blame if that would be the cause of whatever was happening. He knew that was impossible. Rubin had worked right alongside her. Even though they'd taken different parts of the bone, Rubin would have overseen her work.

"You didn't screw anything up, Amaryllis," Rubin assured. "This is Joe Spagnola, a healer like you."

Joe nodded to Amaryllis. "Get up on the bed and come in from the other side."

Malichai would have laughed if he hadn't been the patient. He felt like an experiment with mad scientists gathered around him. Amaryllis crawled up on the bed and lifted her palms up in the same way the others had.

Rubin barely acknowledged her request with more than a slight nod. There was pure concentration on his face and a little frown that boded ill for Malichai.

"Talk, you two," Trap said. "I have to know everything to figure this out."

Trap was the brain, the one Malichai could count on. If there was a puzzle to be solved, Trap was the man to do it.

Light blazed under Amaryllis's palms. Heat increased against his skin, through it, straight to the bone. Malichai felt it like a blast from a laser. He kept his leg still, but it was difficult. The cool stream coming from Rubin was a counterpoint to Amaryllis's heat.

"When you want to power down the energy, you have to breathe from your chi, your life force, feel it move through you into him, and your breath directs how much energy you use on your patient," Joe said unexpectedly.

Immediately, Amaryllis changed her breathing to slow and even, following Joe's instructions, and almost at once, Malichai could feel the difference in heat.

"Do you see how the light is bright, illuminating the bone and all the injuries? The heat and light are two separate things. You have to divide them in your mind. The fridge can continue to run when you turn on the stove."

Amaryllis again followed Joe's tutoring and the heat decreased by several degrees. Joe cleared his throat, his frown going to a scowl. Rubin's face was absolutely inscrutable. Malichai switched his attention from Joe to Amaryllis. Her face had gone very pale.

"Just say it." Ezekiel was the one who ordered it. Malichai couldn't find his voice.

"The bone appears to be disintegrating into hundreds of fractures," Joe said, giving the information to them without softening it in the least. Just straight business, as if Malichai could take knowing his bone was falling apart while they could be in the middle of a very real homegrown terrorist plot.

15

There was a long silence in the room. Malichai feared everyone, with their enhancements, would be able to hear his heart pounding. Ezekiel moved closer to him as if he could somehow protect him from what was happening. He leaned both elbows onto the mattress, up close to Malichai's head, partially shielding him from the others' sight.

"Joe, that isn't helpful information," Trap declared, sounding annoyed. "That doesn't give me a fucking thing to work with. Describe what you're seeing. Is it a fungus causing this? Is the bone weak? Is it brittle? What's happening? The best I can do is look at it and it's not up close like you two see. I get an impression at best."

That was just what Malichai needed. Trap was always going to be that person in the room who took everything back to science. It didn't matter that two people in the room were psychic healers and one was a psychic surgeon. Trap would come up with a way to explain it. Right now, he was Trap being annoyed and short with everyone because they weren't giving him the data he needed to solve the mystery. Malichai was also very aware Rubin hadn't said one word. Not one. He hadn't looked at Malichai or Ezekiel. To Malichai, that was worse than anything Joe could say.

"What we see are hundreds of very small hairline fractures running from his ankle up to his hip. The entire bone is covered. All started from the original wounds. Not all of them, but where the bullets penetrated. Could the bullets have had some kind of coating —"

"Don't speculate," Trap snapped. "Give me facts. The fractures started around the original wounds, but not all of them. What does that mean? I'm sending to Wyatt as well. He might have some questions after."

Malichai found that he could breathe again, and his heart slowed. He wanted to hear as well. Trap reduced everything to possibilities. Rational ones. Ones that meant things could be fixed given the mind of the man working the problem. Wyatt too. Wyatt was at home, guarding the fortress, but he still took the time to be in on the consultation in order to try to save Malichai's leg.

He had good friends. Good family. He looked at his woman. Her expression was every bit as focused as those of the men around her. He had a good woman, a partner, as well. He let out the last of the fear and relaxed into the pain. He had to do his part without freaking out at the thought that like so many other soldiers, he would lose a limb. Like Jerry, who had thrown himself at a grenade to protect his squad, losing both an arm and a leg. So many good men, and he was about to join those ranks.

Ezekiel put a hand on his shoulder but wasn't looking at him, just moved even closer, half sitting on the bed with his hip, his concentration seemingly on Rubin, Joe and Amaryllis.

"The fractures seemed to begin around the larger, deeper wounds, the ones that originally did the most damage, the ones that should have killed him," Rubin said. "His artery was torn. I had to go in while I hauled his ass to the helicopter and hold it together to keep him from bleeding out. At that time, I observed that the wounds were reacting strangely, almost bubbling blood from each of the sites. I had a hell of a time keeping him alive just on that run to the chopper."

Amaryllis gasped and jerked her hands away. She breathed deeply, looking as if she might faint.

"We need that light," Joe snapped.

Malichai opened his mouth to protest the way Joe was talking to her, but Amaryllis simply opened her palms over his legs and whispered a soft apology, shedding that heat and that burning light right through his skin and muscle to his bones.

"What do you mean by bubbling? There was no mention of that, Rubin." Trap sounded more annoyed than ever.

"I was running with Malichai on my shoulder, trying to hold his artery together to keep him from bleeding out and observing the wounds all while running up a very rocky hill. I didn't have much time to observe each wound individually, Trap. I just noticed that the way the blood was coming from several of the wounds was different from normal. It stuck somewhere in the back of my brain."

Rubin sounded the same as always, unruffled, but Malichai knew him. There was just a small underlying warning note, so low one might not hear it, but Ezekiel and Malichai had grown up with him. They exchanged a long look. He was upset, and that meant he was upset on Malichai's behalf. Malichai's stomach did another slow drop. This was bad. His alarm had gone off for a reason.

"Can you tell me how it appeared differently to you?"

"Blood can spray, or ooze, or just leak, pour, stream, but actual bubbling is something I've not really witnessed, not like that, where it was copious amounts." Rubin, again, sounded matter-of-fact, but Malichai knew he didn't want to talk about it.

"Interesting," Trap said. "Did you get that, Wyatt?"

"Yes, and it was as much blood as you would expect from a bullet wound of that size, Rubin?" Wyatt asked. "Even with the field dressing?"

"More. And presenting in a very strange way. Almost like a fountain of blood bubbles."

"You would have thought you would have mentioned that to me," Trap groused.

"He told us when we asked," Wyatt pointed out. "Joe, keep going."

Joe didn't hesitate, sensing the brewing volcano in Rubin. Rubin was a man who was extremely quiet, but if he exploded, he could take the entire team down with him. "There are no fissures starting from any of the lesser wounds. The cracks certainly are throughout the bone, including where those wounds are, but they didn't originate there. In the larger damaged areas, where the bullets tore everything up, there are the beginnings of the fractures in the pitting —"

"Stop," Trap said sharply. "You didn't mention any pitting."

"Sorry, Trap. Around each of those wounds in a large circle —"

"How large," Trap interrupted again.

"Four inches on each of them. A diameter of three inches. Maybe a little larger."

"I have to know exactly. At each wound does the diameter vary? Is it exact?"

Joe was the team leader and respected at all times, but Trap didn't ever seem to notice or pay attention to protocol. He lived in his head, in his research. When he was on the battlefield or running a mission, he was entirely focused. He wasn't a man who would ordinarily ever be part of a team, but he fit with them, and all of them understood his brilliance.

Amaryllis startled everyone by replying. "It's exact. It's a circle of pitting that is three inches out circling the original wound. It doesn't vary, although on two of the five larger wounds where the circle is, it's off, meaning two inches above and one below instead of being exactly centered."

"Damn it," Trap burst out. "Can you fix

what's happening to the bone, Rubin?"

Malichai's heart accelerated and he knew everyone in the room could hear it. He willed his brother not to look at him. He couldn't look at any of them. Everyone had a secret fear. A dread that loomed over them. Since he'd been a child and he'd seen a man, clearly a veteran soldier, begging in the street, one leg gone, just a stub showing, he'd been terrified that he'd end up that way.

"The fracturing is clearly accelerating," Rubin said. He looked down at his hands and then at Malichai. "With Amaryllis and Joe working with me, I believe we have a chance of healing this, but we have before. Amaryllis and I cleared every one of those fractures earlier today after Mills kicked his leg. They should have stayed gone but the time of return seems to be accelerating. Everywhere the pitting is, the fissures in the bone begin, and there's a lot of pitting. We need to find the cause of the return. With the three of us, we can keep the bone clear, but it's imperative to find the actual cause for the fracturing."

"Is his bone brittle? What does he have in him? He has great eyesight. Bird? He swims like a fish. I need to be able to pull up all the data on him." Trap was clearly frustrated.

"His bones aren't hollow," Rubin said. "They're dense. Very dense. More than a normal human, which is why we're careful about taking him to a hospital. We need our own doctors."

"Penguin," Amaryllis guessed. "If he swims like I do."

"Can a regular surgeon fix what's happening to his bone? One of us?"

Malichai closed his eyes. He already knew the answer to Trap's question and he desperately needed comfort. At the same time, he didn't want anyone to touch him. He wasn't going to break down in front of his teammates. How many other men had lost limbs and had to face loved ones? Ask their woman to live with that loss? Ask their children to be okay with it? He was a Ghost-Walker and the government would spend any amount of money to get him back in the field, so he would have a prosthesis very fast, but he would have to come to terms with his worst fear.

"No, Trap, there's no fixing this in an operating room. Amaryllis can watch for it. Examine him every night and any time it starts, the three of us can take care of the problem, but that's not a permanent solution. You and Wyatt are going to have to figure out why this is happening," Rubin said. "I can have him build strength in the leg and we can work on it consistently, but we still need you to figure it out."

"You obviously have a conclusion," Malichai challenged Trap. "Say it. What's causing this, and is there some way to stop it?"

"You know I don't like to speculate . . ." Trap started.

"I don't give a damn," Malichai snapped. "I'm asking you friend to friend, what the fuck is happening to me?"

Trap sighed and ran his fingers several times through his hair in obvious agitation. "If I had to speculate. Just guess — which I don't like to do — I'd say that would be the diameter of the second-generation Zenith patches you used to stop the bleeding and push adrenaline into your body. You used them on the five worst wounds. The ones that could have killed you. That's why each of the circles are exact in diameter, but not in relationship to the wound. You were slapping them on fast, hardly looking at what you were doing. This is some reaction to the Zenith. Wyatt?"

"I came to the same conclusion, but like Trap, I'm not one hundred percent certain."

There was a small silence. Joe and Amaryllis pulled their hands away, immediately taking the heat and light from him. Malichai couldn't have found words if he wanted to. He had slapped those patches on all five of the worst wounds to stop the bleeding in the hopes that he could make it to the helicopter.

"Lily worked on Zenith, to make it safe for us to use. The FDA doesn't even know about this drug. It's not like it can be tested on humans," Trap said. "Wyatt and I took it apart in our lab at Lily's request, although I would have done so anyway. The Zenith should be safe for all of us, but as with any medication, there can be anomalies. You could be allergic. We all have DNA that was placed in us. We don't know, with all of us being different now, what any medication will do to us. Zenith was tested on each individual."

"I used Lily's second-generation Zenith before," Malichai pointed out. "Same leg. I was shot not that long ago, remember? That's why I went with you to your home, Wyatt, to recover from that injury. I used the patch on that injury."

"So, it was the second time on the same leg," Trap mused. "You are most likely — and again, this is a guess off what little data I have — you're most likely having an adverse reaction to the drug."

"An adverse reaction is a rash and swelling," Ezekiel snapped, "not eating away at the bone."

"Actually, Zeke," Trap said, "an adverse reaction is any unintended but harmful effect —"

"Trap." Malichai had to stop him before that darkness welling up in his brother could be let loose. Trap would make a great target, and none of this was his fault.

Trap stopped talking abruptly. Malichai couldn't feel any difference in the buildup of violent energy in his brother, but at least Ezekiel began deep breathing to try to dissipate it on his own without slamming his fists into someone.

Joe stepped between the two men. "We'll start working on the leg and continue twice a day until we figure this out. Trap, can you contact Lily? Wyatt, you've got everything?"

"I'm already sending Trap the files he's going to need," Wyatt said. The audio was so good it sounded as if Wyatt was in the room with them. "Malichai, you've been wounded several times. Since you reported the abuses and discrepancies by Peter Whitney to higher command, you've been targeted by his supporters. You've been sent on missions basically to get rid of you. I know you've been shot several times prior to those two incidents. Did you use second-generation Zenith on you at any other time?"

Amaryllis had gone around to the other side of the bed so she wasn't disturbing Ezekiel, who stayed close. She stretched out beside him, her back to the headboard, just as his was. Malichai threaded his fingers through hers and brought their joined hands to his thigh.

"Lily hadn't perfected the drug then. She was working on it and the original Zenith was too unpredictable, so none of us were using it."

"So, you'd never actually used it before that first time when you used it on your leg?"

"No, when I was wounded prior to Lily perfecting the second-generation Zenith, Rubin, Joe or one of you took care of it, or I did. I've never had to use the patch until that first time our helicopter went down and I was shot. And then this last time, those bullets tore up my leg. I didn't think I was going to make it, I was bleeding so much. It was use the patches or die right there."

"I'm sending all this information to Lily. We're going to have to initiate testing every single GhostWalker again for their reaction to Zenith," Wyatt continued.

"It could be a bad batch as well," Trap suggested. "That happens."

"Or it's reacting specifically to Malichai's DNA," Wyatt said.

"Gentlemen, perhaps it's time for you to take this discussion elsewhere," Joe said. "Rubin, Amaryllis and I have to work on Malichai before the sun comes up. Rubin and I can slip through people unseen as a rule, but in broad daylight with people already speculating about vans, Navy SEALs and hit men in the bed-and-breakfast, I doubt if we'll get away unseen."

"Yeah, that sounds right," Trap said. "Don't worry, Malichai, we'll figure this out."

Malichai lay back, tightening his fingers around Amaryllis's and pressing their joined hands deep into his thigh muscle. They weren't going to figure it out. Wyatt had been his best friend for years. It didn't matter that he was miles away in the swamps of Louisiana, and that he was speaking over a cell, Malichai could read his every nuance. Neither Trap nor Wyatt thought they were going to find a way to save his leg.

"Can you keep me going at least through whatever is happening here in San Diego, Rubin?"

"We'll do our best," Rubin said and looked at Ezekiel.

Not Malichai. Ezekiel. Malichai clenched his teeth so nothing would get out that he would regret. This wasn't anyone's fault. He'd chosen to attack the enemy bunkers like some crazed kamikaze. It seemed the only way at the time, and maybe it had been. He knew he would have done it all over again, even knowing the consequences, in order to bring those soldiers home. He just had to wait until he was alone and then he could do all the necessary swearing and screaming he needed to do.

Amaryllis leaned into him and brushed his jaw with her lips, featherlight, but he felt her touch go through him like a flaming dart. It was all about light, those flames. Solidarity. She was with him. She would be with him through whatever he had to endure. He had that.

The door cracked just enough to allow a shadow to slip into the room and then it was closed again. Cayenne leaned against the thick oak door, her green eyes wide with shock.

"Trap, my water broke. I'm in labor."

Trap nearly leapt across the room, but then he just stood in front of her, raking his hands through his hair. "This is too soon,

Cayenne. You're not supposed to do this yet." His voice was sharp with reprimand but blended with panic.

"Well, I am doing it," she snapped back. "Believe me, I don't want to."

"Cayenne, come here," Ezekiel said, his voice one of complete authority. "Malichai, move all the way over to the other side of the bed. I'm going to have Cayenne hop up for just a minute so I can see what's happening and if the baby is all right. Malichai, do you have a medical kit here in the room?"

He always had one. "It's in the bathroom under the sink. A full kit."

Cayenne looked to Trap to tell her what to do. He stepped back and waved toward the bed. She shook her head. "I want to go home."

"Baby, you're not going to make it home and we can't have the baby in the sky. It's safest here. You're surrounded by doctors. Amaryllis is here as well."

"I don't like anyone touching me. Or poking at me. I'm not sure I can control myself through this, Trap." Cayenne sounded haunted. "What if I hurt someone, or kill them?"

Malichai knew it was a very real possibility. Cayenne's bite was lethal. She had been created in a laboratory and the healthy dose of venom given to her was no joke. She had an hourglass in her hair as a warning, not a decoration.

"We need to get her to the hospital," Joe said. "I'll call an ambulance."

Cayenne turned and rushed for the door. Trap got there just as she tried to pull it open, his large hand above her head, slapping it closed. "Stop, baby. No one's going to make you go anywhere you don't want to go. Get on the bed right now and let Zeke examine you. I'll be right next to you, holding your hand. You have to bite someone, you target me, you understand? I'll be very unhappy if you do anything but what I just told you to do."

Trap poured command into his voice, but at the same time, his tone was velvet soft, low, a sound Malichai had never heard before. Cayenne responded immediately, taking the hand he held out to her and letting him lead her to the bed. She skirted around Joe quickly, as if she were afraid of him, and Malichai knew she wasn't afraid of much. Cayenne was a force to be reckoned with in combat. She could be counted on every time to stand with them. He'd never seen what amounted to terror on her face.

Trap's hands went around her waist and

he lifted her onto the bed and indicated she stretch out beside Malichai.

"I can get up and move to the chair," Malichai offered.

"We might need you," Ezekiel said. "Okay, honey, you know me. I would never do anything to hurt you or your baby. I just want to take a look and see what's happening. Is that okay with you?"

Trap moved in close, keeping possession of her hand. "Look at me, Cayenne. I want you to do this, do you understand me?"

She bit down on her lip but didn't take her gaze from Trap's. To Malichai's horror, her green eyes actually filled with tears. Her nod was nearly imperceptible.

"Go ahead, Zeke," Trap said.

"Need a light over here," Ezekiel snapped.

Amaryllis stepped up beside him with a flashlight. "I know you don't know me, Cayenne, but I'm the same as you. I would never allow experiments on me again either. I give you my word I won't let anyone experiment on you or your child."

She spoke in a low voice, distracting Cayenne as Ezekiel pulled on gloves and slipped a thick pad under Cayenne. Trap had to lift her to do it, but the pad was put in place.

"Zeke is going to help your baby and you.

All of us want to help you. Just please keep in mind that always, you have a sister in the room. A woman that will stand with you no matter what."

Even though Cayenne never took her eyes from Trap's face, Malichai felt the tension ease out of her just a little at Amaryllis's declaration. And she nodded.

"Put your knees up and open them, baby," Trap instructed. He had moved slightly; although he stayed tightly against the mattress, it was clear he was trying to see what Zeke was doing.

Ezekiel had always had that expressionless mask and it stood him in good stead. "Amaryllis, I need heated towels. Can you get them for me? Joe can hold the light. I need them fast as well as hot water. When I say fast, I mean hurry." There was no urgency in his voice, but coming from Ezekiel, Malichai — and everyone who knew Zeke — knew he was declaring an emergency.

Amaryllis handed the flashlight to Joe, and Cayenne nearly came off the bed. If Trap hadn't put his hand on her chest to hold her down, she would have made another run for it.

"No, she can't leave!" Cayenne protested.

"Cayenne, she has to get the things we

need for the baby," Trap said patiently. "Tell Amaryllis it's all right. She'll be back immediately. In the meantime, you have me right here, and Malichai. You know him. You know he'd fight for you. So would Zeke and Joe. We talked about getting upset over nothing. That isn't logical. It's your hormones."

Malichai winced. Most women didn't want anyone talking about hormones being the reason for anything they did. "Honey, I'm right here. I would never allow anyone to take your child from you or harm you in any way," Malichai assured.

"Is it all right if I leave?" Amaryllis asked. "If not, I'll see if I can get someone else to get the heated towels we need."

Cayenne began to pant but she lifted a hand and waved it toward the door, her gaze going from Trap to Malichai just for a moment. Amaryllis took that as a signal to leave.

"How much is she dilated?" Trap asked.

Ezekiel held up his gloved hand. There was blood and other liquids coating the fingers. "She's at eight centimeters, Trap. She's in transition and the contractions are long and very hard." He used his stethoscope to find the baby's heartbeat. It wasn't easy with the shield of silk protecting

Cayenne's insides. Ezekiel was patient, slowly moving the amplifier over her until he suddenly stopped.

The room went silent as he listened. Everyone waited to see if the baby was managing the difficult part of labor without a problem.

"This one is strong. Baby wants out and you're doing an excellent job, Cayenne," Ezekiel encouraged.

So far, Cayenne hadn't made a sound other than to pant quietly, her gaze still clinging to Trap's. He leaned down and brushed a kiss across her forehead. "We're close, baby, so close. Everything is fine. Whitney isn't going to get our child. No one is. No one will take him from us, and they won't get a chance to kill him."

Malichai realized why Cayenne had refused nearly all treatment. She was terrified of someone wanting to kill her child. She had been scheduled for termination. Her experience had been watching others die. She wanted no paper trails following her child. She didn't want any documents anywhere that Whitney or one of his other scientists might have found. She had very real concerns. He wished she'd told them all, but Cayenne had lived her life in a cage, with no family or friends, no relationships.

She was just coming out of her shell and beginning a fragile trust with them.

"No one will get to your child, Cayenne," Malichai added his word. "We're a family. You're part of that. Your children will be ours as well."

Cayenne barely nodded her head, but she did it. She reacted in a positive way, although she never took her eyes from her partner. It was Trap she trusted. Trap she loved. Trap she believed in. Trap was right when he'd said he could never afford to break that trust with her.

"Take another breath now, baby, and let it go," Trap instructed. "We watched a ton of videos, and you know what to do. You're doing great. I'm so proud of you."

His eyes kept straying to Ezekiel. Malichai noticed his face was a little paler than normal. That made him want to smile. Trap was always so removed from the world around him, but clearly, Cayenne having his baby was a huge thing he couldn't quite separate himself from.

Gonna tell this to you straight, Zeke, Trap said, his voice going to all three men. *Anything goes wrong, anything at all, you save Cayenne. I can't live without her. You save her. I'm compatible with blood type. I know Bellisia is Rh-null. She can give blood to anyone. Just letting you know where your priority has to be. She's going to say save the baby . . . but . . .*

Nothing is going wrong. She's going to be fine and so will the baby, Ezekiel shot back. *Cayenne is totally reliant on you, Trap. You can't panic. Slow your breathing down and stop thinking of all the things that could go wrong.*

Trap's mind would go over every possible problem and the solutions to fix them. That was the way he was built. The drawback was, this was Cayenne and it was far too personal for him to retreat into his brain.

Trap made a conscious effort to breathe normally. He kept his gaze glued to Cayenne's as if he could will her to give birth without a single problem. Malichai thought there was something especially beautiful in the way the couple looked at each other.

Amaryllis hurried in with a stack of warm towels and then left to return quickly with two buckets of steaming hot water that she'd boiled.

"How are you doing, Cayenne?" Ezekiel asked. "I'm going to listen to the baby's heartbeat again, just making certain he's doing all right. I want to check your progress again. You seem to be going fast."

Cayenne nodded. "Hurts pretty bad, Zeke."

"You're in transition, honey," Ezekiel said. "You were at eight when I checked you last. Let's see where you are now."

Malichai was proud of his brother. He was in a bad situation but doing his best. Cayenne, even in the condition she was in, was a flight risk. She was terrified of needles. Terrified her child would be taken and used for experiments or just plain killed. Ezekiel had gotten her to respond, which meant she was getting past that fear to allow them all to help her.

Malichai dared to rub her shoulder after a particularly long and hard contraction. She hadn't made a sound, just breathed her way through it and looked at her man. "You're amazing. This childbirth thing isn't for wimps, but it is making me hungry. When Amaryllis gives birth, I might have to have a buffet set up in the room."

To his astonishment, Cayenne turned her head to look at him. There was a hint of laughter in her eyes. "You eat while she's in labor and I can guarantee you that you won't live out the night. If she doesn't do you in, the rest of the women will, including Nonny."

Even Trap laughed. The terrible tension in

the room was dispelled.

Ezekiel suddenly smiled. "There he is. He's so ready to come into the world. Heartbeat is strong and steady. Last contraction slowed him down a little, but nothing to worry about. You're dilated to nine, almost ten. You're going to need to push soon, honey. Do you remember how? Did you watch the videos?"

Cayenne nodded. "I don't want to lie down like this. I'd rather sit."

"Malichai, can you sit against the headboard and let her use your knees as a backrest?" Ezekiel said, very practical, so there was no way Malichai could scramble off the bed and give his brother the bird. "Your leg up to that?"

Ezekiel knew he could bend his leg without a problem. "Wouldn't she feel better with Trap behind her?" he asked hopefully.

"I need to see Trap," Cayenne said. Again, she turned her head to look at him. "Are you okay with it?"

Amaryllis was watching him closely. He felt her moving in him, even though she was standing beside Joe and Ezekiel, keeping the towels warm.

"Sure, honey," he answered Cayenne. "I'll just be sitting here. But when he's born, I get to see him right away, same as you."

"That's a deal," she agreed and then another even harder, longer contraction took her. Immediately her head turned back almost desperately to Trap.

Malichai didn't know many women stronger than Cayenne. She stood on her own two feet. She held her own always. She didn't ask for concessions. Like Trap, he'd tended to think childbirth was something that women could do fairly easily. He was a doctor and he knew all the pitfalls, but for the most part, it was natural and therefore something one didn't really have to worry about. Now, he was worried.

Cayenne had gone very quiet, her eyes closing as if she were falling asleep. Definitely sliding from transition into pushing phase. Her body was resting, waiting for the next big phase.

He was going to rethink the entire having children with Amaryllis idea. They could create a good life together without having kids. Not everyone needed them to complete their families. He had cat DNA in him. Maybe they'd get cats. Tigers. Leopards. Something big to protect his woman with him.

"Malichai, you've gone a little crazy and you're broadcasting loud." Ezekiel's voice dripped with sarcasm.

"I have to go to the bathroom," Cayenne said suddenly, her eyes flying open as she started to sit up.

"That's the baby, putting pressure on you," Trap explained. "I'm going to help you up and tilt you back so you're up against Malichai."

Even as he told her, Trap's hands were gentle on her waist, shifting her as Malichai pulled his knees back to form a backrest for Cayenne, keeping a thin blanket over his legs so she could have something soft to lean against.

"Do you want some ice chips, baby?" Trap asked, as Amaryllis handed him a glass filled with the chips.

Cayenne nodded. "Thanks, I appreciate it." Her eyes met Amaryllis's.

Malichai couldn't help but feel proud of his woman. She had no real knowledge of childbirth either, but she'd thought to break up ice for Cayenne.

Suddenly, Cayenne gasped and clutched at Malichai's leg and Trap's arm. "I have to push. Right now."

Ezekiel shook his head. "Joe, take her right leg up and out of the way. Trap, her left. Drop your chin and breathe him out as you push. Focus. Don't waste a push. Make each one count. You can do this, Cayenne.

This is you and your baby. Help him get out."

He continued to encourage her, telling her he could see hair. The baby had a lot of dark hair with a hint of red in it. "There's his little head. Don't push, Cayenne. Pant for a second while I clear his mouth. Okay, push. That's it. You have a baby. A boy. Your son has arrived and he's looking good."

Joe had immediately released Cayenne's leg and rushed around Amaryllis to get to the baby. It was his job to make certain he was breathing fine and everything looked good. Ezekiel clamped off the cord, made the cut and handed the boy to Joe.

Cayenne and Trap both burst out laughing. Trap leaned down and kissed her. "That was amazing, sweetheart. I can't believe you did that. He didn't look as small as I thought he'd be." He looked up at Ezekiel. "There was no way to see with that shield, but with everyone having multiple births, we were concerned that it was a thing with GhostWalkers."

Malichai's stomach dropped. *Zeke.* He whispered his brother's name into his mind.

Ezekiel closed his eyes briefly and then glanced at Joe. *Draden, Shylah, you need to get me a warmer for a preemie. I don't care how you do it. Steal the fucking thing but get it now. We're going to need it. We can't take them to the hospital, that would tip Whitney off immediately. Arrange for around-the-clock care with the best neonatal nurses possible. All the equipment. We can set up in the basement. It's the best location. Trap has the money for whatever's needed. Joe, how's that one doing?*

He's fine. I'd say a nine on the Apgar. I'm guessing he's weighing in at a five. That's a good size. His lungs are great. This one is going to be fine. Are you certain there's a second one?

Malichai answered for his brother. *I'm certain. All along I thought it was me, or some conspiracy plot in the bed-and-breakfast, but it was Cayenne. Even Trap thought there might be but dismissed it because he didn't want there to be.*

Need scrubs for everyone as an explanation for why we're here. Gives a much better cover, Joe added.

Trap was included in the circle. All of the GhostWalkers heard the alarm with the exception of Cayenne. Very slowly Trap moved back to position himself by his wife's head. He took her hand.

She looked up at him, her expression darkening. "I don't feel very good, Trap."

"Do you feel the need to push again?"

Trap asked.

Cayenne shook her head. "I just feel sick."

"Prep," Ezekiel ordered his team. "Right now. Rubin, I need you to see past her shield to tell me what's happening. Amaryllis, you provide as much light as possible."

Amaryllis didn't argue that Joe would be the better choice. He was needed for the baby. She glanced once at Malichai as if for strength and then she placed both palms over Cayenne's mostly flat stomach. "There's a thin barrier here. Woven tightly."

"Get past it," Ezekiel ordered tersely. He had delivered the first placenta and caught blood clots in a bowl.

"I'm trying," she answered, without raising her voice.

"Don't yell at her, Zeke," Rubin said softly. "I see her now. She's very small. She's alive. Moving. She looks like she's reaching for her brother."

"Direct me. I need to hear her heartbeat," Ezekiel said.

"No, no, more to your left. Right there. She's turned upward so you should hear it." Rubin fell silent to give Ezekiel the chance to listen.

Abruptly he raised his head. "We'll have to get her out now. Let's go."

Joe wrapped the baby boy in warm towels

517

and handed him off to Malichai. Fortunately, they had been using IVs on Malichai, so they had the equipment they needed on hand.

Cayenne looked as if she'd gone to sleep. She had slid down in the bed and the moment Ezekiel seemed finished with her, she'd tried to turn onto her side into the fetal position.

"Sorry, baby." Trap bent close to her, holding her head, looking into her eyes. "Joe needs to get a line into you. There's another baby. She's not responding, and we need to get her out of you. Do you understand what I'm saying? They're going to put a needle in you."

More than anything, Cayenne detested needles. All of them expected her to protest. She frowned. "Are you saying there's still a baby inside me?"

"Rubin says a girl." Trap framed her face between his hands, forcing her to look at him.

Malichai held her arm. Joe found Cayenne's vein and slipped the IV in. He looked up at Trap. "She allergic to anything?"

"Not that I know of. If she is, it wasn't in her file anywhere."

"Get her under," Ezekiel snapped. "Where the hell are Draden and Shylah with the equipment?"

"They aren't miracle workers," Malichai reminded. He slid off the bed, pulled on a pair of drawstring jogging pants, hurriedly scrubbed and pulled on gloves. His leg protested every step he took, but that didn't matter. The life of Trap and Cayenne's daughter was at stake. He was an anesthesiologist and was needed. That was all that mattered. He'd specialized in several types of medicine, as had most of the GhostWalkers, but nearly all of them had gone through the rigorous schooling for an anesthesiologist. More than anything, they were often needed in the field along with surgeons.

"Get her out," Ezekiel repeated. "Amaryllis, I need you right here. You're going to guide me in. I have to get through or around the silk shield and find a way to get the baby out. If I have to, I can go in through her back or side, but that's going to have all sorts of complications." He looked at her. "Can you do it?"

She nodded but glanced back at Joe. "He's probably your better bet."

"I need him for the baby and Rubin to shut down any heavy bleeding I won't see around that shield."

"You can do this, Amaryllis," Malichai said. He knew she could. He absolutely believed she would be able to guide Ezekiel to the infant.

"You promised Cayenne," Trap reminded. "You said anything she needed."

Malichai didn't like the additional pressure being put on Amaryllis, but she just nodded and put both palms over Cayenne's mid-section so he kept his full attention on his patient, making certain she wouldn't feel anything when Ezekiel had to cut her open to take the baby.

They had nothing to give for a local that would work, so they had to put Cayenne out. In some ways, because she was so lethal if she injected her venom into anyone, and if this went wrong, which it very well could, putting her out was the better option.

"The baby is aware, Trap. Sing to her. Talk to her. Let her know you and Cayenne and her brother are waiting for her. That she'll be safe," Ezekiel instructed.

Trap had a good singing voice. He didn't hesitate to use it. He sang to his daughter, sometimes making up the words, telling her about their home and how they were a family, how they'd been waiting for her. They had friends everywhere. People who loved her. She'd heard them talking already. She knew their voices. He went back to singing a lullaby and Ezekiel joined in. Malichai knew the words and he sang softly as well.

"To the right," Amaryllis whispered. "Straight. Keep that cut very straight. If you don't, you'll hit the silk armor and break off the tip."

Ezekiel had the worst job, Malichai knew. He could keep Cayenne just under the surface, safe, not feeling anything. His brother had to perform surgery without any sight. He made the incision and carefully separated the muscles to expose the uterus.

"Now where?"

"She's right there, where you are. You can touch her."

Ezekiel glanced up at Trap. Trap nodded. Malichai tried to send his brother as much unity and goodwill as possible. Draden and Shylah came into the room, pushing a cart filled with equipment. Both wore medical gear, and they closed the door on a couple of curious guests.

Ezekiel turned back to the job of taking the baby. He made the cut carefully, Amaryllis guiding his every movement, and then he was lifting her free, cutting the cord, handing her off to Joe.

She was so tiny Malichai's heart nearly stopped. How could a baby of that size possibly survive? Shylah and Draden worked fast to set up the equipment needed for the little girl.

"Rubin," Ezekiel said suddenly, urgency in his voice.

Trap spun around, going from where Joe had the baby, back to his wife and the blood spilling in crimson globs onto the floor beneath the bed.

Don't you fucking die on me, Cayenne, Trap ordered. *Rubin . . .*

"Don't interrupt his concentration," Ezekiel snapped.

Trap had turned so pale, Malichai feared he was going to faint. He'd never seen Trap so shaken. Even his hands shook as he pushed his fingers continually through his hair over and over. Finally he bent close to Cayenne's ear.

"Baby, listen to me. I'm not much good without you. You know that. Just don't fucking do this. Whatever Rubin is doing, let him. Just let him."

Hearing Trap was heart-wrenching and tore at Malichai. He knew Trap as a man who retreated into his brain, who closed himself off, who would never show emotion in front of others. Seeing him falling apart without his woman was almost too much.

Before Ezekiel could stitch the incision, it was up to Rubin to push the clots from her womb and then clean and cauterize the walls so no excessive bleeding could continue. It wasn't easy working blind. Even Rubin's vision was somewhat obscured by that thick lining of silk. Amaryllis did her best to provide some vision for him, but she knew he saw differently, just as she did, and she doubted if she was helping that much.

No one felt like talking and if they had to, they did so in whispers. Malichai paid close attention to his patient and when he finally did look up, the baby had tubes in her and she was in the little NICU. Her brother was placed close to her, but where he couldn't tear out any of the necessary lines she needed.

Time crawled by. There was never any hurrying Rubin. He never gave off a sense of urgency, yet Malichai knew him well. When he'd first stepped up to help Ezekiel, that strain had been there. Thankfully, it seemed to be fading. He straightened very slowly and looked at Ezekiel and then Trap. He just nodded. That was it. Once. He took a step toward the chairs and then staggered.

Joe caught his arm and helped him to sit. Malichai cursed inwardly. He would be putting more strain on Rubin when it came to once again attempting to heal the bone in his leg.

Ezekiel worked next, using very small

stitches to meticulously close the incision he'd made to separate the muscle and wall of the uterus. He had gone around the silken shield so that was thankfully still intact.

"I don't want Cayenne under so long, Zeke," he told his brother. "I'm backing her out if it's okay with you." He'd barely kept her just below the surface, uncertain how she would do.

Ezekiel nodded and Trap gripped Cayenne's hand. She stirred eventually and turned her head, suddenly vomiting. Both Malichai and Trap had been ready for that. She had a much more delicate system, as she been raised on rations and wasn't used to most foods or drink. When she went out with everyone, she appeared to drink or eat what they did, but she almost always got rid of it because most things made her sick.

Trap had learned that the first time he'd ever been with her. She didn't like beer, but she appeared to drink it because everyone in the bar drank it. He'd tried to teach her that it didn't matter what others thought, but she still always gave the appearance of fitting in. Trap had told them to offer her alternatives whenever they were with her, but if they didn't, she always simply appeared to drink or eat with them.

Malichai looked around his room. It looked like a hospital setting, with a portable NICU and doctors everywhere. His eyes met Amaryllis's. They both shook their heads.

"Malichai," Ezekiel said softly. He once again was taking Cayenne's blood pressure and pulse. "You aren't supposed to be putting any weight on that leg."

The moment his brother pointed it out, his leg throbbed like a son of a bitch. Worse, everyone in the room stared at him. He indicated Cayenne. "I think there's someone a little more important in my bed at the moment."

"Get off the leg, Malichai," Ezekiel and Rubin ordered at the same time.

16

Malichai sat in the basement with Trap and Cayenne waiting for Amaryllis to finish up in the kitchen. Marie had gone with Jacy back to the Fontenots' home in the swamps near New Orleans. They were able to fly in Trap's very luxurious private jet, which made Jacy happy. Nonny was going to make Marie very happy, so Malichai wasn't too worried about the two of them. He was more worried about his leg.

Joe and Amaryllis worked on him in the morning, healing the hairline fractures running through the bone. He didn't say a word to either of them, but all day, his leg ached, and he hadn't done much at all. The basement had been transformed into a mini-hospital, with a bed for Cayenne and the little units for the babies. They had nurses to help, but since Malichai had been forbidden to help Amaryllis around the bed-and-breakfast, and he couldn't stand watching her do all the work, he'd been in the basement, helping Trap and Cayenne with their babies, specifically the little girl. They still hadn't named her. He wanted them to. He felt that the child was aware of everything happening to her.

She was the daughter of two GhostWalkers, two very intelligent, psychically and physically enhanced GhostWalkers. She seemed alert and aware of her surroundings and of everything happening to her. She was cooperative, especially when he spoke softly to her and let her know why he was doing certain things to her. Why she needed the breathing tubes. Why her lungs weren't quite developed, but the shot would help.

Her brother was now named Axel, and Malichai knew the baby was pleased with his name. He should be. Axel had been one of the few men Trap respected. He'd died in the field, saving his fellow Marines and a few of the GhostWalkers who were working on wounded. Trap had been one of those men. Malichai another. Axel was a good, strong name. But the little girl needed a name.

"Trap, what are you waiting for?" he demanded.

Cayenne cradled their little daughter to her protectively. She looked at her husband, but she didn't say anything. Malichai didn't expect her to. Amaryllis would have a lot to say, but Cayenne mostly went along with Trap.

"Waiting for all those tubes to be gone," Trap said gruffly.

"Well, stop waiting, she doesn't like it," Malichai informed him.

Trap turned around slowly. He was pacing up and down the length of the basement, Axel in his arms. "What do you mean, she doesn't like it?"

"She's telepathic. Same as your son. They talk back and forth. She doesn't like that you haven't given her a name. In fact, she thinks you don't want her. Apparently, you don't hold her. Only Cayenne does."

Trap stood very still, a deer caught in the headlights. He raked one hand through his hair, making it stand on end so that he looked like the mad scientist most everyone called him. Then he quickly dropped the hand back to his son so that he clutched the boy as if he might fall at any moment.

"Look at her," he finally burst out. It sounded like an accusation.

For the first time, Cayenne reacted, pulling the baby in closer to her and hunching her body protectively, her eyes on her husband. "I'll name her, Malichai." She looked down at the tiny face and smiled. "I want you, beautiful. I had no idea you were there, lurking in the background. You're like me, aren't you? Axel is like your father, but you're like me. You don't mind being quiet while they stand in front."

"I want her too, Cayenne," Trap said. "You're misunderstanding me. I can't hold her because she's so tiny. I'm afraid I'll crush her. That's what I mean when I tell you to look at her. It's about her being so little. So tiny. Look at my hands and look at her."

Malichai knew Trap. He heard the ring of sincerity in his voice. He loved his little girl and was panicked at the thought of hurting her. Just as he was terrified of losing Cayenne, he was fearful of losing his tiny daughter. That was most likely the real reason he didn't want to name her.

"I've already picked out her name," Trap added gruffly. "I had the name picked out before she was born. Drusilla. I want to call her Drusilla. We talked about this once, Cayenne, and you said it was all right with you." He sounded choked up, which was very unusual for Trap. He wasn't, as a rule, emotional.

"I know I did," Cayenne hedged. "She's like me, Trap. She's quiet, but she's a fighter."

Trap took the seat beside Cayenne and handed Axel to Malichai. He held out his arms for his daughter. "Share, sweetheart. You're not supposed to be holding anything too heavy. In fact, you shouldn't be up yet."

"She's under the weight. Axel is just the weight." Reluctantly, she transferred the baby very carefully into Trap's arms.

Immediately, the little girl's eyes opened. Malichai wanted to point out the intelligence there, but he was certain he didn't have to. Trap would see it. How could he not? He watched Trap swallow hard and then his eyes misted over. He smiled down at his daughter.

"There you are, sweetheart. You are like your mother. Quiet and lethal, and very strong. That's the highest compliment I can pay you." He leaned toward Cayenne. "Kiss me, baby. I know you're upset with good reason, but I'm not being this way because I don't love this little one. She's tiny, and I'm afraid of crushing her. Kiss me, Cayenne."

Cayenne, always, always, gave Trap anything he wanted when he wanted it. She shocked Malichai by hesitating. She really was upset with her man. There were beautiful lacy webs hanging around their bed, giving them privacy, but the ones she'd woven around the portable units had been taken down by a nurse and Trap hadn't protested.

She glanced at Malichai and he put Axel into her arms, lifted a hand and made his way upstairs to the lounge to wait for Amaryllis to finish up in the kitchen. Life was complex with another human being. Trap and Cayenne were made for each other, were perfect for each other and yet there were still complications and misunderstandings. Where did that leave him with Amaryllis? He didn't know the first thing about relationships, and neither did she.

As he took a seat in the lounge, Billy Leven came in, looked around and took the chair closest to him. Billy had definitely bugged the room where the representative for Ideas for Peace from Egypt was going to stay. Marie had made a sudden room change, due to the fact that the GhostWalkers needed the room. She'd placed Draden and Shylah there, stating she'd messed up the bookings, that the couple were supposed to get the larger suite. The suite had been thoroughly cleaned again and the bug was swept away. Most likely Billy had been the source of the bug that had been found in Malichai's room as well.

Marie had acted agitated and then let it

slip that Jacy needed more medical attention and she was going to have to leave. Everyone understood. She'd hired more help so Amaryllis wouldn't be the only one working long hours with the bed-and-breakfast completely full.

"Your leg hurting again?" Billy asked, sounding mournful.

Malichai had noticed he often sounded as if the world were coming to an end. "A little. I overdid the physical therapy. I'm used to training hard and pushing myself. I guess it's not the best thing for me."

"Now that I've got you alone" — Billy lowered his voice to a conspirator's level — "what the hell happened? One minute everything was fine, then you came home in a Navy ambulance and then your friend's wife went into labor . . ."

Malichai shrugged casually. "That's about it. That's what happened. I was shot multiple times and the bone was shattered in multiple places. For some reason it just doesn't want to heal. The bone fragmented and I went down. The Navy guys had a van, not an ambulance, and they got me. They were friends of my friend, the one visiting me. His wife was pregnant but not due for another month. While everyone was trying to figure out what to do with my problem, she suddenly not only went into labor but skyrocketed to delivery. There was no moving her to a hospital and Trap has enough money to buy and sell several planets, so he just set up a hospital right here."

"That's why he has all those guards downstairs," Billy said. "He's rich."

Malichai had to hide his smile. It was clear he'd tried to go down to the basement to spy. He was a very curious man and wanted to know what was going on throughout the inn. "They mean business too. Trap takes the security of his wife and children very seriously. As soon as they can, he'll get them out of here."

"He didn't come for that peace conference?"

"No, he came to see me. I don't get away that often and he thought he'd take the opportunity. I didn't come for it either. I came to see Amaryllis."

"How did you get your leg all shot up?" Billy asked.

Malichai almost dismissed him out of hand, the way he did anyone asking, but something in Billy's voice stopped him. It was more than mere morbid curiosity. It was important to the man to know. Malichai was very certain Billy was mixed up with Callendine, and for some reason knowing what happened was critical to the man.

"I can't give you specifics because it's classified, but I was on a rescue mission. Two of us went in and patched up the real heroes as best we could, but our mission was to take out the heavy guns that were preventing our helicopters from making the pickup. There were a lot of guns. We went in at night and took out a slew of them. Thought we got them all. We didn't realize they had a replacement crew coming in that morning."

He rubbed his thigh. It hurt like a bitch. Before it had taken days and a lot of activity before the pain reached this level. He would bet his last dollar that when Amaryllis went in to look, there would be more hairline fractures.

"They pinned us down when we tried to take the boys up to the rendezvous point. Something had to be done, so I charged the guns and hurtled a few grenades. Shockingly, I survived my idiot charge and started back. The helicopters were already landing, and my partner was helping the wounded to the site. A machine gun opened fire and took me down, by painting a permanent zipper right up the side of my leg."

Just talking about it made his leg hurt even worse. He smelled the gunpowder. The stench of blood and death. Heard the beat of the helicopter rotors. The bark of Rubin's gun. So precise. So deadly. The pain of his shattered bone. It felt shattered all over again.

"You're still in the service," Billy said, respect in his voice.

"I'll always be a soldier," Malichai said.

"Someone called you 'doc.' Said you were a doctor when I asked."

Malichai shrugged. "I'm a soldier and, yes, I'm a doctor because when I go out into the field to see to a wounded soldier, I want to be able to send him home to his wife and family, not his body in a bag, so yeah, I went to school."

"I was in the service as well. Army. Lot of years ago, but Recon. Best years. Good men. A few friends stayed in and they've made great careers for themselves. I should have done that, but my wife was sick, and she needed me at home."

"I'm sorry, Billy, that's tough. I would have gotten out too. Is it okay if I ask —"

"She didn't make it. She had cancer. She lingered for a long time. Three years, and I spent every day with her and am grateful for each of them. But she died and I've been alone since. I spend a lot of time with my online buddies, and my cousins, Tania and

Tommy." He scratched his head. "With all this medical crap going on, you probably missed the hit man story going around."

Malichai lifted an eyebrow. "Hit man?" He sounded skeptical. Inside he was triumphant.

"Yeah, it was in all the papers. Apparently, a local businessman, a stand-up guy by all accounts, churchgoing, had a wife and kids, was a hit man. But someone offed him. The cops arrested another man, accusing him of being a hit man —"

"Wait." Malichai held up his hand. "So, two hit men."

"Yeah, one local. He's dead. The second one, name's Rubin Edon. He's staying right here in this establishment. If Marie were here, I'm sure she'd kick him out, but Amaryllis, poor girl, doesn't have that authority. The cops couldn't hold him. They didn't have enough on him."

"That's crazy," Malichai said, trying to sound noncommittal.

"There's another guy in the hotel, calls himself Gino. Now, he really looks like a hit man. Italian. I'm sure he's Mafia."

"Billy, that's a jump, just because he might be of Italian descent."

"You have to see him, then you tell me what you think." Billy wasn't backing down.

Malichai shrugged. "Are you here for that peace conference?"

"Fuck no!" Billy nearly leapt out of his chair. "Do you think I'm crazy? A bunch of idiot, hippie-dippie people meditating and smoking their weed and talking all night about how cool it would be if the world would just come together in love? Hell no. They can do their drugs and have their orgies and talk until they're blue in the face. You ever been to Burning Man? They say it's all about art. Making a city of art. It's all about women walking around mostly naked and men's asses hanging out of their britches. It's free fucks, free drugs, dirty people doing dirty things. Talk about worthless people. Those are the people you fight for? You almost died for? Makes me want to puke."

Malichai's gut knotted tight, setting off his radar. "I doubt most of them are like that, Billy. A lot of people want to find a way to talk to one another, to find a common ground and maybe some understanding of one another's cultures. You can't put thousands of people from all those countries together and have all of them be dipshits. A few, yes. Those few are probably the camera grabbers, but the majority are really trying to make a difference in the way soldiers do."

Billy shrugged. "Maybe, but they shouldn't associate with drug-addicted hippies."

"You've got a point," Malichai agreed, switching gears. "You still in touch with your buddies in the Army?" Discreetly he rubbed his leg. "If I get booted for medical reasons, it would be nice to think my friends would still stick by me."

"The brothers you make in the military are brothers for life," Billy said staunchly. "You should know that by now."

Malichai rubbed his leg again, this time openly. "Yeah." He flashed Billy a smile. "I guess I was just looking for a little reassurance."

"One of my brothers that goes way back, all the way to boot camp and we served together for several years, is an advisor to the VP. He's climbed that ladder through service and I'm so damned proud of him. He was best man at my wedding. Came looking for me when I went on a bender and stayed drunk for three months after I lost my woman. Got me sobered up and straightened me out. He's never forgotten my anniversary. Calls or comes by to see me. If he can't make it, he sends me a ticket to fly and has me come to him." He grinned at Malichai. "Been to the White House a few times. Who would have thought?"

"That's nice to hear, Billy. Makes me feel better. I don't know what I'd do if I'm not in the military. I suppose being a full-time doctor working on soldiers will have to do, but that doesn't feel the same to me. I haven't even lost my leg yet and I'm whining about it." He pressed his fingers to his eyes briefly. "I worry about what Amaryllis is really going to feel like. I've seen so many good men lose everything when they lose a limb."

"She leaves you, then she's not worth having," Billy said staunchly. "What are you going to be doing when everyone goes to the opening of the ideas on peace or whatever they're calling that nonsense? This place will be deserted."

"My friend is actually a service buddy as well. He's highly decorated, although no one will ever know it. I don't know if he's even shown his wife his medals. He's still in the service. He just got back from saving the world from a virus similar to Ebola. The chances he takes to keep other soldiers and our citizens from harm's way are just plain scary. I told you his wife gave birth prematurely to twins. One is doing well, and they could move him, but the other not so good. I've been helping them. I'll most likely continue with that."

Billy opened his mouth twice and then snapped it closed abruptly. He shook his head. Finally he heaved a sigh. "I don't understand. Why don't they take those kids to the hospital?"

Deliberately, Malichai lowered his voice and looked around. He leaned closer to Billy. "There's a price on his head as well as his wife's. That's why he came here in the dead of night. He wasn't planning on staying, then everything went to hell. If certain factions knew he was here, they would move heaven and earth to assassinate him and his family. He'll leave the moment the babies can fly."

Billy cursed under his breath. "That sucks. He sounds like a good man. A decent man. You've got thousands of useless people sucking down weed and any other drug to make themselves think they're tremendous thinkers, but what they're really doing is partying, and then you have a great man who knows the meaning of hard work and sacrifice and he's stuck in a basement with a price on his head."

"The irony of it all is that he's a true genius. If there is one mind in the world that could solve a few problems if anyone would listen, it would be his."

"You don't see him wasting his time," Billy said. "He chooses to spend it with his wife and family or in service to his country. Few men like that left." He stood up. "I've got an appointment, Malichai. I hope your leg stops hurting and you get to feeling better."

"I'll be fine. Don't worry about me."

Malichai watched Billy go out the front door. Immediately he sent to all GhostWalkers the information, using their telepathic connection.

Billy is involved. Says friend is advisor to VP. Rubin's cover is bought. I said Trap was a very decorated friend in service with price on head as well as on his family. His wife went into labor when they came to visit me at night. Can't leave yet. Billy was visibly upset. Whatever is going to take place I'm afraid will happen on opening day.

Ezekiel answered. *We have been unable to find Callendine or Salsberry. They are legitimately officers in the Army, and they are on assignment. Major General is trying to uncover where they are. This is a Navy town. They're coordinating with us, doing most of the hunt for Callendine and Salsberry. Word is, several Army men in town. That's not unusual, but they don't appear to be here for fun. We've got eyes on them.*

Joe added to the information. *We got one good print off of Salsberry and it comes back legitimate, so I'm going to make that leap and say they were actually ordered here. I don't know who ordered them or why. Major General is demanding answers. The fact that a decorated GhostWalker may lose his leg is helping peel back layers but it's taking too much time. He says the delays appear to be deliberate.*

Malichai had to do some heavy deep breathing at the casual way Joe mentioned that he might lose his leg. If Joe said it, and he would know more than any other, it was closer to the truth than Malichai wanted to know. He forced air through his lungs and with it, brought in the scent of Amaryllis. The moment he took her in, his world changed. Lightened. She could do that, without doing more than existing.

He looked up. She stood there, her blond hair falling around her face and down her back like a waterfall, and her blue eyes like two beautiful jewels glowing at him. She was so beautiful, she seemed to shine from the inside out. She stood in front of him, palm curving around the nape of his neck so gently. She leaned down and then she was kissing him. Taking his breath. Taking away the worst thoughts, forcing them out of his head to make room for her. She tasted sweet — so sweet. He wrapped his arms around her and pulled her down onto his lap. He took over kissing her, letting the fire consume him, knowing it was dangerous to both of them when they were in public, but he needed her. She gave him everything.

The front door was just to the left of the lobby and it opened, the breeze from outside slipping in to ease the heat rising so fast between them. Or maybe it fanned the flames further. Malichai deepened the kiss, his tongue dueling with hers, a tango of fire —

Amaryllis cried out, the sound pouring down his throat, a scream of fear, of pain, of despair. Her body jerked backward, off of him, onto the floor. A huge man stood over her, his face a mask of pure anger, twisted into something evil as he pulled her backward toward the door by her hair. She had both hands up around her hair to try to ease the terrible pressure on her scalp as she scrambled to try to get her feet under her. Her assailant was dragging her too fast.

"What the fuck, you cheating bitch? You think you can run away from me? I told you I would find you anywhere. I'm not alone this time, and your little fuck buddy is a dead man."

Malichai knew immediately who he was

dealing with. He had known Owen Starks before he ever went to work for Whitney. He sent the appropriate SOS to his teammates, especially in light of Starks's declaration that he wasn't alone.

He sprang from the chair, using enhanced strength, uncaring who might see him. Both knees bent to his chest, he flew across the room. At the last possible second, his legs shot out, his boots slamming into Owen's chest, with the force of what had to feel like a freight train. The blow drove the man back so hard he hit the wall, actually splintering the wood. The thud was loud, the force of the jolt shaking the entire house. Two pictures came crashing down, glass shattering across the floor.

Amaryllis staggered to her feet and rushed to Malichai, trying to drag him away. "We have to go. You can't fight him. Really, you can't fight any of them. They have some kind of armor."

Malichai was well aware that Whitney had been experimenting on his supersoldiers. Owen had a thin steel-like plate either beneath his clothing or beneath his skin, but the armor was much like Cayenne's silken shield. When he'd kicked Owen, he'd felt the shock of it rush right back up his body. He'd luckily landed on his feet, but his leg was shaky.

He'd run into Whitney's supersoldiers before. They rarely lasted long, certainly not the five years Amaryllis had said Owen had worked for Whitney. They were tough and they were jacked up. "I want you to go to Trap and Cayenne. Stay there until I come for you." He made it an order. She'd told him there was some kind of reason she couldn't kill Owen Starks. She didn't know why, but he was fairly certain Whitney had made it impossible.

"Honey, if you stay here and fight, I'm staying with you." Amaryllis didn't look at him, only at Owen as he lumbered to his feet, shaking his head and rubbing his chest.

He barely glanced at Malichai. His gaze kept straying to Amaryllis as if he couldn't help himself, or as if he didn't think Malichai was any threat to him. That puzzled Malichai. They knew each other. They'd met. He would have known Malichai was a huge threat.

"Come with me now."

She shook her head. "You hurt me. I'm not going anywhere near you."

"You deserved what you got. Whitney wants you back. You belong to me and you know it. If you care for one single person at this place, you'll come back; otherwise, there's going to be a lot of dead people here."

Malichai knew most of the guests would be returning in another hour if they kept to their usual patterns. He took a few steps to his right to see if that would draw Owen's full attention. So far, Owen didn't seem to recognize him. Owen had always been a smart man. Quick on his feet. Huge ego. He would take in everything and everyone. He wouldn't miss the fact that his opponent was Malichai Fortunes. They had a past. Malichai had a reputation — an even larger one than Owen. Something wasn't right.

The door banged open hard enough that it rocked on its hinges. A very large man filled the doorway. He looked first at Amaryllis, and then his gaze shifted to Malichai. Amaryllis made a single sound of distress and caught at the back of Malichai's shirt, tugging, trying to drag him backward away from the two huge men — men who appeared to be twins. Men who looked exactly alike. Owen Starks didn't have a twin, but this man was an exact replica, right down to the tiny little scar that dissected his eyebrow.

"This isn't good," Gino said, as he joined Malichai. "Are there any others?"

"I've got that feeling in my gut that says

yes," Malichai said.

Gino turned, his gaze running over Amaryllis. "You should get to Cayenne and Trap."

He made it sound like Cayenne might need Amaryllis, and Malichai was grateful for that. In truth, Cayenne was lethal as hell and she would protect Amaryllis.

"I'm not leaving Malichai. In any case, have you noticed, I'm a bit of a distraction? I'm betting when the real deal walks in, I won't be. That's how you're going to know the difference."

Malichai wanted her gone, but he also wanted to get Whitney's clone supersoldiers out of Marie's beautiful home before it was destroyed. He had to get past the goon filling the doorway. She was being stubborn, refusing to retreat. He took another step to his right, sliding his bad leg and struggling to keep from wincing. His opponents would find out soon enough that he had a weakness.

"Amaryllis, come here," the soldier in the doorway said and snapped his fingers at her, as if that would make her mind him.

"That's not going to happen," Malichai said very quietly. "Amaryllis is engaged to me. We're getting married in a few days. You need to tell Whitney to back off."

"Fuck Whitney. Amaryllis is mine. She had no business running off. You need to mind your own business before you get hurt."

Owen the first continued to shake his head and rub his chest. He didn't look at Malichai as he took several steps toward Amaryllis. His brows came together, and his mouth twisted into a frown. "It doesn't have to be this way, Amaryllis. No one has to get hurt."

"I'll take this one," Gino said. "He looks bigger and I haven't had much to eat today. You can have number two in the doorway." He cracked his knuckles and grinned.

We need to get them outside of the house if possible. This is going to get nasty, Malichai said. *If any more show up, we'll need reinforcements.*

He nodded at Gino, skirting around Owen the first, who barely glanced at him. Owen the second continued to be conflicted, not moving from the doorway but going back and forth between staring at Amaryllis as if his life depended on it and flicking his gaze at Malichai from time to time.

Malichai heard the thud of fists as Gino attacked behind him, galvanizing him into action. He hit Owen the second much the same way he'd done Owen the first, wanting to knock him out of the doorway. As his boots hit the second supersoldier square in the chest, he heard Amaryllis cry out. It was a gasping, mewling sound, not loud.

He was already in midair, but he had the flexibility of a cat and he turned, landing in a crouch, almost exactly where Owen the second had been. A third Owen had Amaryllis and she was fighting him in earnest. This had to be the real one. The one he knew from all those years ago. Cunning, calculating, out for himself, this man would use anything or anyone to get what he wanted, including lethal force — and he wanted Amaryllis.

Amaryllis was limited by the small area she had to fight in. Gino couldn't give her any help because he was engaged with Owen the first. The supersoldier was slow, but he was a tank with enormous strength, and he knew how to use it. Amaryllis looked very small in comparison to the real Owen, but she wasn't giving in and she knew what she was doing. She slammed her foot into his ribs, coming under his armor and then spinning in midair to drive her foot down and across his cheek, nearly slamming him to the floor. He had no choice but to let go of her to break his fall.

The two stood facing each other, Owen between Amaryllis and Malichai.

Owen grinned at Amaryllis. "Did you really think you'd get away from me?"

"I managed to escape when you bragged no one could," Amaryllis pointed out, backing up slowly to give herself a little more room.

Malichai could see she was trying to reach the main common room. It was larger and would give her more of an area to avoid Owen. She couldn't afford for him to get his hands on her. She would have to fight him with hard, quick, running strikes. She'd had a lot of time to think how she would take Owen down. Malichai didn't want her to do it alone.

He started toward Owen, when he was hit from behind. The blow felt as if an oak tree had fallen across his back. He staggered forward, nearly fell and caught himself, whirling around to face Owen the second. The supersoldier rushed him, thinking to take advantage while Malichai was off-balance, but Malichai's body was always in perfect balance. He kept turning and caught the soldier coming in with a hard round-house kick to the side of the face, on the chiseled jaw, slashing downward, to drive him to the floor.

Agony blasted through his body. His leg felt as if it had shattered. The pain was so severe, his stomach rebelled, bile rising fast. He fought it down. There was no way he could put that foot on the floor, not yet, not when the explosion of pain was so blinding. He breathed deeply and forced his mind to control his body. He felt Owen the second's eyes on him and knew he had to put his foot on the floor, or the soldier would discover his weakness.

He backed farther into the room, knowing he had to get rid of Owen the second so he could aid Amaryllis. He palmed the knife he kept in his boot and sent a small, silent apology to Marie that her floor was going to be one hell of a mess. He kept the blade hidden along his wrist and the handle in his fist, where it was unseen. Deliberately, he backed away from his opponent, seemingly stumbled, and instantly the supersoldier was on him, his massive fists coming straight at Malichai's face. Getting hit wasn't an option. One punch and he was going down.

Malichai slipped under the punch and slammed the blade of his knife deep into Owen the second's armpit. It was one of the few areas he knew wasn't protected by armor on Whitney's supersoldiers. He twisted the knife as he brought it out and leapt back as blood sprayed across the room.

Owen the second howled, a long wail of

obscenities, and then he rushed Malichai, furious, determined to kill him. He had the original Owen's temper, and it showed. There was fury in his eyes, so much so the eyes glowed a deep red, making him appear diabolical. His big fists punched the air several times around Malichai's head. Once his left hand punched the wall, driving a hole the size of a grapefruit into the wood. Blood spurted from his knuckles and from under his armpit, but he didn't seem to notice.

Malichai kept moving in a loose circle, forcing Owen the second to turn continually with him like a dancer. All the while Malichai waited for another opening. It took patience. He had to block out all thoughts of Amaryllis and what was happening with her, of Marie's guests returning, or of Cayenne and the babies in the basement. He had to think only of his opponent and wait for that one chance to bring him down. He knew Gino was working with that same patience to be able to kill Owen the first.

"What the hell is going on here?" Billy Leven's voice cut in. "Malichai, do you want me to call the police?"

"Stay back," Malichai said, inwardly cursing. The last thing he wanted was for Billy to see Gino fighting with him, or either of them using GhostWalker enhancements, which they were going to need in order to defeat Owen Starks and his clones.

"Amaryllis." Billy almost breathed her name, shocked that anyone would try to punch her, especially a man who appeared to be twice her size.

"Don't get near him, Billy," Amaryllis warned.

Malichai ducked under Owen the second's attack and plunged his knife into the super-soldier's right armpit, again twisting the blade as he brought it out. Blood pumped out with each ragged breath and rushing step the clone took. The walls looked as if an artist had gone a little crazy painting dark red stripes everywhere. Owen the second shuddered and then abruptly sat on the floor, rocking back and forth.

Malichai left him there, rushed past Gino, who was essentially using the same strategy on Owen the first that he'd employed on Owen the second, but the first supersoldier appeared to be a little faster and definitely smarter than the one Malichai had to deal with.

Billy came up behind Owen and pulled his gun, using a two-fisted stance. "Stop right there. If you don't, I'll shoot you." The warning was real. There was no doubt that he would do exactly what he said.

Malichai dove to bring him down, to get him out of harm's way. Owen was on Billy before Malichai, slamming him to the floor, taking the blast in his chest, his armor absorbing the bullet. He grabbed the gun and turned it on Billy as Malichai landed on Owen. Malichai caught Owen's big head in his hands and tried to wrench it.

"Owen, don't!" Amaryllis cried out.

Owen actually shifted his gaze to her, smiling, as he pulled the trigger. He never seemed to notice Malichai using his enhanced strength to try to wrench his neck. Billy's chest exploded into blood and mangled flesh. Owen dropped the gun on the floor right into the pool of blood, all the while looking at Amaryllis. Billy fell back, his gaze on the two combatants as Owen punched Malichai's injured leg repeatedly in an effort to dislodge him.

Amaryllis raced around the two men rolling on the floor to try to stem the blood flowing like a river from Billy. His gaze jumped to her face. He lifted his hand and touched a tear there. "Tell Malichai to get out, his friend too. Get out." His body shuddered and he was dead.

Amaryllis closed her eyes for a moment and then turned her head slowly to see

Owen punching Malichai's leg. Not only was Owen enhanced, but he was bulked up with immense muscles in his arms and chest. The power he generated when he smashed his fist into Malichai's leg was enormous, but Malichai showed no reaction. He kept applying relentless pressure to Owen's neck. Owen was beginning to actually feel it now, that impressive power Malichai had.

She stood up slowly, skirted around Gino, who feinted toward Owen the first with a knife and then circled to his left, giving her the room to get past him. She did, moving without haste. She had the gun in her hand. Billy's gun. The gun Owen had used to shoot a man who had nothing whatsoever to do with Whitney or his pairing schemes. His breeding schemes. Or this latest cloning mess. What did it even mean? Was she supposed to go home with three Owens? One was bad enough.

She went right up to Owen and pressed the gun to his throat. He went still instantly. His throat was one of the few vulnerable places on him. Malichai held his head so it was impossible to move. There was a sudden stillness in the room.

"It would be murder, Amaryllis," Owen said. "You pull that trigger and it's murder."

He didn't struggle. He just waited, his fate in her hands. A small taunting grin slipped over his face. He knew she couldn't pull the trigger. She tried. She tightened her finger, but something stopped her every time she made the effort. She wanted to scream.

A gloved hand reached over her shoulder, took the gun from her. Rubin pushed the barrel against Owen's throat. "Never had any trouble distinguishing between a varmint and a gentleman. Where I come from, we get rid of the varmints." The voice was very soft and carried a slight accent. "Ma'am, I'd appreciate it if you'd look away."

When Amaryllis looked up at him blankly, Rubin gently laid his free hand across her eyes and he squeezed the trigger. The bullet tore through Owen's throat and out the back of his skull. For good measure, Rubin angled the barrel upward and fired a second time to make certain he killed the supersoldier. He dropped the weapon onto the floor and walked away, in keeping with his role of a hit man if anyone was watching.

Malichai sank back onto the floor, breathing through the horrendous pain in his leg. Marie's floors were covered with blood, but the house itself was still intact. Billy was dead, and that was a huge loss. He'd liked the man. Even respected him, but Billy had been mixed up with Callendine and they'd needed him. They'd had a tail on him, but he'd shaken it before he'd met up with his contact, and now they weren't going to have another shot at finding out just what Callendine planned. They could assume he was going to try to blow up the San Diego Convention Center. And they could assume he was going to do so on opening day, but assumptions, when it came to people's lives, didn't cut it. They preferred real data.

Gino joined him, streaks of blood on his chest and face. He flashed a quick grin. "Three of those bastards were three too many."

"I agree." Malichai took Amaryllis's hand as she sank down beside him.

It was too late to do any cleanup before the guests arrived. The Navy sent out their people fast, and they quickly cordoned the entire front of the bed-and-breakfast off so all guests had to come through the back door and couldn't go down the hall to the front. The Navy investigators dealt with the police and fielded questions as they surveyed the damage to the inn. It had been kept to the front room and would have to be repaired as soon as possible.

"I expect poor Marie will never have any

more guests," Amaryllis said. She leaned her head against Malichai's arm.

"Don't underestimate people's morbid curiosity. Most of these guests will return. These are great stories to tell their friends and families, even if they have no idea what's going on."

"If Billy's involved, why would he warn you to leave? He said to tell you and your friend to get out. He was very urgent about it."

"We're certain they plan on having Rubin carry out their hit man's plans to use the bed-and-breakfast as a diversion for whatever the real target is. If all the cops and fire trucks are here, Callendine and his crew will have plenty of time to do whatever it is they're planning and then get away clean. Billy was a man who believed in service to his country, so it's odd that he got caught up in all this. He clearly doesn't want Trap or me to be here when the place is burned to the ground," Malichai mused.

"Can you get up?" Gino asked.

Malichai had been afraid all along someone would ask that question. They were in the way of the Navy people. He shook his head. "Not without a lot of help."

17

There was complete silence in the room. Only the sound of the clock could be heard, and even that was muted. Rubin was the big gun in the room. He'd slipped in, a shadow in the darkness, hidden from all inn guests.

The talent of psychic healing that Amaryllis and Joe possessed was a very rare gift and if Whitney knew they possessed it, he would want them back, but Rubin had the one talent that was prized above all else. He was a psychic surgeon. His talent was protected by every member of the team. No one would ever let it be known what he could do. Whitney would move heaven and earth to acquire him and, most likely, would take his brain apart in order to figure out how he could do surgery on physical bones with his brain.

In the beginning, when it first came out that Malichai would need him, Ezekiel and

Joe had protested Amaryllis knowing his identity, but that had since become a moot point. Malichai planned to marry her. She was a GhostWalker. They either had to trust her enough to make her a part of them, or he would be walking away with her. She would be subject to the same rules all of them were.

Malichai tried to breathe normally, to keep his heartbeat under control as Rubin approached his bed. His hand nearly crushed Amaryllis's.

"It's interesting Owen found you, Amaryllis," Rubin said as he pushed back the thin sheet covering Malichai's leg. Malichai wore shorts that left his leg mostly bare. Rubin ran his hands along the leg but looked at Amaryllis. "Malichai told us how carefully you planned your escape. He admired you greatly for that. I thought your plan was brilliant. You outwitted Whitney and got two of the other women out as well, which actually helped you because they weren't as adept or as certain they wanted to escape, which gave you more time."

Amaryllis nodded. "Sadly, I took that factor into account."

"Not sadly," Rubin corrected. "You were surviving. That's what we do. But Owen found you when he shouldn't have." He closed his eyes, his hands hovering close to the bruising and swelling where Owen had concentrated his punches. "You dealt with Whitney's tracking devices?"

"Yes, of course."

"How did Owen know how to find you? And how did Owen know about Malichai's leg? Malichai assured me he was careful. He hadn't so much as flinched, yet Owen knew."

He fell silent. The room went silent with him. There was no expression on his face, so Malichai couldn't tell what he was thinking, but his gut was churning. Then Rubin's eyes opened, and he was looking at Amaryllis again.

"Owen was so obsessed with you, had he known where you were earlier, he would have come right away. That would lead me to believe he found out recently. Someone contacted him, and they also told him about Malichai and the fact that he'd been shot recently in the leg."

"Who would know about Owen?" Amaryllis asked. "No one knows about him. I only told Malichai. That time in your room, remember? You woke up and thought something was off. Tag had found Lorrie and you wondered how."

"Shit, Malichai," Ezekiel said, for the first

time breaking the silence. "That little snake Billy had bugged your room. You started using a jammer and sweeping it. Callendine tipped off Owen. He probably is on a need-to-know basis and when he sent the information higher up the chain, rather than get Whitney involved, they chose to send in Owen. That would shake things up here and hopefully get rid of the GhostWalker in residence."

Amaryllis avoided his eyes. If Billy had listened to them, he'd heard a lot more than her encounters with Owens. Malichai sent her a wicked little grin, hoping to lighten her mood. Hell, he needed to lighten his mood. He tried to think back. He'd used the jammer because it was ingrained in him, but he always took it with him just in case someone got into his room. He'd slipped it into his pocket. He'd had sex with Amaryllis and then talked about Owen.

"I was at the beach today, minding my own business, reading, when I was contacted by one of Callendine's men," Rubin announced as he continued to assess Malichai's leg. He was at his calf now. "He clearly was a soldier. Army. I sent his photo to Joe to have him identified. He came back under Callendine's command. A man by the name of Sergeant Kolt Michigan. He offered me the job of burning down the bed-and-breakfast. This time, he didn't include Amaryllis or Marie. They switched it to two of the guests. Men by the names of Jay Carpenter and Burnell Strathom. Art dealers out of LA. They wanted them murdered first and their bodies found inside. I was to anonymously call it in. While the police are inside examining the bodies, they'd like the entire bed-and-breakfast to go up in flames."

"Rubin," Amaryllis said softly. "What is wrong with those people? Billy had to have told them that there's two babies in the basement."

"That's why Billy tried warning us to get out, Amaryllis," Malichai reminded her. "He wanted Trap and his family gone, and me to take you out. He didn't want us to be harmed."

"Just everyone else," she said. "I just don't understand."

Frankly, neither did he. Growing up on the streets, Malichai had seen a lot of things that didn't make sense to him, choices made by people who didn't need to make those choices. He understood fear, hunger, desperation, fighting to stay alive, but throwing away homes and families, children, and wives or husbands, intolerance, none of that made sense to him. Not as a child, and not as an adult. He fought for his country, but mostly he fought for the people in his country so they had freedom to make choices. He just hoped they'd be good ones. Murdering the innocent wasn't a good choice any way you looked at it.

"I did offer my services to Cayenne and Trap," Rubin admitted, sounding somewhat embarrassed. As always, his voice was very low and soft, yet those in the room could easily hear him. There was something about the velvet voice that was soothing. Maybe it was the healer in him. Malichai could never quite figure it out. Rubin was both extremely lethal and yet a miracle worker when it came to saving lives.

"They took me up on it. I was able to help Drusilla, the little girl, develop her lungs faster. I just managed to speed things up, they were already well on their way to being ready to go. I wanted them to be able to take those babies and get out of here. Trap is going to move them tonight."

Malichai was relieved to hear it. He could see that same relief on Amaryllis's face. He didn't make the mistake of suggesting she go with Trap and Cayenne, although the urge to do so was strong.

"What about Cayenne?" Joe asked. "Did

she allow you to heal her?"

Rubin sighed. "She did, but Trap all but forced her. I don't feel comfortable in those situations. Cayenne needs to come to us on her terms. She feels safer in the swamp and she's more apt to cooperate when she's there. She has Nonny and Pepper there and she knows they'll have her back. She hasn't quite secured those same bonds with everyone else the way she has with the two of them. It will happen eventually. She's trying to be open to it. I think the babies will help. She definitely wants to go home and be with Nonny, but it wouldn't be wise for the little ones to fly yet."

"Where will they go?" Amaryllis asked.

"Shylah and Draden will escort the family to the safe house and then come back here to help us with Callendine. Trap and Cayenne will stay there until the babies are old enough to fly," Ezekiel said.

"When are you supposed to kill Burnell and Jay?" Malichai asked.

"Day after tomorrow is the big day, the opening of the Ideas for Peace convention. This attack here seems to coincide nicely with it," Rubin said. His hands were still moving up Malichai's thigh with infinite slowness.

Malichai tried to read his expression, but

Rubin was impossible to read. He always had been, even when he'd been a young teenager and he'd first joined the Fortunes brothers on the street, so long ago. He'd been equally as quiet then, and nearly as skilled with a weapon.

"I've been going over the plans for the convention center with Zeke," Joe said. "We're going to have to make more assumptions than we'd like. They'll want to take out the support beams to bring down the buildings. If they can collapse them at the same time, they'll get what they want — the maximum amount of people killed."

"We've got help with this one," Ezekiel assured. "Team Two has arrived from Montana, and the SEALs will be helping us as well. The convention center is huge. It isn't like we can handle this on our own. And given that we expect the attack to happen in two days' time, we don't have a lot of time to prepare."

"Is there a way to stop the conference?" Amaryllis asked.

Ezekiel shook his head. "I'm afraid not. We have no concrete evidence that the conference is actually the target. We've got others looking at some of the political targets around the city that would be more likely. Even the base would be a better target. It's confirmed that there are no political figures invited or appearing even on opening day."

"We can only hope we're wrong," Joe said, "but if we're not, we'll be prepared."

"Rubin," Ezekiel said. "What's going on with Malichai's leg?"

Malichai's heart gave another hard jerk in his chest. He knew the answer was going to be bad. The leg hurt like a mother all the time. *All* the time. Joe and Amaryllis had worked on it continually and it hadn't stopped forming the tiny cracks in the bone. In fact, he was certain the damage was happening at a much faster rate. He knew this was going to be bad, and he dreaded the answer.

He took a deep breath and tried to keep all expression off his face. It took effort not to crush Amaryllis's hand in his.

Rubin glanced up at him, meeting his eyes. There was compassion there. Understanding. Things Malichai didn't want to see. Then Rubin was all business. He didn't speak to Ezekiel or the others in the room, only Malichai.

"I'm going in and repairing the bone again. But I'm only able to repair the damage to the bone itself that is happening at this moment. Whatever the Zenith is doing to the bone is beyond my ability to help. Perhaps Lily has ideas. We just need to keep the bone from fragmenting until we can figure out how to stop that process. You have to baby the leg, Malichai. No more hero stuff. No running. No kicking the crap out of someone. You're in the control room, not in the field. One more stunt like this one and you'll lose the leg. There will be no going back."

The thing about Rubin was he always spoke in a low, velvet-soft southern drawl. He never raised his voice, and by doing that, Malichai knew he meant every word he said. The room went absolutely silent and Malichai's heart dropped. He knew that everyone else would be hopeful, but Rubin wasn't. He had essentially grown up with Rubin. He knew him, all the subtleties of him, and Rubin knew him. Sidelining him when his team was in trouble was asking the impossible of him.

Malichai closed his eyes and just let himself think about Amaryllis while Rubin performed the impossible — psychic surgery. She'd chosen him. She could have chosen anyone with her looks and her intelligence, but she had thrown her lot in with him. Right now, she wore his ring. He put his thumb on the ring he'd given her and rubbed back and forth over the top of it as if it could magically transform his life and what was happening to him.

He thought about the house he'd been building. Had he considered what his woman would want in the house? He had looked at it from every conceivable line of defense. Even the windows. He liked the outdoors and often felt cooped up inside a house, so he needed a ton of windows. Bulletproof windows. Tinted windows. Windows he could see out of, but few could see into.

"If we talk, is that going to disturb him?" Amaryllis whispered.

He shook his head. "Everyone just likes to observe him."

"Observe him?" she echoed. "I can't tell that he's doing anything. Every now and then there's this flash of light and then nothing at all. When Joe heals it's so cool because you can see everything so vividly."

Malichai caught Rubin's small flash of a smile. It was rare to catch a Rubin smile. Malichai had once asked him why there was so little light or heat when he worked. Rubin said he conserved as much energy as possible in case he had to perform multiple surgeries on several patients or just on one. That made sense but it wasn't as flashy.

Rubin explained it wasn't about flash, it was about control. The healer had to get a handle on the gift.

"Should I give everyone the day off that day?" Amaryllis whispered. "All my workers. If they are here, cleaning rooms, or working in the kitchen, they'll be at risk, won't they?"

It was mesmerizing to watch the colors burst out from under Rubin's palms from time to time. It was dark in the room and the color would flash momentarily and then be gone. Because it was impossible to know when the phenomenon was going to occur, Malichai couldn't take his eyes from Rubin and the way he inched his palms over the leg. It felt like laser points moving along in a crooked, almost drunken pattern.

Ezekiel answered Amaryllis. "Honey, Rubin isn't actually going to set the bed-and-breakfast on fire or kill your guests. We might decide it's necessary to fake their deaths, just to draw out Callendine and his crew, but we're not going to set this place on fire. The workers aren't going to be in danger."

Amaryllis laughed nervously. "I didn't think that through. Of course no one is going to set the place on fire."

Malichai brought the ring to his mouth

and kissed her knuckles. "This has been your home for the last year and it's Marie and Jacy's livelihood. Naturally, you'd be worried about it and all those here."

"What do we have on this aide to the vice president?" Mordichai asked.

"Liam Hamilton is the vice president's go-to man. He served with distinction in the Army and has medals and commendations up the wazoo," Gino said. "He was known to be friends with Billy Leven and more than once pulled him out of a bad situation after Billy's wife died of cancer. The vice president in particular thought highly of him for helping his friend."

"You know this how?" Mordichai challenged.

"I'm reading it right out of the newspaper article that was leaked to the press a few years back," Gino said. "Unlike you, I actually do read."

There was a snicker from the back of the room and Malichai managed a smile. They were trying to distract him. He was grateful, but he knew the leg wasn't going to hold and his team needed him. Amaryllis needed him. Rubin might as well have told him to stay in bed. The control room wasn't a place he was comfortable in. He was a soldier. A man of action. He wouldn't know what to do just sitting on his ass.

"Did the vice president issue the order for Callendine to go into the field and take down terrorists?" Ezekiel asked. "Is that how this was sanctioned?"

"Major General was able to get an emergency meeting with the VP and he doesn't believe that any such order was given verbally, but there is a signed order in existence," said Joe. "The VP claims many papers are put in front of him dozens of times a day to sign by his aides and he signs them."

"Without looking at them?" There was both derision and disbelief in Gino's voice.

"It's possible," Ezekiel speculated. "You work with a man long enough, you trust him to have your back. You're in a hurry, you just start signing fast."

"This is the security of our country we're talking about," Gino snapped. "The VP can take time to glance at a paper and see what the hell he's signing, especially if it means sending some of our men to kill innocent citizens."

"I suspect those men are handpicked by Callendine," Joe said. "Just as Violet Smythe despised any female GhostWalker Whitney had spliced insect or snake DNA into, and was determined to stamp them out, I think there is a faction that views anyone opposed to a strong military as treasonous."

Malichai thought Joe could be onto something. Billy had been very disparaging when he talked about anyone who had anything to do with the peace conference. It was simply a way to bring people together to share ideas, and he was opposed to it. On the other hand, he felt very strongly about those in the military. While Callendine hadn't hesitated in issuing the order to kill him, Malichai knew that for a fleeting moment he'd regretted that he had to.

"That's a big leap, Joe," Ezekiel said. "To think the solution is to bring down a convention for ideas on peace and kill hundreds, possibly over a thousand, to make what kind of point?"

"The military goes in, cleans it up, declares it a terrorist attack, we need more money, hell if I know what they're looking for," Joe said. "We all know the military could use money, but that's not the way. That's not the way any of us want to up the budget."

"After talking to Billy," Malichai said, hoping to distract himself from the grimness creeping around Rubin's mouth, "I'd say he practically idolized those in the service. He might do anything to make their lives easier. If his friend at the White House told him they were trying to expand the budget for military families and get equipment that would save the lives of soldiers, but these — he called them hippie-dippie people — were taking that away, I can see Billy deciding that it would be worthwhile to help. Callendine could be persuasive. And this Liam had helped Billy numerous times when he needed it."

"I can't see Callendine buying into that reasoning," Ezekiel said.

"You're right, Zeke. I don't think money for anyone is Callendine's motivation. He isn't all that sympathetic even toward soldiers. He was willing to torture me for information if he had to. He was also willing to kill me. This, for him, isn't about money. I think he despises those people and he wants them dead. He's happy to kill them, and the men with him are like-minded thinkers. Mills had zero hesitation in kicking the shit out of my leg when he knew I'd injured it rescuing soldiers. Callendine and most likely those with him have served their country and taken hits for people for too many years and they feel unappreciated or whatever. I don't know what the hell they want, but the disdain for anyone talking peace is apparent."

"How many men does he have with him?" Gino asked. "Did Major General get that out of the VP?"

"They're looking into it," Joe said. "I would imagine it's a small group. They wouldn't need too many. The less, the better. They wouldn't want anyone talking."

They looked at one another in exasperation. Malichai was beginning to think the vice president knew a little more than he was letting on. "Looking into it" was code for the paperwork was lost and someone else was ultimately going to take the blame if they couldn't bury the entire mess under a top security clearance.

"Can he get to the president?" Ezekiel asked.

Joe shrugged. "My guess is, whatever enemies want to get rid of the GhostWalkers are going to block Major General the way they always do, without even knowing what he wants, from seeing the president. He'll also have whoever Liam Hamilton's friends are blocking him as well. With both keeping him from seeing the president, we're not going to see much help from that direction. The only other thing we can do if we think we're going to need it is to call on the other teams. They can be here immediately, but we'll have to call them in now if we want them. If necessary, one of their commanders may be able to reach the president when Major General can't."

Malichai resisted the urge to rub at his thigh. His leg hurt all the time and with Rubin working on it, the pinpoints of burning heat that moved slowly up his bone turned his stomach, adding to his discomfort, but he would have endured anything to save his leg. He knew Rubin was giving him his best. At times, there was pain etched onto Rubin's face. He hated that for his foster brother. Hated that he had to take on whatever he was healing, if only for a few moments. The breaks in the bone were painful, Malichai could attest to that.

"We can't afford to allow this to get away from us," Ezekiel advised. "I think we should handle it with the ones we've got now. Our team and Team Two, and the SEALs — we're lucky enough to have Ken and Jack know the men running those teams so they're willing to help us out. We need to know the faces of those on our teams. If we don't, one of Callendine's can slip through."

Malichai tried to concentrate on what his brother and Joe were saying. Ezekiel made a good point. They usually worked in a tight unit, with only their own people. They worked fast and efficiently and didn't worry about using their skills or enhancements because all of them were enhanced. They would be in a public situation and some of those they were working with were not classified to know about GhostWalkers and what they were.

He rubbed his temples and immediately Amaryllis put her hand on his jaw, her thumb sliding across his lips. He glanced down and found himself caught by the look in her eyes. She had unusual eyes, shaped like a cat's, so blue they looked as if she wore tinted contacts, but they were real, a deep, shining blue like the deepest sea. Dark lashes, thick and long, only enhanced the feeling of looking into two mysterious, hypnotizing jewels. He blinked and tried to laugh at himself for the nonsense he was thinking, but it was impossible to look away from her.

"We'll stop them, Malichai. Whatever those people are planning, we're going to stop them," she said softly. "Whatever it takes. That's what we do."

In spite of the constant pain in his leg, in spite of the growing fear that he would lose his limb forever, his gut stopped the terrible churning. She was right. They had no choice. They were GhostWalkers. They were soldiers. They stood in front of those who couldn't defend themselves. They would do whatever it took to stop Callendine and his men from blowing up a building with innocent people in it.

Malichai tucked a stray strand of her silky blond hair behind her ear. Just looking at her face gave him a semblance of peace.

"I'm glad you chose our bed-and-breakfast, Malichai," Amaryllis said. "How did you choose us?"

He knew she was trying to continue to distract him from the work Rubin was doing on his leg. It was taking so long. Rubin was so silent, but little beads of sweat had broken out on his forehead and a couple of times, it looked as if he might have swayed with weariness. Ezekiel had moved closer to him, as had Mordichai, just in case he needed support. Neither touched him, or distracted him from his work, but both looked somewhat anxious.

"The girls and Nonny chose," Malichai said. "And the little vipers. They had various places, one in Hawaii, a couple in Florida, I don't know. I was letting them find vacation spots for me because I really didn't care, and they were having a good time doing it. I never heard such laughter and nonsense as those girls trying to send me away."

"That's true," Gino said. "I was with him and even Zara, my wife, was in on it. I love to hear her laugh, and the women were in the kitchen at the table with maps and brochures of resorts, and they had all kinds of plans for Malichai's vacation. I believe ocean fishing was involved. Then they'd go off into some crazy fantasy about what would happen to you, like the fish pulling you overboard, and that one would be nixed, but laughter would ensue big-time."

"Was it Pepper who actually chose San Diego and this bed-and-breakfast?" Malichai asked. "She was there with the little vipers. They're never left out. Thym was on the table next to Cayenne. And little Cannelle, we call her Elle, was sitting in Nonny's lap and Ginger was in a chair, hanging over the table, right by her mom. They were holding court as usual."

"It wasn't actually Pepper," Gino said. "It was Thym. She told them you had to go right here. And she held up the brochure with the bed-and-breakfast advertised. She kept saying it every time someone chose somewhere else. Once, she got tears in her eyes and insisted. Finally, Nonny took the brochure and said Thym had chosen and that was where you were going. Thym's little face lit up like you wouldn't believe."

"That's right," Malichai said. "I forgot that. I knew Nonny had the last word. Thym doesn't talk much. Neither does Elle. Ginger does all the talking for the three of them. It was Thym. Those little girls are gifted."

"Maybe in more ways than we ever suspected," Mordichai said. "You say Thym was very insistent. Is it possible she knew you would meet Amaryllis?"

"How could she know that?" Malichai asked. He tucked Amaryllis's hand close to him, the one with his ring on her finger.

"Hell if I know, Malichai, but how do we do what we do?"

Malichai didn't have an answer. He shrugged. "If that little one can figure out where we can find the right woman, you need to sneak her those little round cinnamon candies she loves so much and Pepper frowns on. Maybe she'll point you in the right direction for finding your woman."

"You just want me to make Pepper mad," Mordichai protested.

"You ever see her angry? Pepper doesn't get upset and she doesn't get angry."

Ezekiel cleared his throat. "When she's in labor, that might not be true," he clarified. "Especially if your name is Wyatt and you were the one who got her pregnant."

"With twins," Gino said. "That seems to

be a trend with GhostWalkers. Quite a few have twins. I'm fairly certain my woman wouldn't be thrilled if I got her pregnant with twins."

Amaryllis tightened her fingers around Malichai. "Yeah, I wouldn't be that happy."

"You remember that," Mordichai said. "Or you'll get yourself in trouble."

The laughter was genuine and eased some of the tension in the room and the pressure in Malichai's chest. "What did Pepper and Wyatt name the twins?"

"Grace, after Nonny, and Fleur, after his mother."

"That's so beautiful," Amaryllis said. "I love their names. I don't have a mother or father." She looked at Malichai.

He shook his head. "I think a lot of little girls are going to be named Grace after Nonny."

Ezekiel inclined his head. "I have to agree with that. She's going to have an entire slew of little grandchildren running around all with the name of Grace."

They laughed, but Malichai thought it might be true. He certainly would want to name a daughter after the woman he admired so much. "How is Pepper doing with all those little girls?"

"I think a better question is, how is Wyatt

doing with all those little girls?" Ezekiel corrected with a grin. "The little viper trio think the babies belong to them and insist they take care of them. Wyatt is concerned about accidental bites. Pepper is exhausted trying to keep up with the feeding. Nonny, as always, is the calm in the center of the storm. Wyatt has at least two little girls on him at all times, although I think Diego is now having to hold babies whether he likes it or not."

Malichai nearly choked on the water he'd been sipping on. Diego? Holding babies? He'd like to see that. He snuck a glance at Rubin, but if Rubin was aware of the conversation floating around him, he showed no signs of it. His face really showed signs of strain now. Of pain. It put things instantly back into perspective for Malichai. Talk of home and family had helped keep the worry of losing his leg at bay, but one look at Rubin, and he knew it was no small battle to try to save his leg.

Hours had passed and Rubin had worked steadily. He'd paused only to drink a little water and rest before taking up the task again. He didn't talk the times he rested. He didn't look at any of them, Malichai included. That was unusual for Rubin and boded ill as far as Malichai was concerned.

Amaryllis had to leave him, going back to work, making certain the guests had dinner and they were all reassured that everything was just fine, and they would be able to use the front entrance very soon. The fight that had broken out concerned the military, and the family would be leaving soon so no other enemies would be trying to get to them.

Because Trap and Cayenne were in the basement and just about every guest was aware someone was down there, and nurses came and went, they decided a good explanation was that Trap was a part of a team terrorists had targeted to assassinate. Those coming after him had been stopped before they could get to him and his family. His family was being moved, and that would take the threat away.

Most guests were very sympathetic and wanted to meet with the hero and shake his hand. That was impossible because his identity and that of his family had to be kept secret. Those who knew Billy were very upset and Tania and Tommy were particularly distraught. They raged at Amaryllis, Tania screaming and crying until only Tommy could comfort her, pulling her into his arms and letting her cry on his shoulder while Amaryllis stood by helplessly. She'd told Malichai she felt terrible, as if she was somehow at fault. She expected the two to leave the inn, but they didn't, they just went to their rooms and refused to come out. The other guests heaped flowers and cards of sympathy at their doors. Amaryllis didn't know whether to leave them there or clean the hallway, so no one tripped or got hurt.

Malichai wished he was up so he could help her. She was already looking tired and strained, having to run the entire inn on her own without Marie. Making decisions for her friend wasn't easy. She texted her often, but knowing the bed-and-breakfast was targeted by Callendine and his crew had to put extra pressure on her. She was worried about the guests — and Malichai.

Trap, Cayenne and little ones are away safely, Draden reported. *Shylah and I are returning to the inn to help out. Will be there in under an hour.*

Malichai breathed a sigh of relief. He hadn't realized how worried he was about those babies. They were in a safe house, surrounded by an army of guards and the best medics the GhostWalkers had. Paul Mangan, the only other psychic surgeon, a young man on Team Three, had been flown from San Francisco to San Diego to help Trap out. With him had come two other members of his team, Javier Enderman and Gideon Carpenter. They looked unassuming, but Malichai knew they were there more for the protection of Paul than anyone else, and both were extremely lethal individuals. He was grateful they were with Trap and his family.

Good hunting, Trap added.

Take care of your family. Malichai couldn't help putting his hand on top of his hip, wondering if the next time he saw Trap he would have a leg or if it would be gone.

Rubin suddenly stepped back and staggered. Ezekiel caught him and guided him down to a chair. Mordichai handed him an open bottle of cold water. The room went eerily silent. Rubin didn't seem to notice that they all waited for his assessment, like he hadn't already given it. Malichai didn't necessarily want to hear it again, not with his brothers in the room. Not with Ezekiel standing so close to him.

He wasn't going to fall apart. He knew what Rubin was going to say because he'd watched his foster brother's face. He knew that bone was Swiss cheese. The damage to it was accelerating. Ezekiel, like Rubin, was going to sideline him, but if he was going to lose his leg permanently, then what difference did it make? He'd rather go out on a mission than lie in a bed feeling sorry for himself.

Rubin drank half the bottle of water and then pressed the cold bottle to his forehead. He stretched his legs out in front of him and leaned back, his eyes closed. "You have one hell of a high pain tolerance, Malichai." There was respect in his voice.

That was the last thing Malichai expected him to say and it embarrassed him. "It does hurt," he conceded. "I guess I should have warned you."

A faint smile curved Rubin's mouth, giving his face that younger look he usually had. Right now, his color was nearly gray. "I don't think even a warning would have prepared me. That bone is disintegrating at a rapid rate. If second-generation Zenith caused this, we all have to stop using it until Lily can figure out why and what happened."

"Could it be I have an unusual reaction to Zenith? An allergy like Trap or Wyatt suggested?" Malichai asked. He didn't know why he wanted the explanation to be a simple one. One he could understand.

"It's possible. That's not my field of expertise. I only repair things that are broken or damaged. The rest of you is strong and healthy, but that bone, which has always been extraordinarily dense, has been chewed through with tiny holes. The attack on it is nothing I've ever seen before. I tried to send the pictures of what I was seeing through Joe to Trap, Wyatt and Lily. I don't know how successful that type of thing is going to be telepathically, but if this destruction is from Zenith, seriously, Malichai, no one should use it."

"How do we prove it, one way or the other?" Malichai asked.

"Hell if I know. That's all Trap, Wyatt and Lily. But your leg." Rubin sighed and rubbed his temples with his fingers, looking down, not straight at Malichai the way he normally would have. He was frowning.

Ezekiel glided closer to Malichai. "What about his leg?" He sounded grim.

Rubin looked up then. He shook his head. "The truth is, I just don't know. We're working with something none of us has ever seen before. Joe and Amaryllis worked on that bone twice before I got to it and already the fracturing was severe."

"Because he had to fight a supersoldier, Rubin," Ezekiel pointed out. "It wasn't like he was lying in bed twiddling his thumbs."

"Zeke," Malichai said softly. "This isn't anyone's fault. Rubin just spent hours trying to save my leg. If I have one at the end of all this, it's due to his work."

"I know that. I do. I'm sorry, Rubin," Ezekiel apologized immediately. "This is just hard to understand. We've been using Zenith, and no one's had a problem. He used it before on that same leg and didn't have a problem."

"We don't actually know that," Rubin contradicted. "The pitting in the bone could have started then, just maybe not as aggressively. Like a buildup of an insect's poison in the system. That happens with some insects. The first time you're fine. The second time makes you sick. The third time kills you." He tipped up the water bottle and drank more.

Malichai was grateful to see that some of the lines of strain were beginning to recede from his face. "Let's just get to what you think the chances of my keeping this leg are, Rubin, and be real. I want to hear real."

Rubin nodded. "I don't know any other way to be. You shouldn't be putting any weight on it. We're going to have to watch you all the time. Joe and Amaryllis will have to be vigilant, checking to see if the hairline fractures start returning even with you babying the leg. If you have to move around, you have to do it on crutches, keeping the weight entirely off the leg. I meant what I said. I think you should be sidelined for this entire mission, but I know that's not going to fly with you, so it's the control room with your leg up."

"Then what? So I rest it. So I stay off it. What is that getting me, Rubin?" Malichai asked before Ezekiel or Joe could tell him he didn't even get to be in the control room. Or the van, as it would more likely be.

"I don't know." Rubin sounded tired and very discouraged.

Malichai had never heard that low, velvety voice so worn. He avoided looking at Ezekiel. His brother knew Rubin every bit as well as he did. If Rubin didn't have a clue how to save his leg, no one did.

"We have to rely on the three brilliant minds to figure out what the hell is going on and how to counteract it and hope that they can do it before whatever is causing this accelerates the damage faster than the three of us can repair it." Rubin's eyes suddenly met his. "Can you take the pain, Malichai? When it's eating through your bone like that, can you take the pain?"

Malichai felt the other members of his team looking at him. His brothers. He felt their compassion. Their anger. Their feelings of helplessness. He felt all those same emotions. Already, his hand was rubbing at the knots on his hip, the knots that formed from trying to ease the ache that was always present in his leg. That ache that would slowly accelerate into a steady pain until it was so bad he could barely think.

He thought of the alternative. That soldier in the street, the one with the sad eyes and the vacant face and no leg, begging for food, just for something to eat. It had been cold and Malichai had been shivering continuously, but Ezekiel had stolen a jacket for him. The soldier had a jacket but no blanket. There were blankets in the space they claimed as their own. There was food. Malichai had made his way there, rolled up his portion of the food in his blanket and returned to the soldier and offered it to him.

At first the man refused to take it, gently shaking his head, not wanting to take from a kid on the street who didn't have much more than him. Malichai had insisted. When he got home that night, he didn't tell Ezekiel what he'd done, but refused to share Zeke's food. When he was shivering so much from the cold and Zeke had snapped at him to get under his blanket, he'd done that, because when Zeke got pissed, you just obeyed.

"I can take it, Rubin," he said. He'd grown up on the streets. He was tough.

18

Malichai thought he'd seen everything. He'd been all over the world. He'd gone to various countries during their celebrations, some with strange rituals and unbelievably extravagant and gorgeous costumes, he'd even seen — on television — the strange and wonderful Comic-Con and Dr. Who conventions, with their seas of people dressed in various attire fitting the themes of their favorite pop culture hero or heroine. What he'd not seen before was the mixture of people from countries around the world coming together dressed in everything from suits to sarongs, women covered in veils from head to toe, and men with turbans and others dressed in nothing but board shorts and sandals. There seemed to be a lot of smiles and nodding, some tried talking in signs; others spoke in halting English or other languages to try to communicate, but they tried.

He noticed phones were out and many people were using apps to translate what they wanted said. He watched the monitors closely. It was impossible to say one person stood out in the crowd because of the way they were dressed. The mix was so strange, with people from different countries dressed in more traditional clothing and some in more religious garb in order to show their solidarity with what the conference was all about. Ideas. Just people bringing together ideas on how to better understand one another and their cultures.

Malichai's job was to identify any of Callendine's men moving through the crowd. The SEAL team had placed vehicles equipped with jammers if needed to stop the remote detonation of any bomb Callendine or his men might set off. If Callendine saw the vehicles out front and around the sides of the building he would know immediately why they were there, but that couldn't be helped. They could only hope the bombs were all about remote detonation, because if they weren't, each bomb would have to be defused. They would have to find every one of them. All team members were looking for bombs in or around every support beam, primarily the major ones.

He hoped they were wrong, but he had a

bad feeling, that nagging one that always told him he was right. He didn't like knowing, but that radar had saved not only him but his fellow GhostWalkers on more than one occasion. He kept looking through the bank of screens, watching carefully not only for Callendine's crew — and he had faces taped to the van's whiteboard stretched just above the bank of screens — but also to catch glimpses of Amaryllis, just to know she was safe. He hadn't seen her in the last few minutes and that made him antsy. He despised that he was sidelined. It didn't matter how important Ezekiel told him this job was, and he knew it was; he wanted to be there, where the action was — and watching over Amaryllis.

"Anything?" Avery, one of the techs assigned to watch as well, asked.

"Not so far," Malichai said. "This is like looking for a needle in a haystack. How do you do it all the time?"

Avery was considered one of the best techs at gathering information. The other team members spoke of him with admiration and respect. Malichai knew the value of a man who took his time and double- and triple-checked all information for his men in the field. He never stopped until he had them back safe at home. Avery was that man. He was also the man who would sit patiently in a van for however long it took, looking into a bank of screens until his eyes wanted to bleed until he discovered the enemy and how best to stop them.

"I could ask you the same thing. Your expertise is the field. You know what you're doing, and you attack it with confidence. This is mine. My world. It's how I can make certain you all come home. It's how I can make the world safer for them." He indicated all the people moving through the multitude of doors as they entered the building.

His gaze never once left the screens, reminding Malichai to keep his eyes on the ones in front of him as well. He had studied the faces of Callendine's crew so long they were burned into his brain. He didn't need to look up at the reminders. These men were the ones Callendine had elected to take on the mission the vice president had sanctioned whether knowingly or unknowingly.

"Man moving out the second door," Avery said suddenly.

Malichai's gaze jumped to the second door. "Yes. Son of a bitch. That's one of them. We're right. We called it. Damn it, they really are going to blow this place up."

The man was named Sergeant Kolt Michigan and he was very militant. He'd been under Callendine's command for several years, just as Mills and Major Roseland Salsberry had. Callendine had spread his influence through his men, along with Liam Hamilton. Someone that connected in the White House, particularly if the vice president was somehow involved as well, would influence the men over years in the direction Callendine wanted them to go. He would be able to see the ones he would have trouble with, and he'd simply have them transferred to another command.

Kolt Michigan coming out of building now. Second door. Bellisia, you're nearest. Can you take him down without anyone noticing you? If Callendine is watching him, he can't be warned, Malichai said. *Wait for confirmation on bomb before you take him. It should be on one of the major supports near the second door. As soon as it's found, let Bellisia know she is cleared to take out her target.*

I'm on it, Ezekiel said.

There was a brief, tense silence.

You have the go, Bellisia, Ezekiel confirmed. *The bomb is here.*

It's a go, Bellisia confirmed.

Bellisia was very small. She had blue eyes and blond hair and was at home in the water. Right now, she was trailing behind

Kolt, very close to him, but she was so small that she was lost in the sea of legs. Malichai caught glimpses of her. At times, small bluish rings rose on her arms, crept up her neck to splash across her skin. Her clothing covered those tell-tale signs of danger. She matched Kolt's pace exactly and as his hand collided with her face, she delivered the deadly bite, but pulled back into the crowd as he swung around.

Kolt frowned, looked at his hand, didn't see anything on his skin. He was wearing gloves and his wrist had just felt a momentary flash, as if a bug had bitten him right over his vein. If he hadn't been so hyper-aware, he wouldn't have noticed. He rubbed the spot and kept walking. He had quite a bit of time to get the hell out of there, but he walked briskly all the same. He didn't want to be anywhere near the place when it blew. There were too many families there, too many children. That bothered him more than he thought it would. Still, they had to be sacrificed. They had to go. He kept walking.

Sweat broke out. For some odd reason, that little vein in his wrist throbbed and his forearm felt numb as he hurried to his car. The parking garage where he'd left his vehicle was a distance away and he had to weave through all the people on the sidewalk making their way to certain death. Just thinking about it made him want to vomit. Every step seemed harder to take. He rubbed at his arm, which had — weirdly — gone numb.

It was becoming harder to breathe. He made his way up the ramp to the second story of the parking garage where his truck was. They had a rendezvous point at a safe house Callendine had taken over as a backup plan. He yanked the door to his vehicle open and crawled inside. Sweat dripped from his forehead into his eyes, stinging. His heart pounded. Maybe he was having a heart attack. He pulled out his phone, but his fingers didn't seem to work and he dropped it.

Kolt found himself slumping over on the seat, unable to move. He stared up at the ceiling of his truck wondering what the hell had happened. His entire body seemed as if it was going numb. He was having trouble breathing. He tried to fight for every bit of air he could. When he began to vomit, he couldn't turn his head to the side, he couldn't move any part of his body. He could only look up and realize he was already dead. He just had to wait until every part of his body shut down.

"You've got to get word to your unit," Avery said. "He's going to get away."

"He's already been dealt with," Malichai assured. "Ezekiel's found the bomb."

For the first time Avery's gaze came up and fixed on him. The tech took a long look and then his gaze was back on the screens.

Remote detonation is the backup. Working on bomb now, Ezekiel said. *Can we get the people out of here?*

We chance Callendine setting off the other bombs. We know there has to be more. Can you get that one, Zeke? Malichai asked, his stomach churning.

All of them had extensive training in explosives, but that didn't mean jack if the bomb was out of their expertise. Too many people were at risk. They'd have to chance Callendine setting off the rest of the bombs. The jammers might work to stop him.

I can get this. Clearly, they're using standard tech, nothing fancy. They didn't expect us to be coming after them.

Malichai could no longer see Bellisia in the crowd, she'd slipped inside where she might have a chance of spotting a member of Callendine's crew. He doubted if any of Callendine's men would know what she looked like or be expecting her, and she was too fast and too good at what she did. So far, it didn't appear as if Callendine knew about the GhostWalker program or who was in it.

"There's suspect number two, James Rodenburg," Avery said. "He's moving fast, coming out of door number four."

Malichai studied his screen to make doubly sure. There couldn't be mistakes. "I've got him."

Shylah, you're up, can you take James Rodenburg? Tall, jeans, tee, about thirty-five, he's to your left, just exited the fourth door. Has a woman and child blocking him at the moment. You need to take him some distance from everyone, and there can't be any trace back to us. Draden, he's just now coming out of the fourth door, so the bomb should be close. Find it fast and give us the go-ahead.

He didn't know Draden's wife as well as the others, but he did know she was reputed to be an assassin few could match up to.

I've got him, Shylah assured. There was absolute confidence in her voice.

Bomb's here, Draden confirmed. *Do not let him walk away.*

Shylah was dressed in jeans and a tee as well. Her wild hair was pulled back in a high ponytail and she was devoid of makeup. Freckles spread across her nose, making her look very young. She smiled at several people and her smile was so engaging, it was impossible not to smile back. She didn't try to hide. She was tall and even memorable. She knew it and she carried herself with confidence. She stayed about fifteen feet behind Rodenburg.

He headed up the street toward the same parking garage Kolt had used. Shylah stopped to look out over the street into a green strip of vegetation just below. She coughed and put her fist over her mouth and turned her head back toward her destination as she took a few steps.

Rodenburg slapped the side of his neck and looked around. His palm came back bloody. Blood poured down the side of his neck to his shirt. He took several steps, not knowing what exactly happened. There was a sting. Nothing else. He found himself on the floor of the parking lot. Several people gathered around him, looking anxious. A young girl bent over him, touched his neck and shook her head.

"I have no idea what's wrong, someone should call an ambulance."

Rodenburg wanted to tell them that it would be futile to call for an ambulance. He was fairly certain that they were all at the bed-and-breakfast where guests and cops were burning or already murdered.

The world just slowly faded away.

It's done, he's down. I'll be back in a few minutes when I can slip into a crowd unseen.

I've got the bomb he left behind. Looks easy enough to dismantle. They gave themselves time to get out. I guess no one wanted to sacrifice their own life for this venture, Draden said.

Get on it, Malichai advised. His gut was churning beyond belief. That was two of the six men Joe had finally confirmed were missing along with Salsberry, Mills and Callendine, all from Callendine's unit. Two. He needed Avery to work his magic.

"All the way to the other side. Coming out. Carter Jorganson," Avery announced in that same calm tone he used. The man was a machine sitting in that van and finding the faces in the midst of so many.

Malichai detested what he had to do next. *Amaryllis. Carter Jorganson, all the way to the left. He's coming out of the building now. He's all in black. Jeans, boots, tee and he's wearing a distinctive black jacket. He even has black hair. Can you take him without being seen? Callendine can't spot you or know Carter is being taken.*

I've got this. Amaryllis sounded cool and very confident.

Malichai had seen her nearly panicked

601

when Owen and his clones had shown up, yet in every other situation she had handled herself with no problem. She hadn't been able to pull the trigger on Owen, yet she was going after Jorganson as if she had no problem with it. He wasn't certain what Whitney had done to her to keep Owen safe, but he hoped it was only Owen.

I've found the bomb, Gino said.

It's a go, Amaryllis. Gino has the bomb.

"Keep looking, Avery. There's three more of these assholes," Malichai said.

He knew the reminder was unnecessary, but it was all he could do when his butt was sidelined and his woman was out there, going up against a trained soldier. She couldn't be seen or recognized by the enemy. Both Joe and Ezekiel had assured him, after talking to her at great length, that she could handle herself, but he wanted to protect her. He wanted to be out there in the field, working with them to make certain they kept every one of those innocent people safe.

The moment they rounded up Callendine's crew, they would shut everything down, but for now, they could only try dismantling the bombs as they found them and hope they had time before Callendine realized his own unit was compromised.

Jorganson had to restrain himself from

pushing his way through the crowd of sheep. That's what they were, nothing but fucking sheep, blatting on and on about peace. There was no peace. There would never be peace. These same people would piss themselves if they were ever in a real situation where they had to fight for themselves or someone else. They wouldn't do it. They would cry like babies and expect someone else to take care of them and then they'd condemn them. Hell was coming and they deserved it.

He managed to keep from shoving an older woman dressed from head to toe in a colorful sari; she walked with grace, but so damn slow he wanted to scream at her. It wasn't like the bomb was going off soon, but Callendine wanted them well away so there was no chance of them being identified or near the convention center when it blew. He wanted them, if possible, on a plane, in the air. He had to get to his car. He'd rented a sports car and had parked it in the parking garage just up the street on the lower floor. He liked the car and looked forward to driving it one last time. He concentrated on that as he moved around another group of people.

Someone jostled him and that pushed him into a young woman. She was a cute little thing with red hair and incredible dark eyes. She caught at his wrist to keep from falling as she stumbled. For one second, he thought he felt a jab through his glove on his left hand, but her fingernails weren't long and she looked almost dainty.

"I'm so sorry," she murmured and moved away, back into the group of peace-minded people.

He was almost sorry she was one of those sheep. He kept walking briskly, now that he was out in the open and he could breathe without taking in the stench of sheep. He made it all the way to his car before he realized he wasn't feeling much in the way of his body. No pain at all, but it was almost as if he was paralyzed. He could barely move. He sank behind the wheel of the sporty car and reached for the starter, but his arms didn't want to work. The paralysis was real. It slowly consumed his entire body until he was incapable of speech or even thinking. It continued until his brain could no longer tell his body to breathe and his heart refused to pump.

It's done. Cone snail venom amped up like only Whitney can do it, Amaryllis confessed. *Coming back in my red wig and nice little getup.*

Malichai didn't want her to come back.

She was much safer away from there. The cameras were picking up all sides of the building and the teams were spread out and moving from main support to support in the hopes of finding more of the bombs. They were certain there would be six of them. Three were being taken care of. There were three more.

"At the back exit. Closer to the hotel. I almost missed him. Ray Valli," Avery identified. "I'm sorry. Can you get your people there in time?"

Bellisia? Can you get to the back exit? Ray Valli is there. White shirt. Jeans. Cowboy boots. He's moving away fast.

I can take him, Bellisia assured.

Malichai nodded to Avery but didn't look away from the screen. *Joe, he's at the back entrance. We knew they would have to block that as well.*

They'd done a mock-up of how they would blow the buildings and take out as many people as possible. Controlling the front and back exits was essential.

I'm on it. Joe's voice was grim. *I was already looking around back here. There's a dark hallway I'm certain he came out of. I heard a door open and close. Damn it, bomb's here, and it's a mother.*

Ray Valli wanted to get away from the

convention center as quickly as possible. He'd questioned the orders more than once to the others. They just didn't make sense to him. He knew the orders had come from the White House. Callendine had told him. The others had reassured him over and over, but these people were citizens of the United States. Okay, not all of them, but the majority. Weren't they the ones they were sworn to protect? He set the bomb just like he was instructed, but he wanted to tell the families to take their kids and run. He didn't. He just stared at them, imagining them with their bodies in pieces. That made him sick. He'd seen enough of that shit in other countries. He didn't need to see it in his own — especially when he was the one responsible.

This was going to be a hard one to live with, but the hell with it. Jorganson was right, they were sheep and they wouldn't listen to reason. They couldn't hear when they were told a simple truth. They wanted to believe everyone in the world was good. Some people really were too stupid to live. That was Jorgey's laughing mantra and it was the truth. He took a deep breath, straightened and began the long walk back to his car. It was on the third floor of the parking garage just up the street.

It was getting hot already, although it wasn't yet afternoon. Sweat broke out and he slapped at an insect on his neck. One nailed him on the inside of his wrist, and he smacked at that one too. He didn't like bugs. He sprayed for them all the time, but he'd never found a bug spray that really deterred mosquitoes. He walked briskly, but after a few minutes he found his arm felt numb and he was having difficulty catching his breath. He didn't want Callendine to see him like that, because he'd make him run for days until he got back in shape. Too much time sitting around watching football and basketball.

By the time he reached his vehicle, his lungs were burning. He put his head back on the seat and closed his eyes, giving himself permission to rest, hoping Callendine didn't have eyes on him. He was just going to stay there for a few minutes . . .

He's down, Bellisia confirmed.

That was four. Malichai glanced at his watch. They'd identified and taken down more than half of them in under five minutes, but Ezekiel was still working on the first bomb. Not one had said they were clear.

"Back entrance, all the way to the left. John Sawyer," Avery said.

Malichai nodded to let Avery know he heard. *Shylah, John Sawyer back entrance, all the way to the left. He's lighting a cigarette on the sidewalk and he just flipped off the building. You see him? You there?*

Yes, he's grinning. Thinks he's getting off scot-free. That's not happening. I'm moving up on him now.

Don't take him close to the center. Callendine probably has eyes on him. If he knows we're onto him, and killing his men, he'll blow this place. We have to find where every bomb is and then get them out.

It was a huge chance they were taking, but they were certain Callendine was prepared to kill everyone if he was discovered.

"You're not supposed to smoke here, sir."

John Sawyer whirled around to see a young girl with freckles spread across her nose looking at him through wide, brown eyes. Her hair was tied back in a ponytail, but even that style failed to tame the mass of waves and wild curls. She was smiling at him with her generous mouth as if she'd given him a compliment instead of telling him, a soldier, a man who had secured her fucking freedom, her right to breathe, what he could and couldn't do.

"Fuck you," he said and flicked the cigarette right at her face.

She was close to him and it should have hit her right in her eye, that glowing end. He'd even stopped to see the results so he could think about them for a long time. He'd had lots of practice hurting the weak, showing them what fools they were and how they should treat men like him with far more respect. Callendine would probably shoot him if he knew some of the shit he'd done, but he'd been careful. He'd like to see this little sweet-faced bitch reach the understanding of just who was in charge.

Somehow, her hand moved with blurring speed. She was so fast he hadn't even blinked yet he didn't see her move and the cigarette hadn't hit her. She caught it and smiled at him. That smile wasn't sweet. Those dark brown eyes were suddenly cool and not at all friendly. She went from looking like a young teen to something altogether different.

Found the bomb, Mordichai confirmed. *Go for it, Shylah.*

"Who are you?" He turned away from her.

Something bit his neck as he turned, and he slapped at it. He walked briskly away, slapping at the insect and then just covering the bite because it throbbed. He felt a trickle of sweat sliding down his neck to soak into his tee and he walked faster. He was almost to the parking garage, but his legs felt rubbery. He made his way to the grass and sank down, thinking he'd just rest for a minute. He found himself lying down, staring up at the sky.

A woman's face swam into view above him. He recognized those freckles. She didn't say anything, she just reached over his body to his neck where the bug had stung him and then she was gone, leaving him in peace to stare up at the sky until everything just faded away.

He's gone. Can they defuse the bomb?

Mordichai's still on it. That's five. We're looking for one more.

Malichai turned to Avery. "Come on, brother, we need the last one. We've got to find that last man." Even as he put it on the tech, he was scanning the screens. There were just so many people. Hundreds. Thousands. Where had they all come from? They'd worked fast, but Callendine would be listening to the scanners, listening for the alerts that would go out for the police to go to the bed-and-breakfast. That had been arranged, although Rubin wasn't at the B and B, he was already in the building searching for the last bomb.

Callendine would be satisfied with the call to the police, but when the fire department and then ambulances weren't called, he would instantly know something wasn't right. He went by the book, by the numbers, and when a mission didn't go right, he hit his fail-safe. They were ensuring the bombs couldn't be detonated by remote, so what was his fail-safe? He might consider that the remotes would be jammed.

"There," Avery said, his voice that same calm. "The last one, Nathan Treadway. He's just now walking out the middle exit back way, he's stopped to talk with a family walking in."

Malichai spotted the man, crouched down beside a double stroller. The parents looked young and they had four children. The older ones were obviously twins, and they looked to be about four or five and the ones in the stroller couldn't have been yet two. Treadway knew he left a bomb inside that building and yet he stopped so casually to talk with children he planned to kill.

Amaryllis, do you see Nathan Treadway? He's right at the middle exit in the back. Crouched down with a family of four children, double stroller. Young parents. He's laughing and talking with the parents, rubbing the curls on the babies in the stroller. He tried to keep his voice impersonal, but even with that, his emotions were there for his entire team to feel.

I've got him. There was complete confidence in Amaryllis's voice.

Malichai saw her now. She moved into position just outside the door, a few feet up the sidewalk, stopping to fiddle with her shoestrings. Treadway got to his feet and with a small, friendly wave at the parents, strode out the door, apparently whistling.

Found the bomb. I'm on it, Rubin said.

I'll be there in two, Ezekiel said. *This one is disarmed.*

It was a beautiful day. Treadway wished he could be there when the building came down. It was huge and the bombs were set to take out the main supports. It would collapse on itself and those inside would be trapped as the ceiling came down. It would be a thing of beauty to watch. He hoped there were outside cameras that would capture the actual fall of the convention center and the slow deaths of those inside. Debris falling. Dirt. Heavy fixtures. Beams. Cement. Brick. The ceiling. It was going to be glorious.

He made his way around a woman tying her shoe without looking at her, although he wanted to swat her ass just because women protested every little thing now, as if men shouldn't even look. He wasn't going to go on a rant about that or be distracted from having the best day. The sun was shining, and the building was coming down on all those idiot people who couldn't think for themselves. They were followers. Every single one of them. They were teaching their children to be followers. They didn't take responsibility for themselves. They lived off the government. They didn't appreciate those who took care of them; in fact, they constantly tore them down. He'd had enough and was fighting back. He knew how to fight. Did they?

Whistling, he walked briskly toward the garage where his rental was parked. He really detested that Callendine had given the order for them to leave, and he even considered pretending there was a problem with his car so he could see the building go up. It didn't seem very fair to plan it all out and then not get to see the actual results. He hoped there was plenty of footage of the bed-and-breakfast burning to the ground as well. If they were lucky, they'd score plenty of victims there too.

As he entered the parking garage, he paused to look around. There was a group of people gathered around someone on the ground. He avoided them and went straight to the stairway leading to the next story where his SUV was parked. It had tinted windows because he didn't give a fuck if he wasn't supposed to have them. He should be able to have them. He sauntered toward the vehicle when he heard a soft sigh behind him.

He spun around. It was the woman from the peace convention center, the one with the shoe that had needing tying. She had red hair and dark eyes. She smiled at him. "You dropped this. You walk so fast, I couldn't catch up with you." She handed him his wallet.

There was a moment he thought he felt a small sensation as he took the wallet when her fingers brushed his palm, but then she was giving him a sweet smile and walking away.

"Wait. Thanks. That was unexpected." It was. She looked like one of those idiots, but she didn't act like one.

"No problem," she said without turning around. "It's a gorgeous day. I think the beach is calling."

He wished he could go to the beach and he was glad she was heading that way instead of back with the sheep. He unlocked the door to the SUV and grabbed the door handle. He missed. It was weird. His hand just fell off. He stared at it, trying to make out the actual grip. He was seeing double. Pain began to shoot from his palm up his arm and it was excruciating. He found he couldn't move his arm, almost as if it was paralyzed.

He tried to turn his head, looking for help, but his neck wouldn't turn. His lungs felt as if they were burning but he couldn't drag in air. He found himself slumping helplessly against the vehicle and then folding in on himself and landing hard on cement half under the car. He couldn't breathe. He couldn't see. Pain engulfed him from head to toe and he had no idea what was happening to him. Then his world just went black.

He's gone, Amaryllis said.

Something in her voice bothered him. Malichai should have been elated. That was Callendine's entire team. *What's wrong, Amaryllis?*

Callendine is here, in the parking garage. I thought he would be closer to the building, but he's up high, on the third floor, overseeing everything from above. He watched all of his men come to the garage, but they never left. He saw me approach Treadway with his wallet and he's on his way to investigate. My guess is, he's going to deploy the fail-safe.

Get everyone out if you can, Malichai.

He wasn't with her. His leg was stretched out, being babied, while she was on the top floor of a parking garage with a man who would shoot her the moment he saw his dead soldier. The GhostWalker teams not busy removing the bomb threats and the SEAL teams immediately began to remove the masses of people as fast but as safely as they possibly could.

Everyone was coming out of the building fast, running. Trying to get away from it. He kept his eyes on the screens, but his mind was with Amaryllis.

Baby, listen to me. He'll shoot first and ask questions later. Meaning, he'll shoot you where it will cause the most pain but not kill you. You can't let him see you. Can you get out of there?

He's at the SUV, crouched beside Treadway, examining him while he's talking into his phone. I'm certain he's trying to blow that building. Get those people out. You have to get them out. He's looking around and he's trying to raise the others. I can hear him calling them.

She was going after him. Malichai knew she was. She wasn't going to let Callendine go. Because he was so completely terrified he was going to lose Amaryllis, that she didn't realize just how ruthless a man she was dealing with, he nearly missed the woman walking out of the building so smugly. Beside her were Tania and Tommy Leven. They were holding hands. Once outside, they separated.

His breath caught in his throat. *Shit. Shit. It's Major Salsberry. She's the fail-safe. She armed a seventh bomb. Get them out of there. Bellisia, Shylah, if either of you are close, she's going out the front entrance right now, to the north, heading away from the parking garage. If you can, one of you get to Amaryllis at the top of the garage, she's hunting Callendine. Tania and Tommy Leven headed toward the parking garage. They're together.*

He was already up and knocking open the van doors. There was no one else. Every single bomb expert was otherwise occupied or on the other side of the building. His brothers. His team. The women. All those innocent people the teams were desperately trying to evacuate without a stampede that would kill everyone. He knew the cost even as he jumped to the ground. He would lose his leg. He had to make that choice. There was no choice. No real other choice, not for a man like him. It might be his worst nightmare, but he couldn't stay in the van and watch those innocent people die.

The moment he landed on his feet, even though he tried to protect his injured leg, Malichai felt the pain rush up from his calf to his thigh like a freight train. Bile rose, but he shoved it down, along with the blackness that edged his vision. He ran, shoving people out of his way, shouting at them to move fast, to get away from the building. He managed to make it inside without mowing anyone down.

Instincts had him turning toward the main support to his right, the main beam they'd all worried about. Ezekiel had already defused the bomb. Salsberry had looked so smug as she'd come out of the convention center, her face portraying her contempt and distaste for the people she was about to kill. She was definitely Callendine's devoted fail-safe. She would have died for him. This wasn't done for money or even because she believed so deeply in the cause, she'd done it for Callendine.

He found the newly planted bomb unerringly and his heart nearly stopped as he flung himself beside it. *Shit, shit. This is bad. Get these people out. Zeke, she's hooked the bombs together. I'm looking it over and she's rewired them both —* He broke off to study the wiring, refusing to look at the minutes counting down so fast. There was so little time and she'd done that deliberately, giving herself just enough time to walk away.

I'm on my way.

That was Zeke, and Malichai wanted him gone. *Get out of here. All of you get out of here. Get these people out.* God. God. There were so many. Too many. He could hear children crying. People screaming. The sounds of chaos. The SEAL teams speaking calmly, trying to bring order into a situation of pure madness.

He had to breathe. He had to get beyond the waves of sickness the excruciating pain in his leg sent up to his brain. He knew the bone was broken. Maybe even shattered into a million pieces, but what did it matter if all these people died? He had to be able to disarm this bomb fast. He'd always been good at this. One of the best. If he could get beyond his own personal discomfort, block the pain and just focus . . .

Shylah was still on the other side of the building to aid the teams removing people through the back exits. Bellisia had stayed just in front to help get the people to leave as fast but as orderly as possible. She was small and she knew few would listen to her, but if she could help in any way, she was determined to do so. Ezekiel and Joe bridged the other GhostWalker team members telepathically, setting up the communication so they all knew what was going on simultaneously.

Major Roseland Salsberry had just condemned hundreds, if not thousands, of innocent men, women and children to death. She'd included the soldiers trying to stop the rogue unit, the GhostWalkers and SEALs, the men from the Navy base, the security men desperately trying to help get the innocent out. Bellisia wasn't about to let her get away with it.

She could see the woman walking so casually while around her the crowd was running. Crying children were pushed to the ground while frantic parents tried to yank them up before they could be trampled over. Salsberry smiled as she surveyed the scene of utter chaos, as if she knew that was what would happen, and she was so happy it had.

Bellisia slipped up beside her, brushed close, close enough to deliver the bite that would end Salsberry's life. It was easy enough to push the venom of the blue-ringed octopus into her system without her even feeling more than an insect sting for a second. The woman was too busy basking in the glory of her success to even notice. It was easy to match those careful, measured steps as they moved away from the crowd and in the opposite direction of the parking garage.

Already the venom was beginning to work. Whitney had made certain to amp up the amount of venom she released into the body of her victim so there was no way they could be saved. Salsberry was obviously feeling something in her hands and arms, most likely numbness or tingling, because she kept rubbing them.

"My name is Bellisia Fortunes," she said softly as they walked together through the crowd. Deliberately, she spoke in a low tone so Salsberry would have to listen. "I don't know if your security clearance is high enough or not, but there's a program in the military known as the GhostWalkers."

She saw by Salsberry's face, that quick glance at her, that she had heard of them. The woman tried to speak, but nothing came out, her voice box was already affected by the poison. It was taking hold fast with the walking, moving it through her system very quickly. In another minute she would go down and there would be nothing anyone could do.

Bellisia smiled at her as if they were co-conspirators. "I see that you have. I'm a

GhostWalker. I'm actually designed to be one of their premier assassins and I'm very, very good at my job, Roseland. I just want you to know that you're dead, and if anyone deserves it, you do." She turned and walked away. Behind her, the body dropped to the sidewalk.

Bellisia hurried back toward the parking garage. She skipped like a child might up the sidewalk, just in case there were cameras on her. It didn't take long to catch up with the couple, Tania and Tommy Leven. They were laughing as they hurried into the garage, on that first floor. They paused, Tommy throwing his arms around Tania and pushing her up against the side of the concrete building to kiss her over and over.

"This was such a rush, Tommy," Tania whispered, "I love you so much."

"I love you too," he said.

Bellisia fell into them. Tommy reached out to steady her. Tania did the same. The small bites were delivered, the venom going in easily. Bellisia smiled up at them, looking for all the world like a pleased child, one with faint blue rings scattered across her skin.

"Thanks."

The two ignored her and, arms around each other, started toward their car. Their pace slowed. Tania staggered and Tommy tried to catch her just as her legs gave out. They both went down. Hard. Neither was able to break their fall. They fell and lay very still.

Amaryllis removed the red wig, rolled it tightly and carefully laid it up against the column closest to the vehicles near Treadway's rented SUV. She backed carefully into the shadows and removed the skirt and blouse, making certain she was out of every camera angle and left that clothing, also rolled as if she were trying to hide it, behind another column. Beneath the attire, she wore her yoga pants and tee, the ones that reflected the background around her, the ones that helped her disappear into any environment. She left her shoes tucked under a car, just barely so they could be seen.

Her hair was already pulled up tightly and slicked back with mesh over it so her wig had stayed on easily. She slipped on soft-soled shoes and looked up at the garage's cameras. Immediately, the energy she sent out short-circuited them. The explosion was dramatic, the sound a loud pop as glass shattered throughout the floor.

Callendine whirled around, his gun out. He looked at the glass on the floor and then up at the camera. He wasn't a coward; he straightened slowly and then, taking his time, walked over to examine the shards, looking to see how the glass had been broken. In doing so, he discovered the red wig rolled so tightly and placed against the wide cement support column. He touched it with the toe of his shoe and then turned, back to the column to search the garage.

He knew he was in a hunt. He spotted the shoes beneath the vehicle several cars down from the dead body of his soldier almost immediately right from where he was standing. She saw him react, his eyes widening, and then once again, searching the garage for other clues. It took several minutes before he spotted the clothing and he had to step out of his comfort zone to ease his way stealthily to get to them. He crouched low, utilizing the vehicles as cover to make his way over to the skirt and blouse to examine them.

Callendine could see that it was a woman who had killed Treadway. He kept shaking his head as if that didn't sit right with him — as if he couldn't believe it. He still couldn't figure out how the man had died. Worse, not one of his soldiers had responded when he had tried to contact them, which meant they were probably dead as well. Amaryllis didn't feel in the least sorry for him. He had been the one to plan and carry out the horrendous attack on innocent people for whatever his reasons, on his own country's soil.

She slipped from one car to the next, creeping closer to him. She knew she had to deliver the toxins into his system before he could pull the trigger and put a bullet in her. She would need a distraction. One small little break. She had to get close and never let him see her. She'd practiced for just such an event as this one. Weeks. Months. Years. It was all about being that close and never letting him see or feel her until it was too late. Whitney had given her the most venomous poison possible and made certain it was extremely fast-acting.

Callendine made the mistake of moving close to his soldier again, once more bending down to try to examine him, looking to see what had killed him. Needing to understand so he wasn't caught in the same trap. Once he stood up again and began to search the garage, she knew she had him. She simply slid beneath the SUV and slithered like a snake over Treadway's body, blending with it so that if Callendine happened to glance down quickly, he would only see Treadway, the body he expected to see.

A car backfired and Amaryllis injected the poison into Callendine's ankle, immediately sliding back beneath the SUV and out the other side. Callendine was distracted momentarily by the loud bang, so that the sting barely registered. Then the pain began to overtake him fast. He started to reach down toward his leg but then looked carefully around again before crouching low to rub at his ankle.

Weirdly, his hand missed his ankle as if his coordination was off. He stared at his hand in fascination. His fingers had multiplied. The gun slipped from his palm to drop to the ground beside Treadway's body. He watched it fall, but there seemed to be two guns clattering to the floor of the garage, not one, and both were so blurred he could barely make them out. His ankle burned and hurt with a fiery pain. He'd never felt anything like it.

Someone crouched down beside him. A woman, yet he couldn't quite make out her face, it was too blurry. He knew it was important to note she was a woman, but he was sliding to the floor right over top of Treadway, which seemed indecent, but he couldn't stop himself, his body was no longer his own to control. He could barely find a way to breathe.

"Malichai Fortunes is my fiancé, Callendine, and I didn't much like you having your man try to kill him. Nor do I take kindly to you and your merry associates attempting to murder innocent people. You didn't get away with it. Not a single one of you."

She got up and sauntered away. He tried to watch her go, but his vision was too blurred, and he was fighting for every breath, his lungs burning and his diaphragm laboring. He lay there for a few more minutes struggling, and then there was silence.

Malichai worked as fast as he could, moving through the wires, grateful whoever had built the bomb had used a much simpler method than the more sophisticated ones that he'd learned to take apart. Those took time they didn't have. He had to block out everything around him but the bomb itself. The people running. Their screams. The sounds of crying children. The fact that Amaryllis was out there somewhere unprotected. The excruciating pain in his leg that caused every nerve ending to send shards of glass through his nervous system.

He ignored his body and concentrated on the bomb, even when Ezekiel threw himself down beside him to disconnect the second bomb Major Roseland Salsberry had attached to the main one to add an extra kick to bringing down the center on top of the innocent people.

He felt sweat trickling down his forehead and more down his chest. He wasn't like the men in the movies who just disarmed bombs so nonchalantly and easily as if they did it daily, yet he'd always had a knack for it. He knew part of that was his psychic gift, his hands moving like the surgeons' might in a body. It was instinctive as well as trained. He was fast because the movement was almost without thought, but yet guided by both training and instinct.

Time passed and he was at the end, cutting the last wire and turning his attention to the bomb Zeke was working on. Ezekiel had it nearly finished with the clock ticking down. Malichai looked at it for a long moment, frowning. Something wasn't quite right. He studied it, staying his brother's hand. Zeke looked at him over his shoulder, but didn't insist he was on the right path, although he'd stopped this bomb once before.

Very cautiously, Malichai used the tip of his snippers to ease open a small door built into the side of the bomb. It was very small and seemingly incongruous. There was no reason for it to be there at all. So why was it there? Two blue wires trailed innocently up to the detonator along with two red ones.

Zeke looked at him. Shook his head and sank back on his heels. "I would have blown us up. How did you know?"

He hadn't. Malichai couldn't tell him why or how his body reacted to explosives, it just happened, and in this case, it had not only saved their lives but also saved the lives of the people not yet evacuated from the building. It wasn't easy getting a couple thousand civilians out of a building, even for military teams working together.

Malichai followed the blue and red wires back to the detonator. All four were twisted around one another and around other wires. Major Salsberry had deliberately made this as difficult as possible. Malichai had to trust his gift — and he did. The timer had counted down far too close to the last minute. He chose a blue wire and snipped it, hearing his brother's gasping protest as he did.

The clock stopped ticking and the two bombs simply sat there looking harmless. Malichai had one moment of euphoria and then pain engulfed him, spread through him, twisting his insides into shards of glass and spewing his guts onto the floor as darkness overtook him.

19

There was the continuous sound of machines beeping in the background. Muted noises that became louder and more persistent until Malichai had little choice but to try and pry his eyes open. For some reason, his eyelids refused to lift. Maybe he was just too damned tired. He was aware of smells. He recognized he was in a hospital, he certainly had been in them enough times. He wasn't in pain. Had he been brought in wounded and fallen asleep? That wouldn't be the first time either.

He tried to assess what was going on while he worked on his sticky eyelids. Memories refused to return to him no matter how hard he reached for them. The world seemed far away at first, but the machines and the persistent beeping annoyed him, refusing to allow him to return to sleep.

"Malichai."

His name. He heard that clearly. Was there

a trace of anxiety in his brother's voice? That was Ezekiel calling out to him. When Zeke called, you always answered. Malichai redoubled his efforts to pry his eyelids open, a little ashamed to be caught sleeping on the job. He managed to open them slightly, mere slits so he could peer around the room.

He was in bed, hooked up to machines, IVs running up his arms to bags of fluids and even blood. What had happened? He forced his gaze to move around the room. Amaryllis's face swam into view. She looked as if she'd been crying. Mordichai was close to her. Rubin and Diego taking her back. Right between them was . . . Nonny. His heart jerked hard. He heard the answering acceleration of a machine. Nonny was there. The machine didn't stop the rapid-fire heartbeat.

Malichai's gaze settled on Ezekiel's face. He was close, right near Malichai's head, ready to block him from the sight of the others. From Amaryllis. This wasn't good. This couldn't be good. He couldn't lift his eyelids any farther. Now he didn't even want to, but he looked at his older brother. Zeke was everything. Father. Brother. Commanding officer. Malichai would follow him into hell. Right now, he needed his father. Ezekiel didn't let him down.

"I'd like to have the room, if you all don't mind," Ezekiel said quietly, which was his way. "Malichai is waking up and I'll need a few minutes to talk to him alone."

"Of course," Mordichai said, before anyone else could say anything.

He took Amaryllis by the hand. Rubin gently put his arm around Nonny. They were careful with the woman. Gentle. Reverent even. The men escorted the two women out of the room, leaving only Ezekiel with Malichai. Now Malichai's heart beat so hard he feared it would explode.

His brother slipped his arm around his chest. "Do you want to try to sit?"

"Just tell me." He knew. He couldn't feel, but he knew. Nonny was there and she wouldn't have come all the way from her beloved swamp at her age if the news wasn't bad — if it wasn't the worst.

God. He felt the burn of tears welling up behind his eyes, choking him in his throat so he could barely breathe, and Ezekiel hadn't said a word.

"They had to take the leg, Malichai. Whatever was causing the bone to disintegrate was creeping higher and higher, almost like a fungus, and there was no stopping it. When you stepped down on it getting out of the van and ran toward the center, the bone itself shattered like glass. It was impossible to repair."

That arm was steady, the way Ezekiel was steady. Always there for Malichai and his brothers. Always would be, no matter how bad things got, and they'd gotten bad. They'd been worse, but not for Malichai. This was his personal nightmare, and then there was Amaryllis. He couldn't — wouldn't — ask her to share this with him.

He wouldn't have cried like a baby in front of the others. He would have been stoic, and not made a single sound, but this was Ezekiel and he just wrapped his arms around his older brother, buried his face in his neck and let his heart shatter. Let his emotions spill like his guts out on his brother's broad shoulders. He sobbed like a baby and didn't even care that he did.

Ezekiel held him tight, never once admonishing him to stop. He simply held him and let him cry, let him mourn his lost leg. When he finally subsided, and Malichai had no idea how long that took, Zeke handed him something to blow his nose with and then pulled up a chair beside the bed.

"You'll have to stay here a little while before we can bring you home. I'll be here. When I have to go home, one of the others will come. Amaryllis wants to stay with you and obviously she can be at the bed-and-breakfast."

Malichai shook his head. "It isn't safe for her there. I don't want to see her either, Zeke . . ."

"Don't be a bonehead. No one is going to be able to stop that girl, least of all me. She earned the right to be in this room with you. You put a ring on her finger, and she knew, just like you did, what you were facing. She's not going away because the worst happened, and don't insult her by even suggesting it. Seriously, Malichai, you're upset, I get that, you're having a first reaction to the news, but you're not going to be an idiot and alienate everyone who loves you because you're depressed and upset."

That was why Ezekiel was his commanding officer as well. He told it like it was and Malichai respected him for it. "Do you remember when I was a kid and it was a bad winter and I gave away my blanket and food? You were so pissed at me?"

Ezekiel ran his fingers through his hair and looked away from Malichai. "Yeah, I remember. It was so damned cold I thought you might freeze to death just getting up to pee. You were so thin, Malichai."

He suddenly turned back and brushed hair from Malichai's forehead. Malichai could feel his fingers trembling, and that was shocking.

"I went to find your blanket for you. I thought someone had taken it from you and I was going to beat the shit out of them. I found the soldier. He wanted to give it back to me. Instead, I told him to keep it. I was so damned proud of you."

To Malichai's astonishment, Ezekiel blinked back tears.

"He told me that you were a great kid and that you had such compassion in you. You always noticed everyone less fortunate on the street and tried to help them. I didn't. I don't know if you realized that or not. I tried to be more like you after that." Ezekiel's fingers continued to move in his hair.

"When I saw him, without his leg, I was terrified that I'd end up like him, an old soldier on the street with no one to care for him after years of service. I had him put in a care home and paid for it when I could, but then . . . I wanted to stay in touch so when it came time, I could bury him. I was in and out of the country so much I just lost sight of him some years ago and he passed away . . ." Malichai trailed off, ashamed that he'd failed the soldier.

Ezekiel looked down at his hands. "I

didn't. You were on a run in the Congo when he passed away and I had him buried with military honors."

"Thanks for that, Zeke."

"You can handle this, Malichai. You're the strongest man I know. You can. It will be a long hard road, but we're all with you. You and I both know that because they've invested so much money in your training, the government is going to want to put a very expensive prosthesis on you so you can continue to go out on missions for them. You can say no. You will still be invaluable to us guarding our women and children at home. You can still be a soldier. Whatever you want to do. It's there for you. In the meantime, Malichai, you just take one day, one step, at a time and know we're all with you."

Malichai knew, intellectually, everything his brother said was true, but emotionally, it was difficult to accept. He still hadn't looked down his body to see his missing leg. He would do that when he was alone. He would rub his hip where he felt that ache still, the one that told him the leg was still present and would hurt for a long, long time.

"The others are going to want to see you, but you don't have to see them until you're ready," Ezekiel assured. "I can put them off, if needed."

There was no judgment in Zeke's voice. There wouldn't ever be from him. Ezekiel would give him all the time in the world to figure it out.

"Just give me a few minutes." He had to look down and see his leg gone. He had to come to terms with it. It would be one thing for his brothers and even Nonny to see him like this, but Amaryllis? No. She was different. He was supposed to be her everything. Whole. Her man. Her protector. Losing his leg didn't fit into his equation of what he was supposed to be for her.

Ezekiel waited for a few minutes and then once again came to the side of the bed to help him sit. He raised the bed just a few inches, forcing Malichai's back up. Still, Malichai didn't look down or take the sheet from his leg. His hip throbbed and the upper part of his thigh throbbed and itched, but he wouldn't touch it. His stomach lurched at the thought. He forced himself to think about Jerry, the soldier they'd rescued in Afghanistan. He'd not only lost his leg, he'd lost his arm as well. Where was he now?

"Would you find someone for me, Zeke?" He dropped his hand to his hip but didn't rub. He just took a deep breath. "His name is Jerry Lannis. Kid took a hit for his team in Afghanistan. Lost an arm and a leg. Rubin helped him out, kept him alive, and he was flown to Germany. Can you find out where he is now and how he's doing?"

He should have done that. Followed up on the kid, maybe gone to see him. How many kids had there been? They'd rescued so many. Brought them home to their loved ones just like this, shattered. He thought because they had loved ones they'd be just fine, but he hadn't considered the cost to their pride. Their manhood. Shit. He pressed his fingers to the corners of his eyes and shook his head.

"I don't know, Zeke. I don't know if I can face her."

"Do you think she'll think less of you?"

"*I* think less of me. Not other soldiers. I look at them and admire their courage. But when I think about facing her, I think about what I'm bringing to the table for her, what I'm offering her."

"You're still the same man."

"Minus a leg." He knew he sounded like he was whining, and it was the last thing he wanted to do, but hell, it was Amaryllis. "I know what you're saying, Zeke." He rubbed his pounding head. He was so damned tired. He just wanted to crawl under the covers and end the entire conversation, wake up and find out it was all a really bad nightmare. "Can you get Nonny for me?"

Ezekiel nodded. "Will do."

Nonny came into the room smelling of sage and lavender, the way she did in the swamp. She looked the same, beautiful and old and wise, never changing, always to be counted on. He wanted to cry the moment he saw her, and yet at the same time, she gave him tremendous courage. She came right to the side of the bed and took his hand, leaning down to brush his cheek with her thin, dry lips.

"Be strong, son. You'll need every bit of courage I know you have, to get you and your girl through this, but you'll do fine because of who you are." She squeezed his hand.

Her skin felt paper-thin, but she had strength. She took the little stool Ezekiel had brought in close to the bed, and Zeke sank into the chair across the room. Malichai knew his brother was still in protection mode just by the fact that he stayed in the room. He was in the shadows, staying still and quiet, but he was there, just in case.

"Thanks for coming, Nonny. I know how

much you love the swamp and the little girls."

She flashed him a smile. "Mostly miss my pipe. No place out here I can just light up without someone saying it isn't healthy."

"That's true," he agreed.

"But I've got you and Trap's little twins, and I got to fly in Trap's jet. Never saw anything like that before. Almost worth giving up the house just to live in that thing."

He had to smile. Nonny would never give up the home her grandsons had built for her. She loved the swamp. It was a huge sacrifice for her to come to see him, but she'd never admit it.

"You've met Amaryllis."

Nonny nodded. "A wonderful girl and very devoted to you. She's a stayer. She's going to be there through the lean times, Malichai, that's the kind of girl she is. Like Zara and Pepper. Like Cayenne and Bellisia. She'll stay with you and make a home with you the way I did with my Berengere." There was love in her voice when she mentioned the name of her husband. "She's a good woman, but then you boys tend to find you the good ones."

"Don't like thinking about her having to deal with this," he said gruffly and tried glancing down, but couldn't quite make himself do it.

Nonny's fingers tightened around his. "If she lost her leg, Malichai, would you stay with her and deal with it? Would you think she was less than who she is?"

"No, but that's different."

"Why?"

"I'm a man. I'm supposed to protect her. Have two legs to support her and keep bastards like Whitney from coming at her."

"What about if she had to have a hysterectomy or she gets breast cancer? She had to have her breasts removed. Does that make her less than a woman in your eyes?"

"Hell no." He had a visceral reaction to that. He would never want Amaryllis to think he wouldn't want her because she had to have a breast removed or she had to have a hysterectomy and couldn't have children. "Amaryllis is important to me, not because of all those things, but because of who she is." And he meant it. She wasn't her breasts or her womb. He got Nonny's point. He couldn't help how he felt, no matter how sexist it was or how ridiculous, and he knew it was. It was a gut reaction. Maybe others didn't have it, but he did.

"Malichai, you're going to have times when you'll be depressed and you're going to want to send Amaryllis away, but you have to fight those inclinations. This can tear your relationship apart or strengthen the two of you until you're unbeatable. She'll stand with you. I can guarantee you that she will. You have to let her because if you do, the two of you will have something so special all the way to the end of your days."

He believed her because Nonny would know. She had a gift. If she said Amaryllis would give that to him, and he to her, it would be so. He just had to overcome this problem he had, this idea that he was inferior because he didn't have a leg. He tried again to look and he just couldn't quite make himself do it, but his hand slid from his hip to his thigh. Down just a little farther. His heart went crazy. There wasn't much there. Even enough left for a prosthesis? How much of a stub did one need? Because they needed something.

"Take a breath, Malichai," Ezekiel's voice came out of the shadows. Steady. Reasonable. Not in the least upset. He was breathing in and out. Malichai followed because he always followed his brother wherever he led.

The sound of the machine he was hooked to stabilized. Went back to a regular rhythm. He glanced at Nonny, a little ashamed. She gave him her familiar grin. That helped to steady him as well.

"Are you ready to see your girl? She's been very anxious to see you. She has something she wants to talk to you about and she says it's very important."

Malichai knew he couldn't continue to put Amaryllis off. He didn't want her hurt. The doctors would be coming in soon and he needed to see her alone. He had to "read" her. To make certain for himself that she wanted to stay with him and go through the long process he knew it was going to be for recovery.

"I'm ready." He wasn't. He looked at his brother and saw Ezekiel's quick look at him. If anyone knew him, it was Zeke. Ezekiel knew he'd just lied to Nonny. That probably earned him a place in hell.

Nonny took him at his word and went to the door to call Amaryllis in. Then she was there, his woman, smelling the way she always did, a breath of fresh air in the midst of the hospital smells. She looked beautiful, but again, he could see that she'd been in tears. She smiled at him, and came straight to him, leaning down to brush several kisses across his lips.

"You scared me, Malichai. You really did," she said softly.

"Not any more than you scared me, going after Callendine, Amaryllis," he said. "Were you able to get him?"

"Absolutely. He died right there in the parking garage. Every one of them was taken down. Including Tania and Tommy Leven. They were in on it too. Bellisia caught up with them making out in the parking garage after coming out of the convention center with Salsberry. Apparently Tania is Tommy's wife, not his sister. She contacted Linda online because Linda and her sisters volunteer for nearly all the various conventions and she figured they would know just about everything about the buildings, including how to get in and out of them fast."

"And Linda's gay," Ezekiel said. "And fell for it."

Amaryllis nodded. "Yes. She's very upset that she did. The military police were able to collect tons of evidence. I think they were happy as well, other than they couldn't really explain the strange poisons in the men who died."

"Wouldn't worry about it," Ezekiel said. "Someone higher up will bury the entire thing."

"I hope they'll at least get to the aide who sanctioned them," Amaryllis said. "And the vice president."

"That's not going to happen," Ezekiel said. "We all know that, but the president's been warned."

"Do you think he knew about this?" Malichai asked.

"No, I don't believe he did. I think he was honestly outraged," Ezekiel said. "Joe flew to Washington along with Major General to speak with him, and Joe has a way of knowing who is lying and who's telling the truth. He believed the president, and that's good enough for me."

Malichai circled Amaryllis's waist with his arm. She was on the side where his leg was gone, and he didn't like that. He didn't want her looking, yet at the same time, she needed to see what she'd be dealing with for the rest of her life if she stayed with him. "Babe, I want you to know, if you want out, now's the time to say so, no hard feelings, just walk away and I'm okay with it." He forced himself to make the offer.

There was a long silence. She didn't respond. He could hear the sound of the machines beeping and coughing as they did their jobs, spitting out information to the room and the nurses down the hall. He had no choice but to look up at her. Amaryllis looked down at him with her amazing blue eyes. She searched his face for a long time.

"Do you really think I'd leave you, Malichai? Do you think I'm that shallow? I love you. Absolutely love you and I'd do anything for you. In fact, now that you've brought the subject up, I've had . . . no . . . we've had an offer. Dr. Whitney called me a few nights ago and had a long talk with me about some research and work he's been doing lately. I followed it up by looking into the things he was saying, and everything checked out."

Ezekiel stood up and came around to the other side of the bed. "Amaryllis, you can't trust a thing Whitney says. He's very self-serving."

"Yes, I know that. I know that's true, other than when it comes to his GhostWalker program. He wants that to be successful. Any mistakes he makes when it comes to a GhostWalker preys on him. He's OCD about it and can't seem to let it go. I believed everything he said to me, although I'm certain he was twisting some facts to suit him."

Malichai didn't like the fact that Whitney knew how to get in touch with her, but there was no hiding the Owen deaths, or the military investigations or the bomb threats. Amaryllis was involved with the bed-and-breakfast. She was surrounded by Ghost-Walkers and Whitney would see that, but he also would know how to find her.

"This isn't on him. He didn't have anything to do with second-generation Zenith or my reaction to it," Malichai said. "If that's even the problem."

"Trap says that's it," Ezekiel said. "He's been working on it when he's not been helping Cayenne with the twins. He says the problem appears to be with your bones and the DNA in them. So Amaryllis would have a similar problem using second-generation Zenith. The first time you used it just set you up for the fall. He can explain the entire sequencing thing to you and how it happened, because Trap loves that kind of thing, but I'd prefer not to go there."

Malichai didn't care one way or the other as long as it stopped right there. "Is it going to continue throughout my body?"

"From what he says, no. They stopped it climbing up your leg. It was aggressive because you had so many bullet holes and used five patches. That was a lot of the Zenith, and the exposure was all the way up the bone. The bone just disintegrated. Believe me, brother, Rubin examined every single bone in your body to ensure there wasn't a problem anywhere else."

That was a huge relief. Malichai had worried that eventually whatever was eating his bones was going to continue right through his body like a cancer.

"Why didn't you tell me Whitney had called you, Amaryllis?" Ezekiel asked.

As head of the family, he was used to making decisions or at least being consulted. As one of the GhostWalkers' commanding officers, he was in a position of leadership.

Amaryllis shrugged. "Before I said anything to anyone about Whitney's proposal, I wanted to see if it had any merit. I lived in his compound for years. I grew up there. I watched him. I know him fairly well. This seemed like it could be the truth, but I didn't want to give Malichai and the rest of you false hope."

Malichai immediately noticed that she had distanced herself from them. It wasn't Malichai and her. Or the GhostWalkers and her. It was Malichai and the GhostWalkers without her. He didn't like it, but this time he managed to control his heart rate and kept the rhythm steady.

"There's a little salamander that lives in water, called the axolotl, with the largest genome ever fully sequenced. Universities are very interested in this particular salamander. In fact, it's becoming very popular because it has the ability to grow any limb back, including eyes. They can regenerate spinal cords, any limb you cut off, even parts of the brain, but most salamanders can do that."

Malichai had a feeling he knew where this was going. He glanced at his brother. Another Whitney experiment. Whitney was always a step ahead of science because he was willing to step on the toes of others in their fields and also to try things before they had been tested to see if they were safe. What would Malichai be willing to do for another leg? His own leg? Would he be willing to try an untested method? An unexperimented one? A part of him didn't want Amaryllis to go any further. He was tired and he could barely keep his eyes open. His nonexistent leg throbbed and burned and itched. He couldn't look down at it. He didn't want her to. He hadn't yet gotten to the point of acceptance. She couldn't offer him a way out and expect that he wouldn't take it.

"He says that the axolotls use stem cells to regenerate and he's completed the sequencing of the genome. He claims he has unlocked a method to signal the pathway between genes and activate the ability to regenerate the genetic material and ultimately tissue. In other words, he can get Malichai to regrow his leg using some drug or gene-editing tool such as the one he already used on him. He would turn all of this technology over to Lily if Malichai would be willing to be the first to be experimented on."

Ezekiel shook his head. "You know better than that, both of you. Whitney is a genius and he's further ahead in gene-splicing and gene sequencing than just about anyone on the planet, I'm not arguing with that. He steals from other researchers and steps on them to get ahead and never feels bad about it. We know that because he used Zara to steal from researchers and she was very good at it. I've certainly heard of the axolotl salamander. I believe Trap keeps some in his laboratory there at his house. He says they can regenerate new limbs in three weeks without scarring. He believes they'll be the ones to aid humans in the future, but Whitney? Letting him back into your life for any reason? No way. That's disaster. Trusting him? It isn't going to happen, Malichai."

It was his leg. His body. Malichai wanted to shout that at his brother, but he knew he would sound like a child. This was his first day and he had to take a breath and really think things through. Ezekiel was right. Any bargain with Whitney was always a steep one. He had a price and sometimes that cost was hidden, but it was there, and you had to figure it out. He was willing to let Whitney put any kind of animal or insect DNA in him if that was the cost, ramp up his testosterone or give him silk armor, whatever it took to grow back his own leg. That was his choice, and no one had a say in that but him.

"What else did he say?" Malichai asked, ignoring his brother's outburst because Whitney would have said more than what Amaryllis was giving him.

"It doesn't matter because you aren't doing it," Ezekiel snapped.

Malichai had been looking at Amaryllis, not his brother, and there was something that came and went on her face very fast. One moment there, the next gone, but he caught it. Yeah. Whitney had given her a price.

"Baby," he said softly. "Tell me what he said to you."

Just his tone alone kept Ezekiel silent.

She shrugged. "He said I had to come back." She sounded nonchalant, as if it wasn't the biggest sacrifice in the world. As if she hadn't planned her escape so carefully to get out. "He wants to study how I can heal others in exchange for you regenerating your own limb." She knew if Whitney got his hands on her again, there would be no way out for her. He would put her in his breeding program and her life would be hell. She would do that — for him. Give up her life in order for him to have a leg.

Malichai felt anger welling up. That was so Whitney. He'd challenged Amaryllis, dared her to show him whether or not she loved Malichai enough to save his leg by returning to him.

He was silent, counting to a hundred slowly, not wanting to sound like Ezekiel, a dictator, not wanting to tell Amaryllis what she could or couldn't do. That wasn't the right way, not with her, not with anyone, but especially not with her. He lay back and closed his eyes, so tired he wasn't certain he could ever open them again, but he kept his arm around her. Needing her. Needing the closeness. The connection.

"He doesn't know us, does he? He doesn't know how much I love you or how much I need you. Or you me. I'd never give you up for a leg. For any body part. You wouldn't trade me either." He poured absolute belief into his voice. "The truth is, Amaryllis, I'm a GhostWalker. My training alone is worth millions of dollars to the government. They aren't going to let a little thing like my leg being amputated stop me from deploying when they need me. I'm going to have the best prosthesis available, most likely the most futuristic one, if Whitney hasn't already given Trap or Lily his research on this salamander. It doesn't matter to us what they do or how they do it. Crawl up on the bed with me and lie down. I just need you close."

That was the best he could do. He did need her close. He didn't open his eyes because he couldn't. He knew sleep was going to overtake him very soon. He wanted to make certain Ezekiel knew to watch out for her. He hoped he'd said enough, that she knew they were better together than apart.

Amaryllis came around to the other side of the bed. "You know I'm going to get into trouble with the nurses, don't you?"

"I'll protect you," he promised. He thought he smiled, but he couldn't tell, he was too tired.

She climbed up onto the bed and lay on the sheet, fitting her body next to his, like a glove. She felt good. Right.

"Screw Whitney," he said softly, turning his head so he could press his lips to the silk of her hair. "I'll always have this. I'll always have you. I love you so much, baby."

"I love you, Malichai. Go to sleep, honey, I'll watch over you."

Nice, brother. I'm proud of you.

Sometimes Ezekiel didn't know when to leave it alone. The burn of tears was back just because he was too damned emotional. Now it wasn't about his leg. It might be later, but thanks to Whitney and his games, this was all about keeping Amaryllis. She would have gone. She would have traded her life for his leg. He saw that clearly on her face, read it in her mind. She loved him that much. Who would ever be that stupid, that selfish, to trade that kind of love for a body part?

Malichai drifted off to the sound of machines and the scent of Amaryllis's hair. One arm was around her waist, the other, his hand was on his hip, feeling the pain all the way down his nonexistent leg. He let go of that reality and just hung on to Amaryllis.

"Is he asleep?" Ezekiel asked.

"He appears to be," she answered softly. "It's hard to say."

"I hate this for him. Thank you for loving him enough to make that offer, but stay for him. He needs you with him. Especially now more than ever. He needs to know he's worth it to you to stay with him in spite of the fact that he doesn't have a leg."

Amaryllis stroked a light caress along Malichai's rib cage. "I'd give him anything, Ezekiel," she admitted. "Anything at all. Owen was this larger-than-life adversary that I couldn't overcome. Maybe Whitney and Owen had conditioned me not to be able to best him, certainly I couldn't use my venom on him, but still, I should have been able to pull the trigger of a gun, yet I froze. I did every time that I faced him. Even when Malichai needed me to shoot him. I failed him then and I promised myself I would never do it again."

"You know that Whitney plants shit in our heads, right? Most likely when he chose Owen as his golden boy and he knew you women had poisons that could kill his number-one protector — or him — he made certain you couldn't kill either of them. That would only make sense, Amaryllis, or he would have been dead a long time ago. Had you talked to Malichai about it, he would have explained that to you."

Amaryllis looked around the room. "Are there cameras in here? Audio?"

Ezekiel shook his head. "We made certain of it. We clear it out three times a day just to be certain. What are you worried about?"

"One of the girls I escaped with, a girl by the name of Coral, showed up at the bed-and-breakfast. She asked to stay with Marie. I like her, but I can't be certain that Whitney didn't get ahold of her and send her back for a reason. You know the games he plays. If I recommend her to Marie, she'll be treated like family. Marie's that way. If not, she won't get the job. I'd hate that, because she looks like she really needs it."

"You want us to check her out?" Ezekiel was cautious. This was the first time Amaryllis had made an actual request of the team. They would have checked out the newcomer anyway. They'd all but adopted Marie and her daughter, Jacy, as their own, so anyone working for her on a long-term basis was going to come under scrutiny, but having Amaryllis ask was a huge breakthrough.

"If you don't mind."

"Of course not," Ezekiel said. "We're going to have to be here for a while. We can't move Malichai back home until he's ready for that. He's got to go through his care here and then therapy and finally home care. It's a long process. He'll need you to be strong for him."

"Are the others going back?"

"Yes, they need to get back home," Ezekiel

said. "Bellisia, my wife, will be staying. She'll help Cayenne and Trap with the babies. Drusilla is healing fast and will be ready to travel soon. Trap wants to get them home. Cayenne doesn't like the nurses telling her what she can and can't do with her own little ones."

Amaryllis frowned. "Like what? I wouldn't like it either."

"She makes the most beautiful lacy webs and hangs them for privacy, like curtains. If she puts them around the babies at all, the nurses rip them down. Cayenne has been good about it, but Trap can see that her patience is wearing thin. He can't tell them to leave the webs alone because to them they see a giant spider somewhere close, not beautiful lace curtains."

"I see. That could be bad."

"That's why it's good Bellisia is staying. She isn't the closest to Cayenne, but she'll help the situation. Zara is the one who kind of throttles everyone back. She's more like Nonny in that way. She has this kind of gentle mediation thing she does, and everyone just gets along, especially the little ones. Cayenne seems to react very well to the way Zara mediates as well. Bellisia is more of an 'in your face' kind of girl." He grinned when he said it.

Amaryllis couldn't help smiling. "You like that."

He shrugged. "She's a little spitfire. She's my little warrior. She'll stand up for anything or anyone she believes in."

"What's Shylah like, Draden's wife?"

"She's harder to explain. She's kind. Very compassionate. And she'll drop you in two seconds if you're her target. Pepper is Wyatt's wife and she's the nicest woman you'll ever want to meet. She was scheduled for termination along with the triplets, Wyatt's little girls. Pepper can get brain bleeds around violence, although she will back us up and protect the babies fiercely if need be. She has something on her skin that if touched, can make someone crazy for her, so there's a continual sexual thing that she has to counteract all the time. It's a difficult life for her. Nonny's been a great help there."

"And Cayenne?"

"You met her. She was raised in a tiny cell. Never had a family, raised only on rations. Used only to train in situations of life or death. She wasn't treated very well ever by anyone. Trap was the one who got her out, got her clear. She came back and helped Wyatt and Pepper get the little girls clear, but none of us knew if it was because she felt bad for the girls or if she was repaying Trap. Then she disappeared. Rumors started about a thief robbing some bad people of money on their way home from the bars. They never could remember much. Trap became convinced it was Cayenne. He was right."

"How terrible for her. She must have been so frightened."

"I guess she was. We were all a little afraid of her. She was lethal, Amaryllis. She knew how to use her silk and her venom, and she didn't hesitate. She could paralyze and she could kill. Naturally, Nonny felt bad for her. She would have taken in every lame duck in the swamp that needed a home if Wyatt had let her. But it was Trap that found a way to bring Cayenne in."

"It couldn't have been easy."

"No, especially because Trap didn't trust anyone either. He's on the autism spectrum and everyone he'd ever loved had been ripped away from him — murdered. Many of his family members by his own father. It has always been easier for him to retreat into his head and just push others away with rude behavior. If someone does act as if they want him, it has always turned out it's for his money, which he has plenty of. Cayenne had to rely on him for everything, and that in turn made him a better man. He had to learn to adjust, to talk, to give her his best. He made a lot of mistakes in the beginning and he still makes them, but he makes them only once and then he doesn't again because she's his entire world."

"I saw that. It looked like she thought he was her world."

"She does think he's her world, that's for sure," Ezekiel said. He sighed and stood up, stretching. "This is going to be a very long, hard road, Amaryllis. It won't be easy for Malichai. I believe this is the one thing he's always feared."

"He's strong. Nonny whispered that to me when we were out in the waiting room. She said he's strong and that I needed to be as strong or stronger for him. I am and I will be," she said resolutely. "You don't have to worry, I'll stand with him."

Ezekiel came to the other side of the bed and leaned down to brush his brother's cheek with his lips and then he cupped the side of Amaryllis's face. "I know you will. I'm counting on that. We all are." He turned and walked out of the room.

Amaryllis stared up at the ceiling, grateful her heart wasn't hooked to the monitor the way Malichai's was. It would have been beating a million miles an hour, not because she was going to stay with a man whose leg had been amputated, but because she had considered leaving before she'd talked to him and she would have missed her chance to be loved for the rest of her life by an extraordinary human being.

20

"I'd sure like to know what kind of hardware you have in that leg, because this is bullshit, Malichai," Jerry Lannis said, wiping the sweat from his forehead and downing half a bottle of water while he studied Malichai's face.

Malichai raised an eyebrow. "It's not my fault you haven't been training. I run hills every day while you're kicking back trying to get your woman to rub your back or some such fool thing."

Jerry spewed water out his nose. "It's not my fault that your woman kicks your ass if you don't run. The last time you were lagging behind on time I half expected her to come out onto the road and flog the skin right off your back for being lazy. You're right, mine does like to pamper me." He flashed a little grin and wiggled his eyebrows.

"In any case," Malichai said, "we've got

another half hour on this run. I've got to swim after this. You going with me or backing off for the day?"

Swimming was a chore for Jerry at times. He was still getting used to his new arm prosthesis. He pushed himself in spite of Malichai's teasing. Malichai knew he went through periods of depression because he would call and Malichai would meet him somewhere to talk. If they weren't in close vicinity, they'd talk on the phone. They'd made that pact with each other. At Ezekiel's insistence, Malichai had consulted with a counselor and that counselor had told him to have someone he trusted he could talk to.

There were more than fifteen hundred soldiers who'd lost limbs in Iraq or Afghanistan. Ezekiel wanted his brother to not only have the best physical care but have the best mental health care as well. That meant leaning on those soldiers who had carved this path before him. They'd already suffered depression and knew that downward spiral. Malichai wanted those same advantages for Jerry and he'd reached out to him and his family. The two stayed close through their recoveries.

Malichai usually trained every day with his team or Amaryllis unless Jerry was visiting. He and his family lived near the Washington base, but his wife wanted to relocate the family to a different state once Jerry was out of the military. She felt that seeing his friends continue without him was even more depressing for him. Training with Malichai seemed to boost his spirits, and she wanted him closer.

Malichai was all for that. They'd found a home in New Orleans that they loved, but before they purchased it, Malichai wanted them to experience the humidity and heat. Washington had rain and a different climate altogether. New Orleans had rain and heat. The owners had agreed to rent to them for a couple of months to see how they liked living there before they actually purchased.

"I think I'll swim with you. I'm trying to get this arm to work for me. My daughter thinks it's the coolest thing ever. She wants one."

Malichai laughed. "I've found that the children make things seem much simpler and uncomplicated. I like being around them. I thought we could use Trap's pool."

Jerry's face lit up. "Do you think he'd mind?"

"Trap couldn't care less. We'll have the lanes, but the kids might be in the shallow pool. They know better than to get into the deep pool, especially if any adult is training, but they'll watch. Just so you're warned. They have opinions."

"I should have brought my kids."

"I told you to. Amaryllis enjoys visiting with Denise, and your two girls would have fun with the little vi— with Wyatt's daughters."

"Why do you call them that? The vipers? I've heard you refer to them like that before."

They jogged up the hill together and along the trail in the swamp. Malichai was grateful the tree branches had closed around them. He couldn't help looking around. "Never say that out loud. Pepper might hear you. Those three little munchkins bit hard when they were cutting their teeth and we would tease them. Pepper didn't like it. We still slip up."

"I'll be careful," Jerry agreed as they made their way through the swamp along the path that led to Trap and Cayenne's home.

The water felt good on Malichai's skin and he stayed swimming long after Jerry went home. He swam lap after lap. Jerry was right, the hardware in his leg was revved up, the best that could be given to him, so that he could still run and jump with blurring speed. He didn't have the stealth he'd once had, but he was working on that. His hands were every bit as steady, so he couldn't complain.

Much later, Amaryllis joined him, swimming with him, and he appreciated the sight of her in a small bikini he'd talked her into buying and wearing when they were alone. She wasn't that girl who showed off her body, but for him, she did. The children were gone, and no one was around but the two of them and the royal blue triangle was cut to curve right up her cheeks, revealing how perfectly shaped she was, riding the center and curving downward and low on her hips. He loved looking at her from the back just to see that view.

Then there was the delicious side view she gave him. He loved her generous breasts. She had them and he could look at them all day. More than once, in the hospital, when he thought he might go insane with phantom pain and itching, she had suddenly given him something else to think about, revealing the sexiest bra beneath her top, all lace with her nipples peeking through at him. Because she was actually very modest, and he knew what it cost her, he appreciated it all the more. He also bought into the distraction more.

She'd let him buy that top, nothing really

but strings, beautiful royal blue rolled cord to frame her rounded breasts, with a tiny scrap of material barely managing to cover her nipples. When she was wet from the pool, the way she was now, she might as well not be wearing a thing. She looked like a wild temptress rising out of the water and turning to wade toward him with her deep-sea blue eyes and that beautiful, generous mouth of hers. He was a lucky man and he knew it.

He reached out and caught her by the straps of her top and pulled her into him. She immediately looked at their surroundings.

"We're completely alone, Amaryllis. I wouldn't want another man looking at you. Trap is in his lab, which means Cayenne is as well. Everyone else has gone home. It's us and this pool. I can turn the lights off." He made the suggestion gently. He wasn't going to push it one way or the other. He was a little more adventurous than she was, but if she wasn't comfortable, he was fine with taking what they had indoors. Everything they did was beautiful and sexy to him.

"I would very much like you to turn the lights off," she agreed, even as she shrugged her shoulders and one strap slid down.

His breath caught in his throat. That small movement had taken those cords right off that round curve, so her nipple stood out starkly, begging for attention. He couldn't help himself. He had to touch her, his thumb strumming her nipple gently before he forced himself to turn away, climb the stairs and hit the light switch, plunging them into darkness.

The pool itself was still lit with a dim, opalescent light. That light quickly turned to a pinkish, almost radiant light spilling upward from beneath the water. Amaryllis looked down at the light display and then up at him, laughing.

Malichai laughed. "That's so Trap. He'll probably have unicorns galloping on the bottom of the pool before Drusilla is two."

"It is beautiful," she pointed out.

"You're beautiful," he corrected, dipping his head, his mouth finding her bare breast while he removed the little complicated corded bikini top. Her breast was cool from the water, but full and sexy, her nipple a tight, responsive bud in his mouth.

He tugged with his teeth and rolled with his tongue, using his fingers on her other breast. He loved waking up to her. Loved going to bed with her. She made him laugh all the time. Amaryllis was so perfect for him. When she had her mouth on his cock, it was pure heaven. No one could take him there like she could. When he was moving in her body, her tight sheath clamped down around him like a silken fist, she could take him all the way to paradise.

There in the water, he wrapped his arm around her waist and lifted her, as he untied the cord at her hips and let her bikini bottom float away. She immediately wrapped her legs around his waist, tilting her hips to his eagerly. He loved that about her as well. She might not go for public displays of affection the way some of the other women did, but she never said no to him. She was always ready for him, looking for ways to be with him.

Then he was moving in her and there was nothing in his mind but Amaryllis and the way she made him feel. That heat bursting through him. The fire she brought, burning him from the inside out. The love that ran through the lust and beauty of their coming together any way he took her. Water splashed around them. He heard her soft little cries, that music she made that seemed to add to the flames licking over his skin joining them together.

Then they were soaring together in the way they seemed to do so easily. He could barely breathe with loving her. When the world returned and he was aware of the night and the stars and the changing lights around them, that it wasn't Amaryllis's magic dazzling his eyes, he let himself just feel how much he loved her. He held her there in the pool for a long time. She didn't move, her arms around him, not asking a single question, not demanding he let her go, just holding him the way he was her, content to let the ever-changing lights play over them as Malichai came down from his Amaryllis high.

Eventually he brushed kisses against her neck. "I told Trap we'd meet him in the lab."

"You have to find my suit. It floated off somewhere and I've got to shower and get dressed."

"You don't want the kids to find little scraps of cloth at the bottom of the pool tomorrow?" he teased.

She flashed a grin at him and walked up the stairs naked. He watched her go the entire way because Amaryllis naked was a sight to behold.

"Whitney, you are so full of shit," Trap snapped. "There are thirty-two *billion* base pairs in the genome of an axolotl salamander and scientists in Vienna, Heidelberg and

Dresden were the first to actually completely map out the genome, which will be a huge leap forward for limb regeneration in humans, but we're not there yet. You weren't the first to map that out, they did. I'm not sending you Malichai to experiment on. It isn't happening because if you tell one lie, everything else is built on that lie, which means you're full of absolute shit."

"Do you really think I'd use one of my very few GhostWalkers as my first human experiments in limb regeneration?" Whitney demanded. "You think so much of yourself, Dawkins. You always have. You're depriving Malichai of his own leg, one of bone and tissue, one completely regenerated, because you don't think it's possible because *you can't do it.*"

Malichai was tired of the argument between Trap and Whitney. It seemed like it went on day in and day out, but this was the first time it alarmed him. This was the first time Whitney had made references to experimenting on other humans — and when he experimented on human beings it was always on young girls or women. He believed they were inferior, and their only value was to science.

"Whitney." Trap sounded interested now. "When Sergej Nowoshilow was speaking expressly about having the map for complicated structures such as limbs to be regrown, such as human legs, it was noted that the human PAX3 gene, which is *essential* during muscular and neural growth, is missing, with the axolotl PAX7 taking its place."

"Which makes sense since a salamander needs its own stem cells and we need our own stem cells. You're splitting hairs, Trap," Whitney said. It was shocking that he referred to Trap by his first name rather than as Dawkins. "I'm telling you, I can get Malichai to regenerate his own leg, without scarring. His own tissue, muscular and neural growth."

"We'll get there, but we're years away, even with our greatest scientists working on this," Trap objected, the voice of reason. "Even with you stepping on the backs of geniuses, which you've been doing for years, you can't pull this off."

"You're so damn stubborn, you always think you're right. I'll send you the proof of it if you don't believe me. I get tired of you arguing with me."

Malichai's heart clenched hard in his chest. His eyes met Trap's and then he looked at Amaryllis. She looked every bit as apprehensive as Malichai felt. Her tongue moistened her lower lip.

"What kind of proof, Whitney?" Trap asked.

"The kind even an asshole like you can't deny, Dawkins," Whitney snapped. There was a loud buzzing and the connection was lost.

Amaryllis scooted closer to Malichai until she was practically sitting in his lap. "What do you think he meant by that?"

"I don't know, honey," he said gently. "It doesn't matter. My leg is doing great just the way it is. I'm getting stronger every single day." He didn't want to think about regeneration and whether it was possible. He wanted to quit hearing about it because then he would dream about it. Anyone would.

"What he meant" — Cayenne said, coming out of the shadows where she often stayed, and moving right into Trap so that he pulled her into him, her back to his front, his arms around her — "is that he used one of us. Or more than one. He cut off an arm or a leg, or more than one arm or leg, and he tried to regrow it. More than likely he did it several times. He failed and he did it again and again until he was successful because that's the kind of man he is."

She turned around and leaned into Trap,

her head on his chest as if for comfort, her slender arms around his neck. The fixture above spilled light over her, turning her hair a gleaming black and revealing the red hourglass that sometimes showed in the thick strands of silk. She looked very small next to Trap, and when he locked his arms around her, he looked very protective.

Malichai closed his eyes against that terrible truth. Whitney had most likely done exactly that to some little girl in order to perfect his miracle of regeneration for his GhostWalker teams. For his soldiers. For those he deemed worthy of his miracles. If others benefited, he didn't mind, but he really did it for them. The ones he made suffer in order to perfect it didn't matter. They should be grateful they had given so much toward science and in service of their country. Not only did he believe that, but he raised the girls to think that way. To him they were worth nothing but what he used them for — his experiments.

There was a small, miserable silence. "I really despise that man," Malichai said. "With every breath I take." He stood up and reached down to extend his hand to Amaryllis.

She took it and he pulled her up.

"I think we all do," Trap acknowledged.

"Did you get a good workout swimming?"

"We did. Thanks for allowing us to use the pool," Malichai said. "I'm walking my woman home. Tomorrow we're getting married. I'm reminding you, Trap, in front of Cayenne so she'll get you there."

"I'm the one who puts everything on the calendar," Trap said indignantly.

Cayenne turned around, a small smile forming. "True, he does, but then he never looks at the calendar. I do that. I'll get him there, no worries."

"Thanks, hon," Malichai said. "Nonny's cooking up a feast, so if he won't come for the festivities, bring him for the food."

"Nonny frowns on missing things like weddings," Cayenne said seriously. "She told both of us events like that were important to the people we care about and we needed to always show up. So we'll be there." She looked up at Trap. "For certain. With gifts. Dressed nicely."

He cupped her face in his hands. "We'll be there," he agreed, looking down at her.

Malichai couldn't help grinning. He wasn't altogether certain Trap and Cayenne knew they were still in the room. "We're taking off now. We'll see you later."

Trap lifted a hand as they left the laboratory and then he was kissing Cayenne.

Amaryllis fit just under his shoulder, her arm circling his waist as she matched his steps. "I clocked your run after Jerry took a break, Malichai, you're getting faster. Is the prosthesis still rubbing when you're running that fast?"

"No, that last adjustment made it perfect."

She was silent for a moment and Malichai's gut tightened. He knew it was inevitable that she would ask the question, and he didn't really know what his answer was going to be.

"Do you want to try Whitney's experimental process to regrow your leg, Malichai?"

He shook his head. "I don't know the answer to that, Amaryllis. I really don't. Right now, I'm working hard to build my body back up again so I can get into the field and be of use to my team. I don't know what I'm going to do beyond that. I knew Whitney was harassing Trap with this nonsense about being able to regenerate an entire limb, but Trap, Lily and Wyatt have all assured me that the technology is still a good fifty years away. I'm not going to waste my time on dreams. I need to work with what I've got."

He stopped there on the narrow trail that led back to the Fontenot house. Their home wasn't quite finished. It was coming along, and the sound of hammers often rang out until sunset, but for now, they were staying with Wyatt, Pepper, Nonny and the five little girls who seemed to be like quicksilver, running everywhere. He pulled Amaryllis into his arms.

"I have you, babe. I love you more than anything else in this world. When I look ahead to our future, it's always bright and happy. It's always surrounded with love because you're in it. Of course there's always those stacks of romance books we're going to be reading at night, but that's a good thing because I'll be taking all the best ideas out of them."

Malichai framed her face with both hands and bent to take her mouth. She looked like an angel, kissed like sin and loved him as only Amaryllis could. She was everything he'd ever wanted in a woman, and leg or no leg, he was counting himself a very lucky man.

ABOUT THE AUTHOR

Christine Feehan is the #1 *New York Times* bestselling author of the Carpathian series, the GhostWalker series, the Leopard series, the Shadow Riders series, and the Sea Haven novels, including the Drake Sisters series and the Sisters of the Heart series. She lives in the beautiful mountains of Lake County, California. Please visit her website at www.christinefeehan.com.

The employees of Thorndike Press hope you have enjoyed this Large Print book. All our Thorndike, Wheeler, and Kennebec Large Print titles are designed for easy reading, and all our books are made to last. Other Thorndike Press Large Print books are available at your library, through selected bookstores, or directly from us.

For information about titles, please call:
  (800) 223-1244

or visit our website at:
  gale.com/thorndike

To share your comments, please write:
  Publisher
  Thorndike Press
  10 Water St., Suite 310
  Waterville, ME 04901